THE GIRL WHO OWNED A CITY

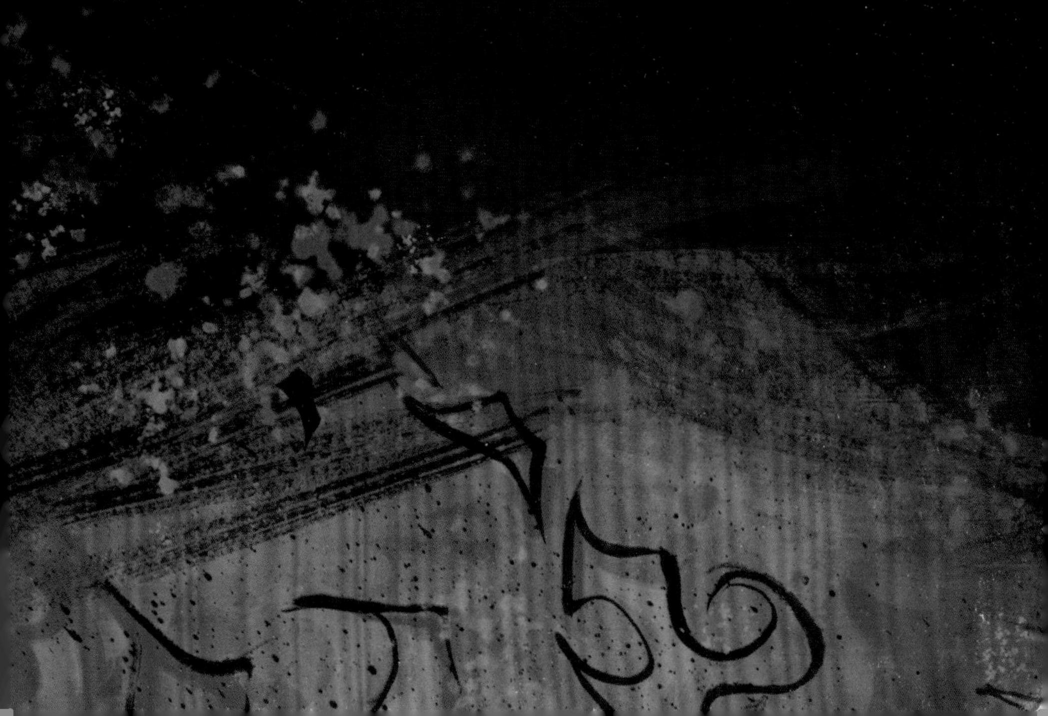

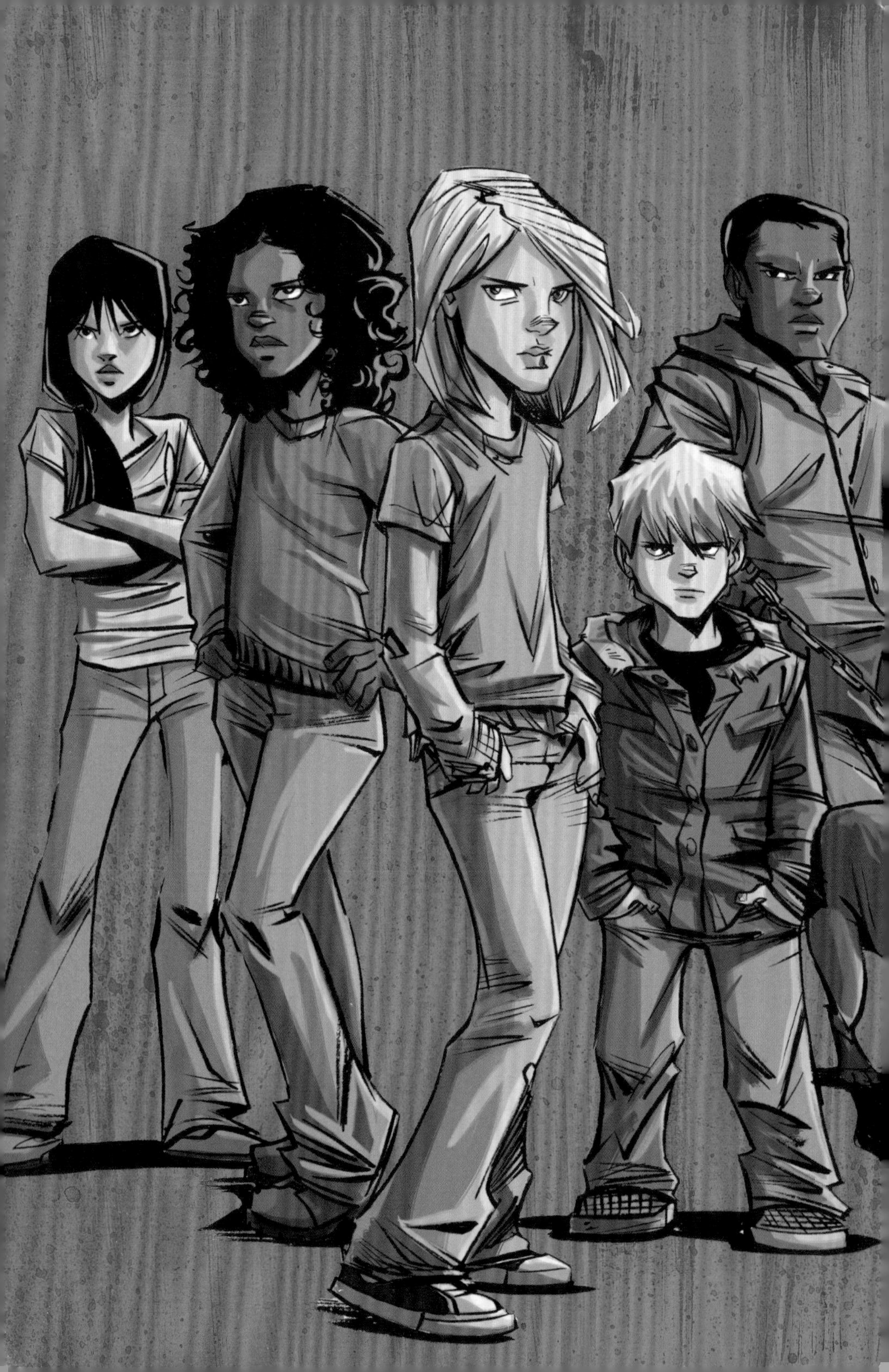

THE GIRL WHO OWNED A CITY

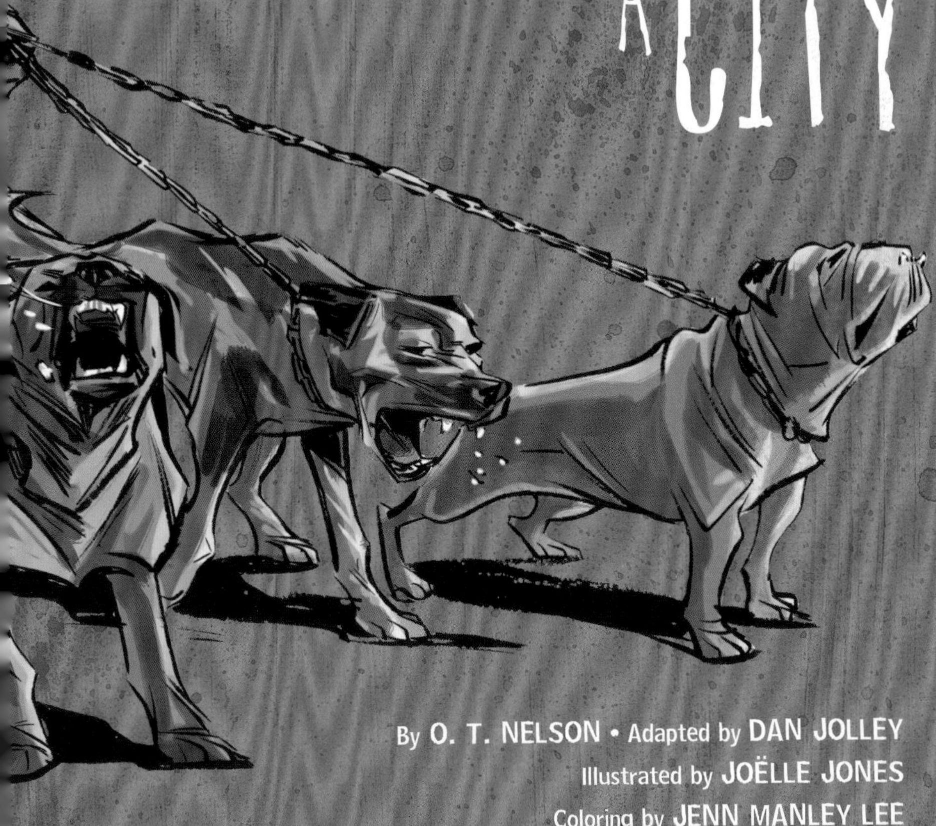

By O. T. NELSON • Adapted by DAN JOLLEY
Illustrated by JOËLLE JONES
Coloring by JENN MANLEY LEE

GRAPHIC UNIVERSE™ • MINNEAPOLIS • NEW YORK

FOR LISA AND TODD
—O. T. NELSON

STORY BY O. T. NELSON
ADAPTED BY DAN JOLLEY
PENCILS AND INKS BY JOËLLE JONES
COLORING BY JENN MANLEY LEE
LETTERING BY GRACE LU

GRAPHIC UNIVERSE™
A DIVISION OF LERNER PUBLISHING GROUP, INC.
241 FIRST AVENUE NORTH
MINNEAPOLIS, MN 55401 USA

FOR READING LEVELS AND MORE INFORMATION, LOOK UP THIS TITLE AT WWW.LERNERBOOKS.COM.

MAIN BODY TEXT SET IN MEANWHILE.
TYPEFACE PROVIDED BY COMICRAFT/ACTIVE IMAGES.

LIBRARY OF CONGRESS CATALOGING-IN-PUBLICATION DATA

JOLLEY, DAN.
        THE GIRL WHO OWNED A CITY : THE GRAPHIC NOVEL / BY O. T. NELSON ; ADAPTED BY DAN
    JOLLEY ; ILLUSTRATED BY JOËLLE JONES.
            P.   CM.
        SUMMARY: WHEN A PLAGUE SWEEPS OVER THE EARTH KILLING EVERYONE EXCEPT CHILDREN
    UNDER TWELVE, LISA NELSON ORGANIZES A GROUP TO REBUILD A NEW WAY OF LIFE.
        ISBN: 978-0-7613-4903-7 (LIB. BDG. : ALK. PAPER)
        ISBN: 978-0-7613-8750-3 (EB PDF)
        1. GRAPHIC NOVELS. [1. GRAPHIC NOVELS. 2. SURVIVAL—FICTION. 3. SCIENCE FICTION.]
    I. JONES, JOËLLE, ILL. II. NELSON, O. T. GIRL WHO OWNED A CITY. III. TITLE.
    PZ7.7.J65GI 2012
    741.5'973—DC22   2009033270

MANUFACTURED IN THE UNITED STATES OF AMERICA
3 – PC – 5/1/15

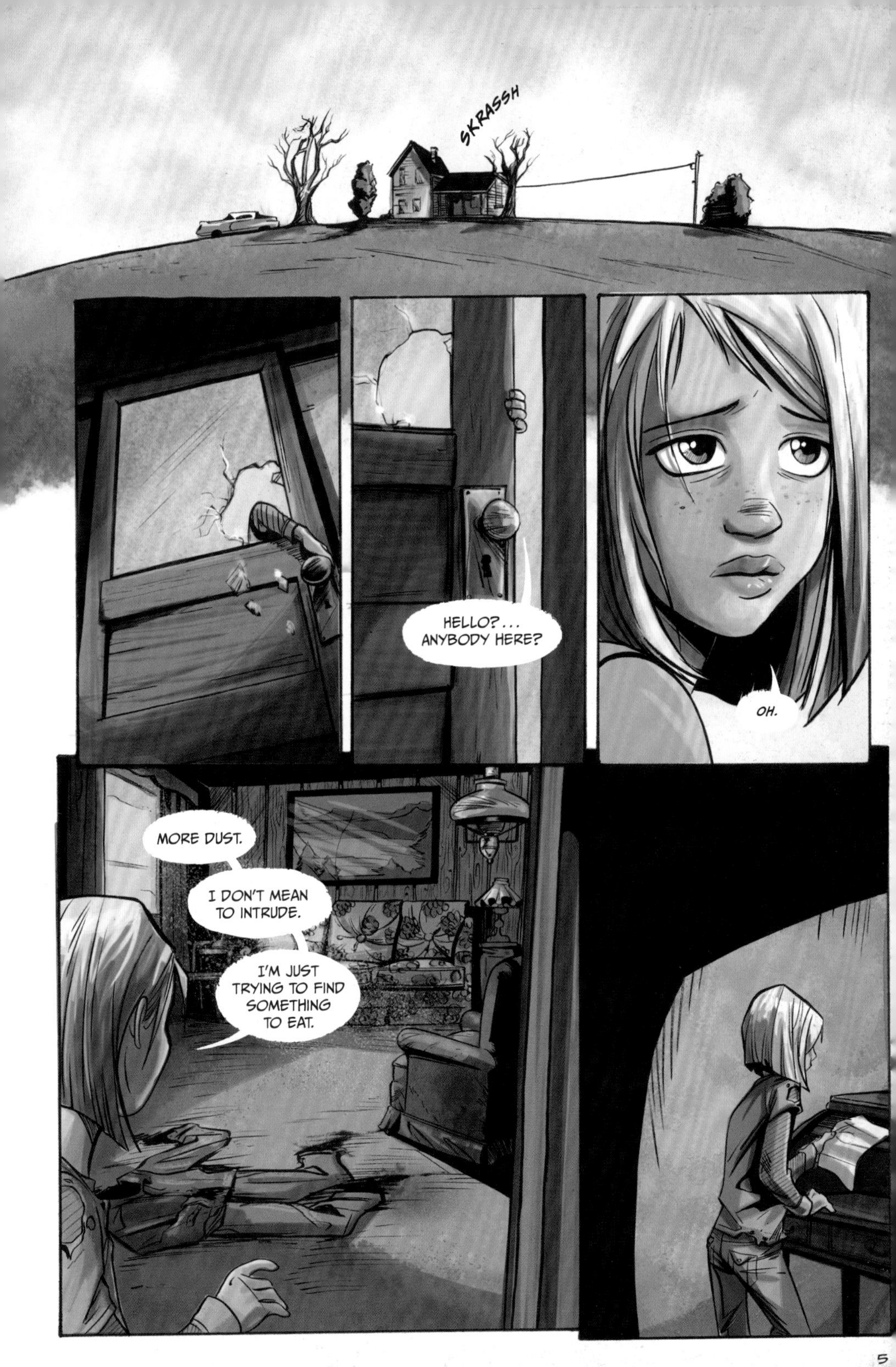
SKRASSH
HELLO?... ANYBODY HERE?
OH.
MORE DUST.
I DON'T MEAN TO INTRUDE.
I'M JUST TRYING TO FIND SOMETHING TO EAT.

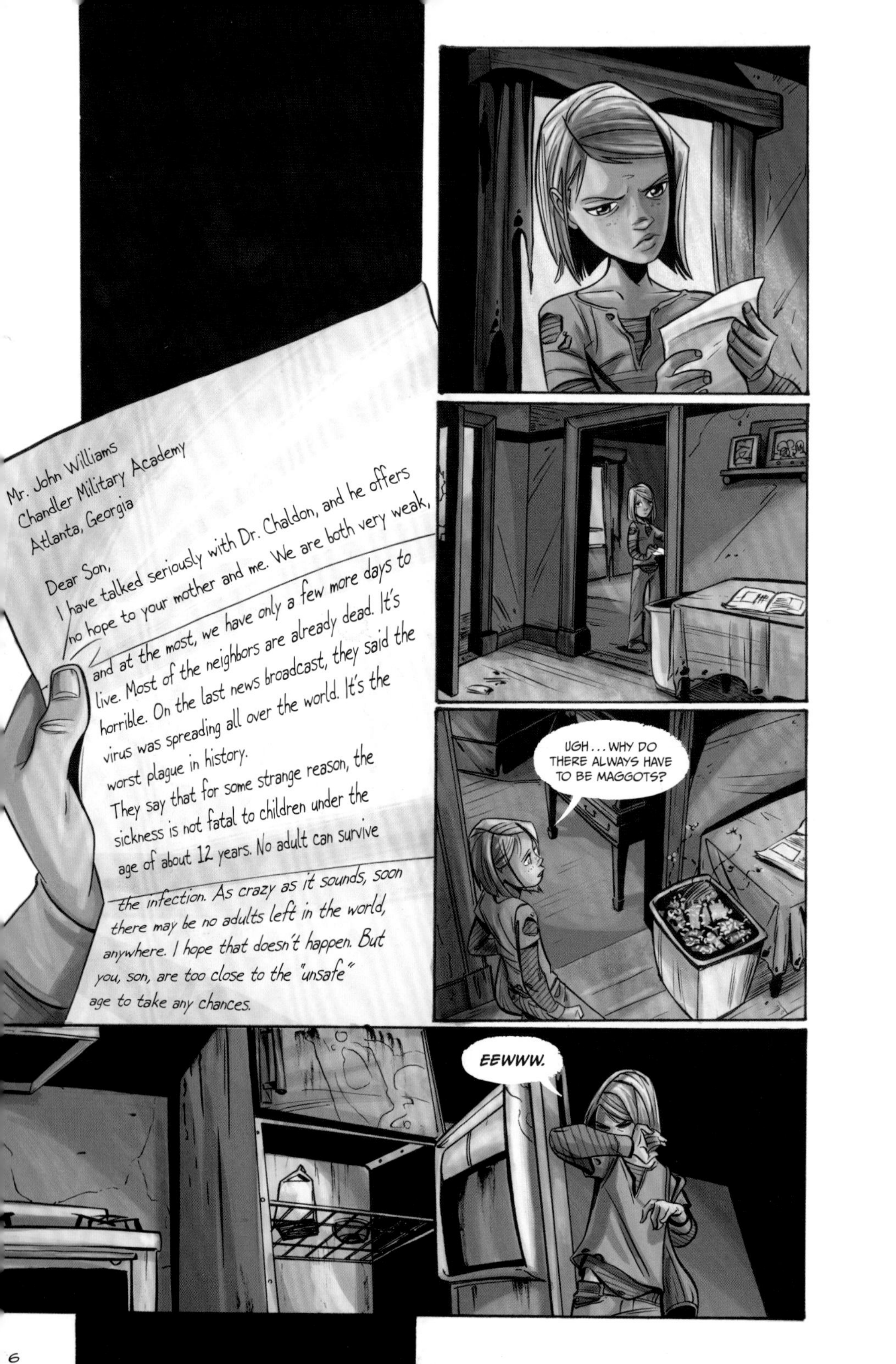

Mr. John Williams
Chandler Military Academy
Atlanta, Georgia
Dear Son,
I have talked seriously with Dr. Chaldon, and he offers no hope to your mother and me. We are both very weak, and at the most, we have only a few more days to live. Most of the neighbors are already dead. It's horrible. On the last news broadcast, they said the virus was spreading all over the world. It's the worst plague in history.
They say that for some strange reason, the sickness is not fatal to children under the age of about 12 years. No adult can survive the infection. As crazy as it sounds, soon there may be no adults left in the world, anywhere. I hope that doesn't happen. But you, son, are too close to the "unsafe" age to take any chances.
UGH... WHY DO THERE ALWAYS HAVE TO BE MAGGOTS?
EEWWW.

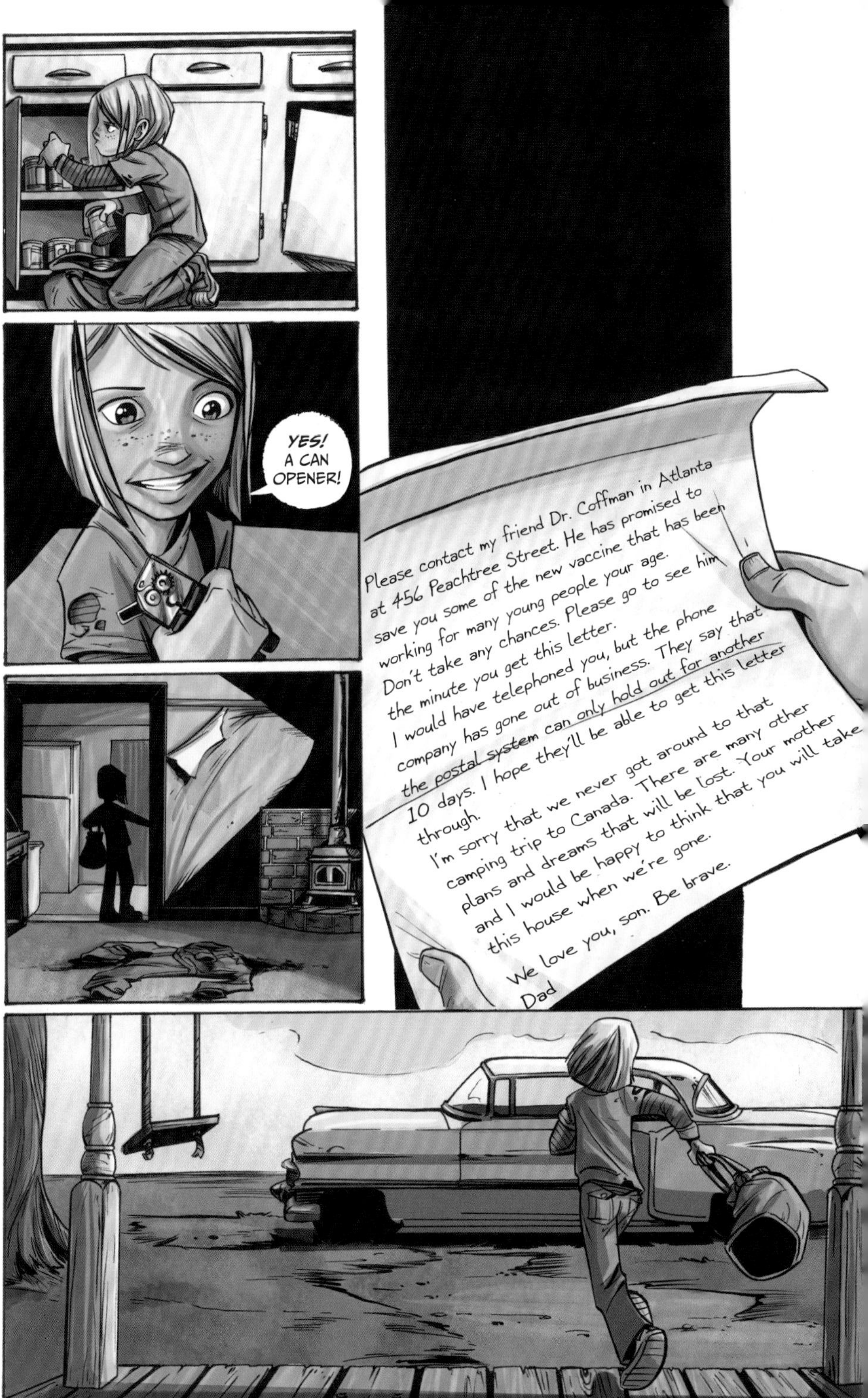
YES! A CAN OPENER!
Please contact my friend Dr. Coffman in Atlanta at 456 Peachtree Street. He has promised to save you some of the new vaccine that has been working for many young people your age. Don't take any chances. Please go to see him the minute you get this letter.
I would have telephoned you, but the phone company has gone out of business. They say that the postal system can only hold out for another 10 days. I hope they'll be able to get this letter through.
I'm sorry that we never got around to that camping trip to Canada. There are many other plans and dreams that will be lost. Your mother and I would be happy to think that you will take this house when we're gone.
We love you, son. Be brave.
Dad

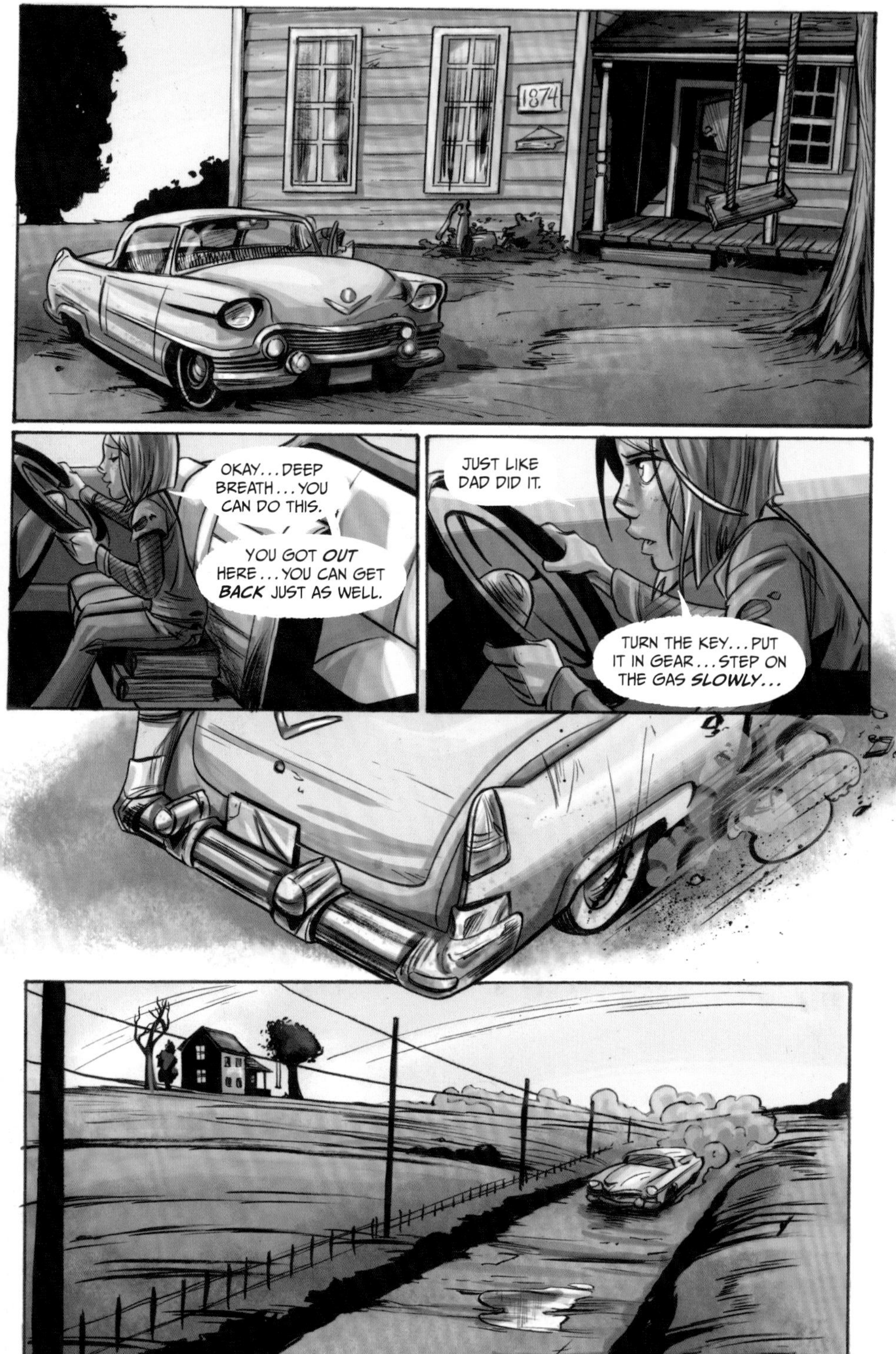
1874
OKAY... DEEP BREATH... YOU CAN DO THIS.
YOU GOT OUT HERE... YOU CAN GET BACK JUST AS WELL.
JUST LIKE DAD DID IT.
TURN THE KEY... PUT IT IN GEAR... STEP ON THE GAS SLOWLY...

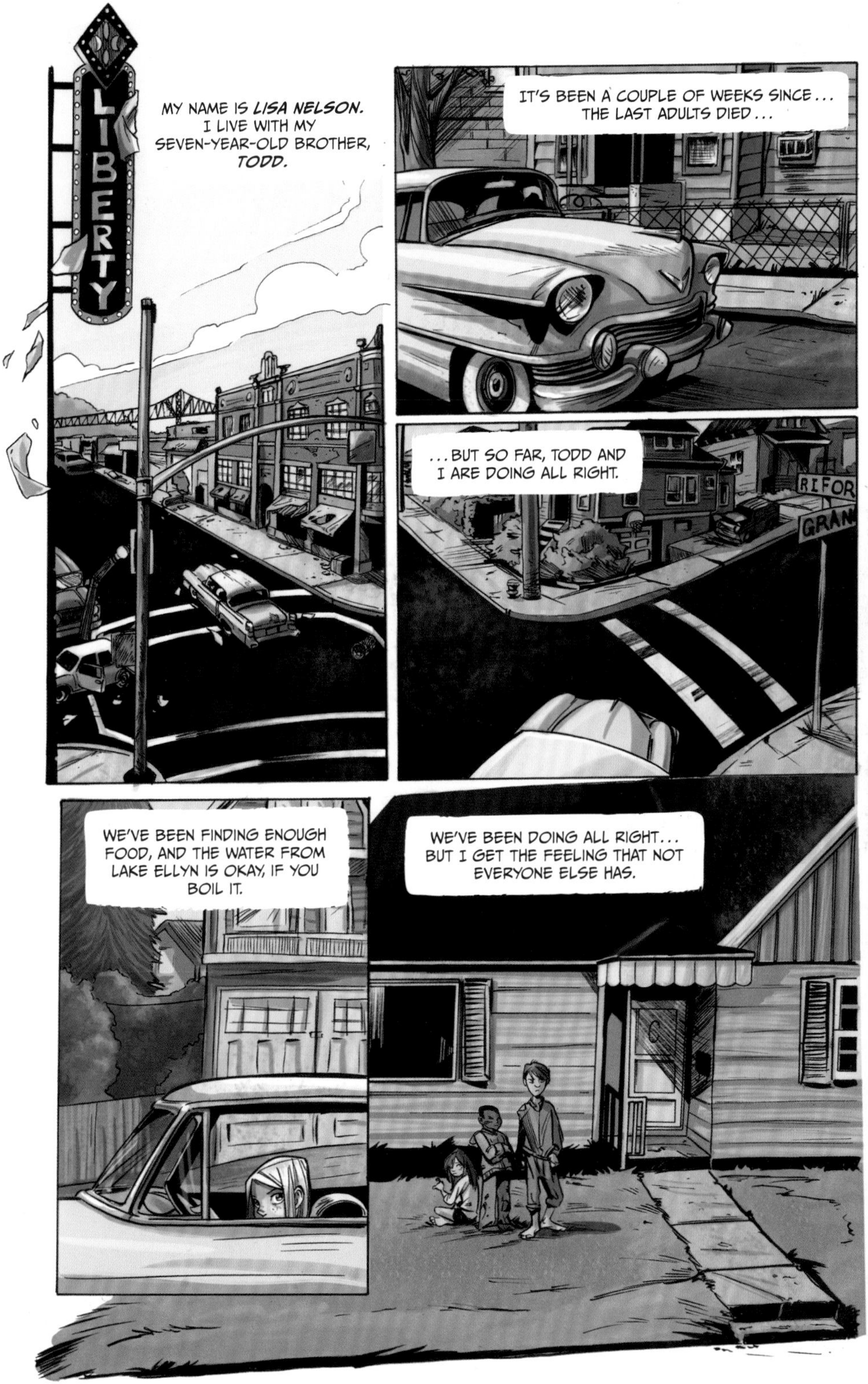

LIBERTY
MY NAME IS LISA NELSON. I LIVE WITH MY SEVEN-YEAR-OLD BROTHER, TODD.
IT'S BEEN A COUPLE OF WEEKS SINCE... THE LAST ADULTS DIED...
...BUT SO FAR, TODD AND I ARE DOING ALL RIGHT.
WE'VE BEEN FINDING ENOUGH FOOD, AND THE WATER FROM LAKE ELLYN IS OKAY, IF YOU BOIL IT.
WE'VE BEEN DOING ALL RIGHT... BUT I GET THE FEELING THAT NOT EVERYONE ELSE HAS.

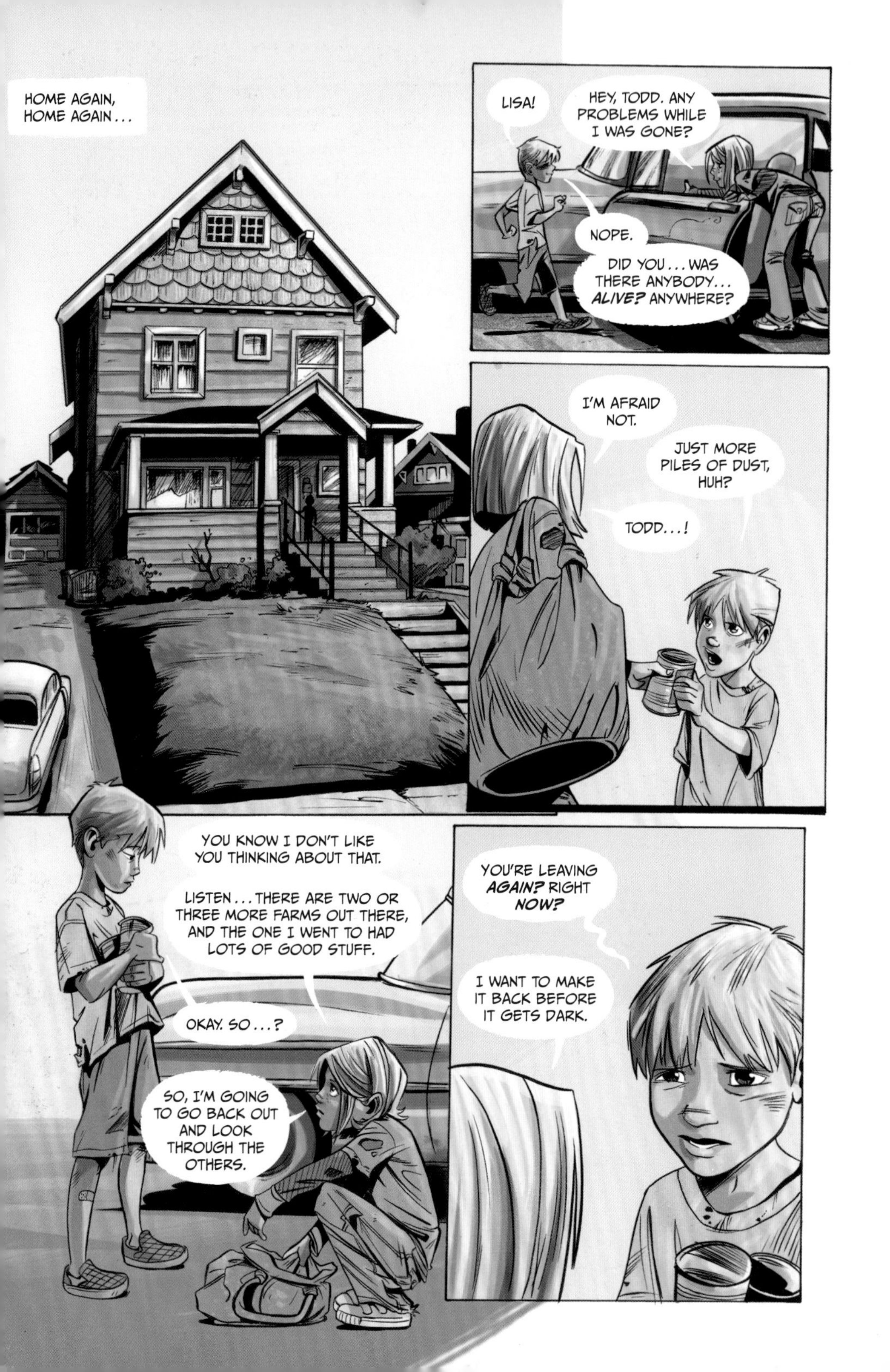
HOME AGAIN, HOME AGAIN...
LISA!
HEY, TODD. ANY PROBLEMS WHILE I WAS GONE?
NOPE.
DID YOU... WAS THERE ANYBODY... *ALIVE?* ANYWHERE?
I'M AFRAID NOT.
JUST MORE PILES OF DUST, HUH?
TODD...!
YOU KNOW I DON'T LIKE YOU THINKING ABOUT THAT.
LISTEN... THERE ARE TWO OR THREE MORE FARMS OUT THERE, AND THE ONE I WENT TO HAD LOTS OF GOOD STUFF.
OKAY. SO...?
SO, I'M GOING TO GO BACK OUT AND LOOK THROUGH THE OTHERS.
YOU'RE LEAVING *AGAIN?* RIGHT *NOW?*
I WANT TO MAKE IT BACK BEFORE IT GETS DARK.

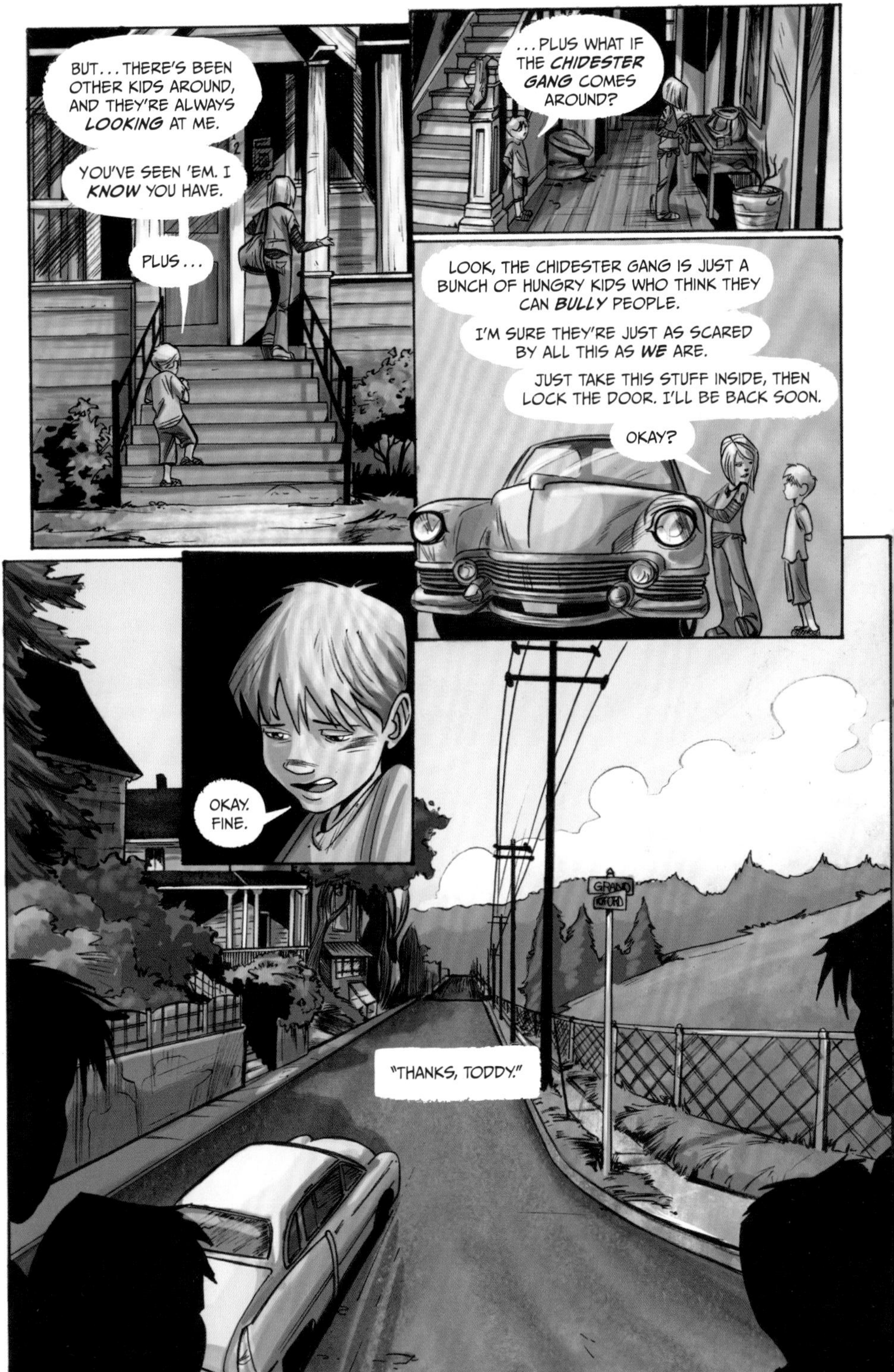
BUT... THERE'S BEEN OTHER KIDS AROUND, AND THEY'RE ALWAYS LOOKING AT ME.
YOU'VE SEEN 'EM. I KNOW YOU HAVE.
PLUS...
...PLUS WHAT IF THE CHIDESTER GANG COMES AROUND?
LOOK, THE CHIDESTER GANG IS JUST A BUNCH OF HUNGRY KIDS WHO THINK THEY CAN BULLY PEOPLE.
I'M SURE THEY'RE JUST AS SCARED BY ALL THIS AS WE ARE.
JUST TAKE THIS STUFF INSIDE, THEN LOCK THE DOOR. I'LL BE BACK SOON.
OKAY?
OKAY. FINE.
GRAND
"THANKS, TODDY."

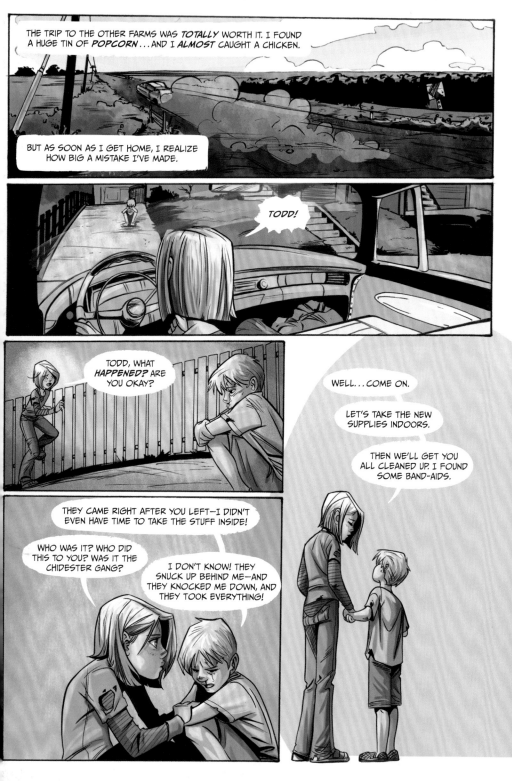

THE TRIP TO THE OTHER FARMS WAS *TOTALLY* WORTH IT. I FOUND A HUGE TIN OF *POPCORN*... AND I *ALMOST* CAUGHT A CHICKEN.

BUT AS SOON AS I GET HOME, I REALIZE HOW BIG A MISTAKE I'VE MADE.

TODD!

TODD, WHAT *HAPPENED?* ARE YOU OKAY?

WELL... COME ON.

LET'S TAKE THE NEW SUPPLIES INDOORS.

THEN WE'LL GET YOU ALL CLEANED UP. I FOUND SOME BAND-AIDS.

THEY CAME RIGHT AFTER YOU LEFT—I DIDN'T EVEN HAVE TIME TO TAKE THE STUFF INSIDE!

WHO WAS IT? WHO DID THIS TO YOU? WAS IT THE CHIDESTER GANG?

I DON'T KNOW! THEY SNUCK UP BEHIND ME—AND THEY KNOCKED ME DOWN, AND THEY TOOK EVERYTHING!

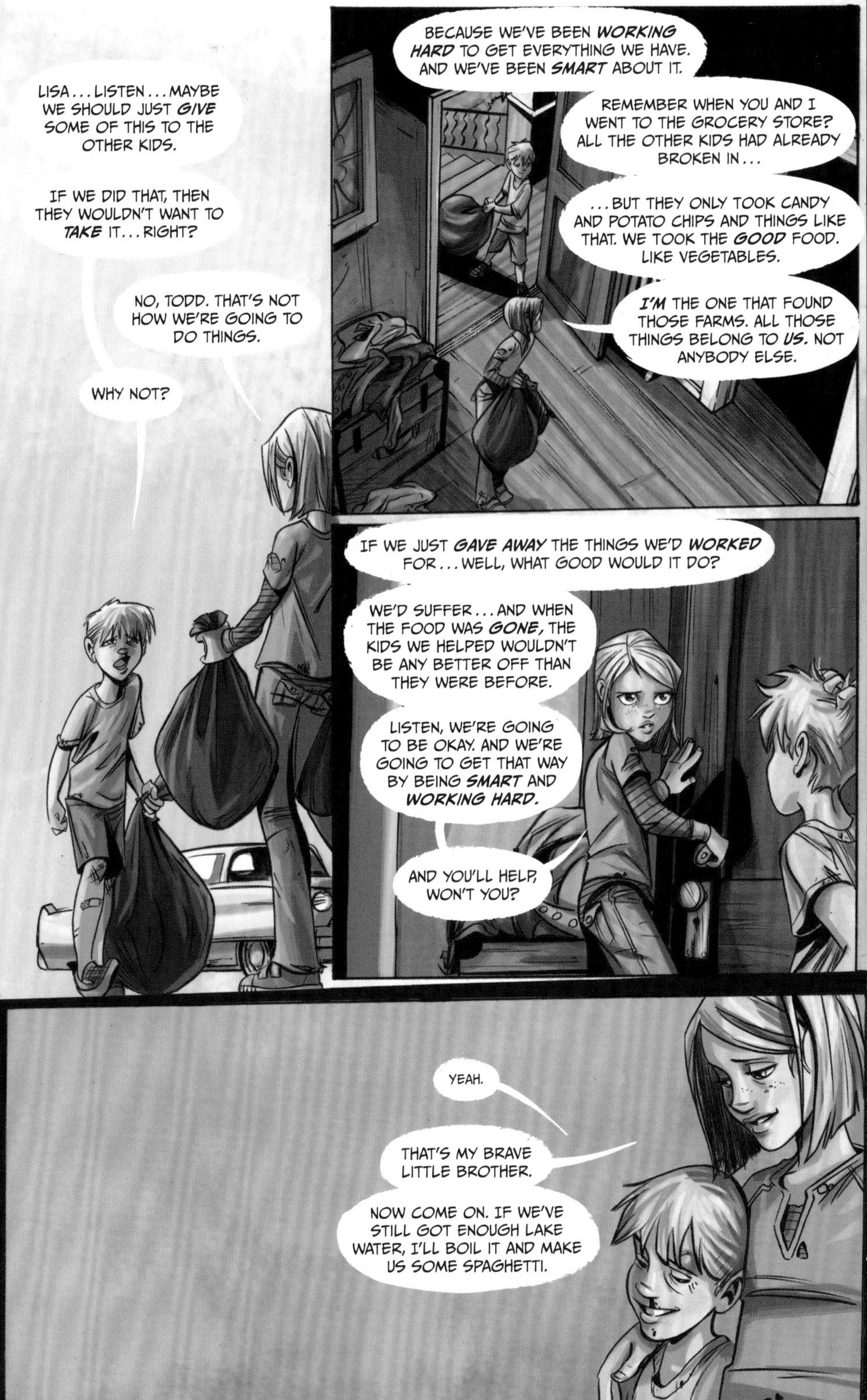
LISA... LISTEN... MAYBE WE SHOULD JUST *GIVE* SOME OF THIS TO THE OTHER KIDS.
IF WE DID THAT, THEN THEY WOULDN'T WANT TO *TAKE* IT... RIGHT?
NO, TODD. THAT'S NOT HOW WE'RE GOING TO DO THINGS.
WHY NOT?
BECAUSE WE'VE BEEN *WORKING HARD* TO GET EVERYTHING WE HAVE. AND WE'VE BEEN *SMART* ABOUT IT.
REMEMBER WHEN YOU AND I WENT TO THE GROCERY STORE? ALL THE OTHER KIDS HAD ALREADY BROKEN IN...
...BUT THEY ONLY TOOK CANDY AND POTATO CHIPS AND THINGS LIKE THAT. WE TOOK THE *GOOD* FOOD. LIKE VEGETABLES.
I'M THE ONE THAT FOUND THOSE FARMS. ALL THOSE THINGS BELONG TO *US.* NOT ANYBODY ELSE.
IF WE JUST *GAVE AWAY* THE THINGS WE'D *WORKED* FOR... WELL, WHAT GOOD WOULD IT DO?
WE'D SUFFER... AND WHEN THE FOOD WAS *GONE,* THE KIDS WE HELPED WOULDN'T BE ANY BETTER OFF THAN THEY WERE BEFORE.
LISTEN, WE'RE GOING TO BE OKAY. AND WE'RE GOING TO GET THAT WAY BY BEING *SMART* AND *WORKING HARD.*
AND YOU'LL HELP, WON'T YOU?
YEAH.
THAT'S MY BRAVE LITTLE BROTHER.
NOW COME ON. IF WE'VE STILL GOT ENOUGH LAKE WATER, I'LL BOIL IT AND MAKE US SOME SPAGHETTI.

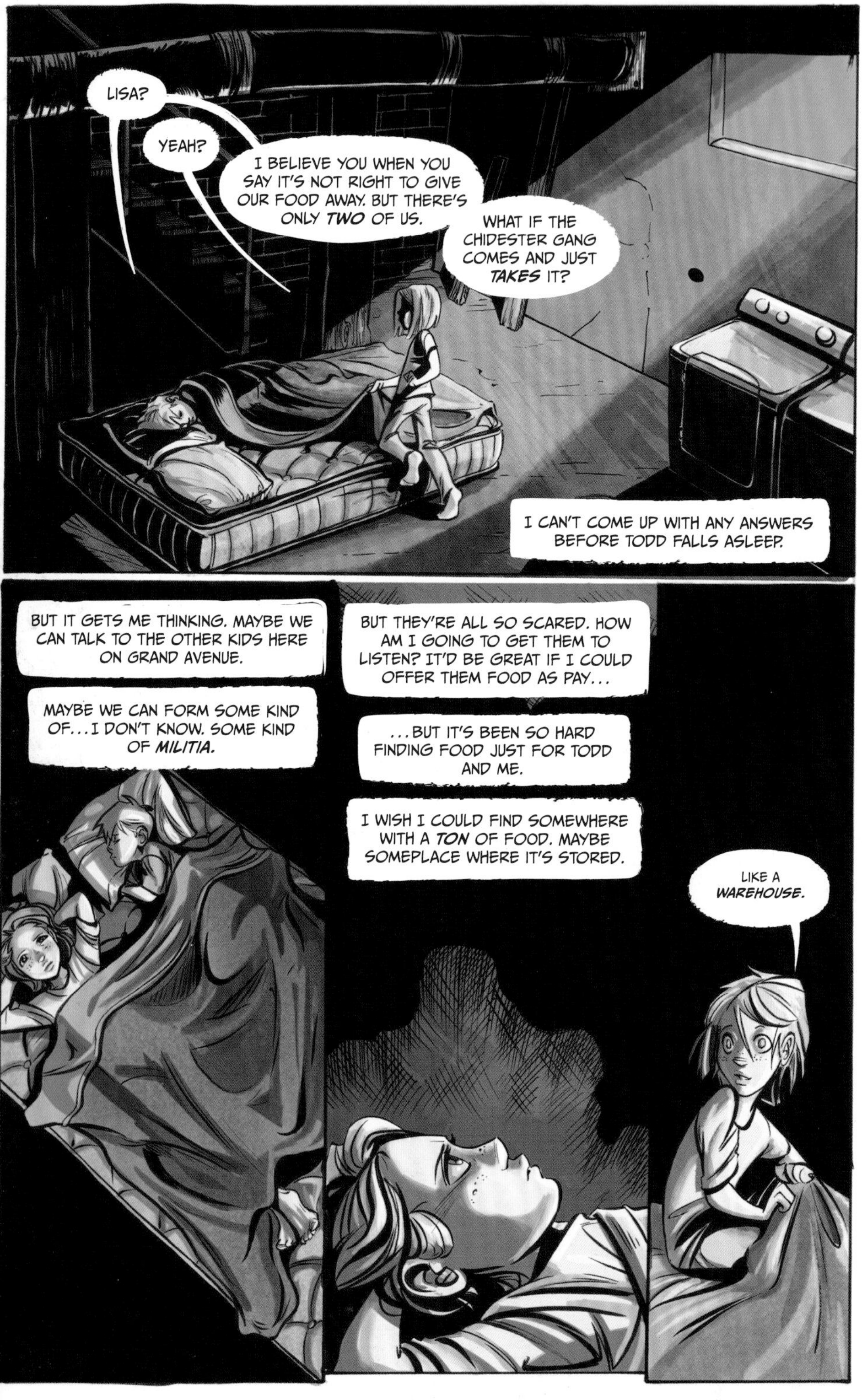
LISA?
YEAH?
I BELIEVE YOU WHEN YOU SAY IT'S NOT RIGHT TO GIVE OUR FOOD AWAY. BUT THERE'S ONLY *TWO* OF US.
WHAT IF THE CHIDESTER GANG COMES AND JUST *TAKES* IT?
I CAN'T COME UP WITH ANY ANSWERS BEFORE TODD FALLS ASLEEP.
BUT IT GETS ME THINKING. MAYBE WE CAN TALK TO THE OTHER KIDS HERE ON GRAND AVENUE.
MAYBE WE CAN FORM SOME KIND OF... I DON'T KNOW. SOME KIND OF *MILITIA.*
BUT THEY'RE ALL SO SCARED. HOW AM I GOING TO GET THEM TO LISTEN? IT'D BE GREAT IF I COULD OFFER THEM FOOD AS PAY...
...BUT IT'S BEEN SO HARD FINDING FOOD JUST FOR TODD AND ME.
I WISH I COULD FIND SOMEWHERE WITH A *TON* OF FOOD. MAYBE SOMEPLACE WHERE IT'S STORED.
LIKE A *WAREHOUSE.*

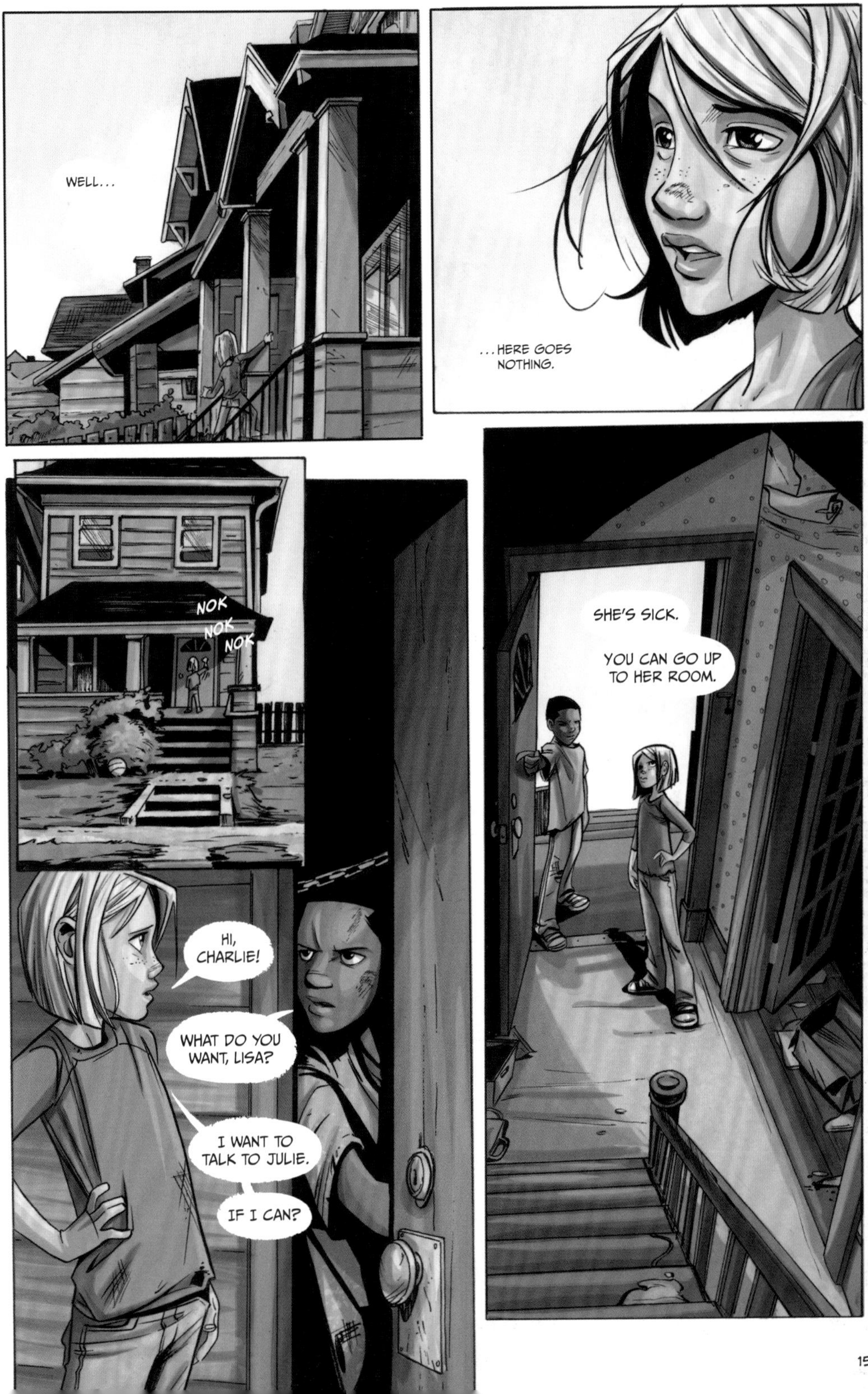
WELL...
...HERE GOES NOTHING.
NOK
NOK
NOK
HI, CHARLIE!
WHAT DO YOU WANT, LISA?
I WANT TO TALK TO JULIE.
IF I CAN?
SHE'S SICK.
YOU CAN GO UP TO HER ROOM.

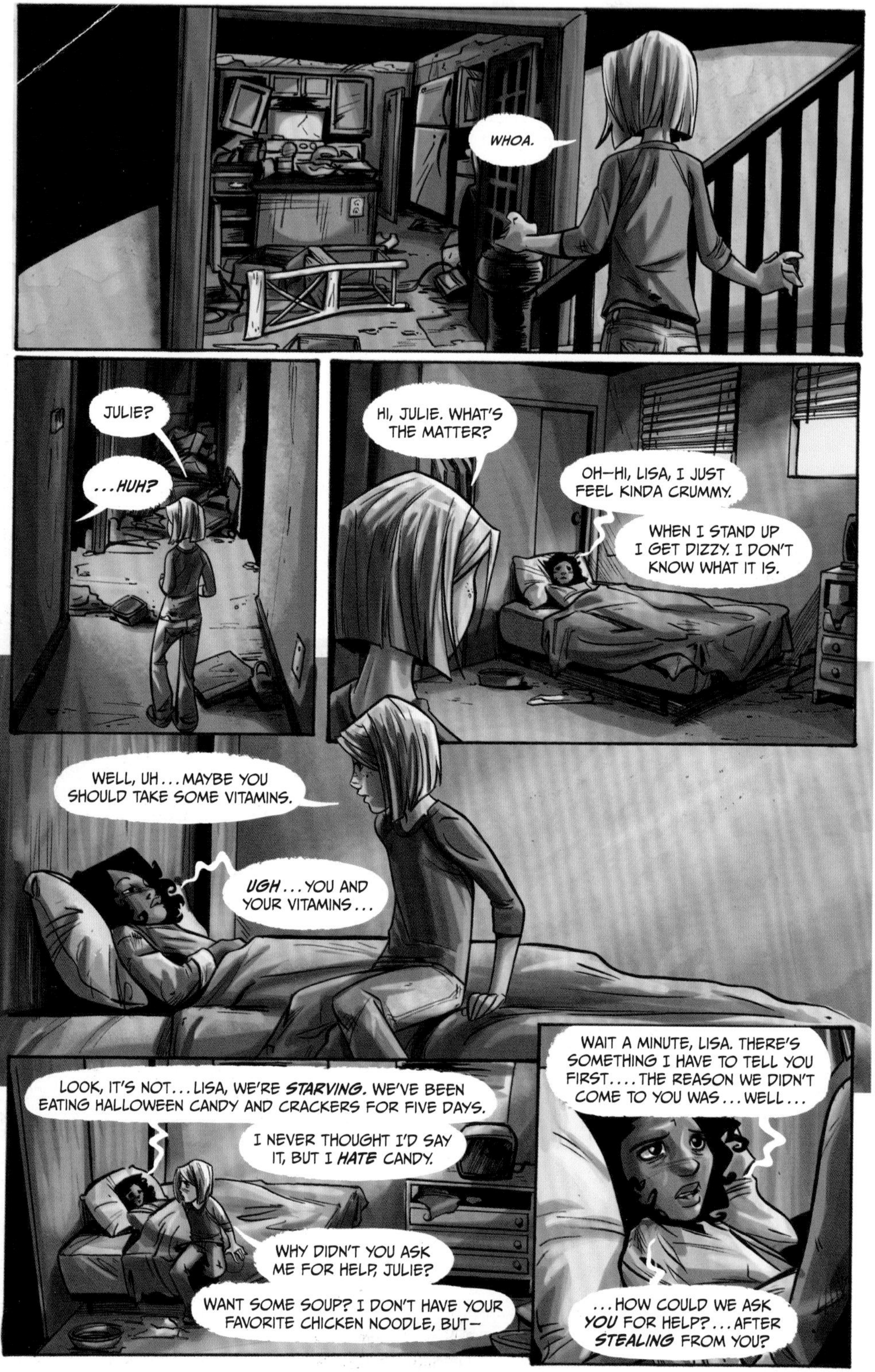
WHOA.
JULIE?
...HUH?
HI, JULIE. WHAT'S THE MATTER?
OH—HI, LISA, I JUST FEEL KINDA CRUMMY.
WHEN I STAND UP I GET DIZZY. I DON'T KNOW WHAT IT IS.
WELL, UH...MAYBE YOU SHOULD TAKE SOME VITAMINS.
UGH...YOU AND YOUR VITAMINS...
LOOK, IT'S NOT...LISA, WE'RE STARVING. WE'VE BEEN EATING HALLOWEEN CANDY AND CRACKERS FOR FIVE DAYS.
I NEVER THOUGHT I'D SAY IT, BUT I HATE CANDY.
WHY DIDN'T YOU ASK ME FOR HELP, JULIE?
WANT SOME SOUP? I DON'T HAVE YOUR FAVORITE CHICKEN NOODLE, BUT—
WAIT A MINUTE, LISA. THERE'S SOMETHING I HAVE TO TELL YOU FIRST....THE REASON WE DIDN'T COME TO YOU WAS...WELL...
...HOW COULD WE ASK YOU FOR HELP?...AFTER STEALING FROM YOU?

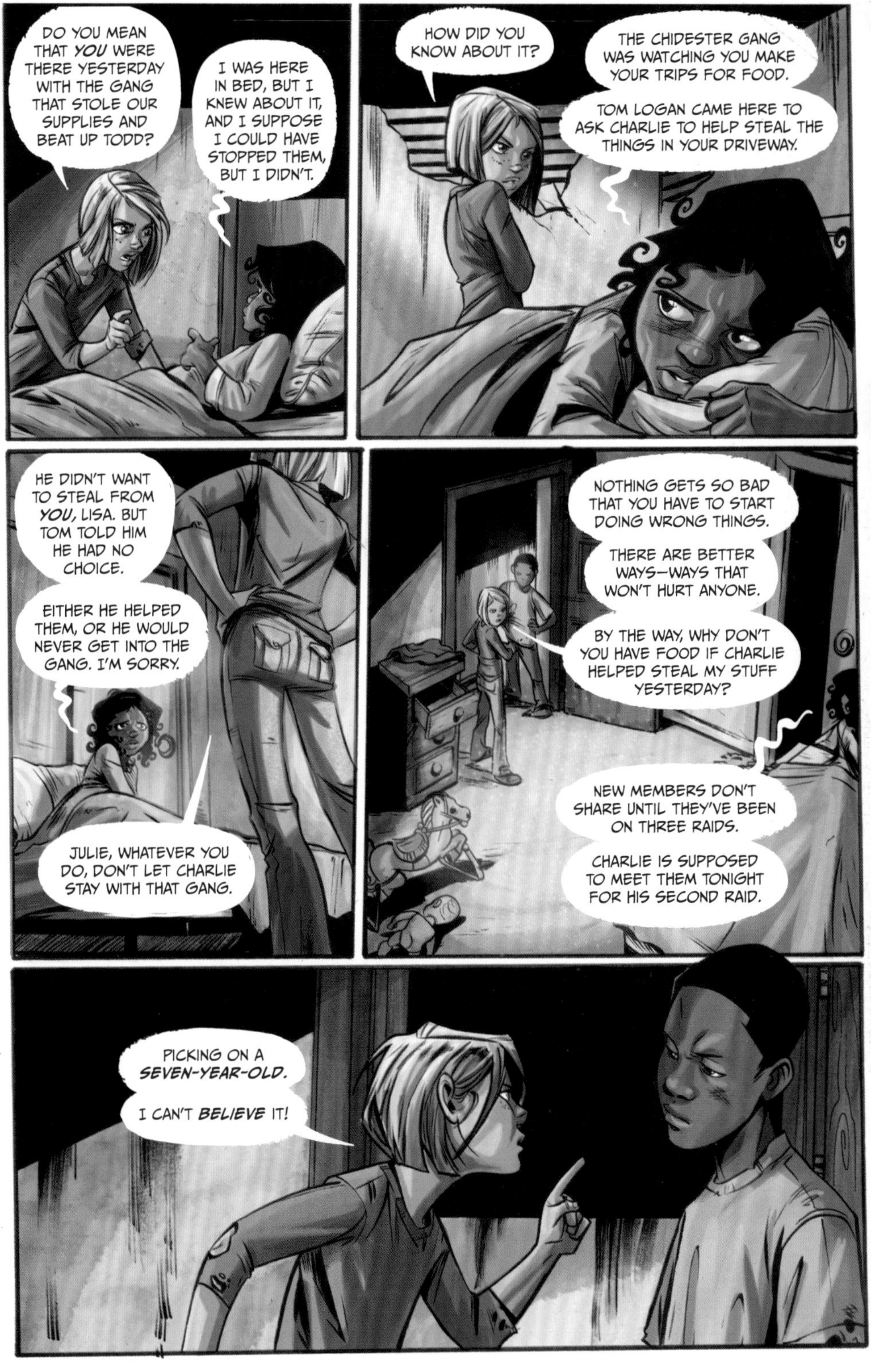
DO YOU MEAN THAT *YOU* WERE THERE YESTERDAY WITH THE GANG THAT STOLE OUR SUPPLIES AND BEAT UP TODD?
I WAS HERE IN BED, BUT I KNEW ABOUT IT, AND I SUPPOSE I COULD HAVE STOPPED THEM, BUT I DIDN'T.
HOW DID YOU KNOW ABOUT IT?
THE CHIDESTER GANG WAS WATCHING YOU MAKE YOUR TRIPS FOR FOOD.
TOM LOGAN CAME HERE TO ASK CHARLIE TO HELP STEAL THE THINGS IN YOUR DRIVEWAY.
HE DIDN'T WANT TO STEAL FROM *YOU,* LISA. BUT TOM TOLD HIM HE HAD NO CHOICE.
EITHER HE HELPED THEM, OR HE WOULD NEVER GET INTO THE GANG. I'M SORRY.
JULIE, WHATEVER YOU DO, DON'T LET CHARLIE STAY WITH THAT GANG.
NOTHING GETS SO BAD THAT YOU HAVE TO START DOING WRONG THINGS.
THERE ARE BETTER WAYS—WAYS THAT WON'T HURT ANYONE.
BY THE WAY, WHY DON'T YOU HAVE FOOD IF CHARLIE HELPED STEAL MY STUFF YESTERDAY?
NEW MEMBERS DON'T SHARE UNTIL THEY'VE BEEN ON THREE RAIDS.
CHARLIE IS SUPPOSED TO MEET THEM TONIGHT FOR HIS SECOND RAID.
PICKING ON A *SEVEN-YEAR-OLD.*
I CAN'T *BELIEVE* IT!

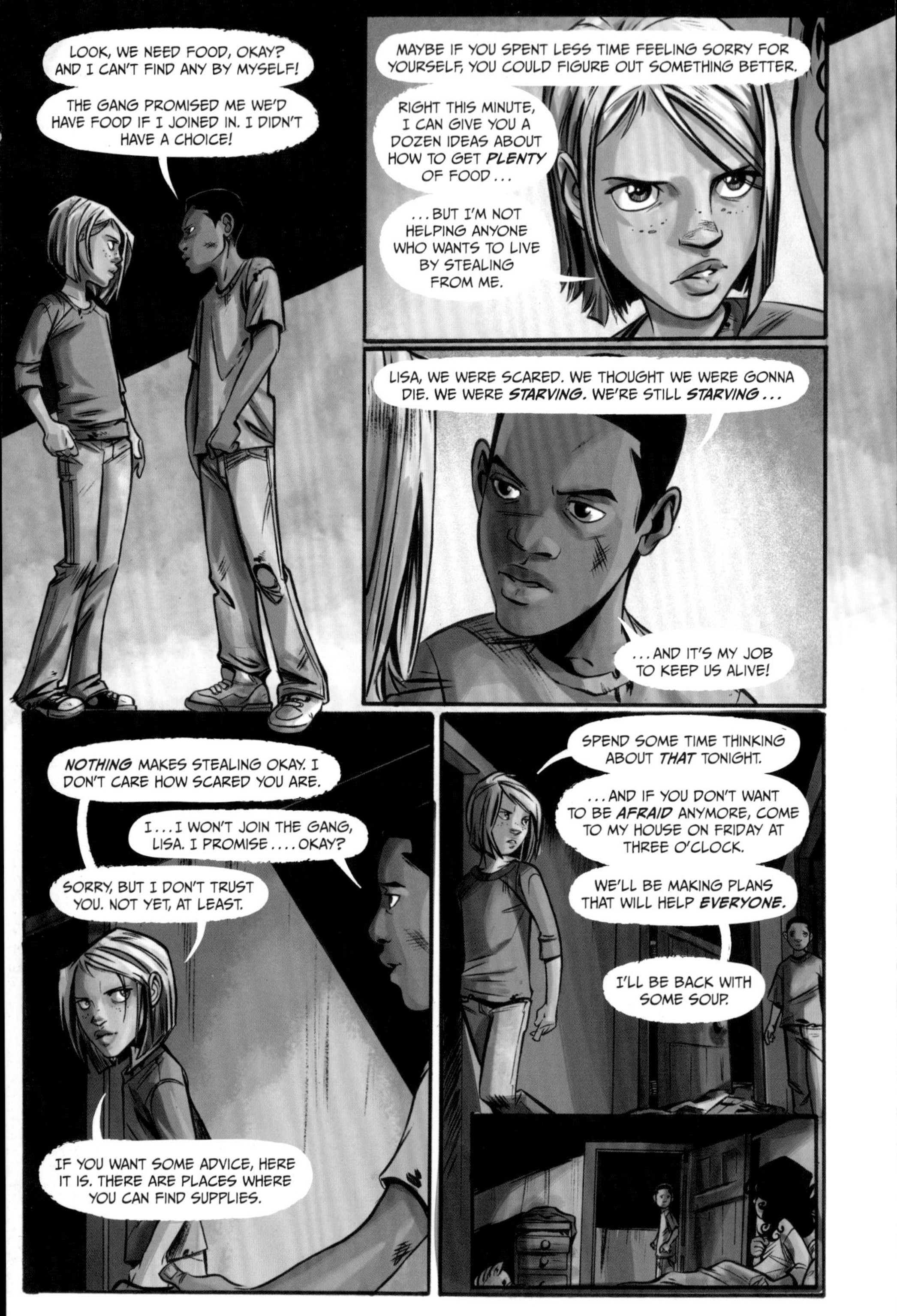
LOOK, WE NEED FOOD, OKAY? AND I CAN'T FIND ANY BY MYSELF!
THE GANG PROMISED ME WE'D HAVE FOOD IF I JOINED IN. I DIDN'T HAVE A CHOICE!
MAYBE IF YOU SPENT LESS TIME FEELING SORRY FOR YOURSELF, YOU COULD FIGURE OUT SOMETHING BETTER.
RIGHT THIS MINUTE, I CAN GIVE YOU A DOZEN IDEAS ABOUT HOW TO GET PLENTY OF FOOD . . .
. . . BUT I'M NOT HELPING ANYONE WHO WANTS TO LIVE BY STEALING FROM ME.
LISA, WE WERE SCARED. WE THOUGHT WE WERE GONNA DIE. WE WERE STARVING. WE'RE STILL STARVING . . .
. . . AND IT'S MY JOB TO KEEP US ALIVE!
NOTHING MAKES STEALING OKAY. I DON'T CARE HOW SCARED YOU ARE.
I . . . I WON'T JOIN THE GANG, LISA. I PROMISE . . . . OKAY?
SORRY, BUT I DON'T TRUST YOU. NOT YET, AT LEAST.
IF YOU WANT SOME ADVICE, HERE IT IS. THERE ARE PLACES WHERE YOU CAN FIND SUPPLIES.
SPEND SOME TIME THINKING ABOUT THAT TONIGHT.
. . . AND IF YOU DON'T WANT TO BE AFRAID ANYMORE, COME TO MY HOUSE ON FRIDAY AT THREE O'CLOCK.
WE'LL BE MAKING PLANS THAT WILL HELP EVERYONE.
I'LL BE BACK WITH SOME SOUP.

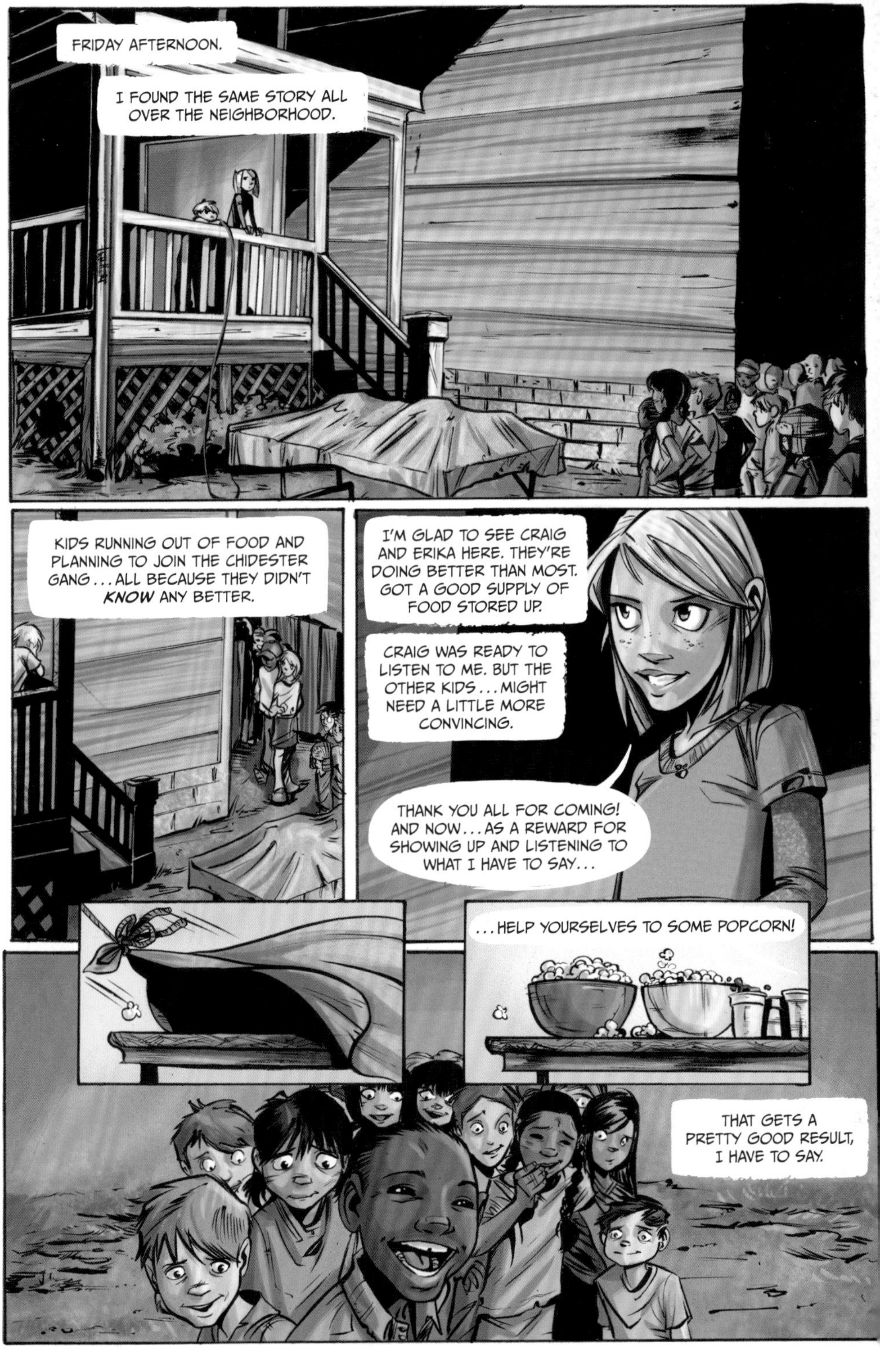
FRIDAY AFTERNOON.
I FOUND THE SAME STORY ALL OVER THE NEIGHBORHOOD.
KIDS RUNNING OUT OF FOOD AND PLANNING TO JOIN THE CHIDESTER GANG . . . ALL BECAUSE THEY DIDN'T *KNOW* ANY BETTER.
I'M GLAD TO SEE CRAIG AND ERIKA HERE. THEY'RE DOING BETTER THAN MOST. GOT A GOOD SUPPLY OF FOOD STORED UP.
CRAIG WAS READY TO LISTEN TO ME. BUT THE OTHER KIDS . . . MIGHT NEED A LITTLE MORE CONVINCING.
THANK YOU ALL FOR COMING! AND NOW . . . AS A REWARD FOR SHOWING UP AND LISTENING TO WHAT I HAVE TO SAY . . .
. . . HELP YOURSELVES TO SOME POPCORN!
THAT GETS A PRETTY GOOD RESULT, I HAVE TO SAY.

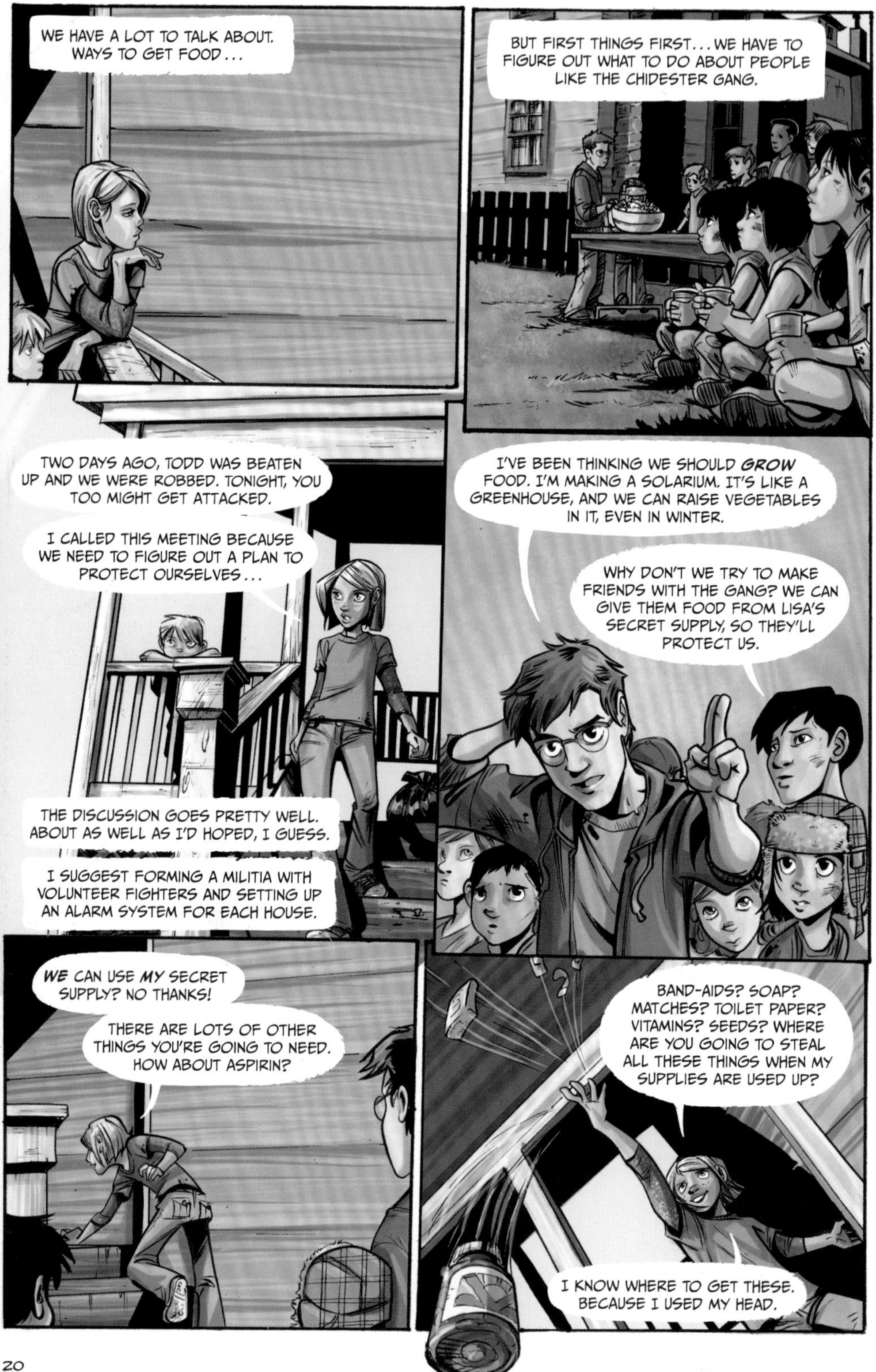
WE HAVE A LOT TO TALK ABOUT. WAYS TO GET FOOD . . .
BUT FIRST THINGS FIRST . . . WE HAVE TO FIGURE OUT WHAT TO DO ABOUT PEOPLE LIKE THE CHIDESTER GANG.
TWO DAYS AGO, TODD WAS BEATEN UP AND WE WERE ROBBED. TONIGHT, YOU TOO MIGHT GET ATTACKED.
I CALLED THIS MEETING BECAUSE WE NEED TO FIGURE OUT A PLAN TO PROTECT OURSELVES . . .
THE DISCUSSION GOES PRETTY WELL. ABOUT AS WELL AS I'D HOPED, I GUESS.
I SUGGEST FORMING A MILITIA WITH VOLUNTEER FIGHTERS AND SETTING UP AN ALARM SYSTEM FOR EACH HOUSE.
I'VE BEEN THINKING WE SHOULD **GROW** FOOD. I'M MAKING A SOLARIUM. IT'S LIKE A GREENHOUSE, AND WE CAN RAISE VEGETABLES IN IT, EVEN IN WINTER.
WHY DON'T WE TRY TO MAKE FRIENDS WITH THE GANG? WE CAN GIVE THEM FOOD FROM LISA'S SECRET SUPPLY, SO THEY'LL PROTECT US.
WE CAN USE ***MY*** SECRET SUPPLY? NO THANKS!
THERE ARE LOTS OF OTHER THINGS YOU'RE GOING TO NEED. HOW ABOUT ASPIRIN?
BAND-AIDS? SOAP? MATCHES? TOILET PAPER? VITAMINS? SEEDS? WHERE ARE YOU GOING TO STEAL ALL THESE THINGS WHEN MY SUPPLIES ARE USED UP?
I KNOW WHERE TO GET THESE. BECAUSE I USED MY HEAD.

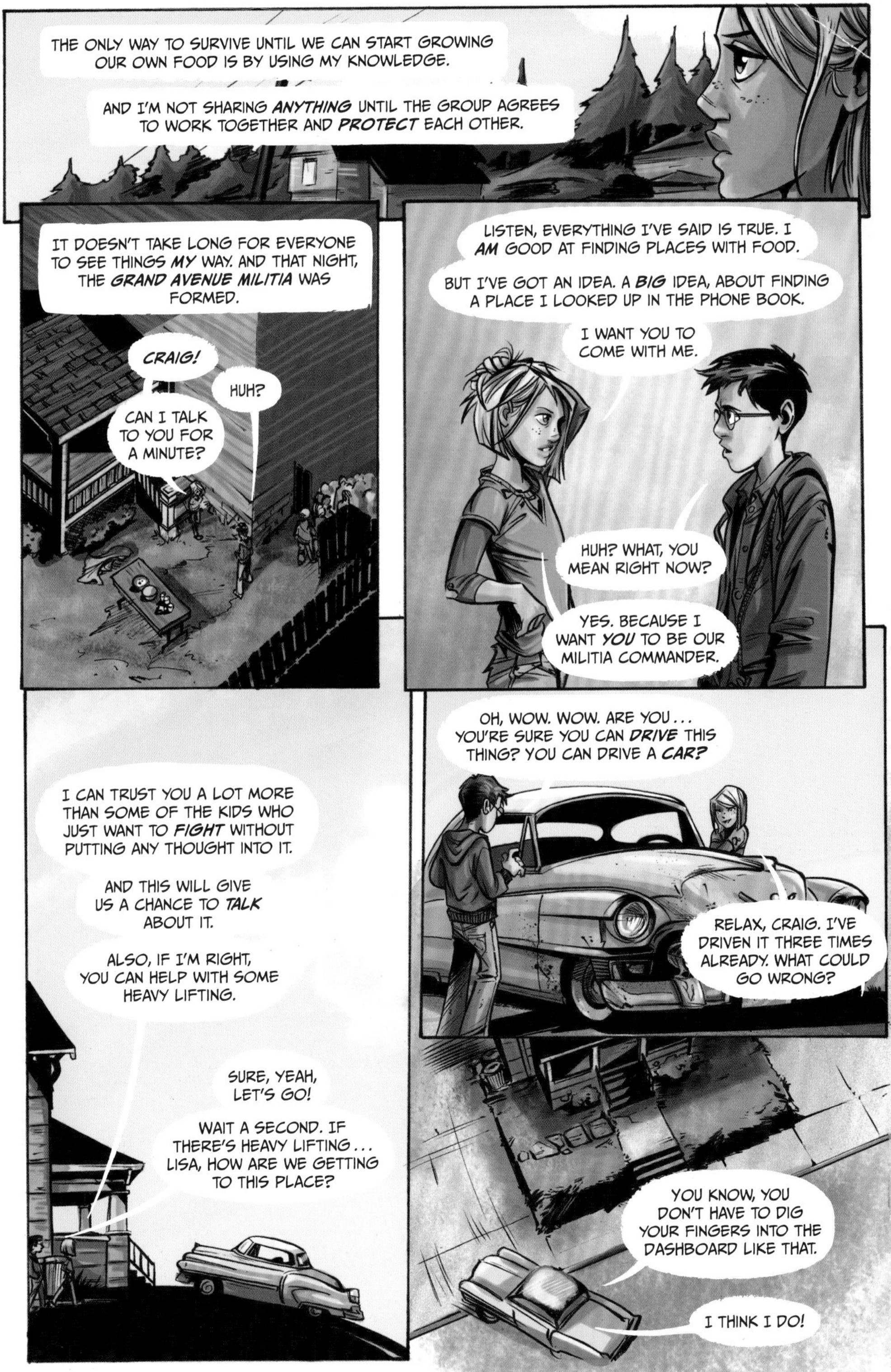
THE ONLY WAY TO SURVIVE UNTIL WE CAN START GROWING OUR OWN FOOD IS BY USING MY KNOWLEDGE.
AND I'M NOT SHARING ANYTHING UNTIL THE GROUP AGREES TO WORK TOGETHER AND PROTECT EACH OTHER.
IT DOESN'T TAKE LONG FOR EVERYONE TO SEE THINGS MY WAY. AND THAT NIGHT, THE GRAND AVENUE MILITIA WAS FORMED.
CRAIG!
HUH?
CAN I TALK TO YOU FOR A MINUTE?
LISTEN, EVERYTHING I'VE SAID IS TRUE. I AM GOOD AT FINDING PLACES WITH FOOD.
BUT I'VE GOT AN IDEA. A BIG IDEA, ABOUT FINDING A PLACE I LOOKED UP IN THE PHONE BOOK.
I WANT YOU TO COME WITH ME.
HUH? WHAT, YOU MEAN RIGHT NOW?
YES. BECAUSE I WANT YOU TO BE OUR MILITIA COMMANDER.
I CAN TRUST YOU A LOT MORE THAN SOME OF THE KIDS WHO JUST WANT TO FIGHT WITHOUT PUTTING ANY THOUGHT INTO IT.
AND THIS WILL GIVE US A CHANCE TO TALK ABOUT IT.
ALSO, IF I'M RIGHT, YOU CAN HELP WITH SOME HEAVY LIFTING.
SURE, YEAH, LET'S GO!
WAIT A SECOND. IF THERE'S HEAVY LIFTING... LISA, HOW ARE WE GETTING TO THIS PLACE?
OH, WOW. WOW. ARE YOU... YOU'RE SURE YOU CAN DRIVE THIS THING? YOU CAN DRIVE A CAR?
RELAX, CRAIG. I'VE DRIVEN IT THREE TIMES ALREADY. WHAT COULD GO WRONG?
YOU KNOW, YOU DON'T HAVE TO DIG YOUR FINGERS INTO THE DASHBOARD LIKE THAT.
I THINK I DO!

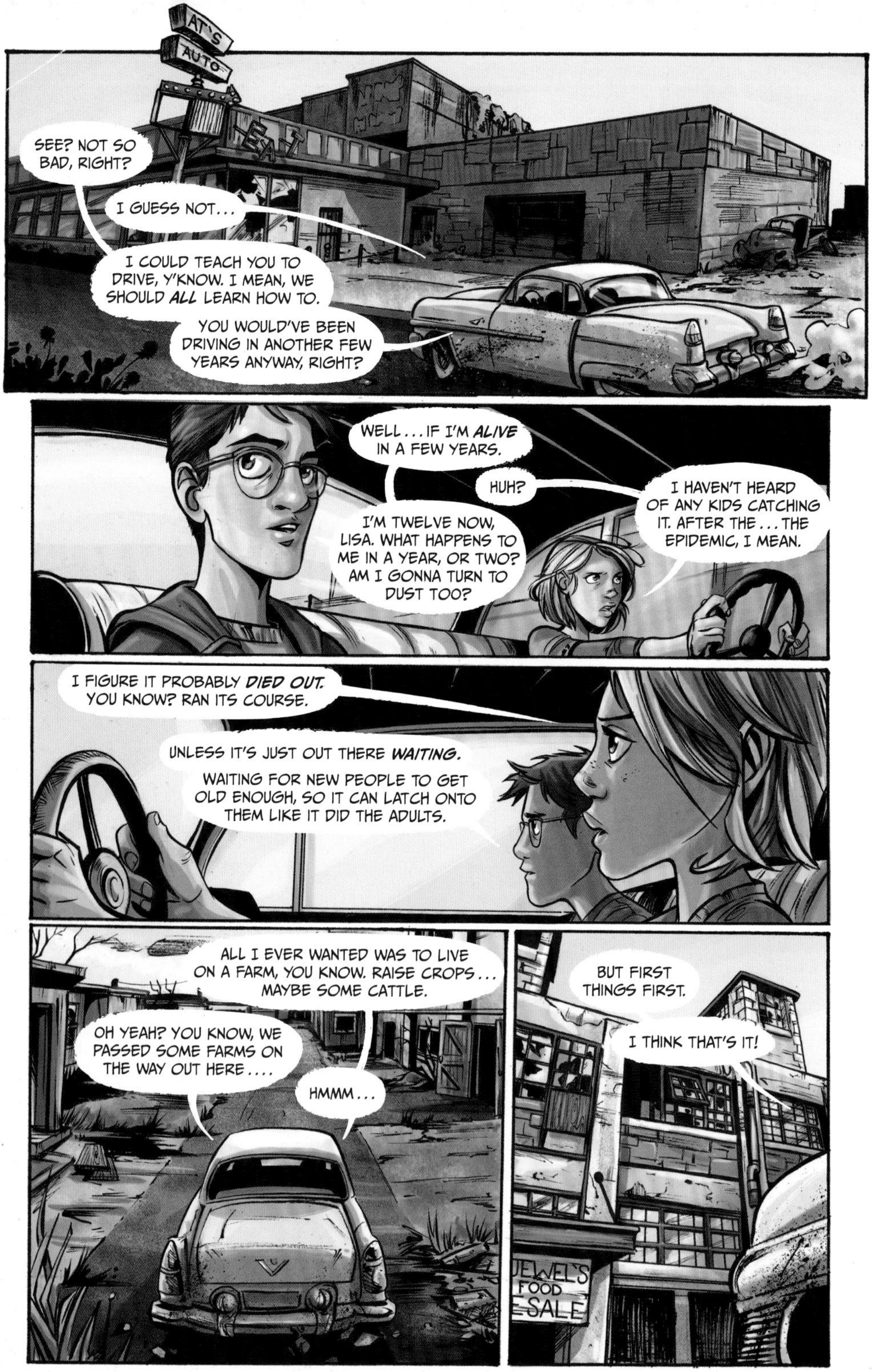
AT'S
AUTO
EAT
SEE? NOT SO BAD, RIGHT?
I GUESS NOT...
I COULD TEACH YOU TO DRIVE, Y'KNOW. I MEAN, WE SHOULD ALL LEARN HOW TO.
YOU WOULD'VE BEEN DRIVING IN ANOTHER FEW YEARS ANYWAY, RIGHT?
WELL... IF I'M ALIVE IN A FEW YEARS.
HUH?
I'M TWELVE NOW, LISA. WHAT HAPPENS TO ME IN A YEAR, OR TWO? AM I GONNA TURN TO DUST TOO?
I HAVEN'T HEARD OF ANY KIDS CATCHING IT. AFTER THE... THE EPIDEMIC, I MEAN.
I FIGURE IT PROBABLY DIED OUT. YOU KNOW? RAN ITS COURSE.
UNLESS IT'S JUST OUT THERE WAITING.
WAITING FOR NEW PEOPLE TO GET OLD ENOUGH, SO IT CAN LATCH ONTO THEM LIKE IT DID THE ADULTS.
ALL I EVER WANTED WAS TO LIVE ON A FARM, YOU KNOW. RAISE CROPS... MAYBE SOME CATTLE.
OH YEAH? YOU KNOW, WE PASSED SOME FARMS ON THE WAY OUT HERE....
HMMM...
BUT FIRST THINGS FIRST.
I THINK THAT'S IT!
JEWEL'S
FOOD
SALE

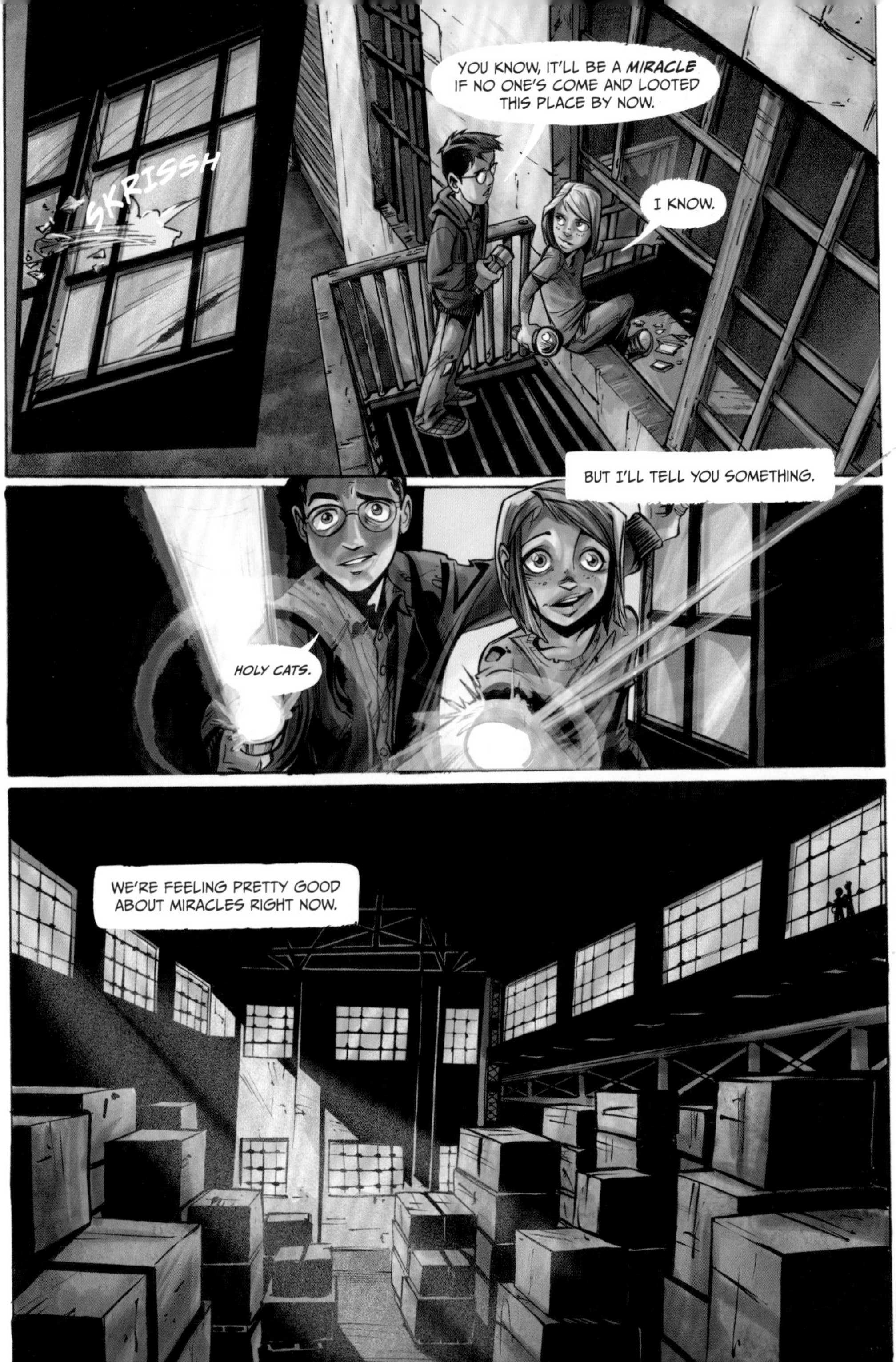
SKRISSH
YOU KNOW, IT'LL BE A *MIRACLE* IF NO ONE'S COME AND LOOTED THIS PLACE BY NOW.
I KNOW.
BUT I'LL TELL YOU SOMETHING.
HOLY CATS.
WE'RE FEELING PRETTY GOOD ABOUT MIRACLES RIGHT NOW.

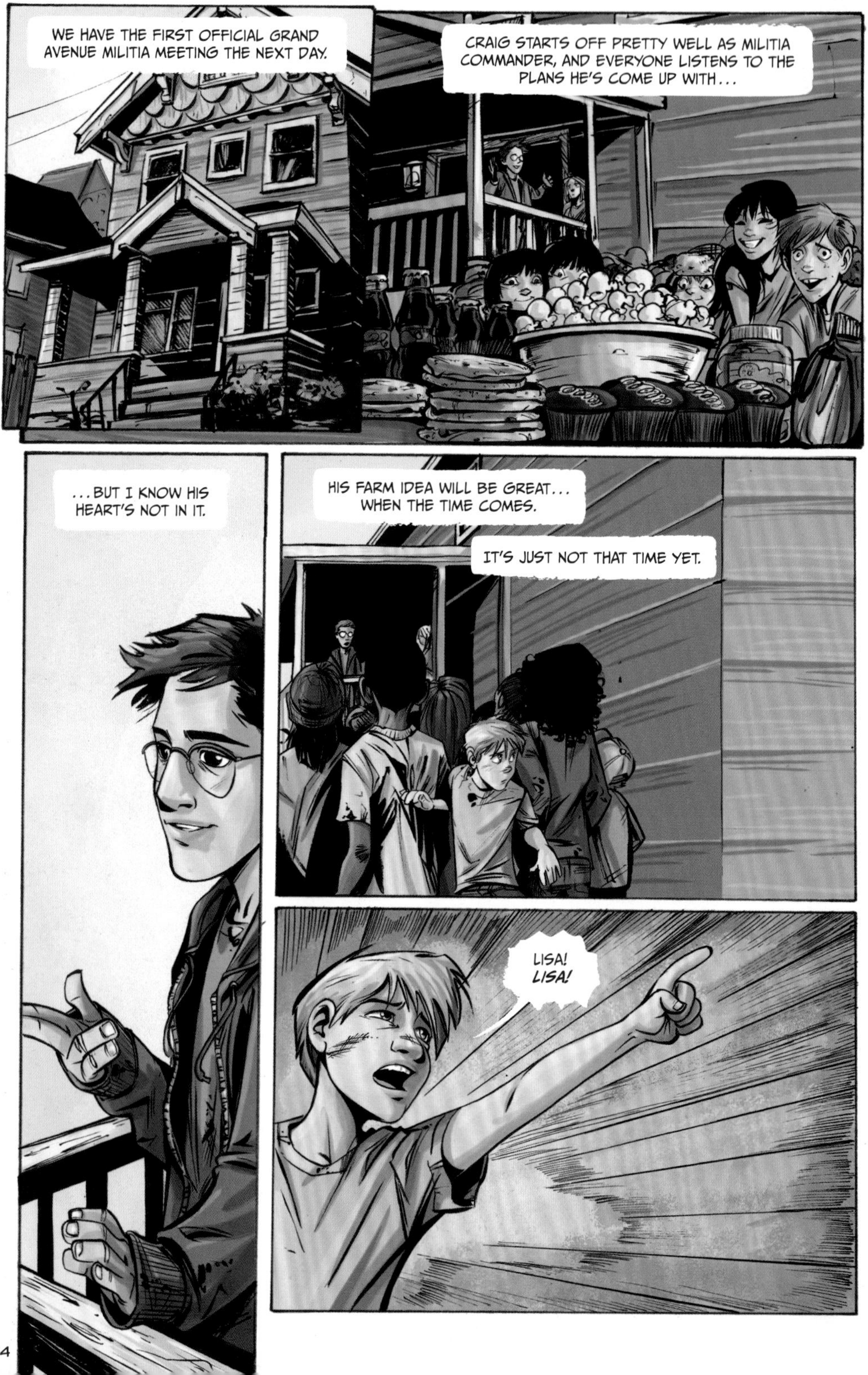
WE HAVE THE FIRST OFFICIAL GRAND AVENUE MILITIA MEETING THE NEXT DAY.
CRAIG STARTS OFF PRETTY WELL AS MILITIA COMMANDER, AND EVERYONE LISTENS TO THE PLANS HE'S COME UP WITH...
...BUT I KNOW HIS HEART'S NOT IN IT.
HIS FARM IDEA WILL BE GREAT... WHEN THE TIME COMES.
IT'S JUST NOT THAT TIME YET.
LISA! *LISA!*

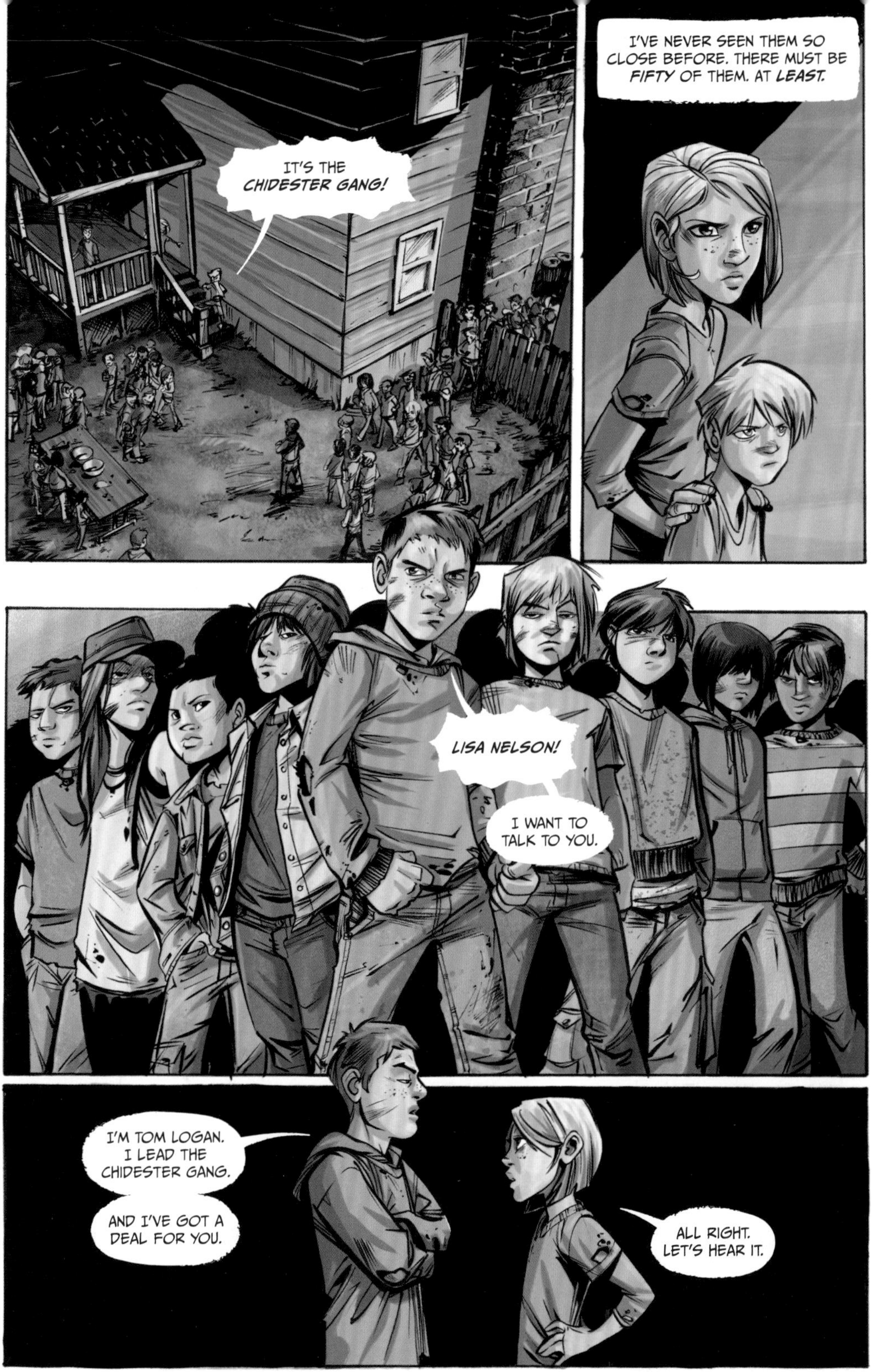
IT'S THE *CHIDESTER GANG!*
I'VE NEVER SEEN THEM SO CLOSE BEFORE. THERE MUST BE *FIFTY* OF THEM. AT *LEAST.*
LISA NELSON!
I WANT TO TALK TO YOU.
I'M TOM LOGAN. I LEAD THE CHIDESTER GANG.
AND I'VE GOT A DEAL FOR YOU.
ALL RIGHT. LET'S HEAR IT.

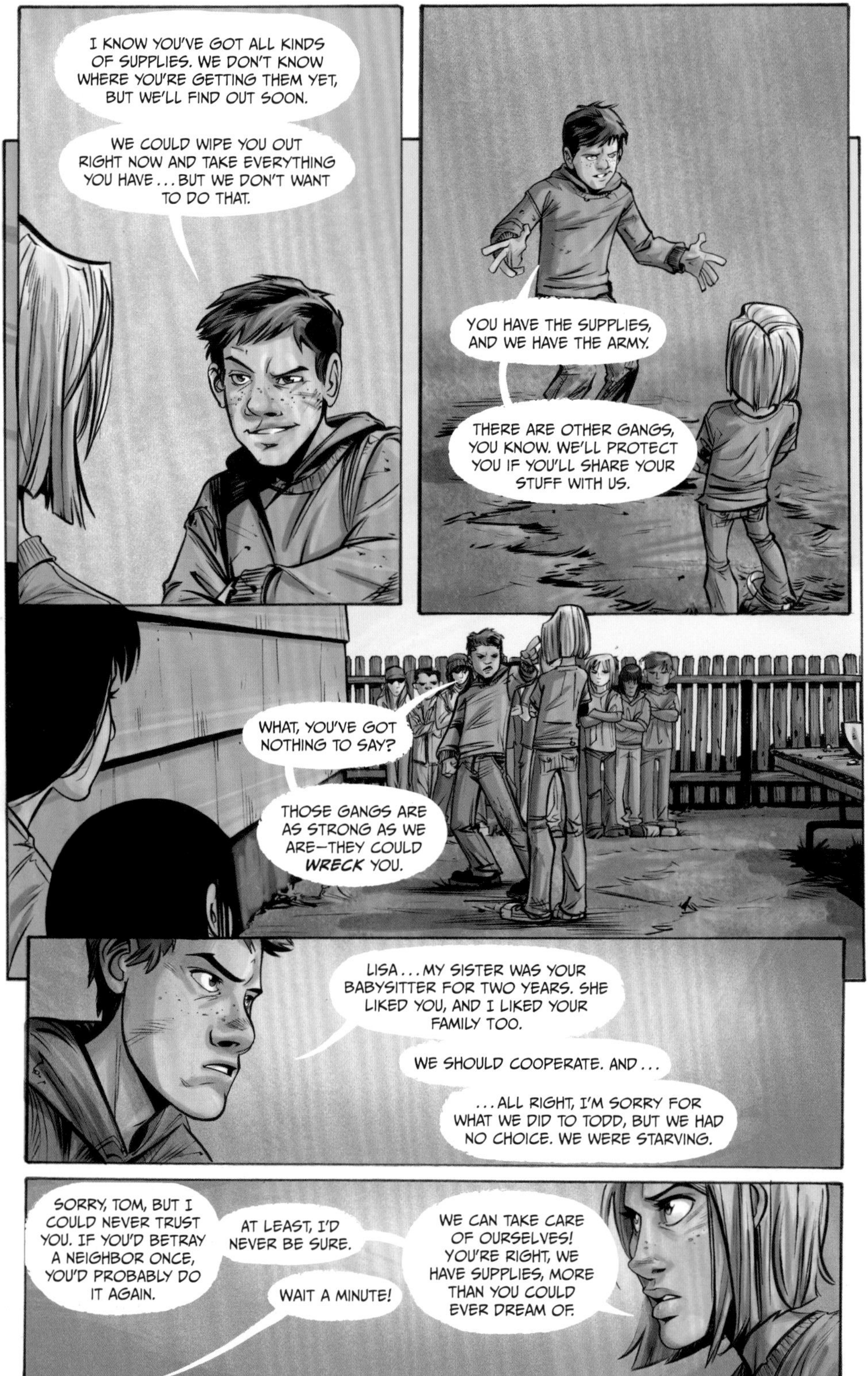

I KNOW YOU'VE GOT ALL KINDS OF SUPPLIES. WE DON'T KNOW WHERE YOU'RE GETTING THEM YET, BUT WE'LL FIND OUT SOON.
WE COULD WIPE YOU OUT RIGHT NOW AND TAKE EVERYTHING YOU HAVE . . . BUT WE DON'T WANT TO DO THAT.
YOU HAVE THE SUPPLIES, AND WE HAVE THE ARMY.
THERE ARE OTHER GANGS, YOU KNOW. WE'LL PROTECT YOU IF YOU'LL SHARE YOUR STUFF WITH US.
WHAT, YOU'VE GOT NOTHING TO SAY?
THOSE GANGS ARE AS STRONG AS WE ARE—THEY COULD ***WRECK*** YOU.
LISA . . . MY SISTER WAS YOUR BABYSITTER FOR TWO YEARS. SHE LIKED YOU, AND I LIKED YOUR FAMILY TOO.
WE SHOULD COOPERATE. AND . . .
. . . ALL RIGHT, I'M SORRY FOR WHAT WE DID TO TODD, BUT WE HAD NO CHOICE. WE WERE STARVING.
SORRY, TOM, BUT I COULD NEVER TRUST YOU. IF YOU'D BETRAY A NEIGHBOR ONCE, YOU'D PROBABLY DO IT AGAIN.
AT LEAST, I'D NEVER BE SURE.
WE CAN TAKE CARE OF OURSELVES! YOU'RE RIGHT, WE HAVE SUPPLIES, MORE THAN YOU COULD EVER DREAM OF.
WAIT A MINUTE!

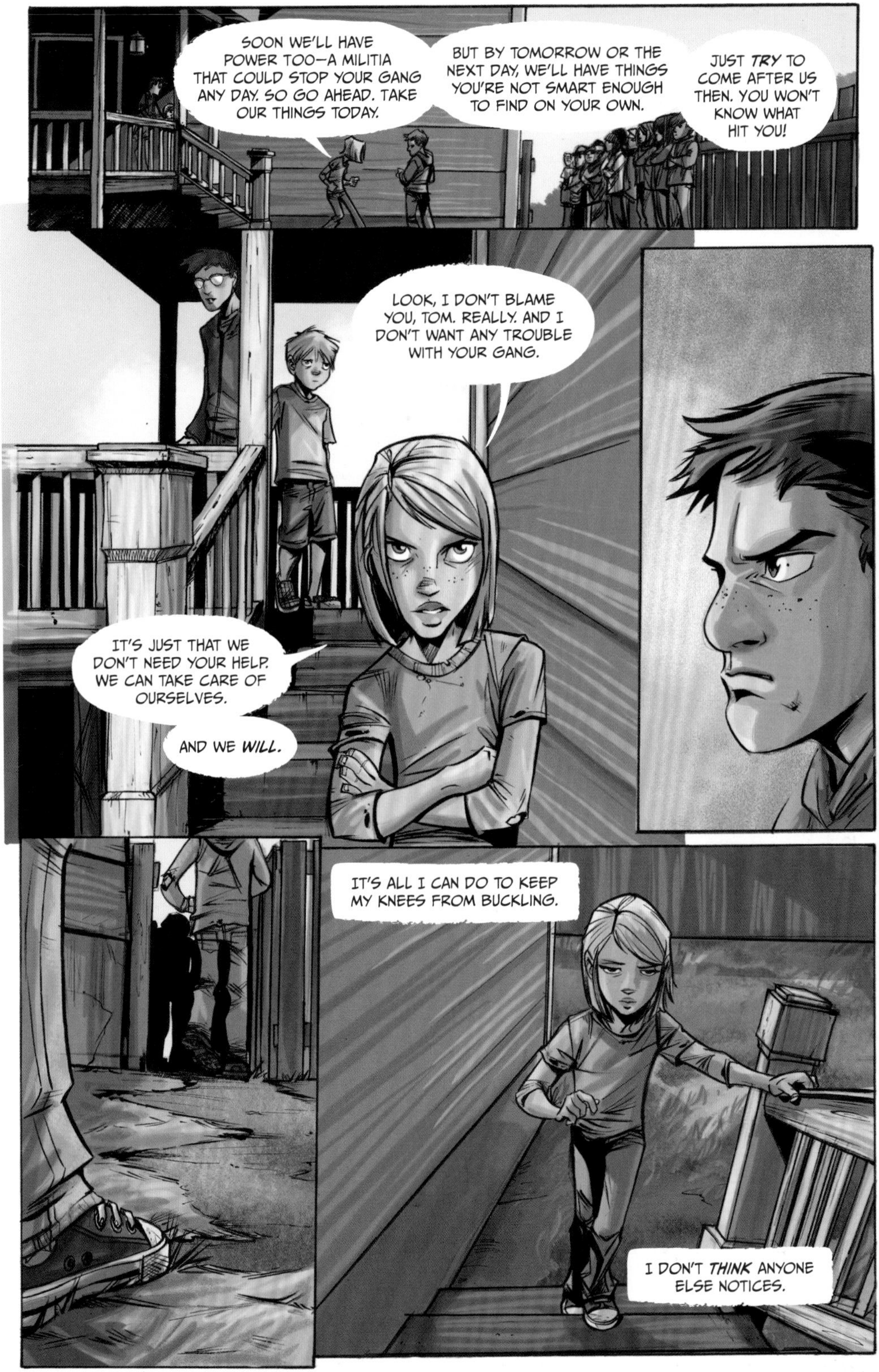
SOON WE'LL HAVE POWER TOO—A MILITIA THAT COULD STOP YOUR GANG ANY DAY. SO GO AHEAD. TAKE OUR THINGS TODAY.
BUT BY TOMORROW OR THE NEXT DAY, WE'LL HAVE THINGS YOU'RE NOT SMART ENOUGH TO FIND ON YOUR OWN.
JUST *TRY* TO COME AFTER US THEN. YOU WON'T KNOW WHAT HIT YOU!
LOOK, I DON'T BLAME YOU, TOM. REALLY. AND I DON'T WANT ANY TROUBLE WITH YOUR GANG.
IT'S JUST THAT WE DON'T NEED YOUR HELP. WE CAN TAKE CARE OF OURSELVES.
AND WE *WILL.*
IT'S ALL I CAN DO TO KEEP MY KNEES FROM BUCKLING.
I DON'T *THINK* ANYONE ELSE NOTICES.

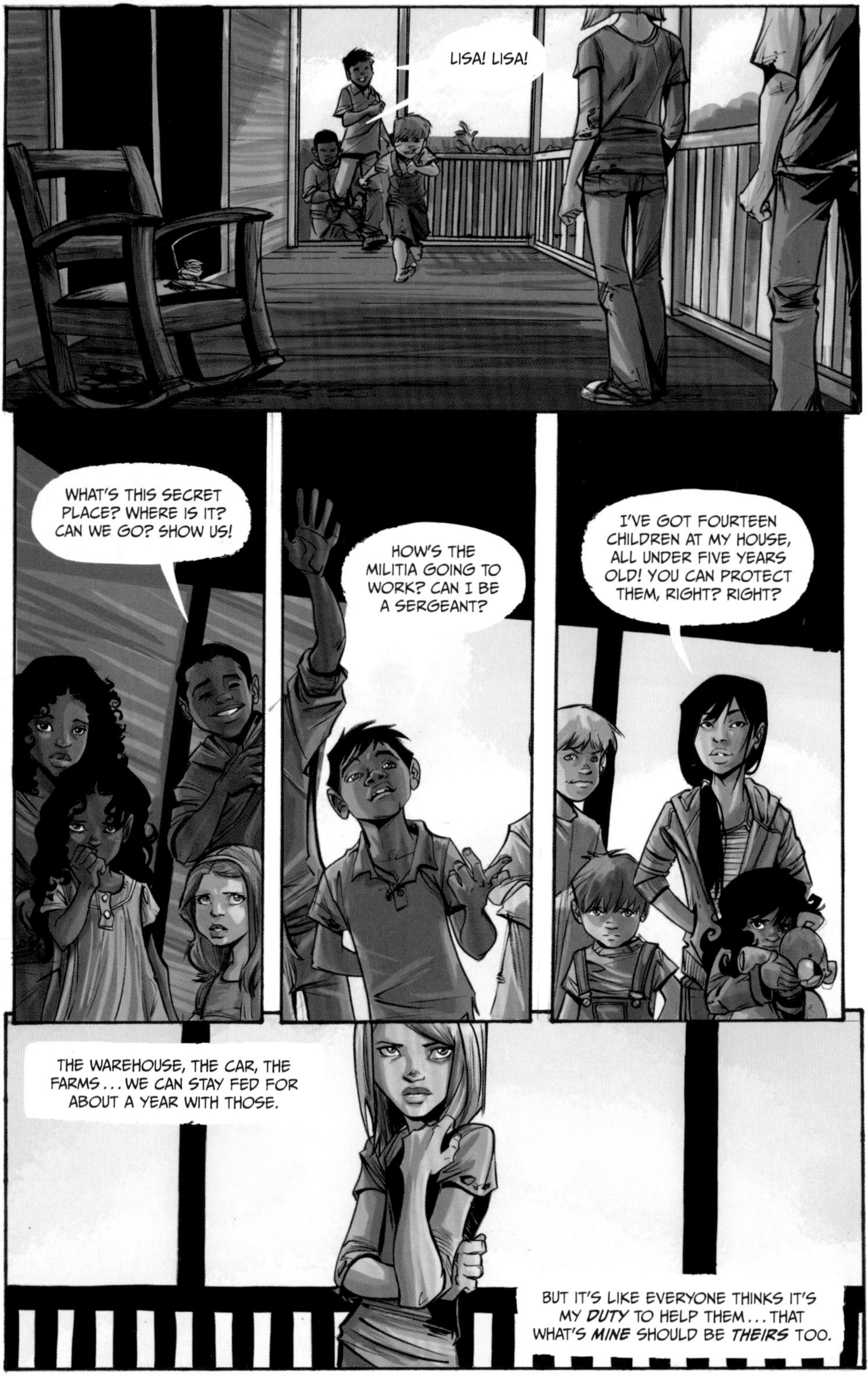
LISA! LISA!
WHAT'S THIS SECRET PLACE? WHERE IS IT? CAN WE GO? SHOW US!
HOW'S THE MILITIA GOING TO WORK? CAN I BE A SERGEANT?
I'VE GOT FOURTEEN CHILDREN AT MY HOUSE, ALL UNDER FIVE YEARS OLD! YOU CAN PROTECT THEM, RIGHT? RIGHT?
THE WAREHOUSE, THE CAR, THE FARMS . . . WE CAN STAY FED FOR ABOUT A YEAR WITH THOSE.
BUT IT'S LIKE EVERYONE THINKS IT'S MY *DUTY* TO HELP THEM . . . THAT WHAT'S *MINE* SHOULD BE *THEIRS* TOO.

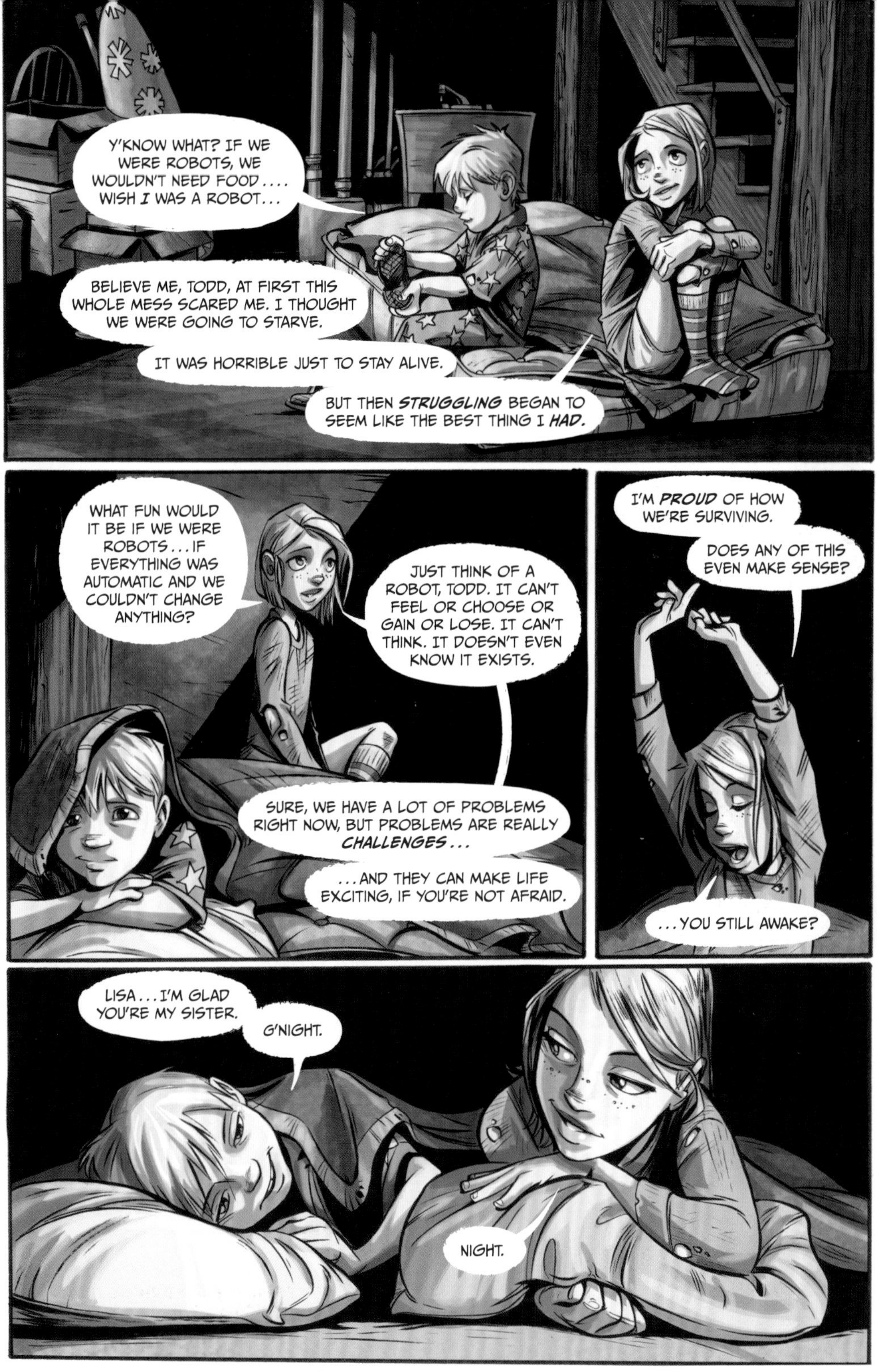
Y'KNOW WHAT? IF WE WERE ROBOTS, WE WOULDN'T NEED FOOD.... WISH *I* WAS A ROBOT...
BELIEVE ME, TODD, AT FIRST THIS WHOLE MESS SCARED ME. I THOUGHT WE WERE GOING TO STARVE.
IT WAS HORRIBLE JUST TO STAY ALIVE.
BUT THEN ***STRUGGLING*** BEGAN TO SEEM LIKE THE BEST THING I ***HAD.***
WHAT FUN WOULD IT BE IF WE WERE ROBOTS... IF EVERYTHING WAS AUTOMATIC AND WE COULDN'T CHANGE ANYTHING?
JUST THINK OF A ROBOT, TODD. IT CAN'T FEEL OR CHOOSE OR GAIN OR LOSE. IT CAN'T THINK. IT DOESN'T EVEN KNOW IT EXISTS.
SURE, WE HAVE A LOT OF PROBLEMS RIGHT NOW, BUT PROBLEMS ARE REALLY ***CHALLENGES...***
...AND THEY CAN MAKE LIFE EXCITING, IF YOU'RE NOT AFRAID.
I'M ***PROUD*** OF HOW WE'RE SURVIVING.
DOES ANY OF THIS EVEN MAKE SENSE?
...YOU STILL AWAKE?
LISA... I'M GLAD YOU'RE MY SISTER.
G'NIGHT.
NIGHT.

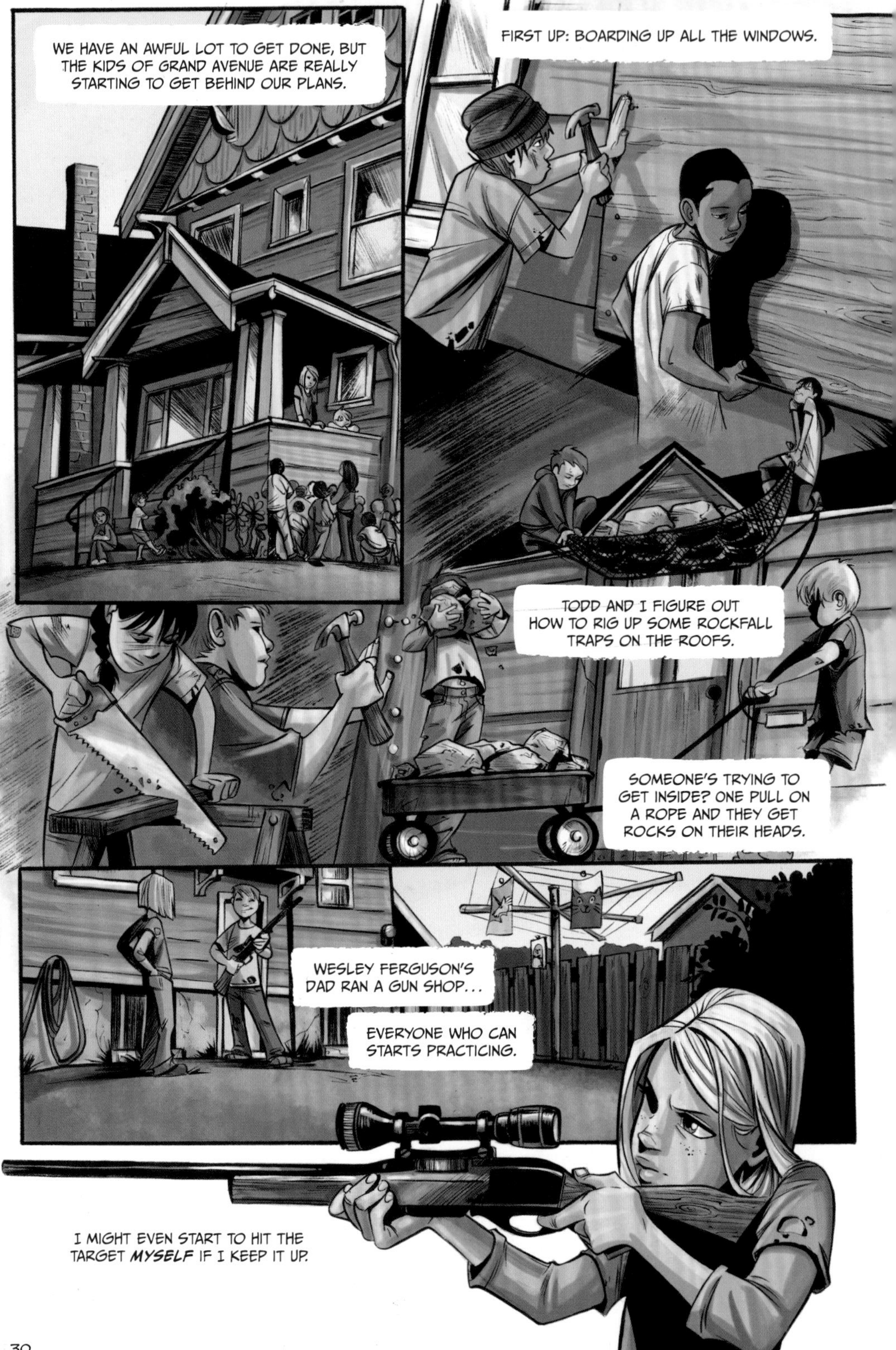

WE HAVE AN AWFUL LOT TO GET DONE, BUT THE KIDS OF GRAND AVENUE ARE REALLY STARTING TO GET BEHIND OUR PLANS.
FIRST UP: BOARDING UP ALL THE WINDOWS.
TODD AND I FIGURE OUT HOW TO RIG UP SOME ROCKFALL TRAPS ON THE ROOFS.
SOMEONE'S TRYING TO GET INSIDE? ONE PULL ON A ROPE AND THEY GET ROCKS ON THEIR HEADS.
WESLEY FERGUSON'S DAD RAN A GUN SHOP...
EVERYONE WHO CAN STARTS PRACTICING.
I MIGHT EVEN START TO HIT THE TARGET ***MYSELF*** IF I KEEP IT UP.

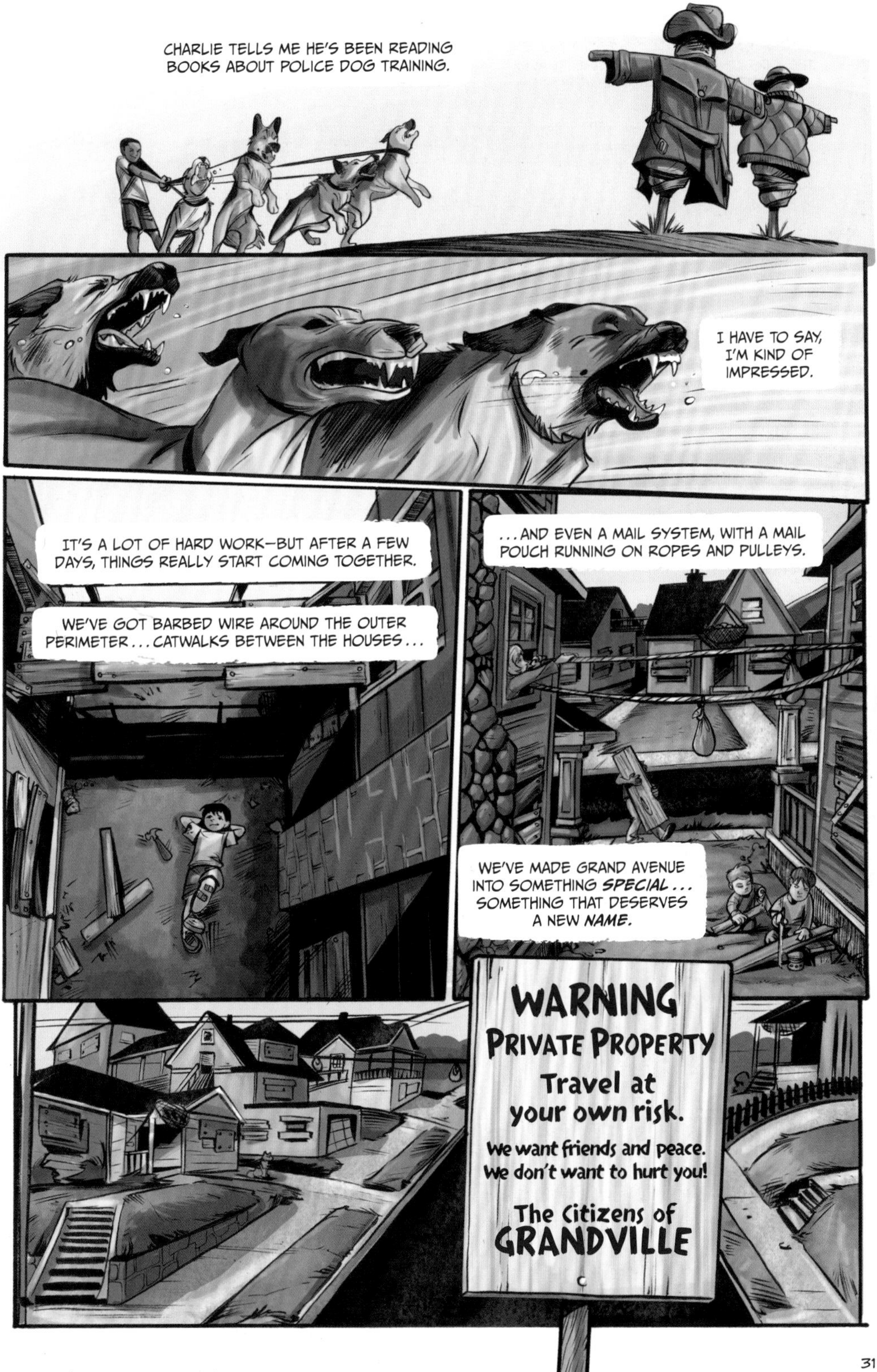
CHARLIE TELLS ME HE'S BEEN READING BOOKS ABOUT POLICE DOG TRAINING.
I HAVE TO SAY, I'M KIND OF IMPRESSED.
IT'S A LOT OF HARD WORK—BUT AFTER A FEW DAYS, THINGS REALLY START COMING TOGETHER.
WE'VE GOT BARBED WIRE AROUND THE OUTER PERIMETER . . . CATWALKS BETWEEN THE HOUSES . . .
. . . AND EVEN A MAIL SYSTEM, WITH A MAIL POUCH RUNNING ON ROPES AND PULLEYS.
WE'VE MADE GRAND AVENUE INTO SOMETHING SPECIAL . . . SOMETHING THAT DESERVES A NEW NAME.
WARNING
PRIVATE PROPERTY
Travel at your own risk.
We want friends and peace. We don't want to hurt you!
The Citizens of GRANDVILLE

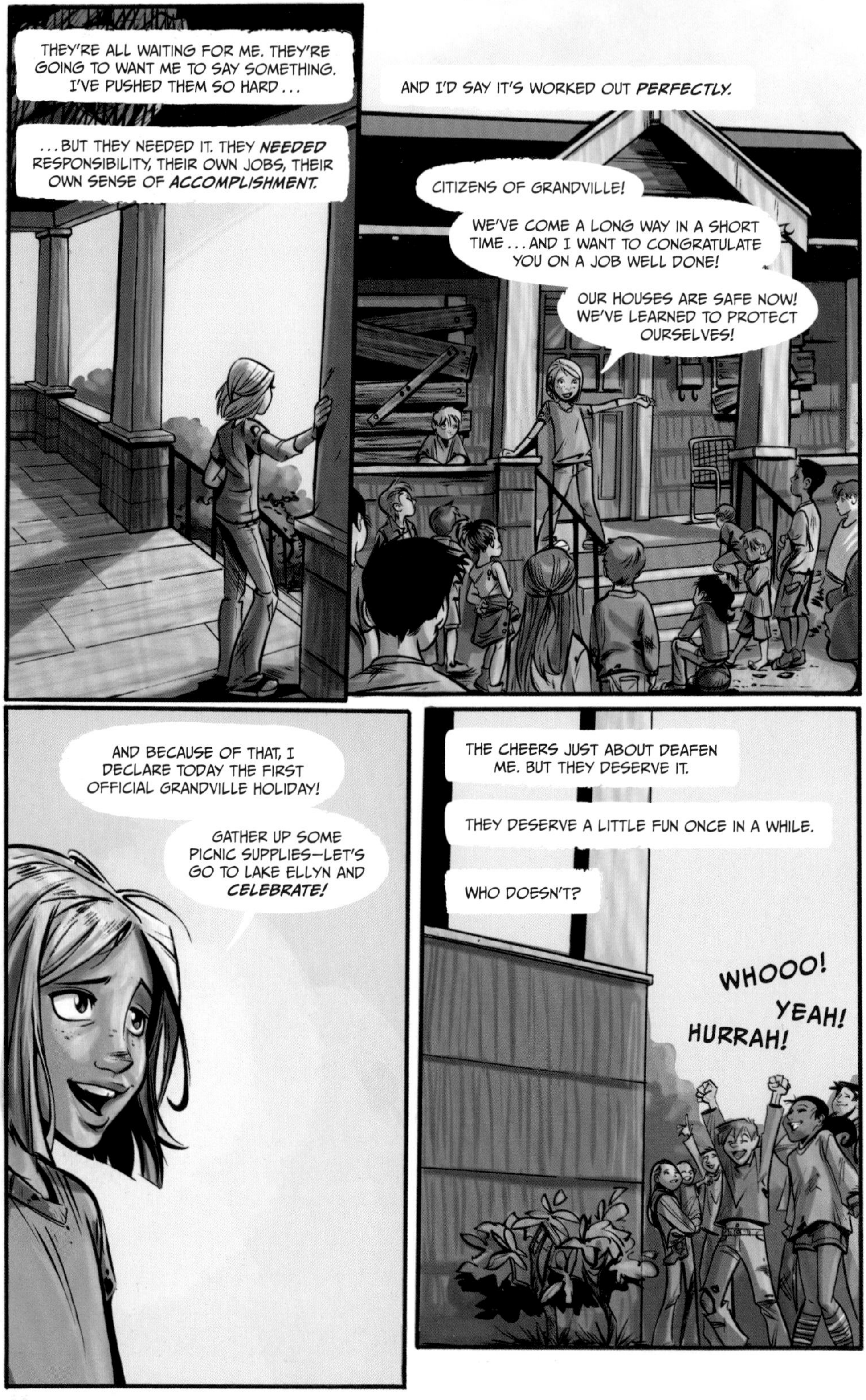
THEY'RE ALL WAITING FOR ME. THEY'RE GOING TO WANT ME TO SAY SOMETHING. I'VE PUSHED THEM SO HARD . . .
. . . BUT THEY NEEDED IT. THEY NEEDED RESPONSIBILITY, THEIR OWN JOBS, THEIR OWN SENSE OF ACCOMPLISHMENT.
AND I'D SAY IT'S WORKED OUT PERFECTLY.
CITIZENS OF GRANDVILLE!
WE'VE COME A LONG WAY IN A SHORT TIME . . . AND I WANT TO CONGRATULATE YOU ON A JOB WELL DONE!
OUR HOUSES ARE SAFE NOW! WE'VE LEARNED TO PROTECT OURSELVES!
AND BECAUSE OF THAT, I DECLARE TODAY THE FIRST OFFICIAL GRANDVILLE HOLIDAY!
GATHER UP SOME PICNIC SUPPLIES—LET'S GO TO LAKE ELLYN AND CELEBRATE!
THE CHEERS JUST ABOUT DEAFEN ME. BUT THEY DESERVE IT.
THEY DESERVE A LITTLE FUN ONCE IN A WHILE.
WHO DOESN'T?
WHOOO!
YEAH!
HURRAH!

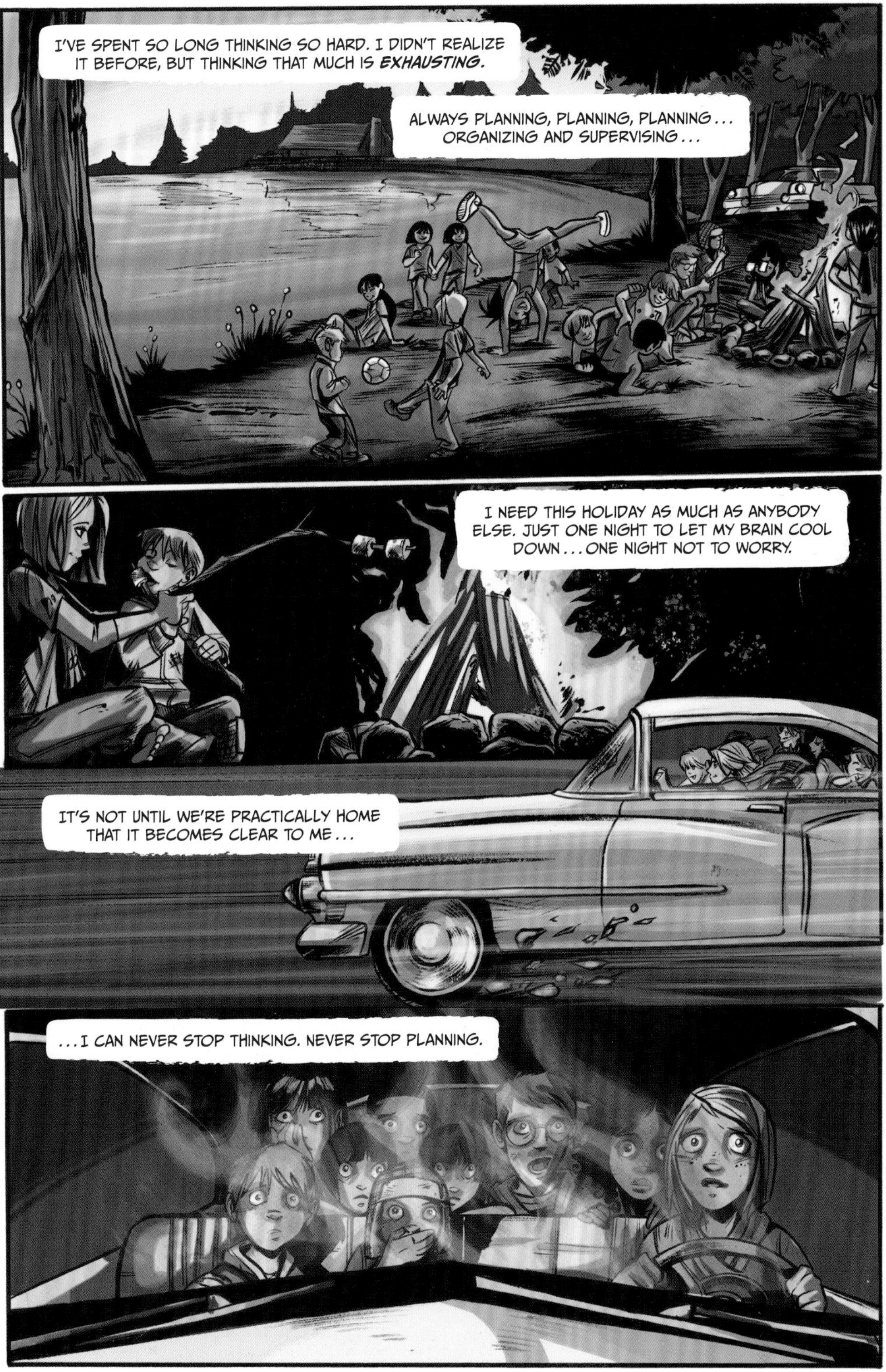
I'VE SPENT SO LONG THINKING SO HARD. I DIDN'T REALIZE IT BEFORE, BUT THINKING THAT MUCH IS EXHAUSTING.
ALWAYS PLANNING, PLANNING, PLANNING... ORGANIZING AND SUPERVISING...
I NEED THIS HOLIDAY AS MUCH AS ANYBODY ELSE. JUST ONE NIGHT TO LET MY BRAIN COOL DOWN... ONE NIGHT NOT TO WORRY.
IT'S NOT UNTIL WE'RE PRACTICALLY HOME THAT IT BECOMES CLEAR TO ME...
...I CAN NEVER STOP THINKING. NEVER STOP PLANNING.

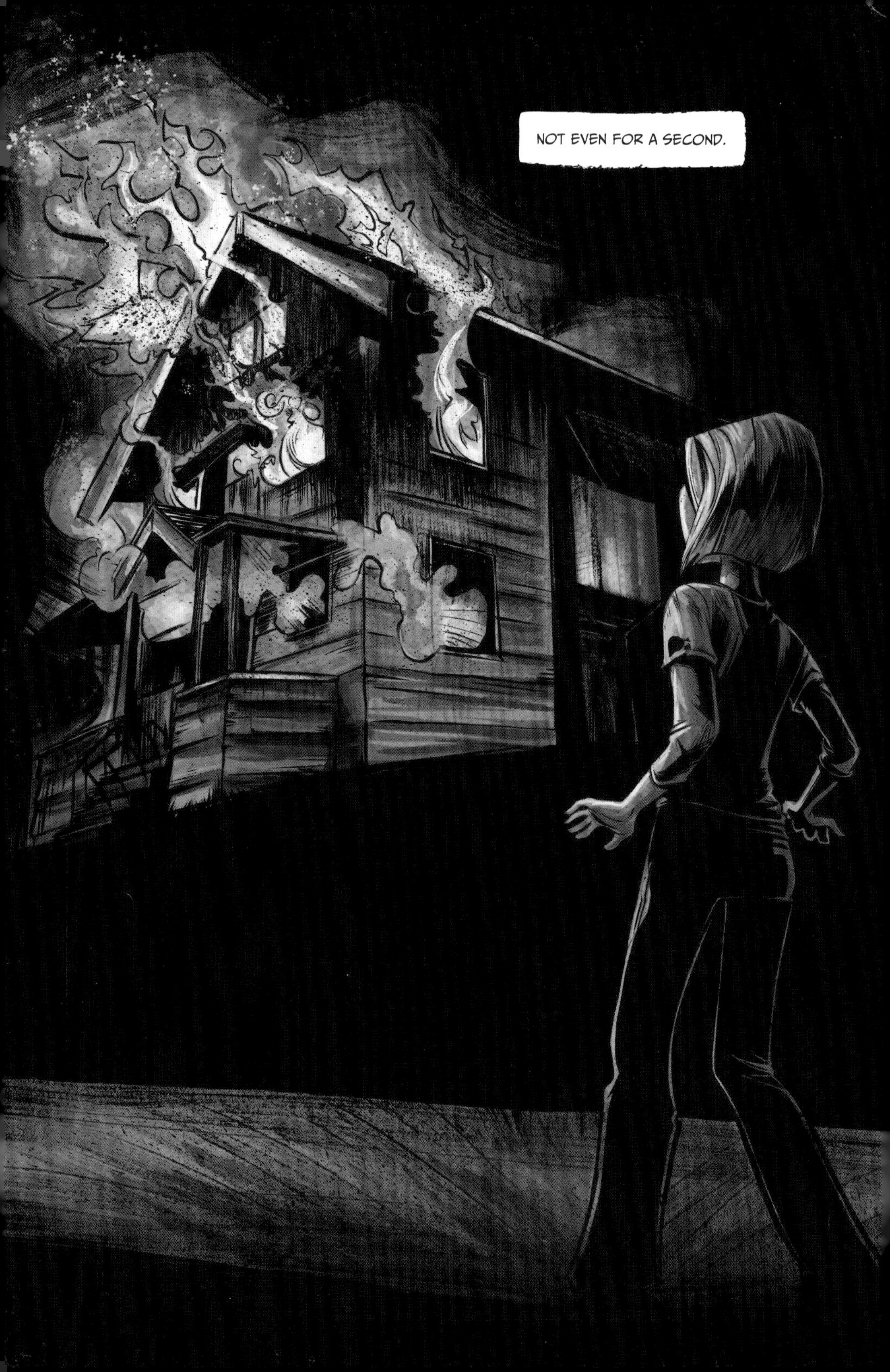
NOT EVEN FOR A SECOND.

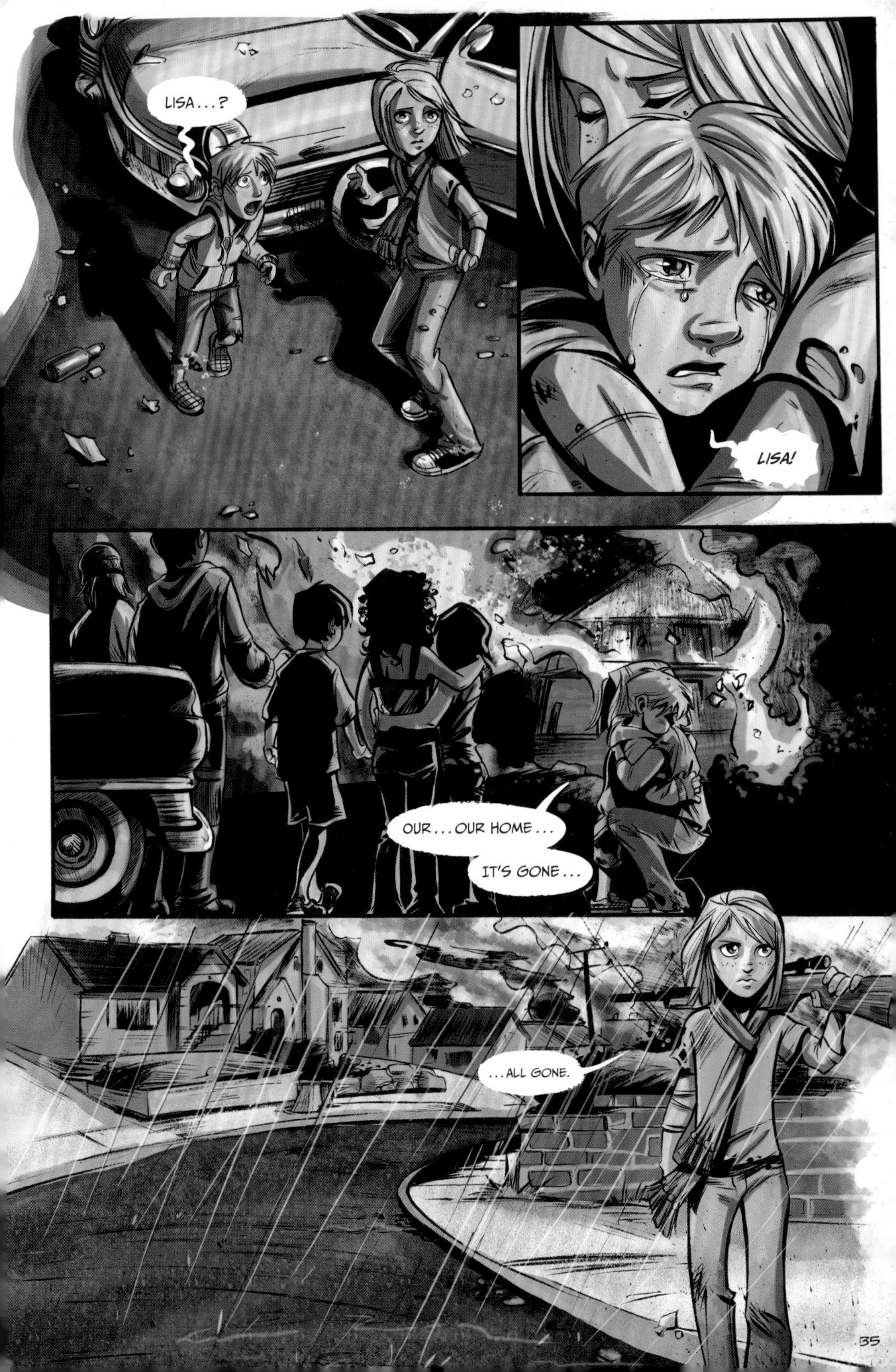
LISA...?
LISA!
OUR... OUR HOME...
IT'S GONE...
...ALL GONE.

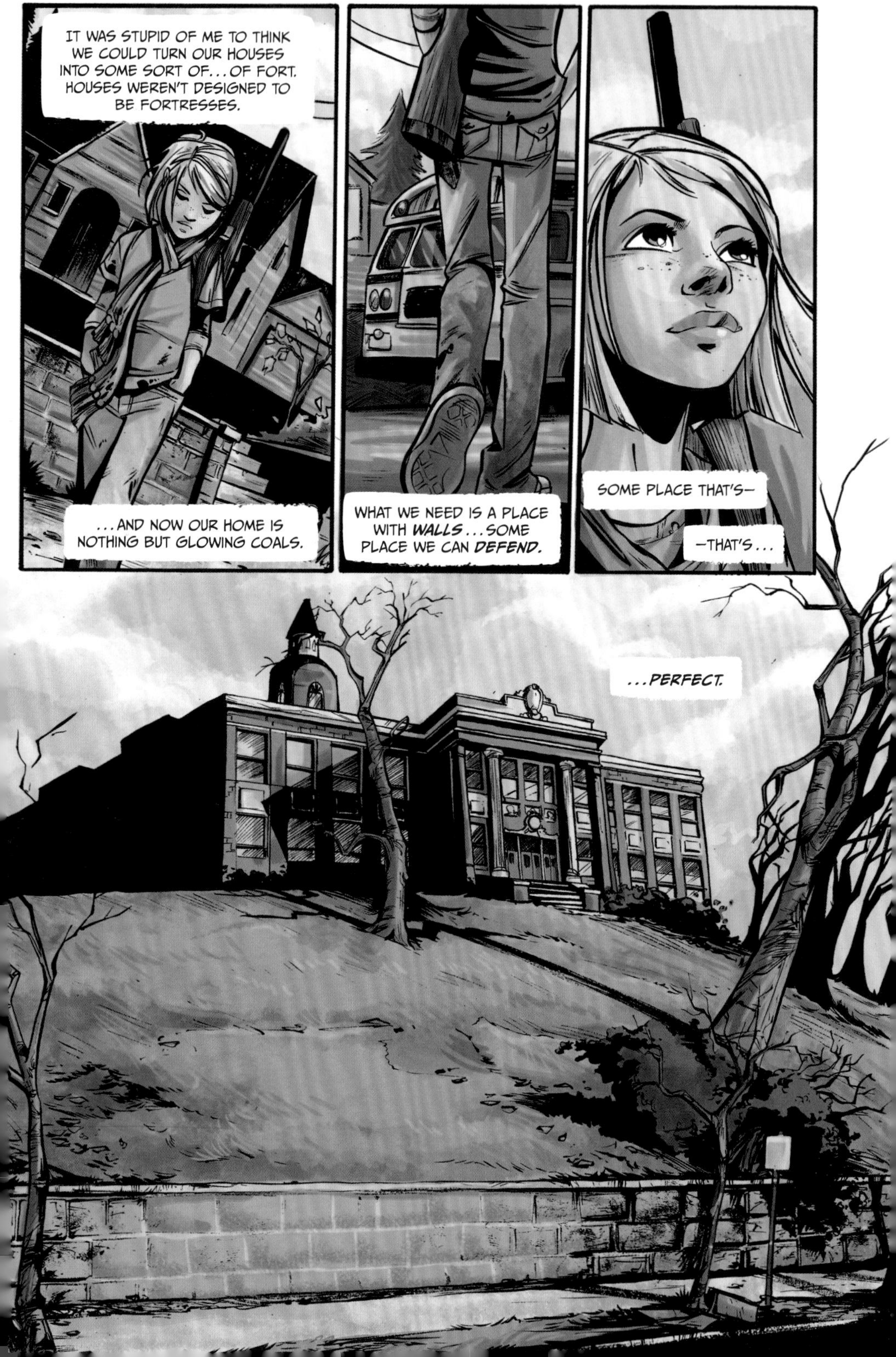
IT WAS STUPID OF ME TO THINK WE COULD TURN OUR HOUSES INTO SOME SORT OF... OF FORT. HOUSES WEREN'T DESIGNED TO BE FORTRESSES.
...AND NOW OUR HOME IS NOTHING BUT GLOWING COALS.
WHAT WE NEED IS A PLACE WITH *WALLS*... SOME PLACE WE CAN *DEFEND.*
SOME PLACE THAT'S—
—THAT'S...
...*PERFECT.*

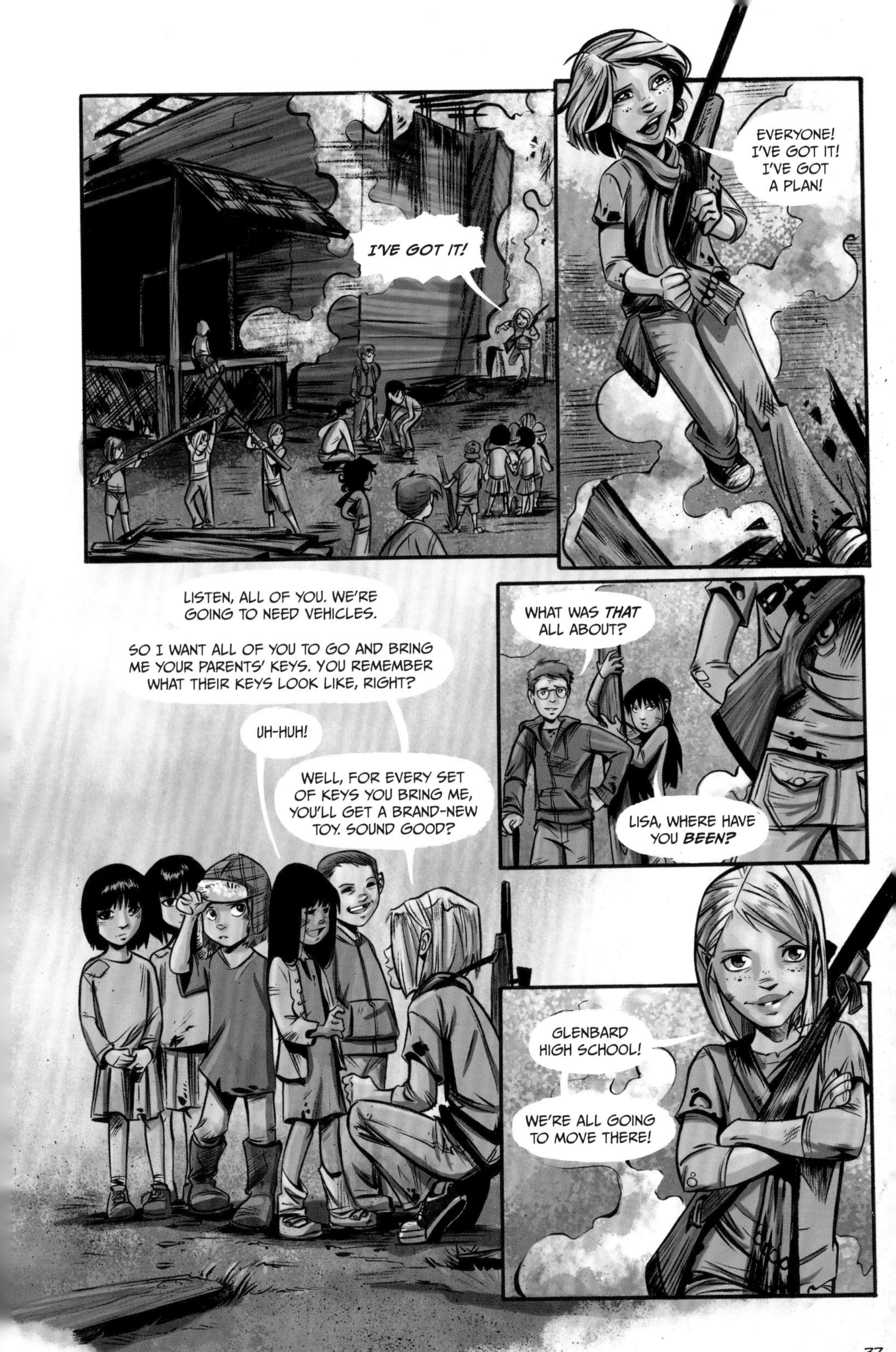
I'VE GOT IT!
EVERYONE! I'VE GOT IT! I'VE GOT A PLAN!
LISTEN, ALL OF YOU. WE'RE GOING TO NEED VEHICLES.
SO I WANT ALL OF YOU TO GO AND BRING ME YOUR PARENTS' KEYS. YOU REMEMBER WHAT THEIR KEYS LOOK LIKE, RIGHT?
UH-HUH!
WELL, FOR EVERY SET OF KEYS YOU BRING ME, YOU'LL GET A BRAND-NEW TOY. SOUND GOOD?
WHAT WAS *THAT* ALL ABOUT?
LISA, WHERE HAVE YOU *BEEN?*
GLENBARD HIGH SCHOOL!
WE'RE ALL GOING TO MOVE THERE!

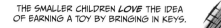
THE SMALLER CHILDREN *LOVE* THE IDEA OF EARNING A TOY BY BRINGING IN KEYS.

ALL THEIR FIGHTING AND ARGUING AND WHINING AND COMPLAINING DRIES UP WHEN THEY'VE BEEN GIVEN *JOBS* TO DO.

I'M GLAD TO SEE IT. BECAUSE IF MY PLAN WORKS OUT, *EVERYONE* IS ABOUT TO HAVE *PLENTY* OF RESPONSIBILITY.

LISA, I COULDN'T FIND ANY KEYS, BUT I THINK I CAN HELP ANYWAY....

IT'S OKAY, EILEEN. WHAT DID YOU HAVE IN MIND?

MY DAD'S BIG GARAGE IS ON GENEVA ROAD. HE MADE ROADS! IT'S GOT DUMP TRUCKS... AND BULLDOZERS...

THERE MIGHT BE SOME KEYS THERE. DON'T YOU LIKE BULLDOZERS, LISA?

...CAN I STILL HAVE A TOY?

HOW'S YOUR PLAN SO FAR, LISA?

IT MIGHT HAVE JUST GOTTEN A LOT BETTER.

NOW WE'VE GOT BIG TRUCKS AND BULLDOZERS TOO.

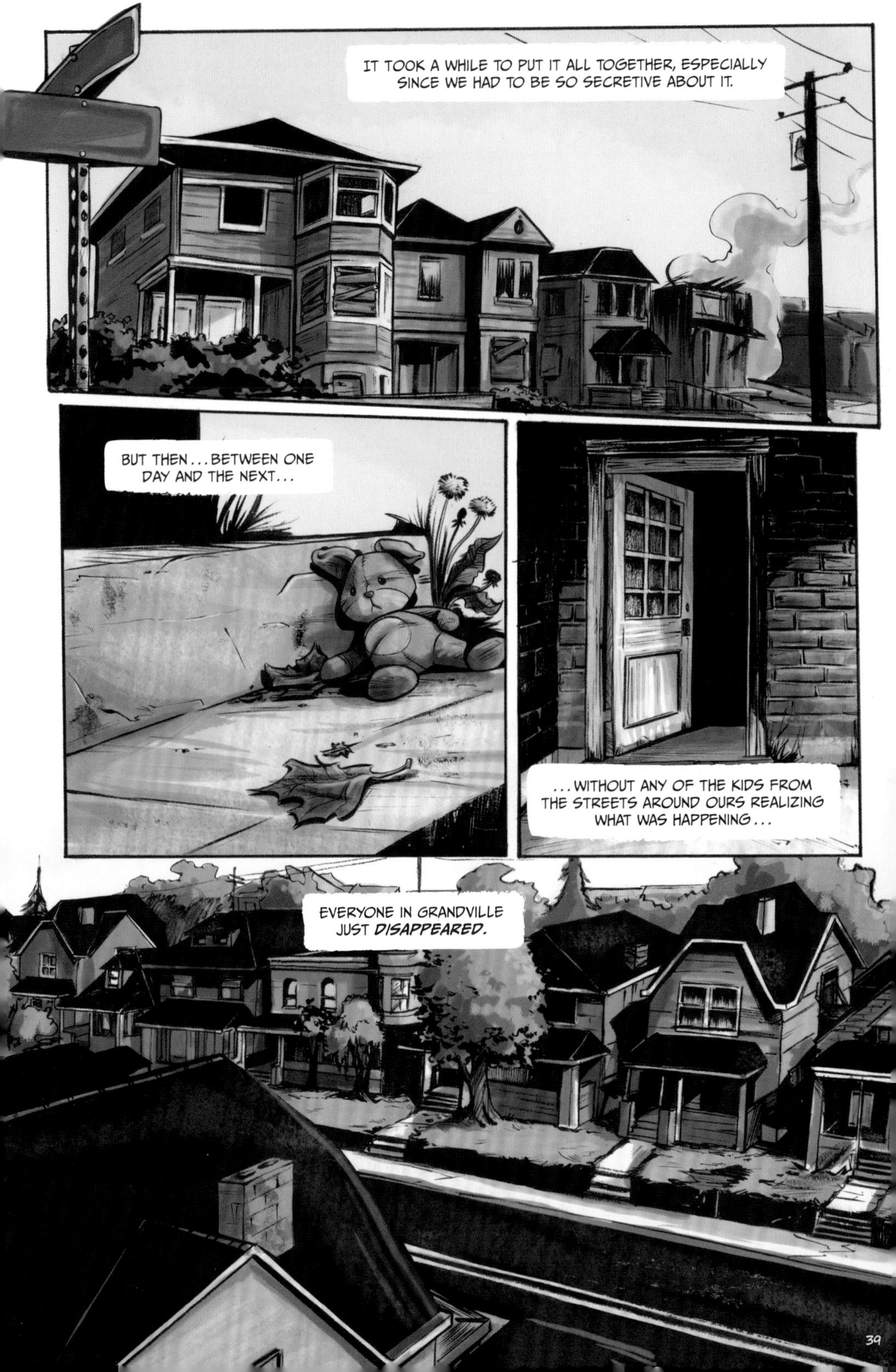
IT TOOK A WHILE TO PUT IT ALL TOGETHER, ESPECIALLY SINCE WE HAD TO BE SO SECRETIVE ABOUT IT.
BUT THEN . . . BETWEEN ONE DAY AND THE NEXT . . .
. . . WITHOUT ANY OF THE KIDS FROM THE STREETS AROUND OURS REALIZING WHAT WAS HAPPENING . . .
EVERYONE IN GRANDVILLE JUST *DISAPPEARED.*

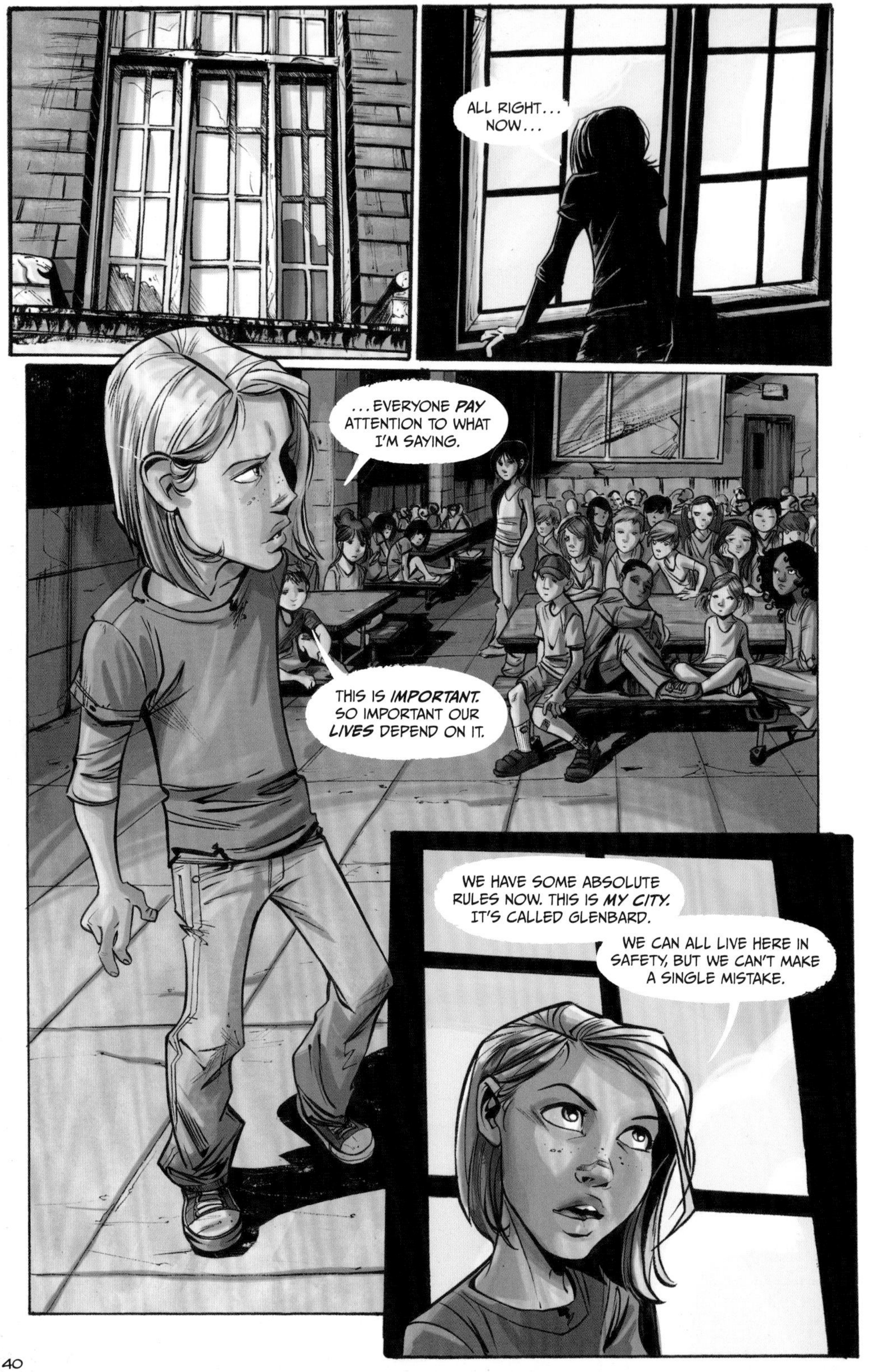
ALL RIGHT...
NOW...
...EVERYONE PAY ATTENTION TO WHAT I'M SAYING.
THIS IS IMPORTANT. SO IMPORTANT OUR LIVES DEPEND ON IT.
WE HAVE SOME ABSOLUTE RULES NOW. THIS IS MY CITY. IT'S CALLED GLENBARD.
WE CAN ALL LIVE HERE IN SAFETY, BUT WE CAN'T MAKE A SINGLE MISTAKE.

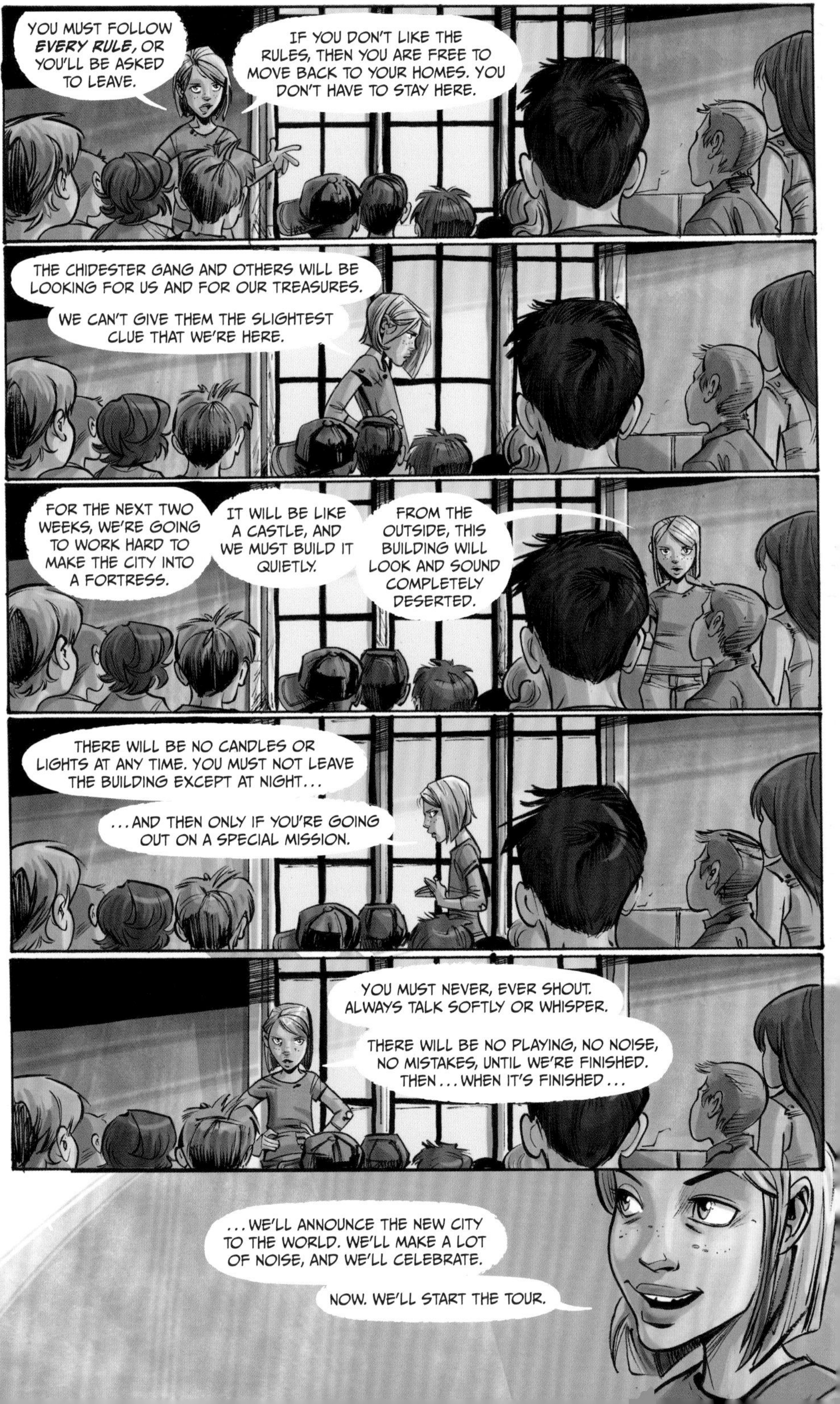
YOU MUST FOLLOW EVERY RULE, OR YOU'LL BE ASKED TO LEAVE.
IF YOU DON'T LIKE THE RULES, THEN YOU ARE FREE TO MOVE BACK TO YOUR HOMES. YOU DON'T HAVE TO STAY HERE.
THE CHIDESTER GANG AND OTHERS WILL BE LOOKING FOR US AND FOR OUR TREASURES.
WE CAN'T GIVE THEM THE SLIGHTEST CLUE THAT WE'RE HERE.
FOR THE NEXT TWO WEEKS, WE'RE GOING TO WORK HARD TO MAKE THE CITY INTO A FORTRESS.
IT WILL BE LIKE A CASTLE, AND WE MUST BUILD IT QUIETLY.
FROM THE OUTSIDE, THIS BUILDING WILL LOOK AND SOUND COMPLETELY DESERTED.
THERE WILL BE NO CANDLES OR LIGHTS AT ANY TIME. YOU MUST NOT LEAVE THE BUILDING EXCEPT AT NIGHT...
...AND THEN ONLY IF YOU'RE GOING OUT ON A SPECIAL MISSION.
YOU MUST NEVER, EVER SHOUT. ALWAYS TALK SOFTLY OR WHISPER.
THERE WILL BE NO PLAYING, NO NOISE, NO MISTAKES, UNTIL WE'RE FINISHED. THEN...WHEN IT'S FINISHED...
...WE'LL ANNOUNCE THE NEW CITY TO THE WORLD. WE'LL MAKE A LOT OF NOISE, AND WE'LL CELEBRATE.
NOW. WE'LL START THE TOUR.

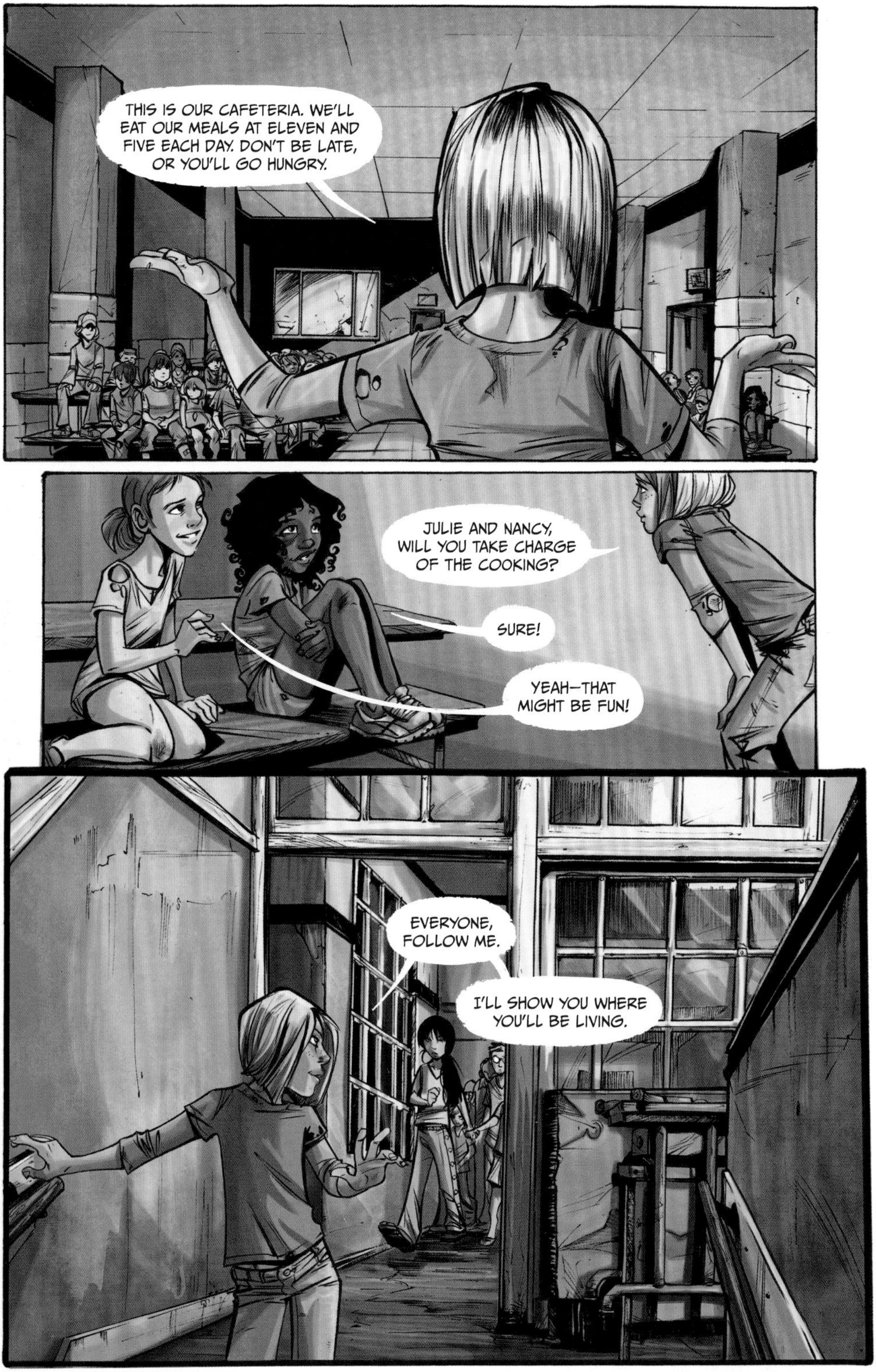
THIS IS OUR CAFETERIA. WE'LL EAT OUR MEALS AT ELEVEN AND FIVE EACH DAY. DON'T BE LATE, OR YOU'LL GO HUNGRY.
JULIE AND NANCY, WILL YOU TAKE CHARGE OF THE COOKING?
SURE!
YEAH—THAT MIGHT BE FUN!
EVERYONE, FOLLOW ME.
I'LL SHOW YOU WHERE YOU'LL BE LIVING.

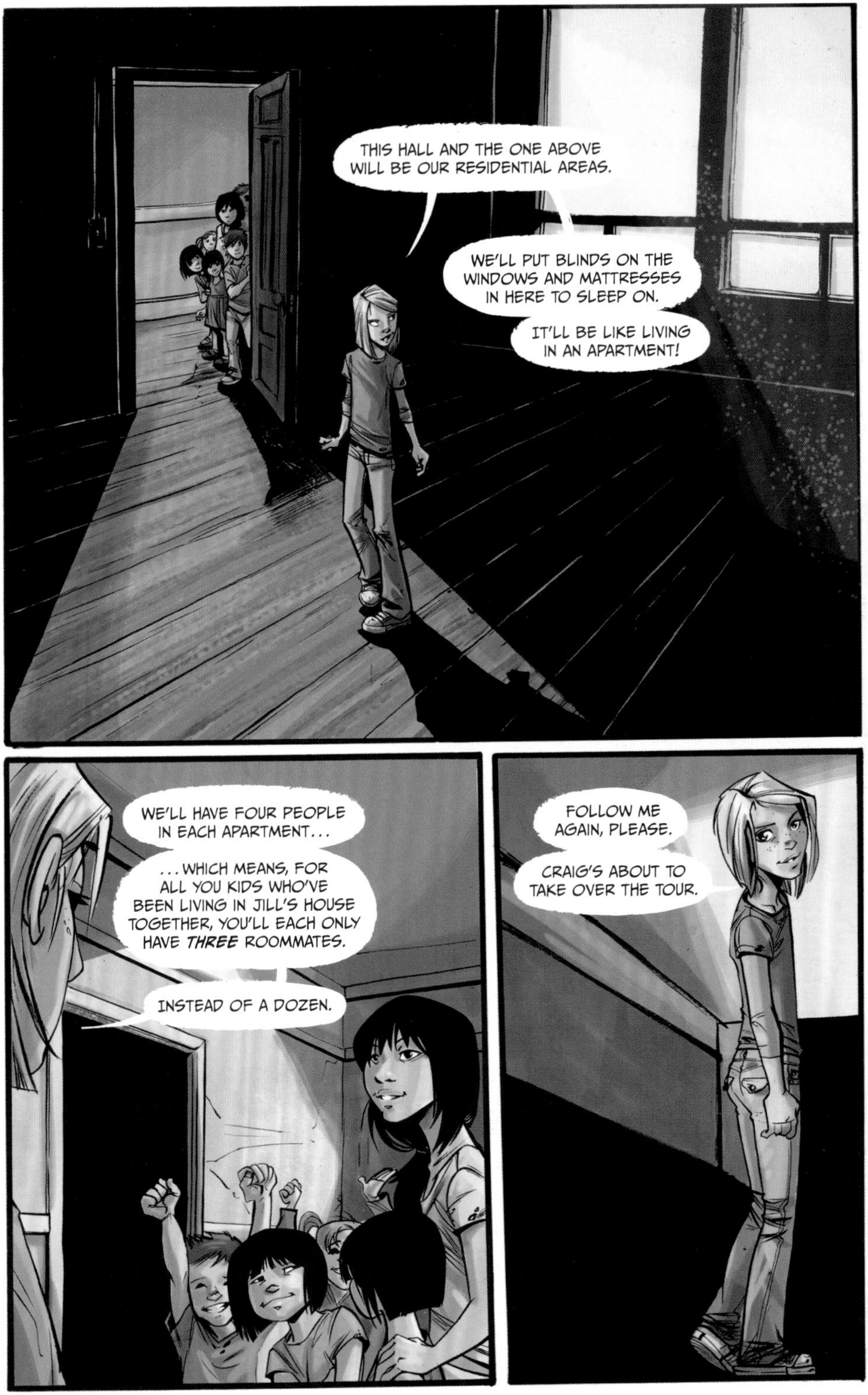
THIS HALL AND THE ONE ABOVE WILL BE OUR RESIDENTIAL AREAS.
WE'LL PUT BLINDS ON THE WINDOWS AND MATTRESSES IN HERE TO SLEEP ON.
IT'LL BE LIKE LIVING IN AN APARTMENT!
WE'LL HAVE FOUR PEOPLE IN EACH APARTMENT...
...WHICH MEANS, FOR ALL YOU KIDS WHO'VE BEEN LIVING IN JILL'S HOUSE TOGETHER, YOU'LL EACH ONLY HAVE *THREE* ROOMMATES.
INSTEAD OF A DOZEN.
FOLLOW ME AGAIN, PLEASE.
CRAIG'S ABOUT TO TAKE OVER THE TOUR.

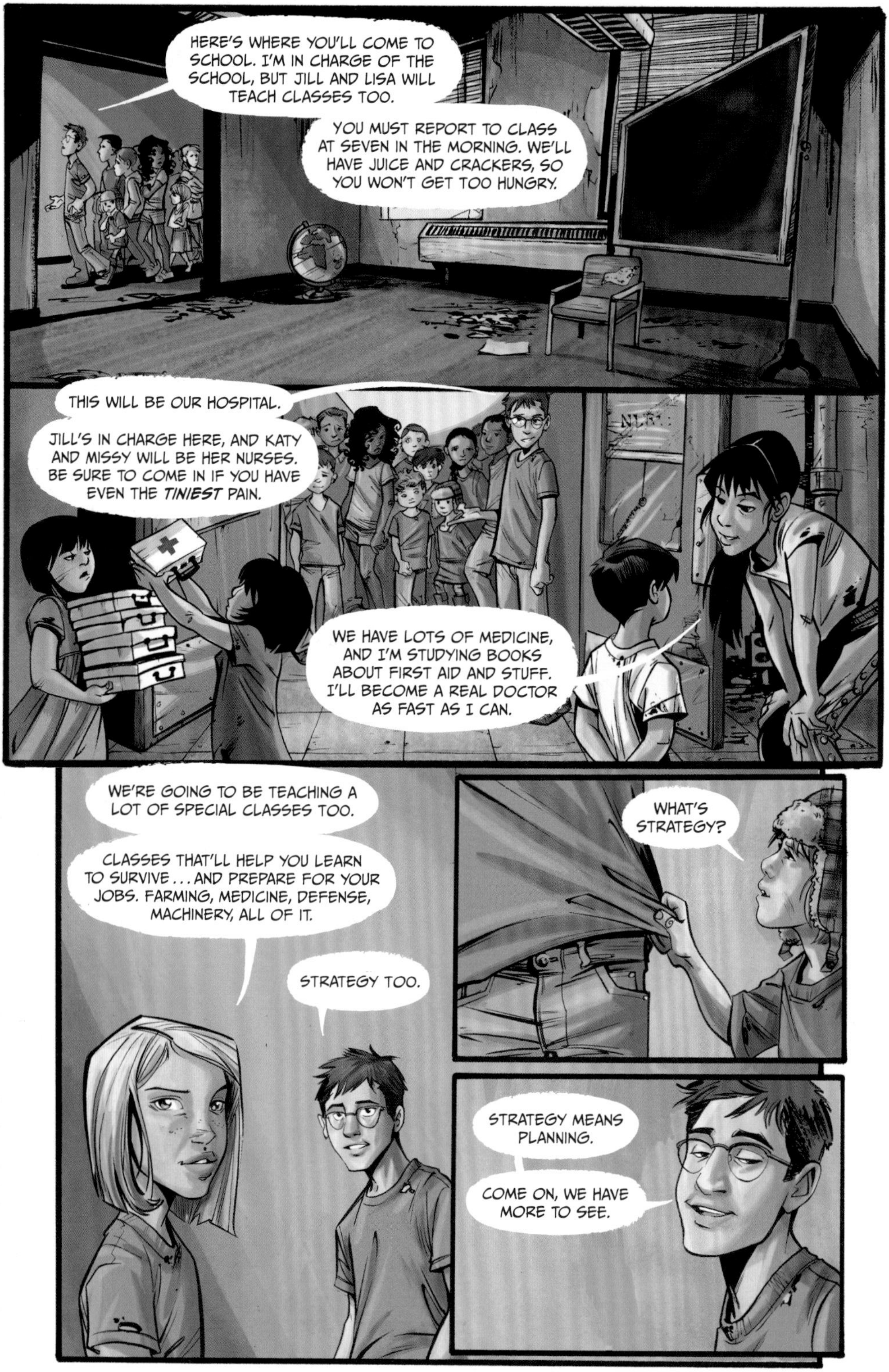
HERE'S WHERE YOU'LL COME TO SCHOOL. I'M IN CHARGE OF THE SCHOOL, BUT JILL AND LISA WILL TEACH CLASSES TOO.
YOU MUST REPORT TO CLASS AT SEVEN IN THE MORNING. WE'LL HAVE JUICE AND CRACKERS, SO YOU WON'T GET TOO HUNGRY.
THIS WILL BE OUR HOSPITAL.
JILL'S IN CHARGE HERE, AND KATY AND MISSY WILL BE HER NURSES. BE SURE TO COME IN IF YOU HAVE EVEN THE *TINIEST* PAIN.
WE HAVE LOTS OF MEDICINE, AND I'M STUDYING BOOKS ABOUT FIRST AID AND STUFF. I'LL BECOME A REAL DOCTOR AS FAST AS I CAN.
WE'RE GOING TO BE TEACHING A LOT OF SPECIAL CLASSES TOO.
CLASSES THAT'LL HELP YOU LEARN TO SURVIVE . . . AND PREPARE FOR YOUR JOBS. FARMING, MEDICINE, DEFENSE, MACHINERY, ALL OF IT.
STRATEGY TOO.
WHAT'S STRATEGY?
STRATEGY MEANS PLANNING.
COME ON, WE HAVE MORE TO SEE.

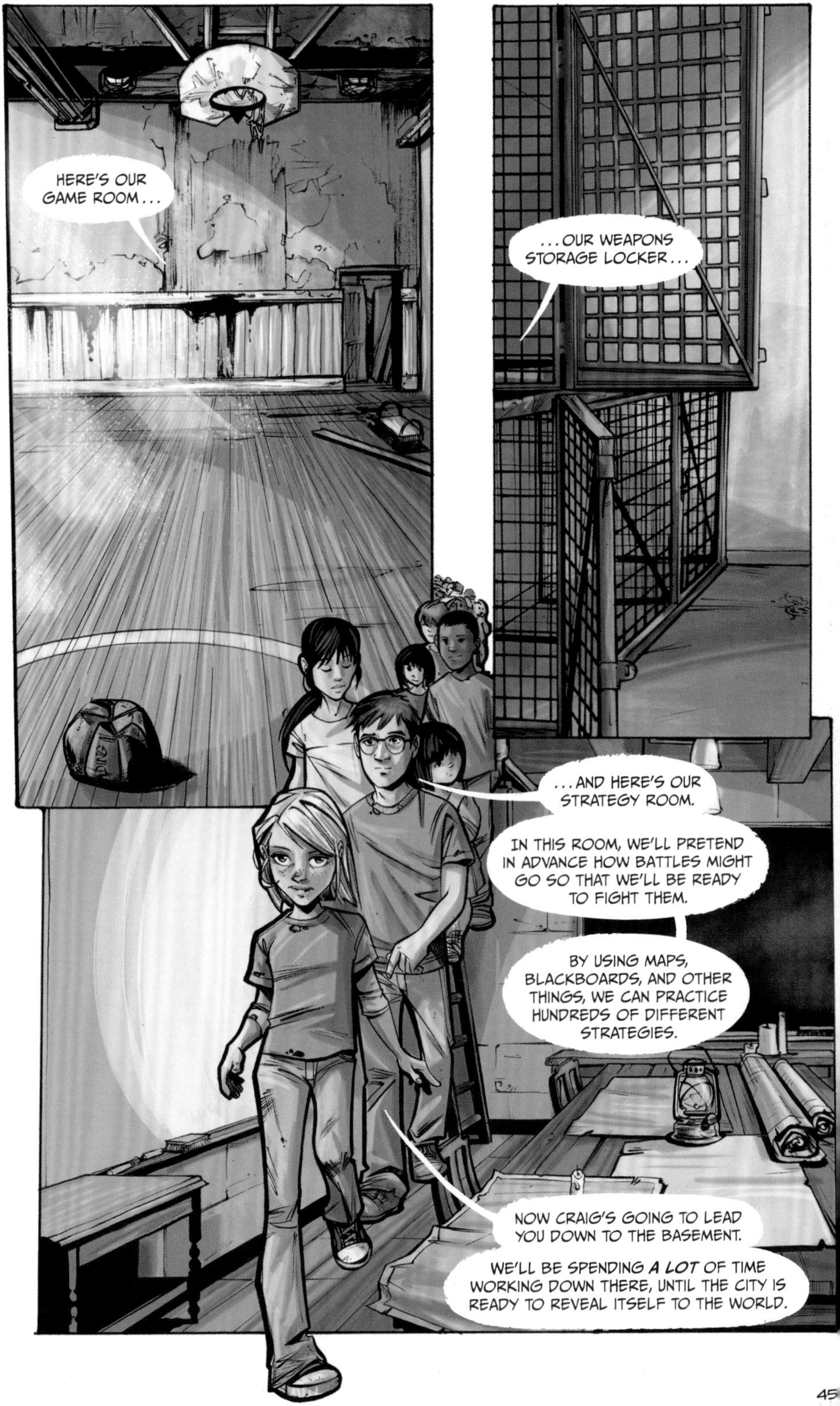
HERE'S OUR GAME ROOM...
...OUR WEAPONS STORAGE LOCKER...
...AND HERE'S OUR STRATEGY ROOM.
IN THIS ROOM, WE'LL PRETEND IN ADVANCE HOW BATTLES MIGHT GO SO THAT WE'LL BE READY TO FIGHT THEM.
BY USING MAPS, BLACKBOARDS, AND OTHER THINGS, WE CAN PRACTICE HUNDREDS OF DIFFERENT STRATEGIES.
NOW CRAIG'S GOING TO LEAD YOU DOWN TO THE BASEMENT.
WE'LL BE SPENDING *A LOT* OF TIME WORKING DOWN THERE, UNTIL THE CITY IS READY TO REVEAL ITSELF TO THE WORLD.

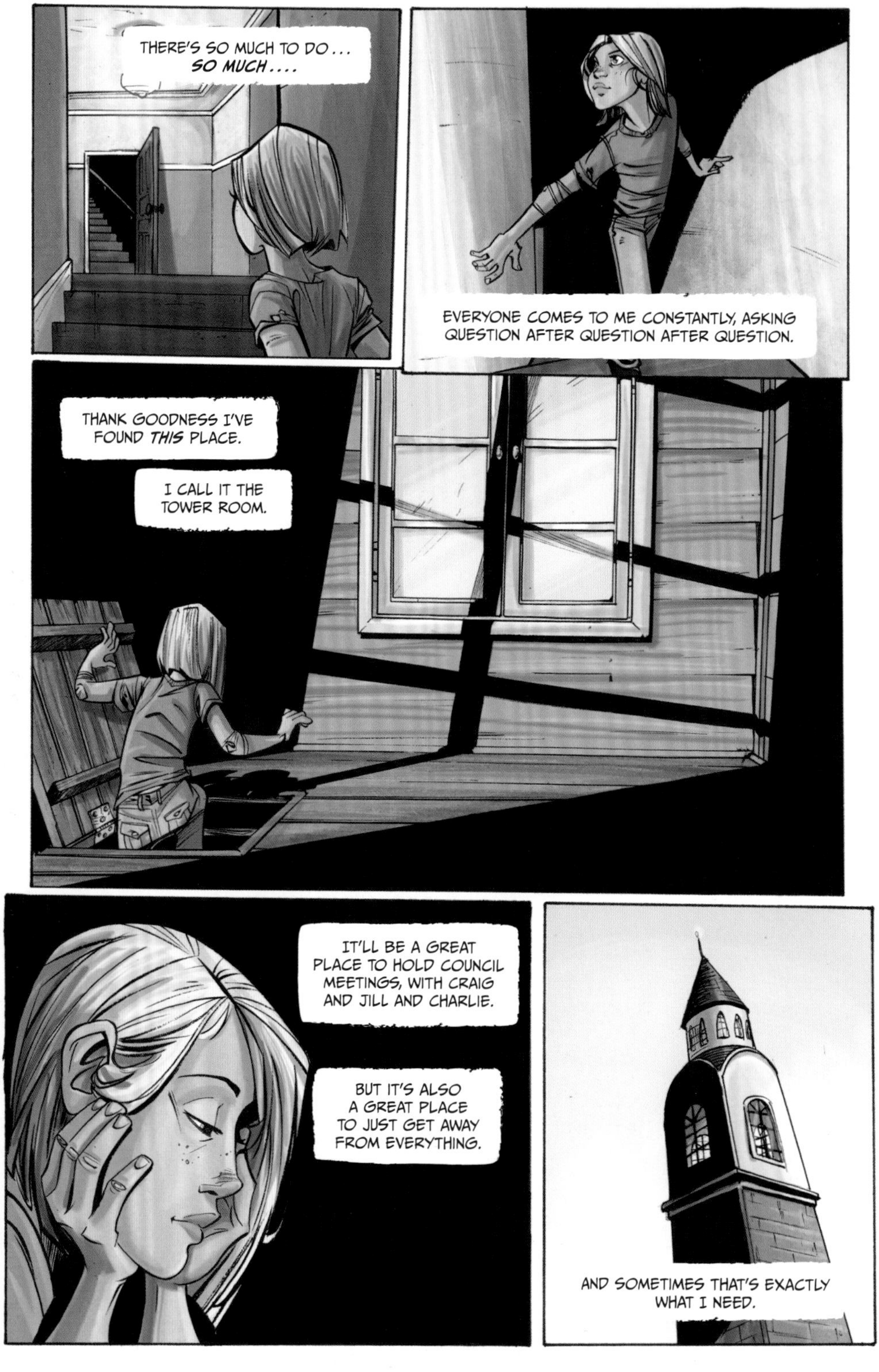
THERE'S SO MUCH TO DO . . . *SO MUCH* . . . .
EVERYONE COMES TO ME CONSTANTLY, ASKING QUESTION AFTER QUESTION AFTER QUESTION.
THANK GOODNESS I'VE FOUND *THIS* PLACE.
I CALL IT THE TOWER ROOM.
IT'LL BE A GREAT PLACE TO HOLD COUNCIL MEETINGS, WITH CRAIG AND JILL AND CHARLIE.
BUT IT'S ALSO A GREAT PLACE TO JUST GET AWAY FROM EVERYTHING.
AND SOMETIMES THAT'S EXACTLY WHAT I NEED.

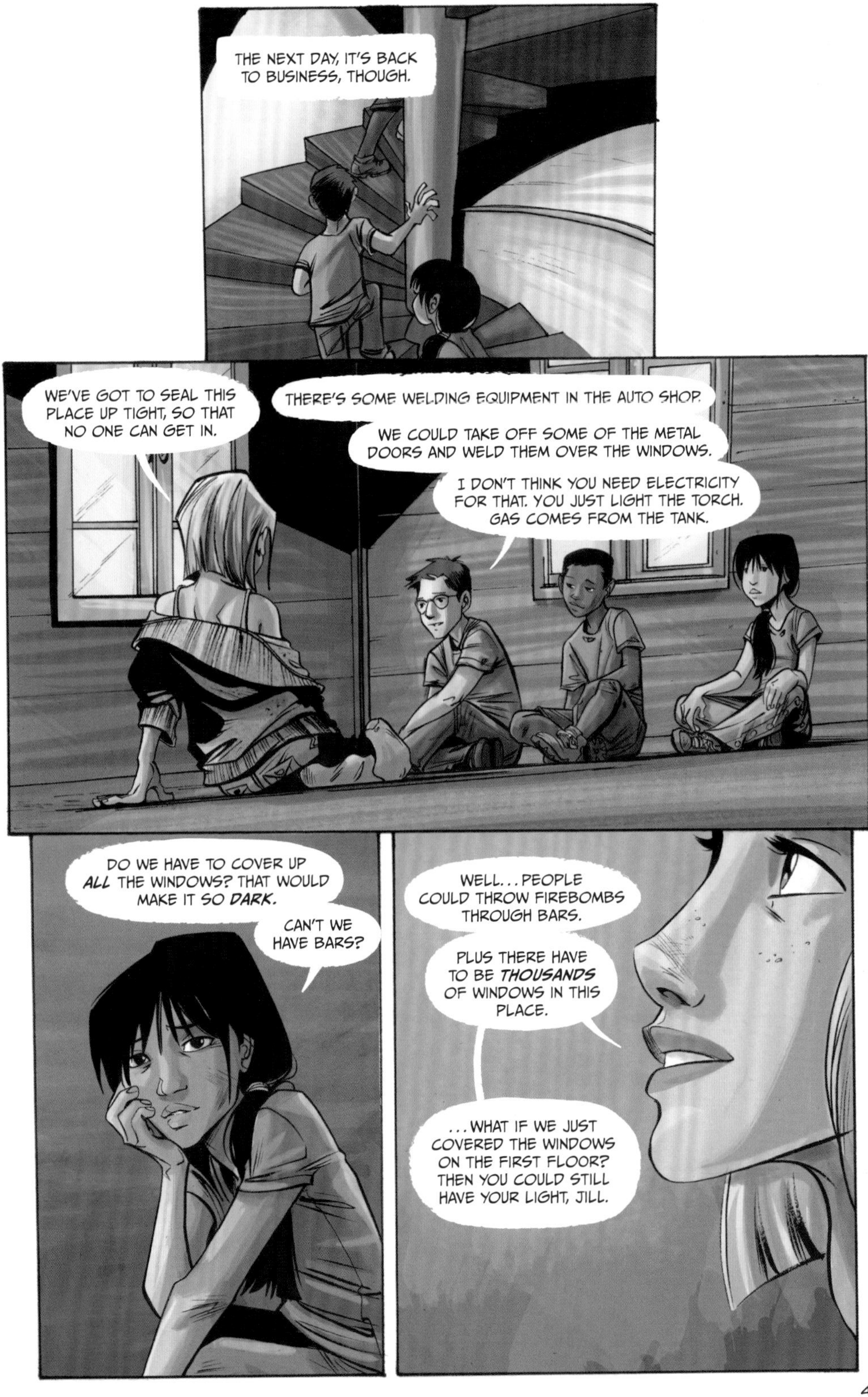
THE NEXT DAY, IT'S BACK TO BUSINESS, THOUGH.
WE'VE GOT TO SEAL THIS PLACE UP TIGHT, SO THAT NO ONE CAN GET IN.
THERE'S SOME WELDING EQUIPMENT IN THE AUTO SHOP.
WE COULD TAKE OFF SOME OF THE METAL DOORS AND WELD THEM OVER THE WINDOWS.
I DON'T THINK YOU NEED ELECTRICITY FOR THAT. YOU JUST LIGHT THE TORCH. GAS COMES FROM THE TANK.
DO WE HAVE TO COVER UP ***ALL*** THE WINDOWS? THAT WOULD MAKE IT SO ***DARK.***
CAN'T WE HAVE BARS?
WELL... PEOPLE COULD THROW FIREBOMBS THROUGH BARS.
PLUS THERE HAVE TO BE ***THOUSANDS*** OF WINDOWS IN THIS PLACE.
...WHAT IF WE JUST COVERED THE WINDOWS ON THE FIRST FLOOR? THEN YOU COULD STILL HAVE YOUR LIGHT, JILL.

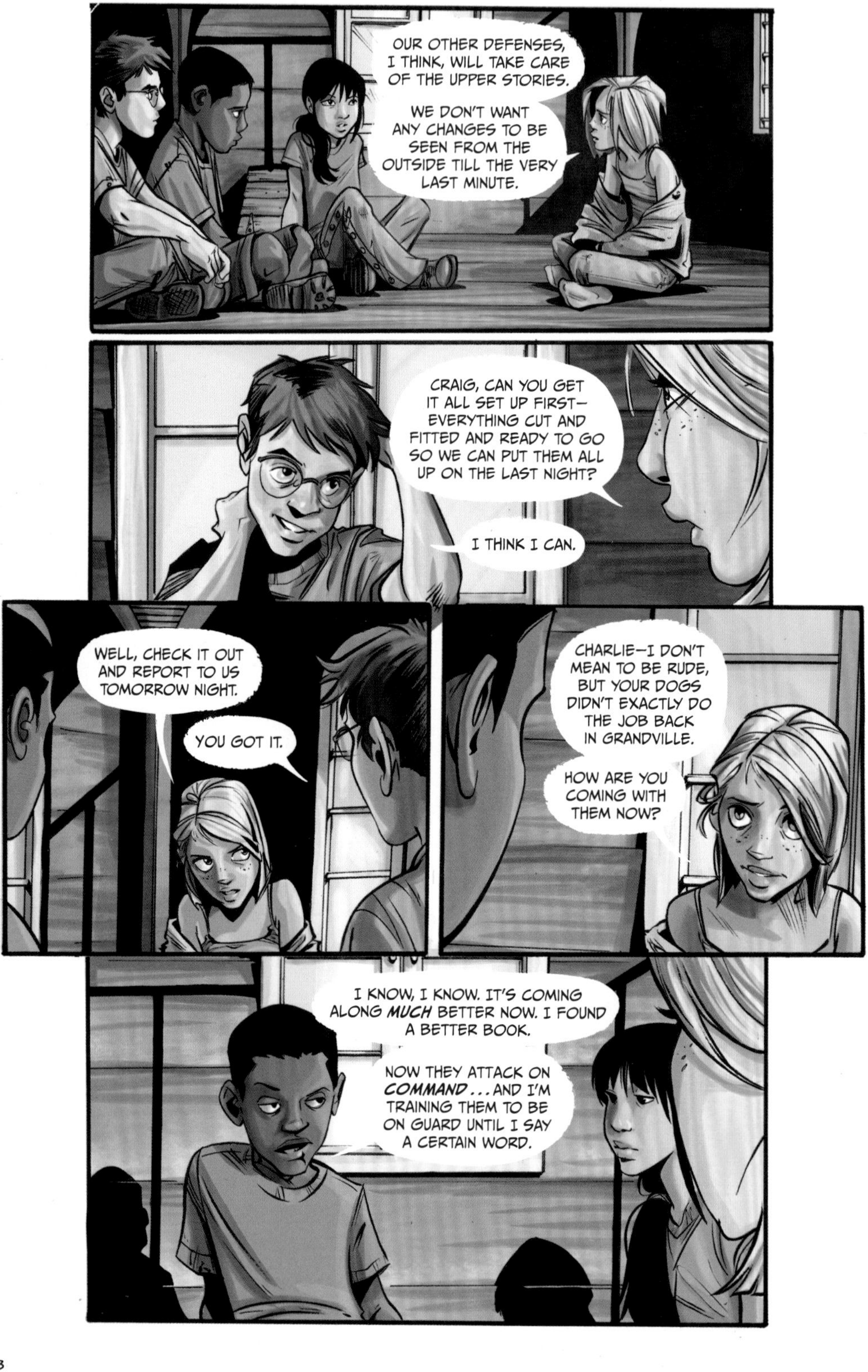
OUR OTHER DEFENSES, I THINK, WILL TAKE CARE OF THE UPPER STORIES.
WE DON'T WANT ANY CHANGES TO BE SEEN FROM THE OUTSIDE TILL THE VERY LAST MINUTE.
CRAIG, CAN YOU GET IT ALL SET UP FIRST— EVERYTHING CUT AND FITTED AND READY TO GO SO WE CAN PUT THEM ALL UP ON THE LAST NIGHT?
I THINK I CAN.
WELL, CHECK IT OUT AND REPORT TO US TOMORROW NIGHT.
YOU GOT IT.
CHARLIE—I DON'T MEAN TO BE RUDE, BUT YOUR DOGS DIDN'T EXACTLY DO THE JOB BACK IN GRANDVILLE.
HOW ARE YOU COMING WITH THEM NOW?
I KNOW, I KNOW. IT'S COMING ALONG *MUCH* BETTER NOW. I FOUND A BETTER BOOK.
NOW THEY ATTACK ON ***COMMAND*** . . . AND I'M TRAINING THEM TO BE ON GUARD UNTIL I SAY A CERTAIN WORD.

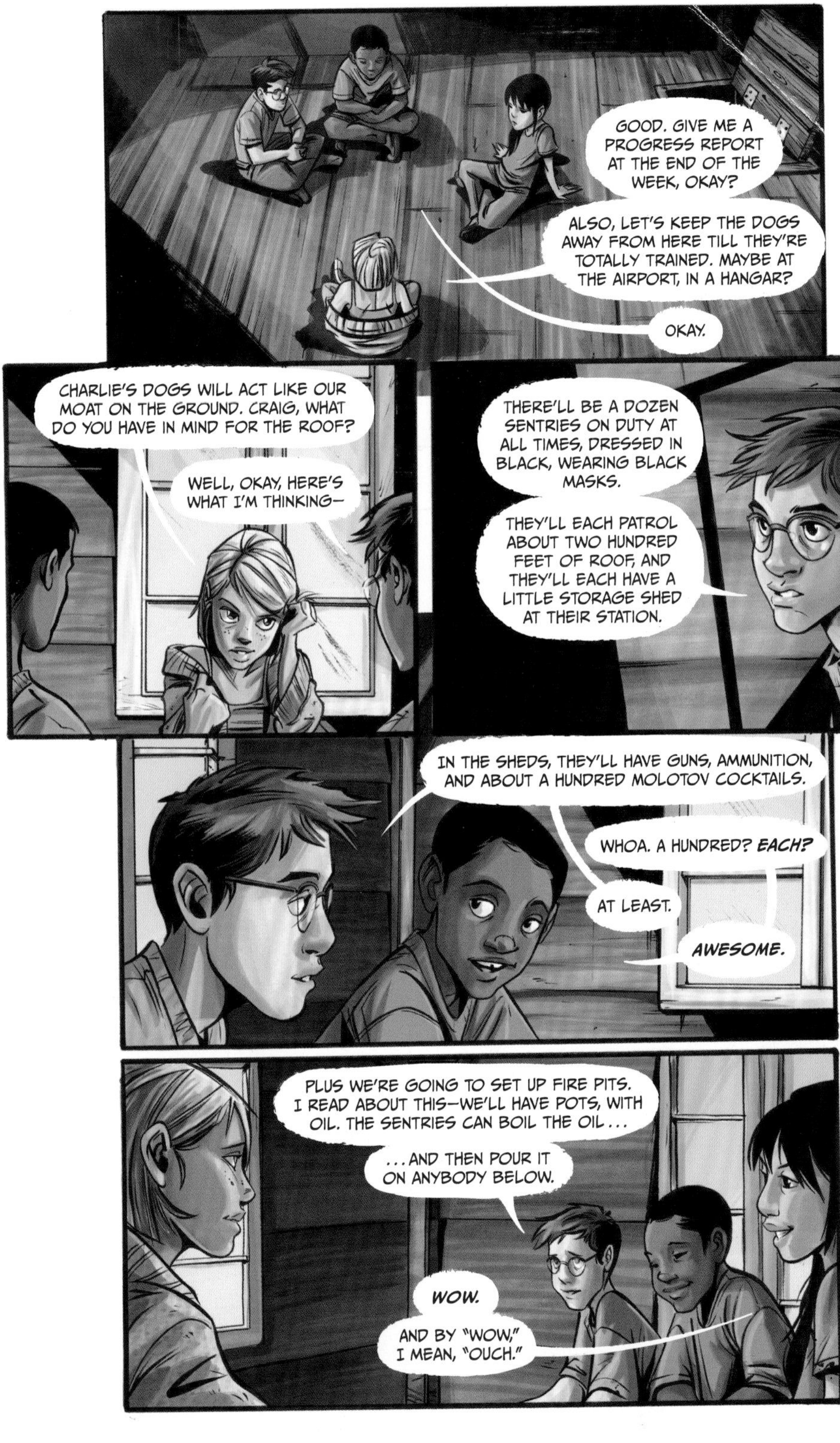
GOOD. GIVE ME A PROGRESS REPORT AT THE END OF THE WEEK, OKAY?
ALSO, LET'S KEEP THE DOGS AWAY FROM HERE TILL THEY'RE TOTALLY TRAINED. MAYBE AT THE AIRPORT, IN A HANGAR?
OKAY.
CHARLIE'S DOGS WILL ACT LIKE OUR MOAT ON THE GROUND. CRAIG, WHAT DO YOU HAVE IN MIND FOR THE ROOF?
WELL, OKAY, HERE'S WHAT I'M THINKING—
THERE'LL BE A DOZEN SENTRIES ON DUTY AT ALL TIMES, DRESSED IN BLACK, WEARING BLACK MASKS.
THEY'LL EACH PATROL ABOUT TWO HUNDRED FEET OF ROOF, AND THEY'LL EACH HAVE A LITTLE STORAGE SHED AT THEIR STATION.
IN THE SHEDS, THEY'LL HAVE GUNS, AMMUNITION, AND ABOUT A HUNDRED MOLOTOV COCKTAILS.
WHOA. A HUNDRED? *EACH?*
AT LEAST.
AWESOME.
PLUS WE'RE GOING TO SET UP FIRE PITS. I READ ABOUT THIS—WE'LL HAVE POTS, WITH OIL. THE SENTRIES CAN BOIL THE OIL . . .
. . . AND THEN POUR IT ON ANYBODY BELOW.
WOW.
AND BY "WOW," I MEAN, "OUCH."

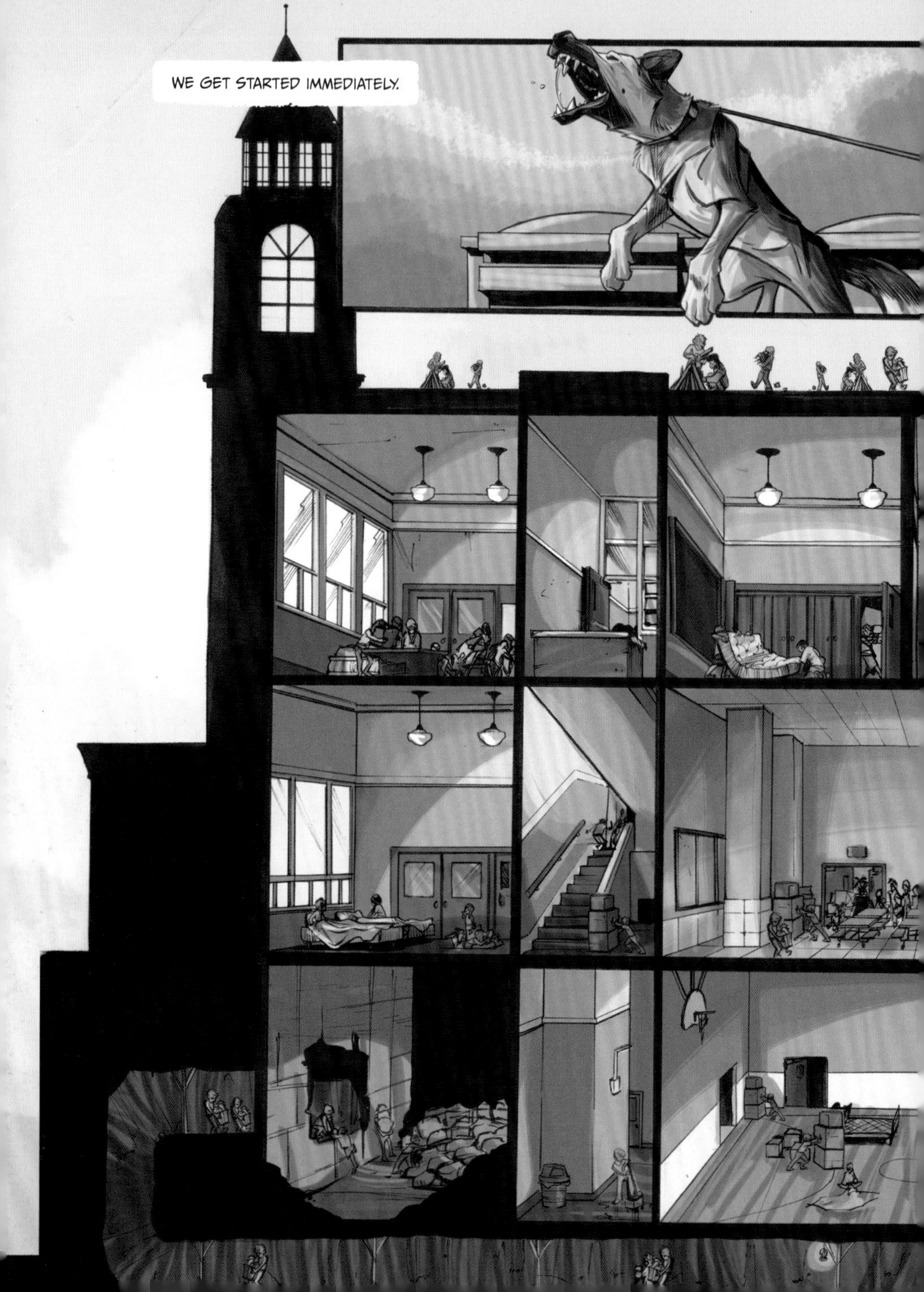
WE GET STARTED IMMEDIATELY.

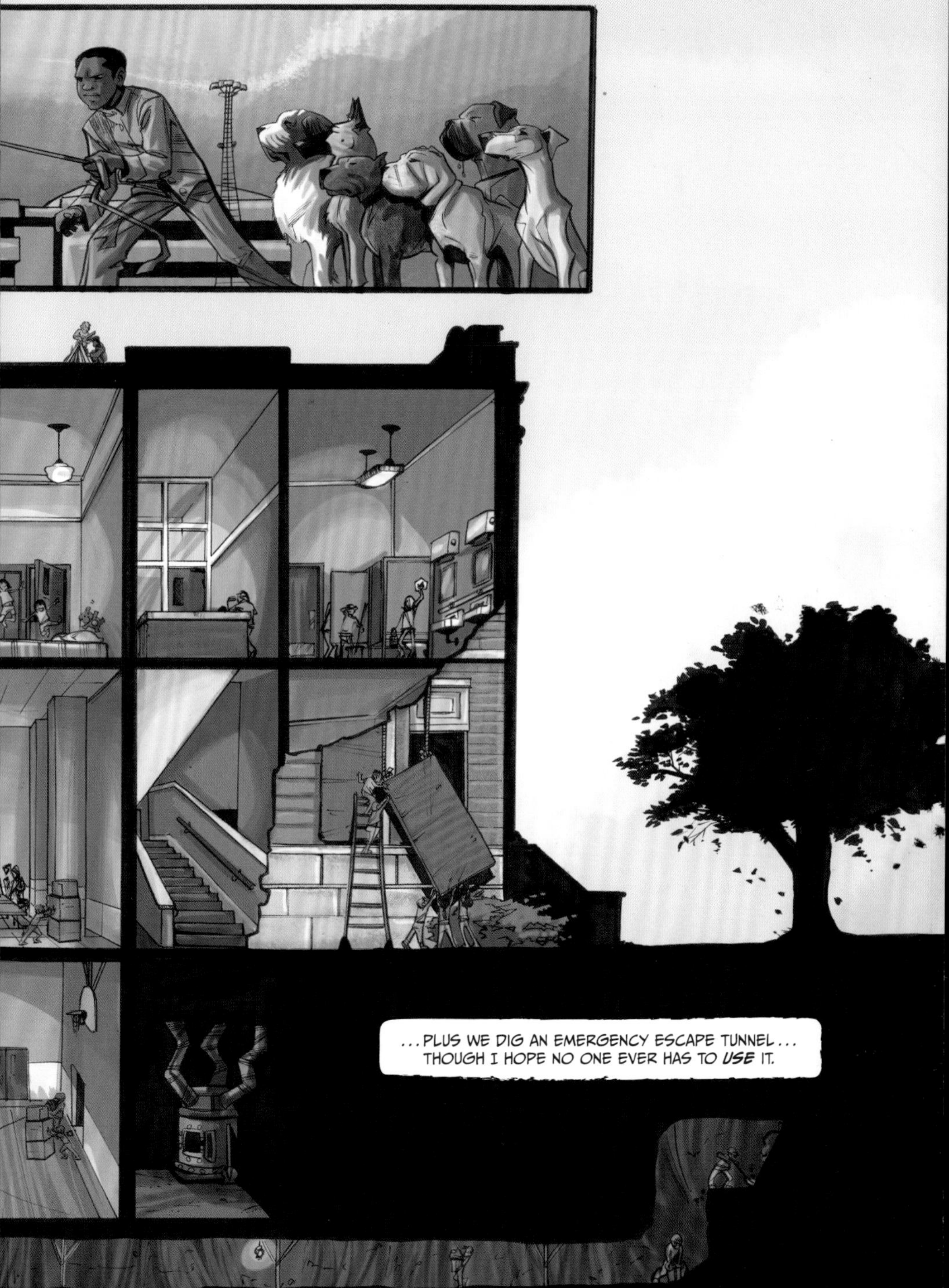
...PLUS WE DIG AN EMERGENCY ESCAPE TUNNEL...
THOUGH I HOPE NO ONE EVER HAS TO *USE* IT.

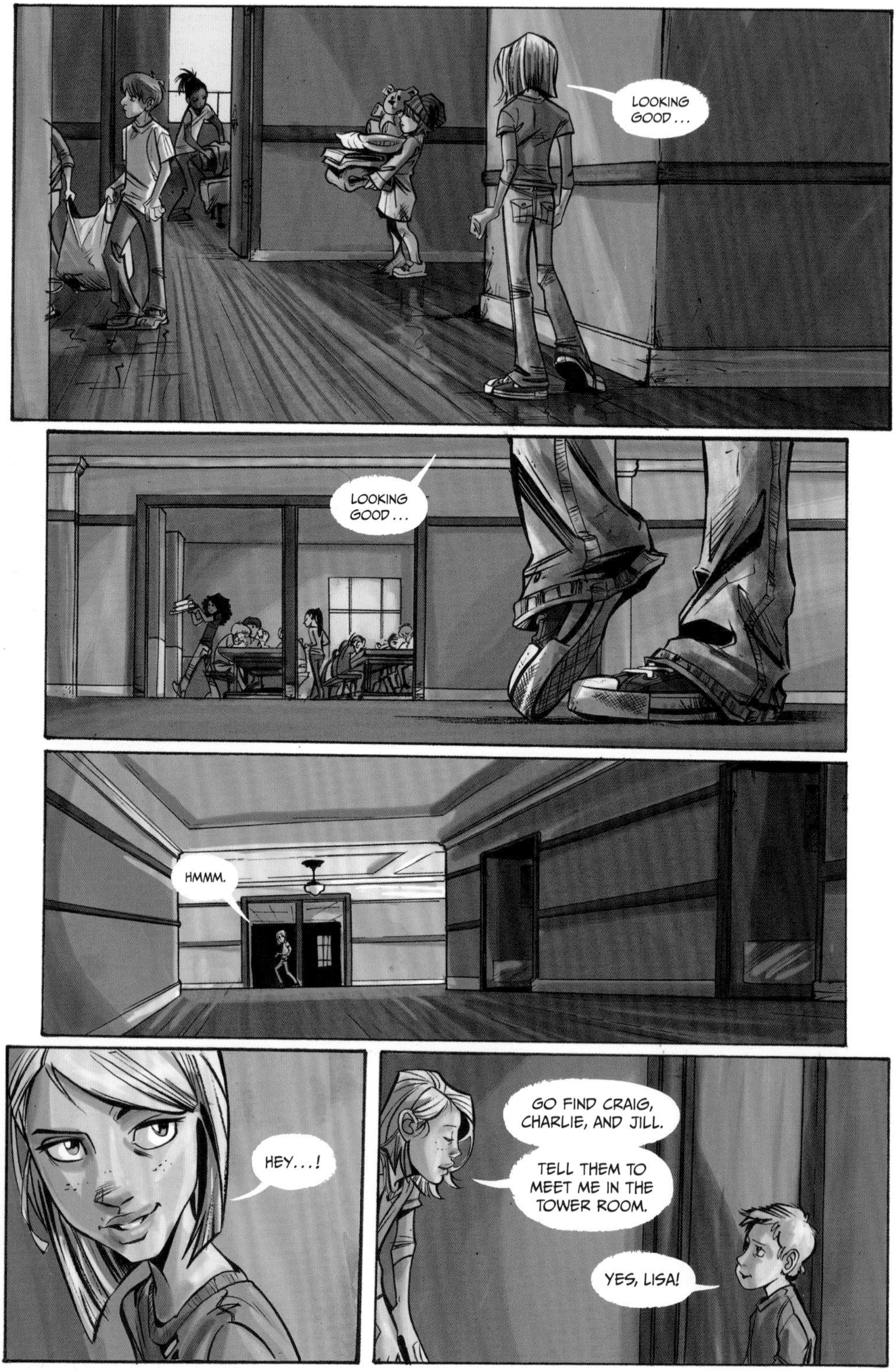
LOOKING GOOD . . .
LOOKING GOOD . . .
HMMM.
HEY . . . !
GO FIND CRAIG, CHARLIE, AND JILL.
TELL THEM TO MEET ME IN THE TOWER ROOM.
YES, LISA!

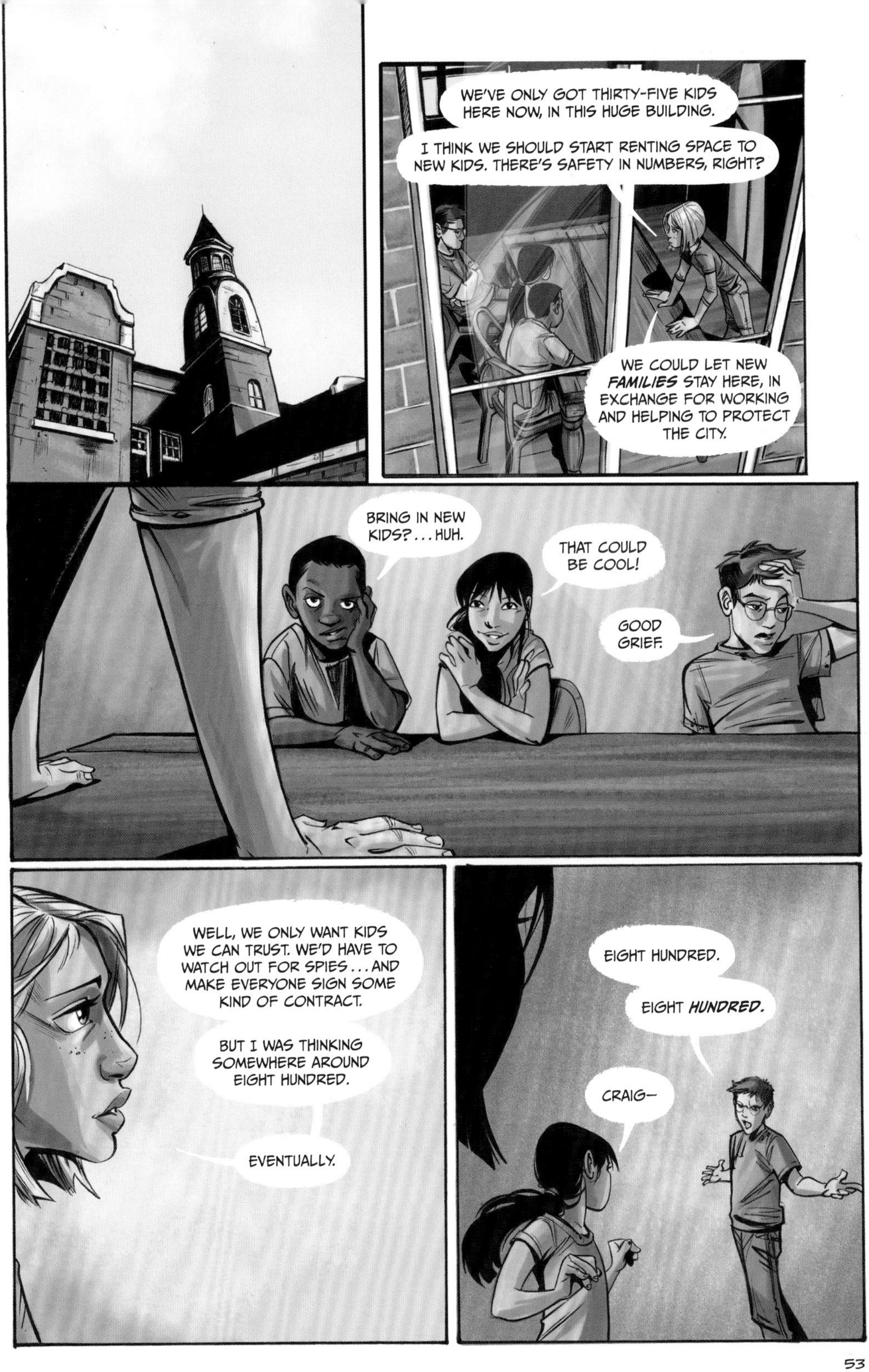
WE'VE ONLY GOT THIRTY-FIVE KIDS HERE NOW, IN THIS HUGE BUILDING.
I THINK WE SHOULD START RENTING SPACE TO NEW KIDS. THERE'S SAFETY IN NUMBERS, RIGHT?
WE COULD LET NEW *FAMILIES* STAY HERE, IN EXCHANGE FOR WORKING AND HELPING TO PROTECT THE CITY.
BRING IN NEW KIDS? . . . HUH.
THAT COULD BE COOL!
GOOD GRIEF.
WELL, WE ONLY WANT KIDS WE CAN TRUST. WE'D HAVE TO WATCH OUT FOR SPIES . . . AND MAKE EVERYONE SIGN SOME KIND OF CONTRACT.
BUT I WAS THINKING SOMEWHERE AROUND EIGHT HUNDRED.
EVENTUALLY.
EIGHT HUNDRED.
EIGHT ***HUNDRED.***
CRAIG—

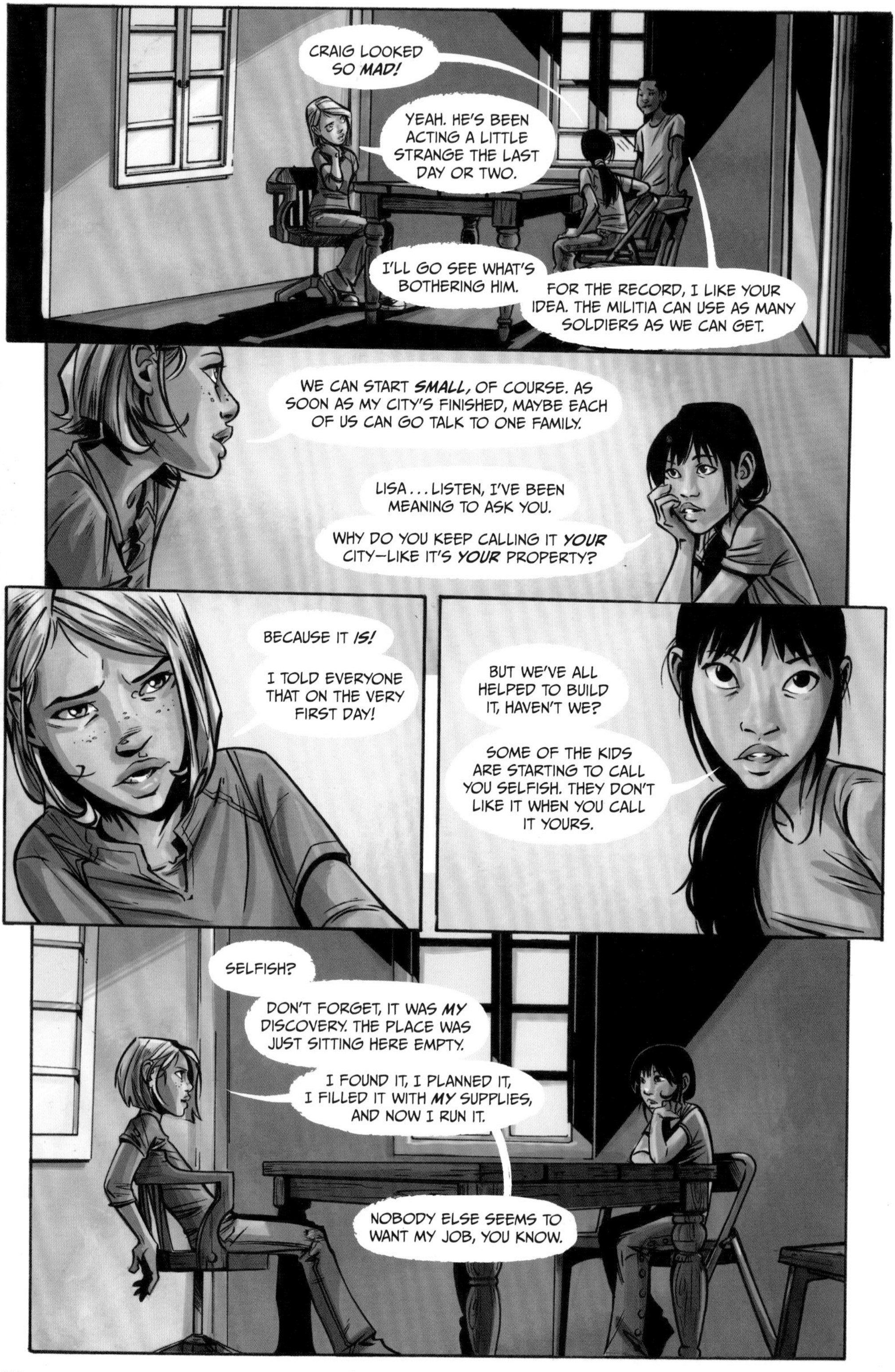
CRAIG LOOKED SO *MAD!*
YEAH. HE'S BEEN ACTING A LITTLE STRANGE THE LAST DAY OR TWO.
I'LL GO SEE WHAT'S BOTHERING HIM.
FOR THE RECORD, I LIKE YOUR IDEA. THE MILITIA CAN USE AS MANY SOLDIERS AS WE CAN GET.
WE CAN START *SMALL,* OF COURSE. AS SOON AS MY CITY'S FINISHED, MAYBE EACH OF US CAN GO TALK TO ONE FAMILY.
LISA . . . LISTEN, I'VE BEEN MEANING TO ASK YOU.
WHY DO YOU KEEP CALLING IT *YOUR* CITY—LIKE IT'S *YOUR* PROPERTY?
BECAUSE IT *IS!*
I TOLD EVERYONE THAT ON THE VERY FIRST DAY!
BUT WE'VE ALL HELPED TO BUILD IT, HAVEN'T WE?
SOME OF THE KIDS ARE STARTING TO CALL YOU SELFISH. THEY DON'T LIKE IT WHEN YOU CALL IT YOURS.
SELFISH?
DON'T FORGET, IT WAS *MY* DISCOVERY. THE PLACE WAS JUST SITTING HERE EMPTY.
I FOUND IT, I PLANNED IT, I FILLED IT WITH *MY* SUPPLIES, AND NOW I RUN IT.
NOBODY ELSE SEEMS TO WANT MY JOB, YOU KNOW.

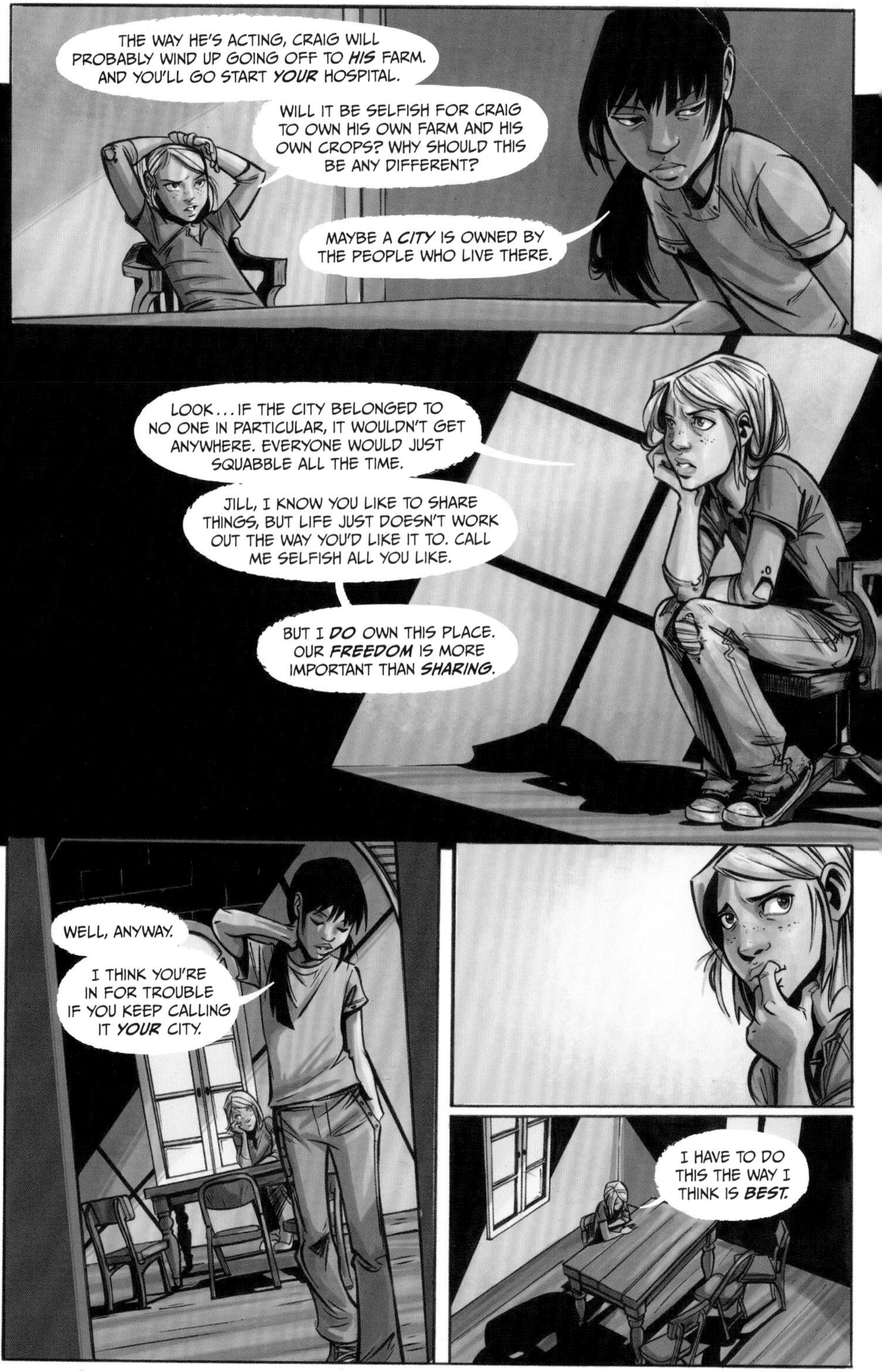
THE WAY HE'S ACTING, CRAIG WILL PROBABLY WIND UP GOING OFF TO *HIS* FARM. AND YOU'LL GO START *YOUR* HOSPITAL.
WILL IT BE SELFISH FOR CRAIG TO OWN HIS OWN FARM AND HIS OWN CROPS? WHY SHOULD THIS BE ANY DIFFERENT?
MAYBE A *CITY* IS OWNED BY THE PEOPLE WHO LIVE THERE.
LOOK... IF THE CITY BELONGED TO NO ONE IN PARTICULAR, IT WOULDN'T GET ANYWHERE. EVERYONE WOULD JUST SQUABBLE ALL THE TIME.
JILL, I KNOW YOU LIKE TO SHARE THINGS, BUT LIFE JUST DOESN'T WORK OUT THE WAY YOU'D LIKE IT TO. CALL ME SELFISH ALL YOU LIKE.
BUT I *DO* OWN THIS PLACE. OUR *FREEDOM* IS MORE IMPORTANT THAN *SHARING*.
WELL, ANYWAY.
I THINK YOU'RE IN FOR TROUBLE IF YOU KEEP CALLING IT *YOUR* CITY.
I HAVE TO DO THIS THE WAY I THINK IS *BEST*.

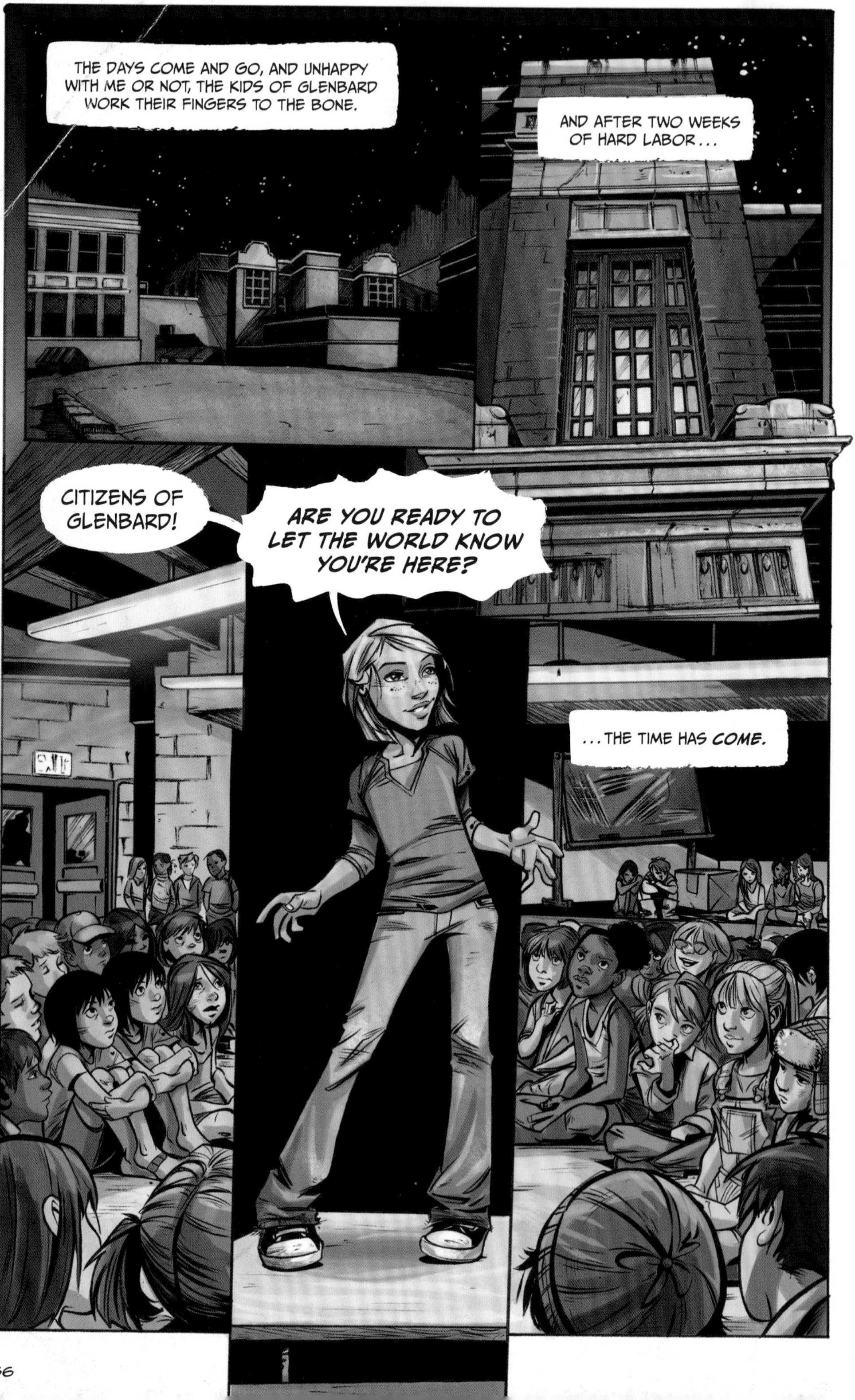
THE DAYS COME AND GO, AND UNHAPPY WITH ME OR NOT, THE KIDS OF GLENBARD WORK THEIR FINGERS TO THE BONE.
AND AFTER TWO WEEKS OF HARD LABOR...
CITIZENS OF GLENBARD!
ARE YOU READY TO LET THE WORLD KNOW YOU'RE HERE?
...THE TIME HAS COME.

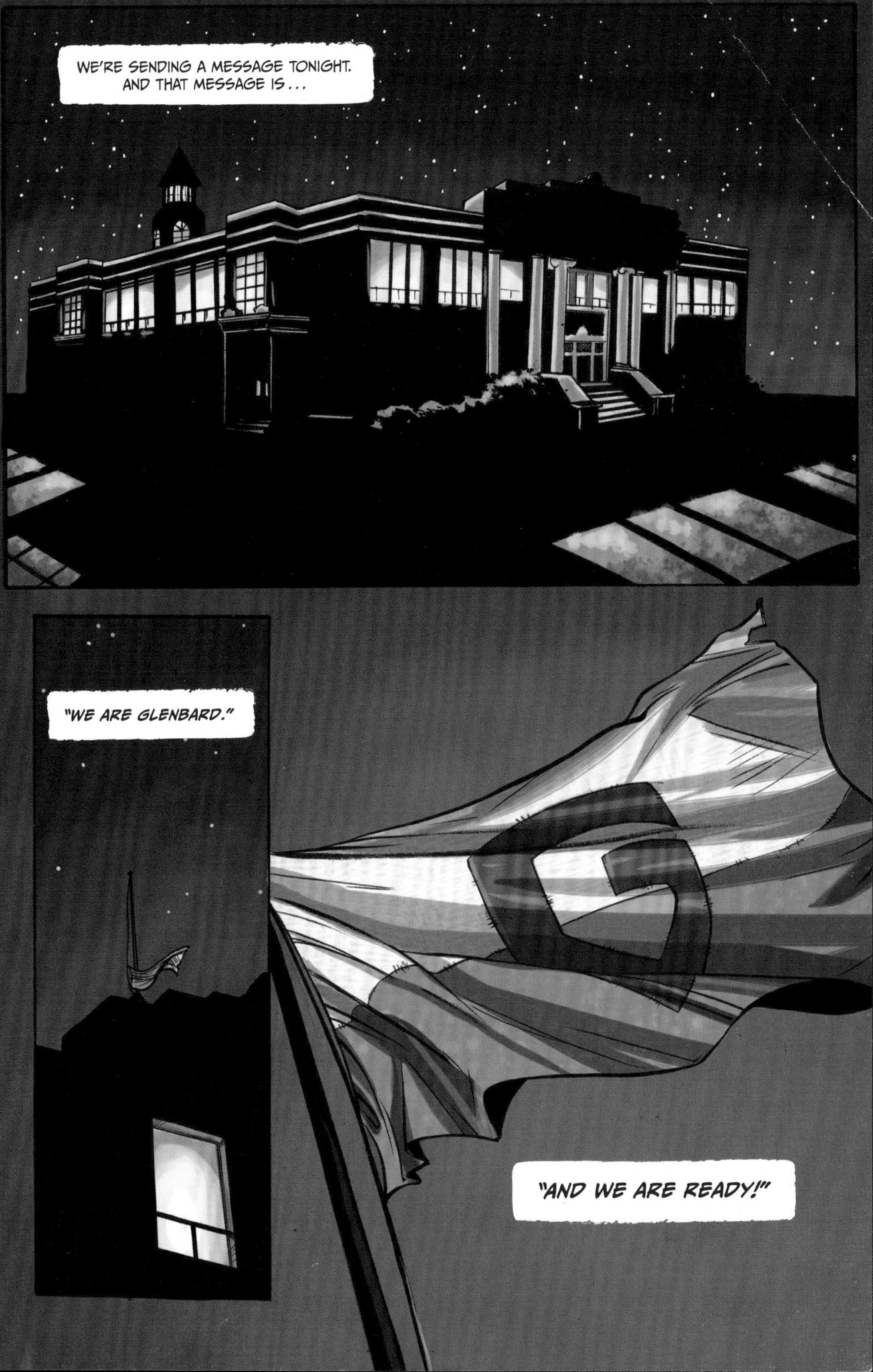
WE'RE SENDING A MESSAGE TONIGHT. AND THAT MESSAGE IS . . .
"WE ARE GLENBARD."
"AND WE ARE READY!"

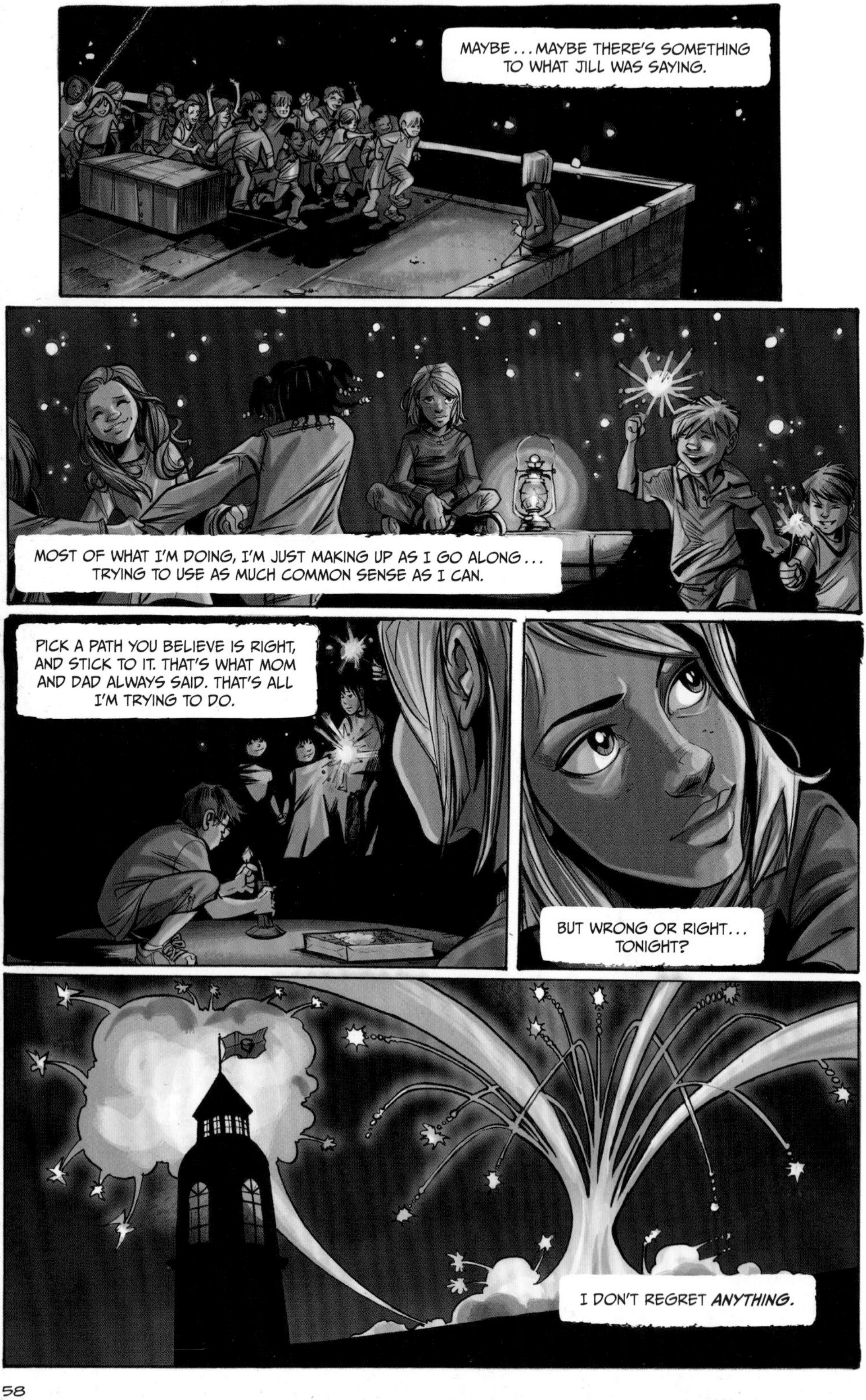
MAYBE . . . MAYBE THERE'S SOMETHING TO WHAT JILL WAS SAYING.
MOST OF WHAT I'M DOING, I'M JUST MAKING UP AS I GO ALONG . . . TRYING TO USE AS MUCH COMMON SENSE AS I CAN.
PICK A PATH YOU BELIEVE IS RIGHT, AND STICK TO IT. THAT'S WHAT MOM AND DAD ALWAYS SAID. THAT'S ALL I'M TRYING TO DO.
BUT WRONG OR RIGHT . . . TONIGHT?
I DON'T REGRET *ANYTHING.*

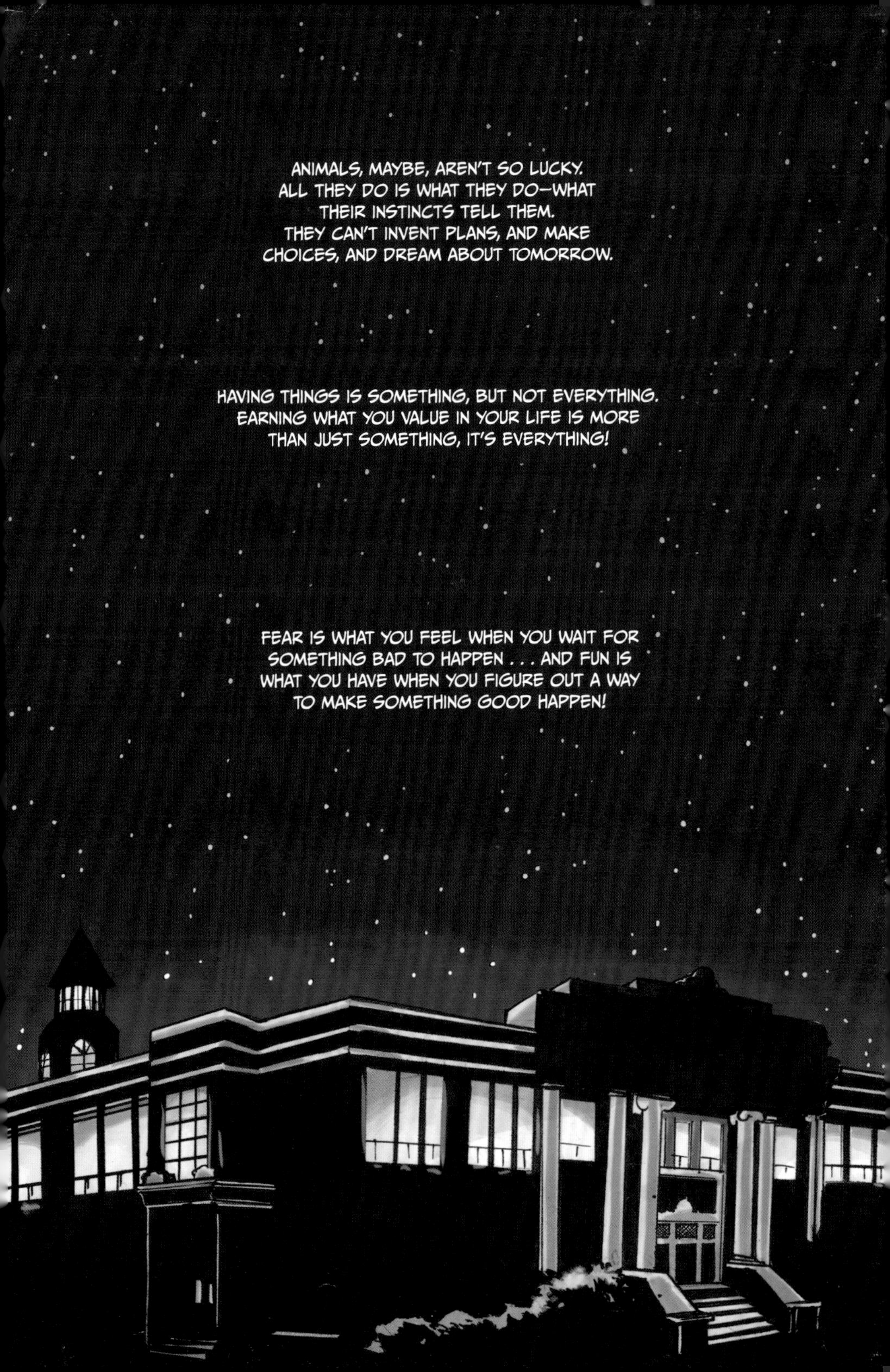
ANIMALS, MAYBE, AREN'T SO LUCKY. ALL THEY DO IS WHAT THEY DO—WHAT THEIR INSTINCTS TELL THEM. THEY CAN'T INVENT PLANS, AND MAKE CHOICES, AND DREAM ABOUT TOMORROW.
HAVING THINGS IS SOMETHING, BUT NOT EVERYTHING. EARNING WHAT YOU VALUE IN YOUR LIFE IS MORE THAN JUST SOMETHING, IT'S EVERYTHING!
FEAR IS WHAT YOU FEEL WHEN YOU WAIT FOR SOMETHING BAD TO HAPPEN . . . AND FUN IS WHAT YOU HAVE WHEN YOU FIGURE OUT A WAY TO MAKE SOMETHING GOOD HAPPEN!

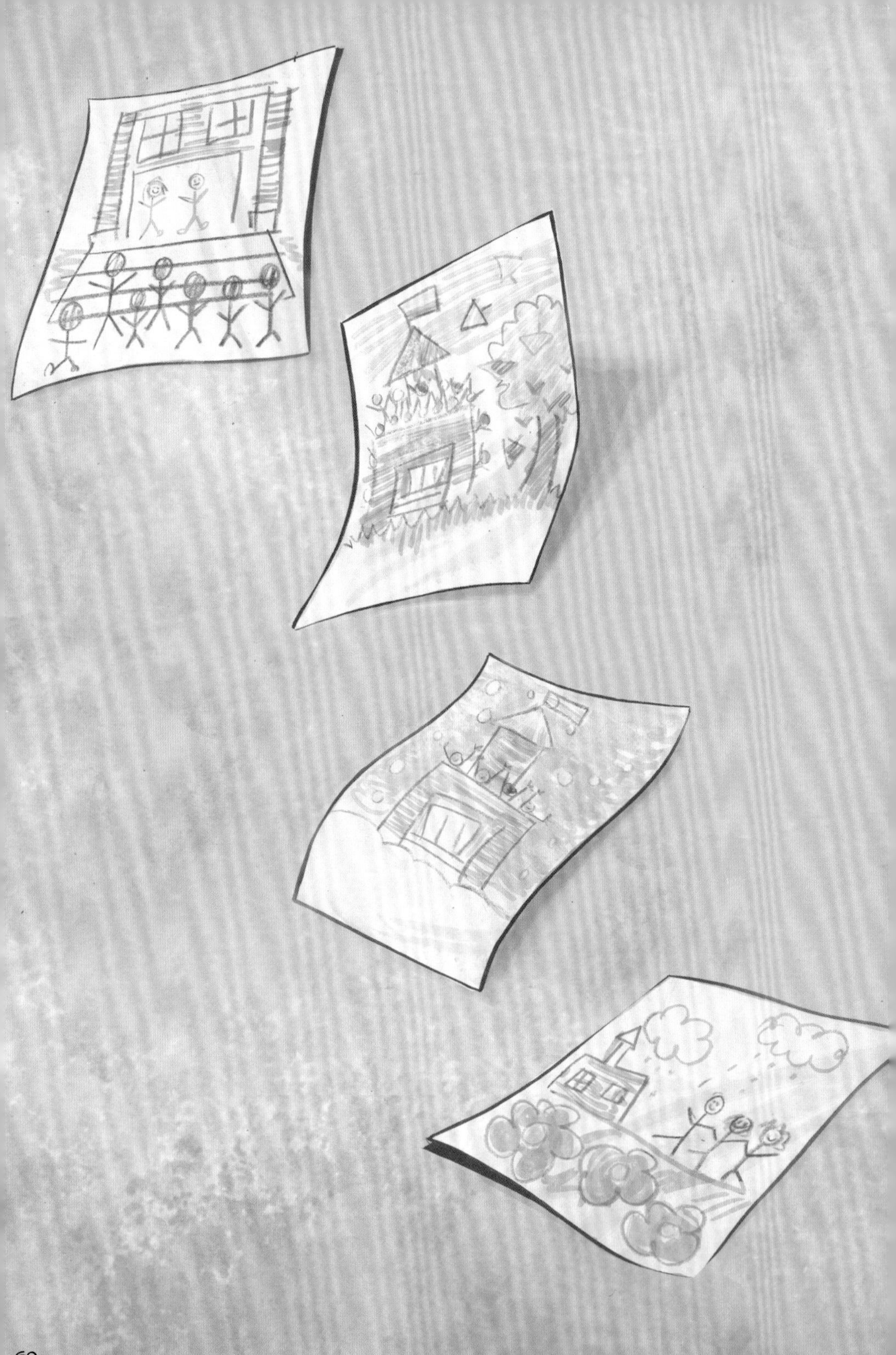

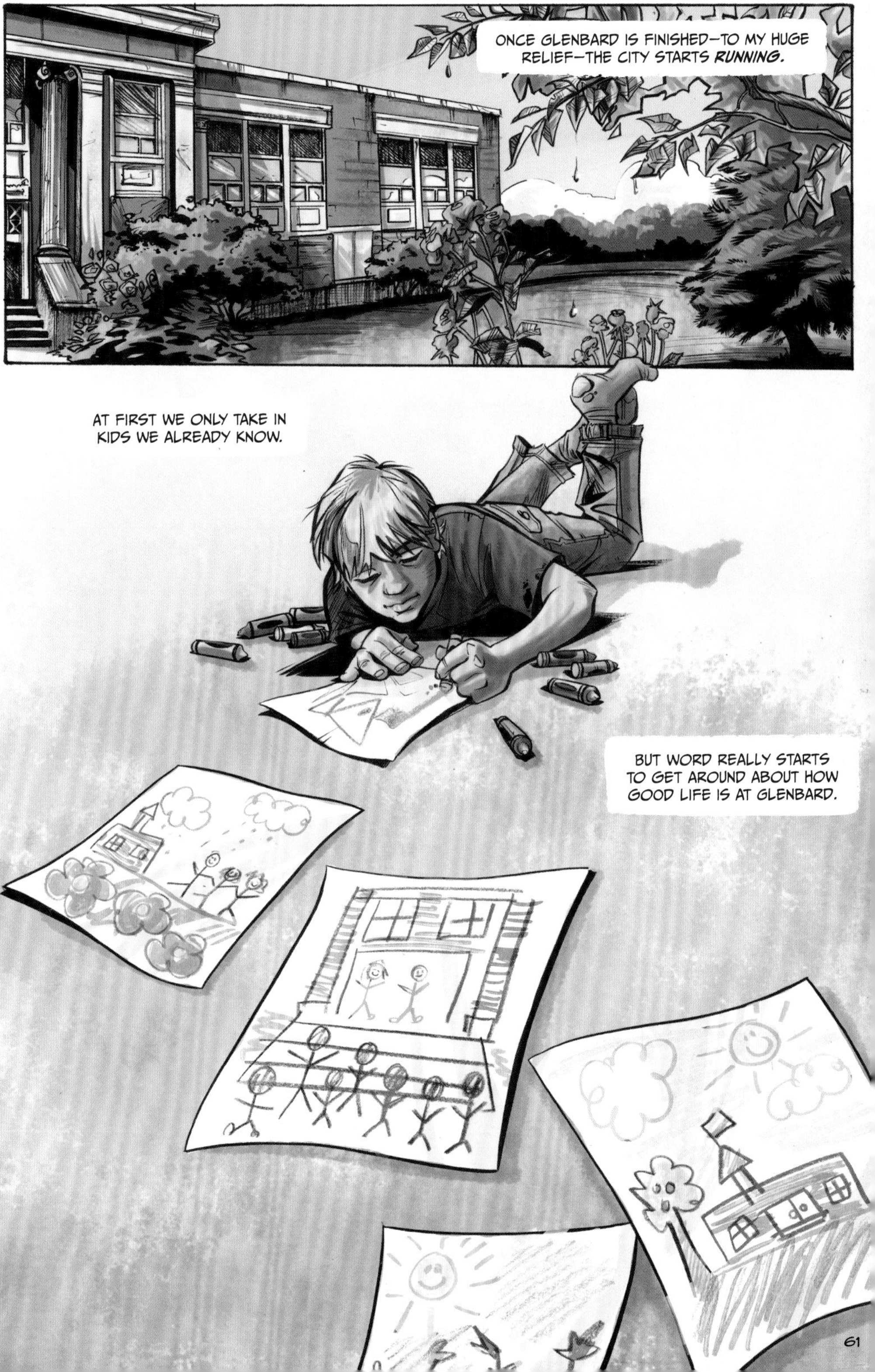

ONCE GLENBARD IS FINISHED—TO MY HUGE RELIEF—THE CITY STARTS *RUNNING.*
AT FIRST WE ONLY TAKE IN KIDS WE ALREADY KNOW.
BUT WORD REALLY STARTS TO GET AROUND ABOUT HOW GOOD LIFE IS AT GLENBARD.

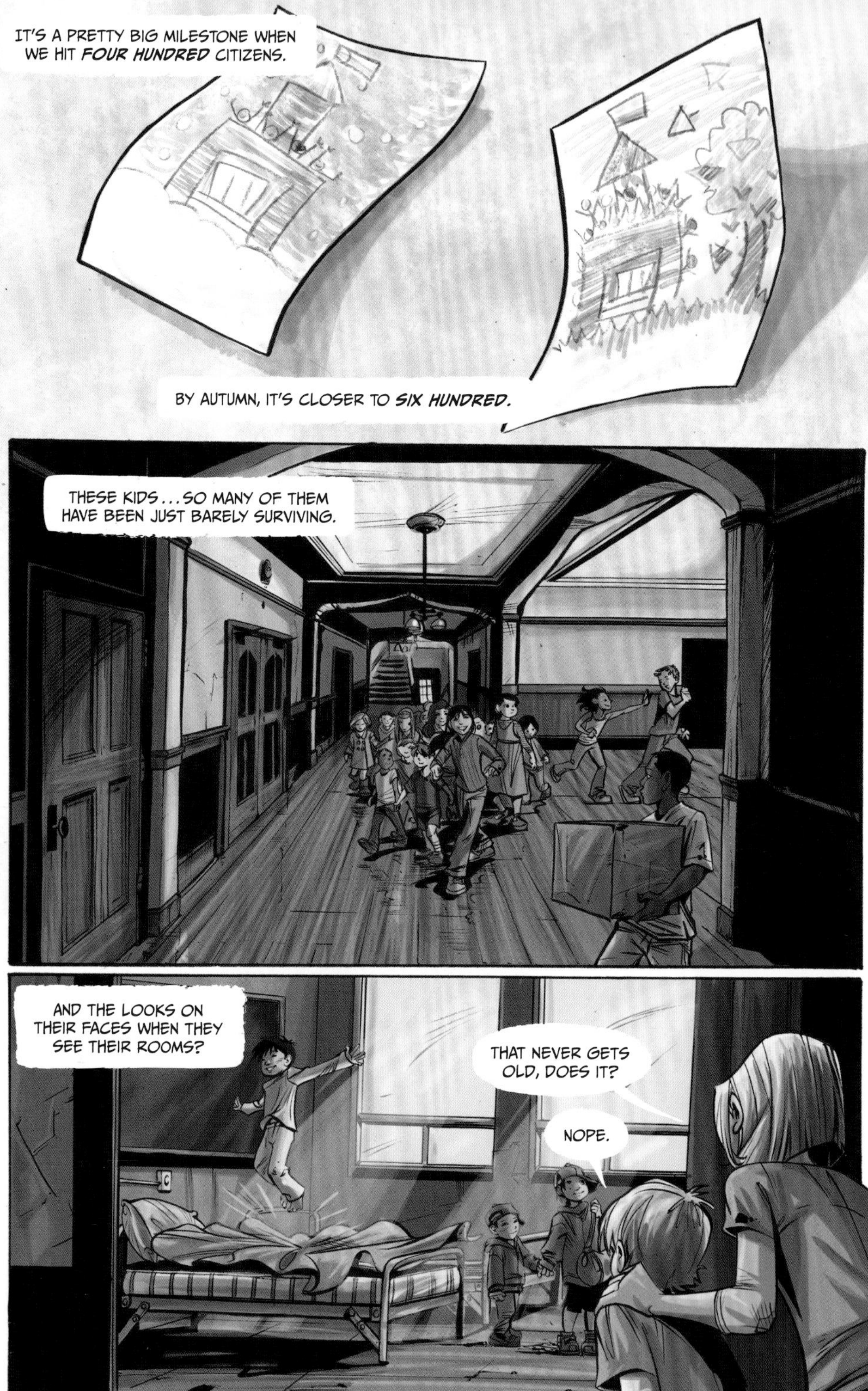
IT'S A PRETTY BIG MILESTONE WHEN WE HIT *FOUR HUNDRED* CITIZENS.
BY AUTUMN, IT'S CLOSER TO *SIX HUNDRED.*
THESE KIDS . . . SO MANY OF THEM HAVE BEEN JUST BARELY SURVIVING.
AND THE LOOKS ON THEIR FACES WHEN THEY SEE THEIR ROOMS?
THAT NEVER GETS OLD, DOES IT?
NOPE.

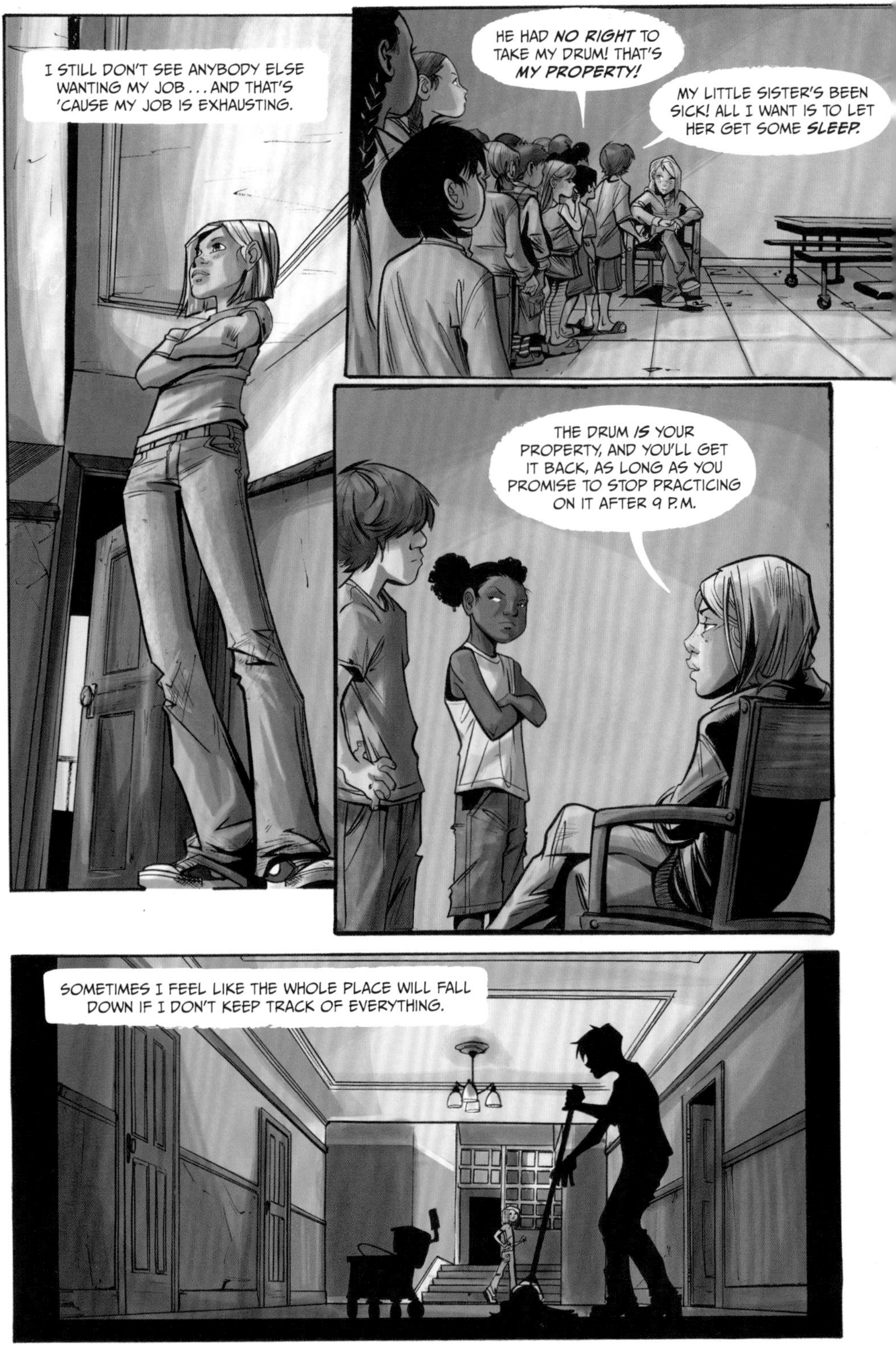
I STILL DON'T SEE ANYBODY ELSE WANTING MY JOB . . . AND THAT'S 'CAUSE MY JOB IS EXHAUSTING.
HE HAD NO RIGHT TO TAKE MY DRUM! THAT'S MY PROPERTY!
MY LITTLE SISTER'S BEEN SICK! ALL I WANT IS TO LET HER GET SOME SLEEP.
THE DRUM IS YOUR PROPERTY, AND YOU'LL GET IT BACK, AS LONG AS YOU PROMISE TO STOP PRACTICING ON IT AFTER 9 P.M.
SOMETIMES I FEEL LIKE THE WHOLE PLACE WILL FALL DOWN IF I DON'T KEEP TRACK OF EVERYTHING.

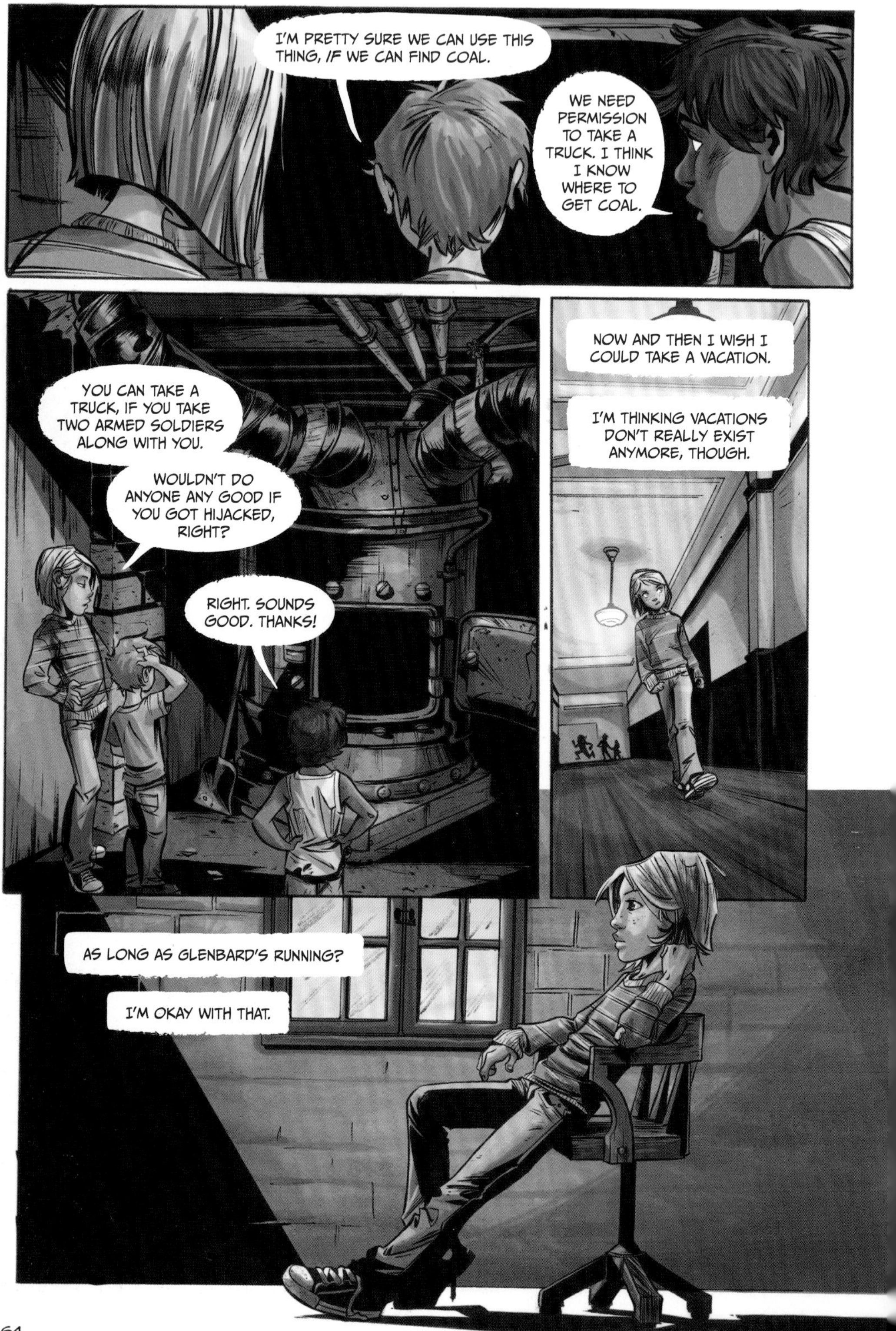

I'M PRETTY SURE WE CAN USE THIS THING, *IF* WE CAN FIND COAL.
WE NEED PERMISSION TO TAKE A TRUCK. I THINK I KNOW WHERE TO GET COAL.
YOU CAN TAKE A TRUCK, IF YOU TAKE TWO ARMED SOLDIERS ALONG WITH YOU.
WOULDN'T DO ANYONE ANY GOOD IF YOU GOT HIJACKED, RIGHT?
RIGHT. SOUNDS GOOD. THANKS!
NOW AND THEN I WISH I COULD TAKE A VACATION.
I'M THINKING VACATIONS DON'T REALLY EXIST ANYMORE, THOUGH.
AS LONG AS GLENBARD'S RUNNING?
I'M OKAY WITH THAT.

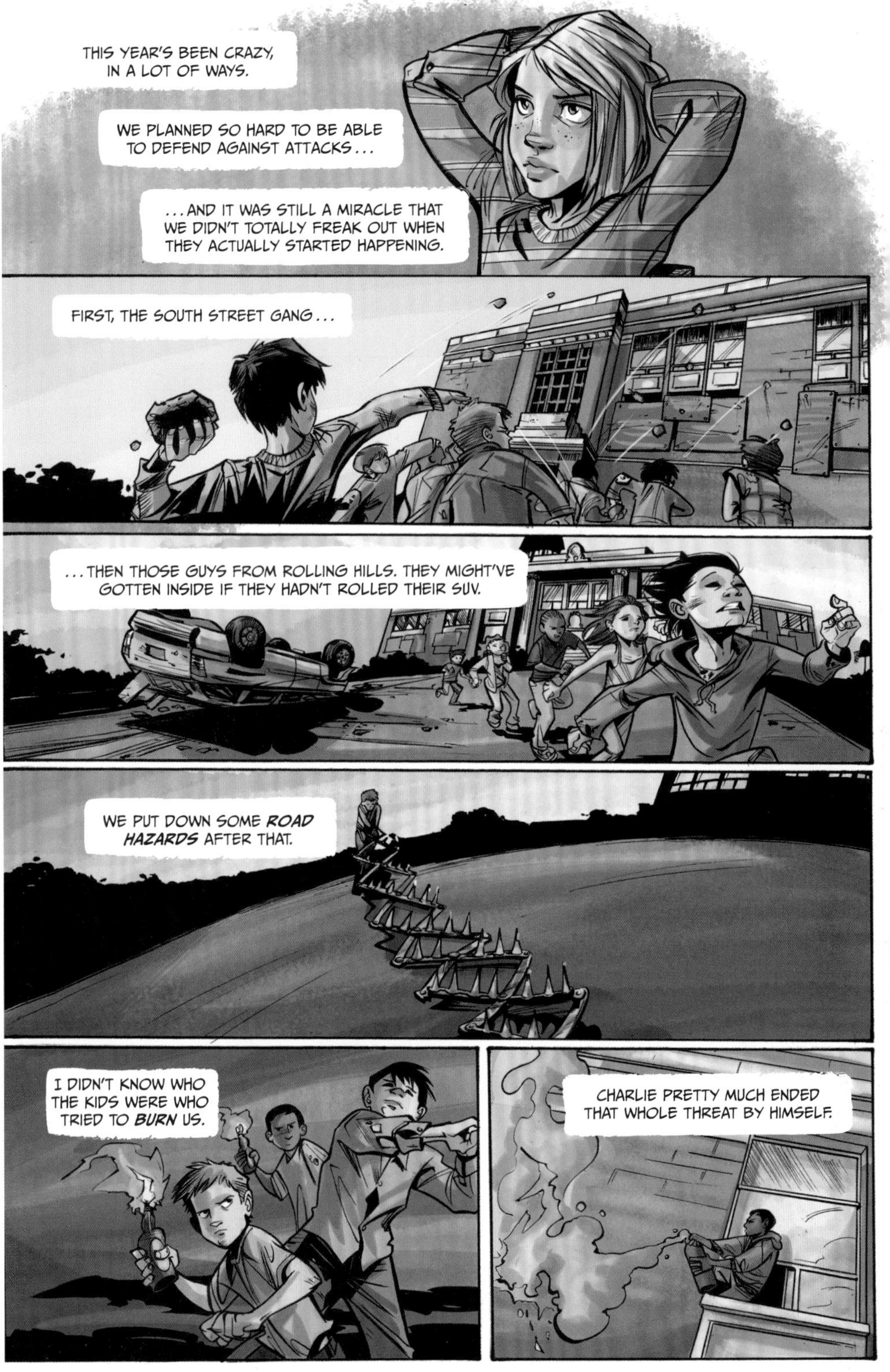
THIS YEAR'S BEEN CRAZY, IN A LOT OF WAYS.
WE PLANNED SO HARD TO BE ABLE TO DEFEND AGAINST ATTACKS...
...AND IT WAS STILL A MIRACLE THAT WE DIDN'T TOTALLY FREAK OUT WHEN THEY ACTUALLY STARTED HAPPENING.
FIRST, THE SOUTH STREET GANG...
...THEN THOSE GUYS FROM ROLLING HILLS. THEY MIGHT'VE GOTTEN INSIDE IF THEY HADN'T ROLLED THEIR SUV.
WE PUT DOWN SOME ***ROAD HAZARDS*** AFTER THAT.
I DIDN'T KNOW WHO THE KIDS WERE WHO TRIED TO ***BURN*** US.
CHARLIE PRETTY MUCH ENDED THAT WHOLE THREAT BY HIMSELF.

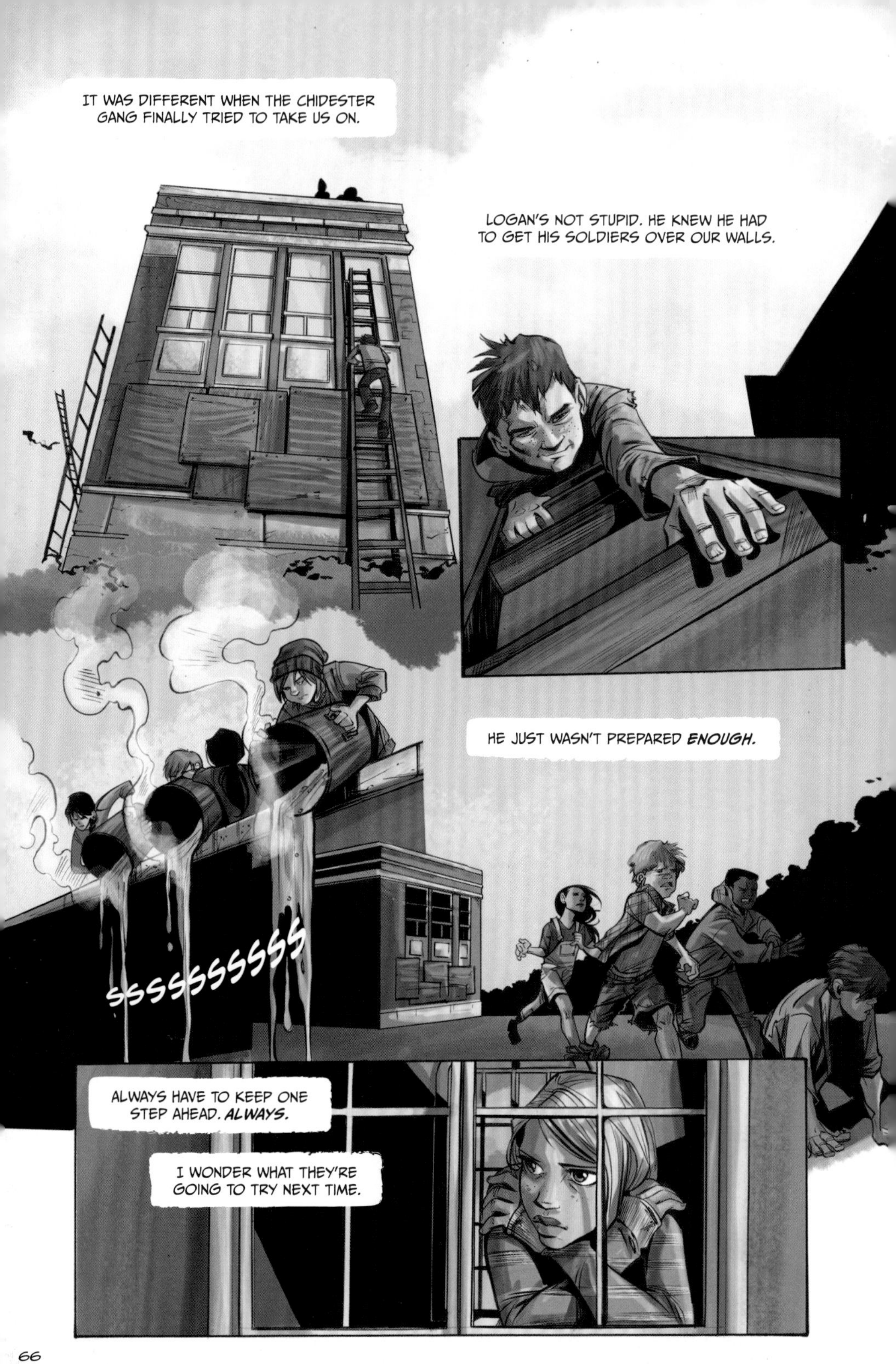
IT WAS DIFFERENT WHEN THE CHIDESTER GANG FINALLY TRIED TO TAKE US ON.
LOGAN'S NOT STUPID. HE KNEW HE HAD TO GET HIS SOLDIERS OVER OUR WALLS.
HE JUST WASN'T PREPARED ENOUGH.
SSSSSSSSSS
ALWAYS HAVE TO KEEP ONE STEP AHEAD. ALWAYS.
I WONDER WHAT THEY'RE GOING TO TRY NEXT TIME.

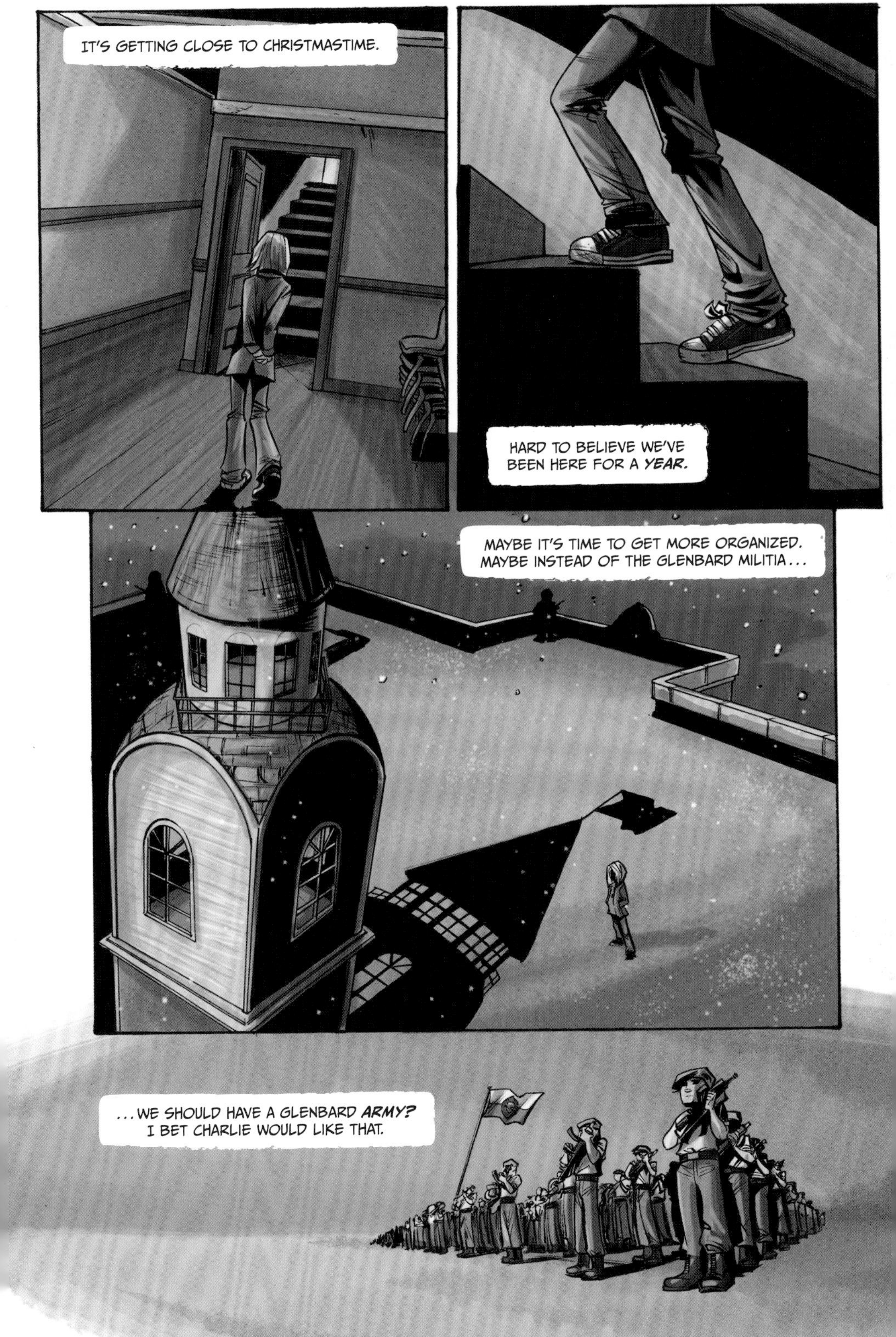
IT'S GETTING CLOSE TO CHRISTMASTIME.
HARD TO BELIEVE WE'VE BEEN HERE FOR A *YEAR.*
MAYBE IT'S TIME TO GET MORE ORGANIZED. MAYBE INSTEAD OF THE GLENBARD MILITIA...
...WE SHOULD HAVE A GLENBARD *ARMY?* I BET CHARLIE WOULD LIKE THAT.

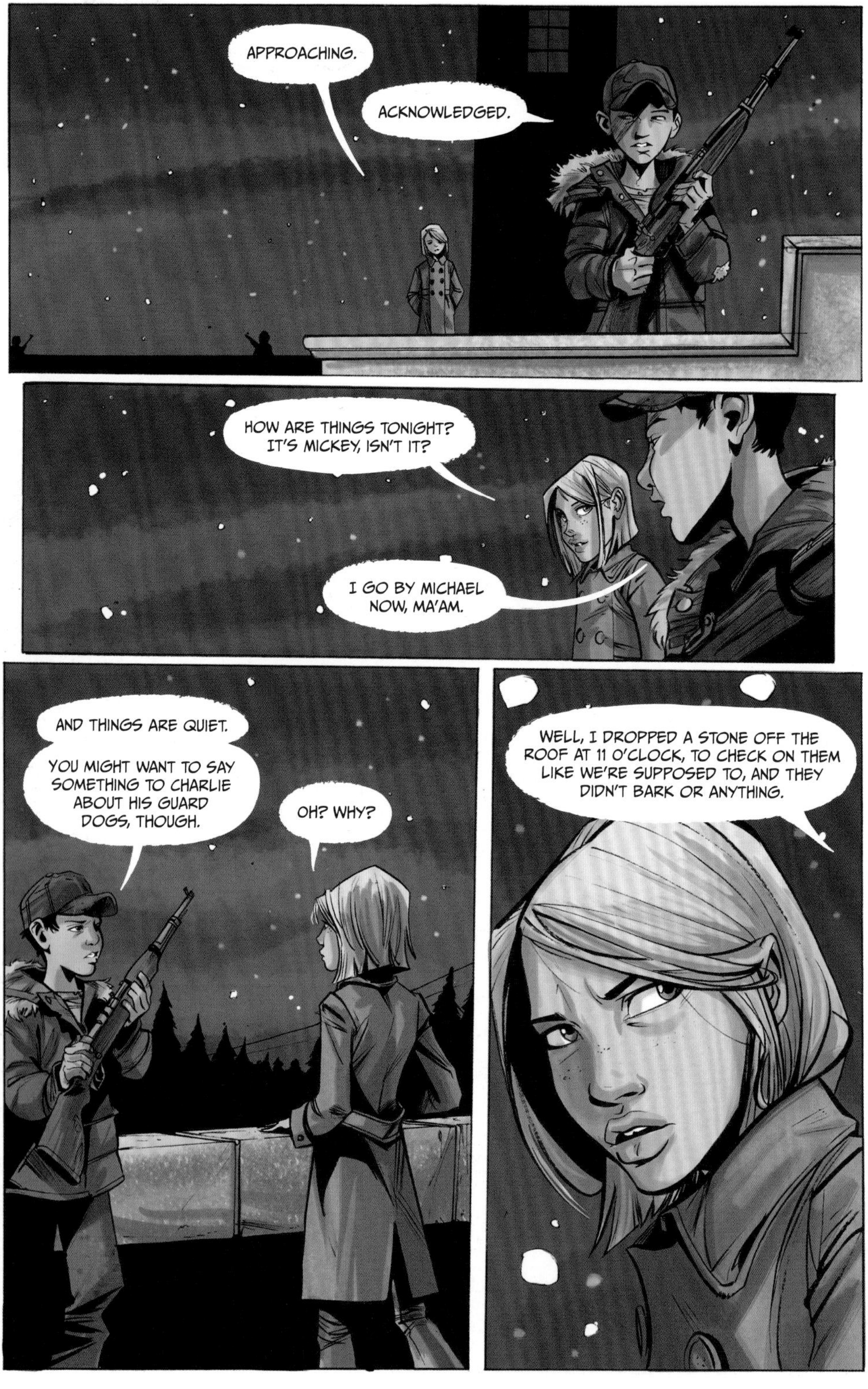
APPROACHING.
ACKNOWLEDGED.
HOW ARE THINGS TONIGHT? IT'S MICKEY, ISN'T IT?
I GO BY MICHAEL NOW, MA'AM.
AND THINGS ARE QUIET.
YOU MIGHT WANT TO SAY SOMETHING TO CHARLIE ABOUT HIS GUARD DOGS, THOUGH.
OH? WHY?
WELL, I DROPPED A STONE OFF THE ROOF AT 11 O'CLOCK, TO CHECK ON THEM LIKE WE'RE SUPPOSED TO, AND THEY DIDN'T BARK OR ANYTHING.

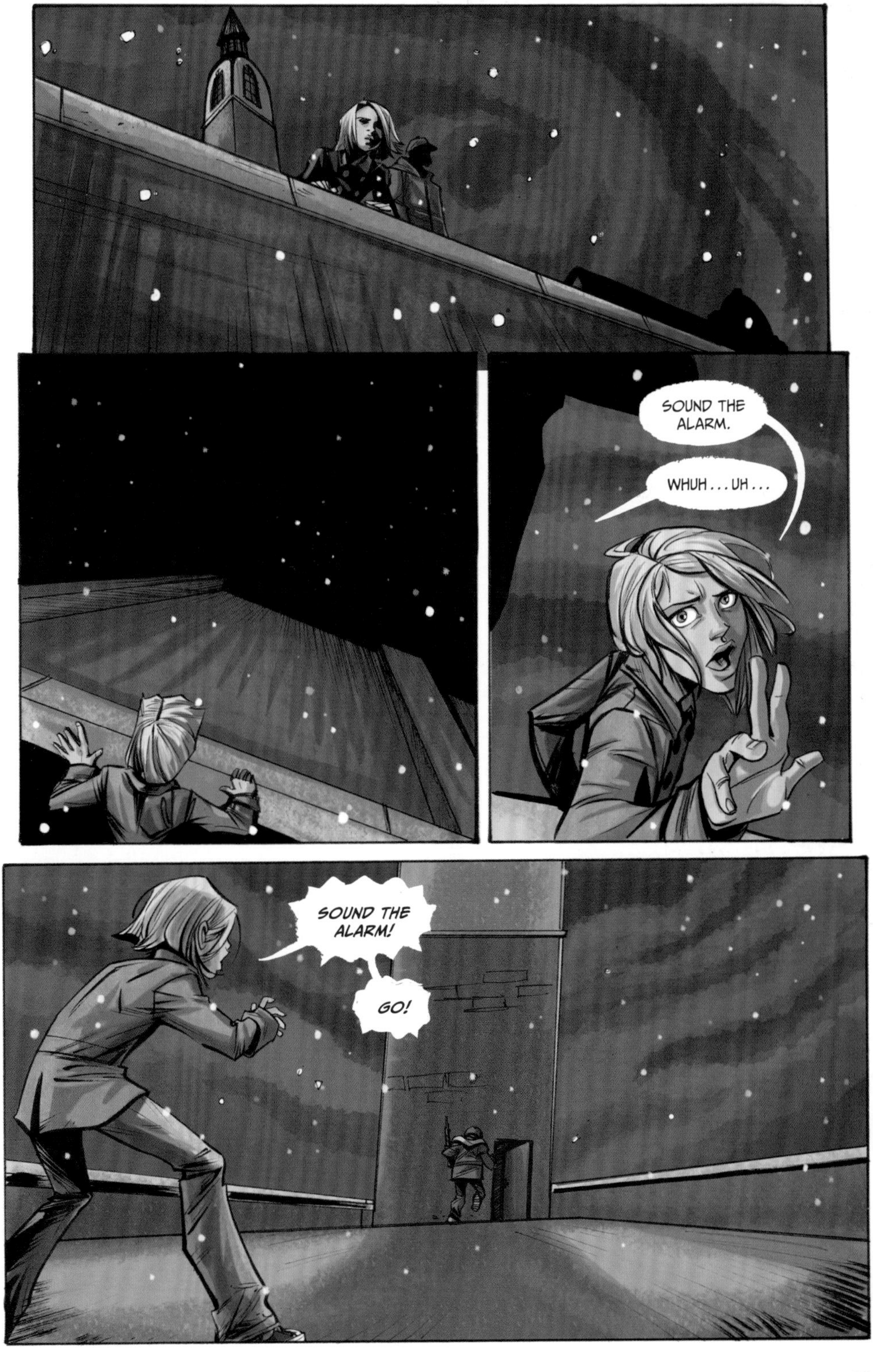
SOUND THE ALARM.
WHUH . . . UH . . .
SOUND THE ALARM!
GO!

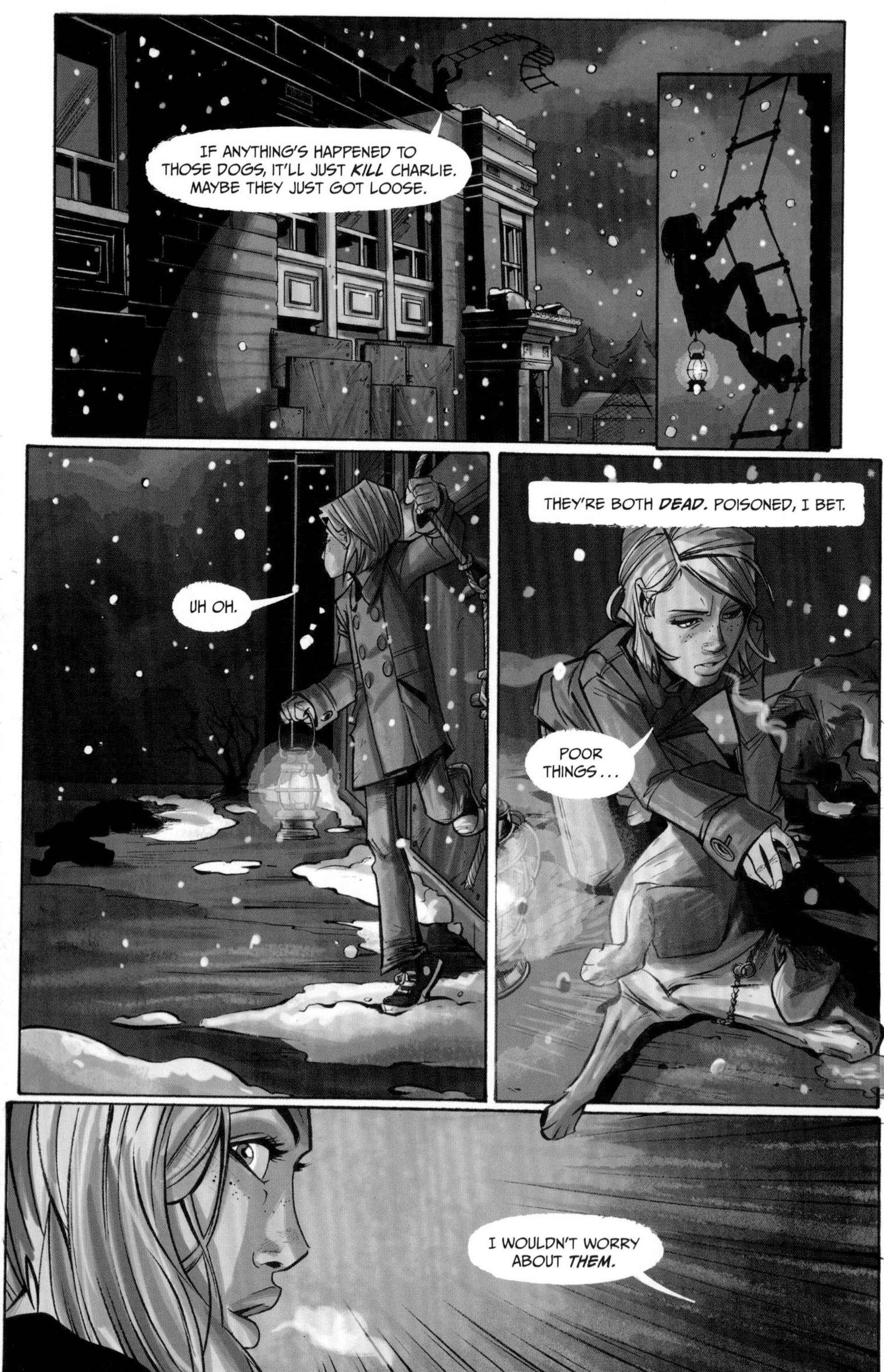
IF ANYTHING'S HAPPENED TO THOSE DOGS, IT'LL JUST KILL CHARLIE. MAYBE THEY JUST GOT LOOSE.
UH OH.
THEY'RE BOTH DEAD. POISONED, I BET.
POOR THINGS . . .
I WOULDN'T WORRY ABOUT THEM.

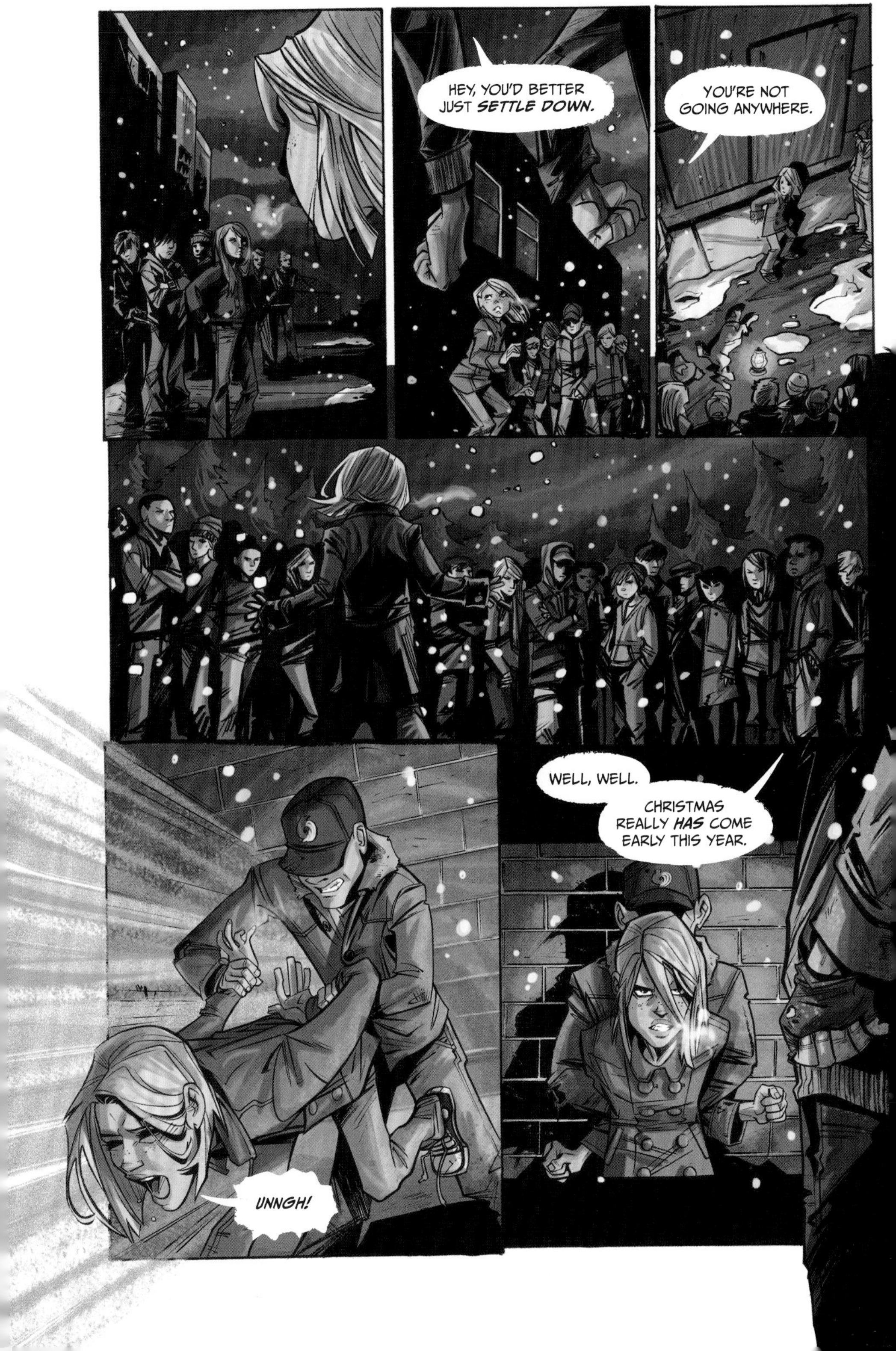
HEY, YOU'D BETTER JUST SETTLE DOWN.
YOU'RE NOT GOING ANYWHERE.
UNNGH!
WELL, WELL.
CHRISTMAS REALLY HAS COME EARLY THIS YEAR.

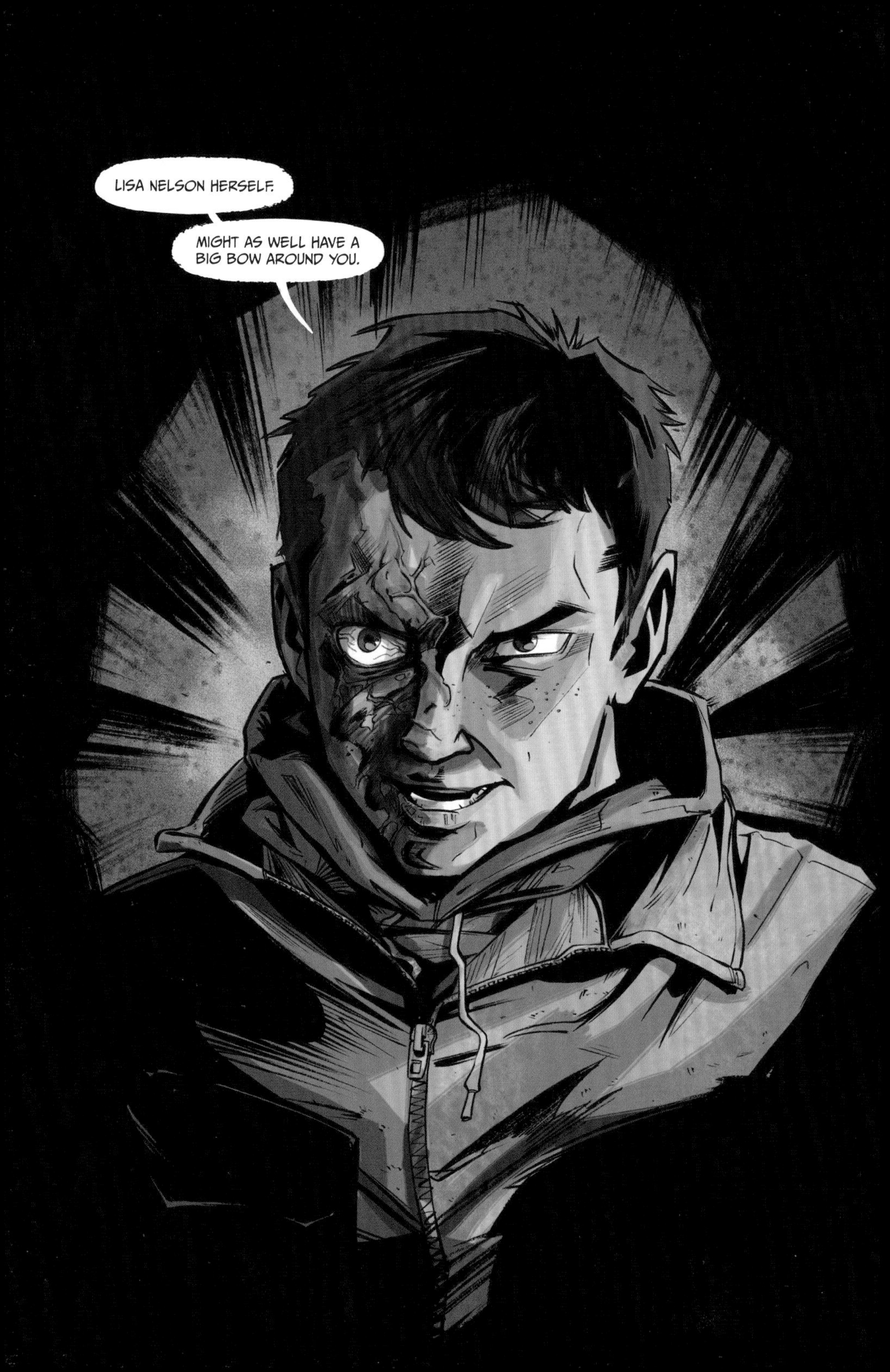
LISA NELSON HERSELF.
MIGHT AS WELL HAVE A BIG BOW AROUND YOU.

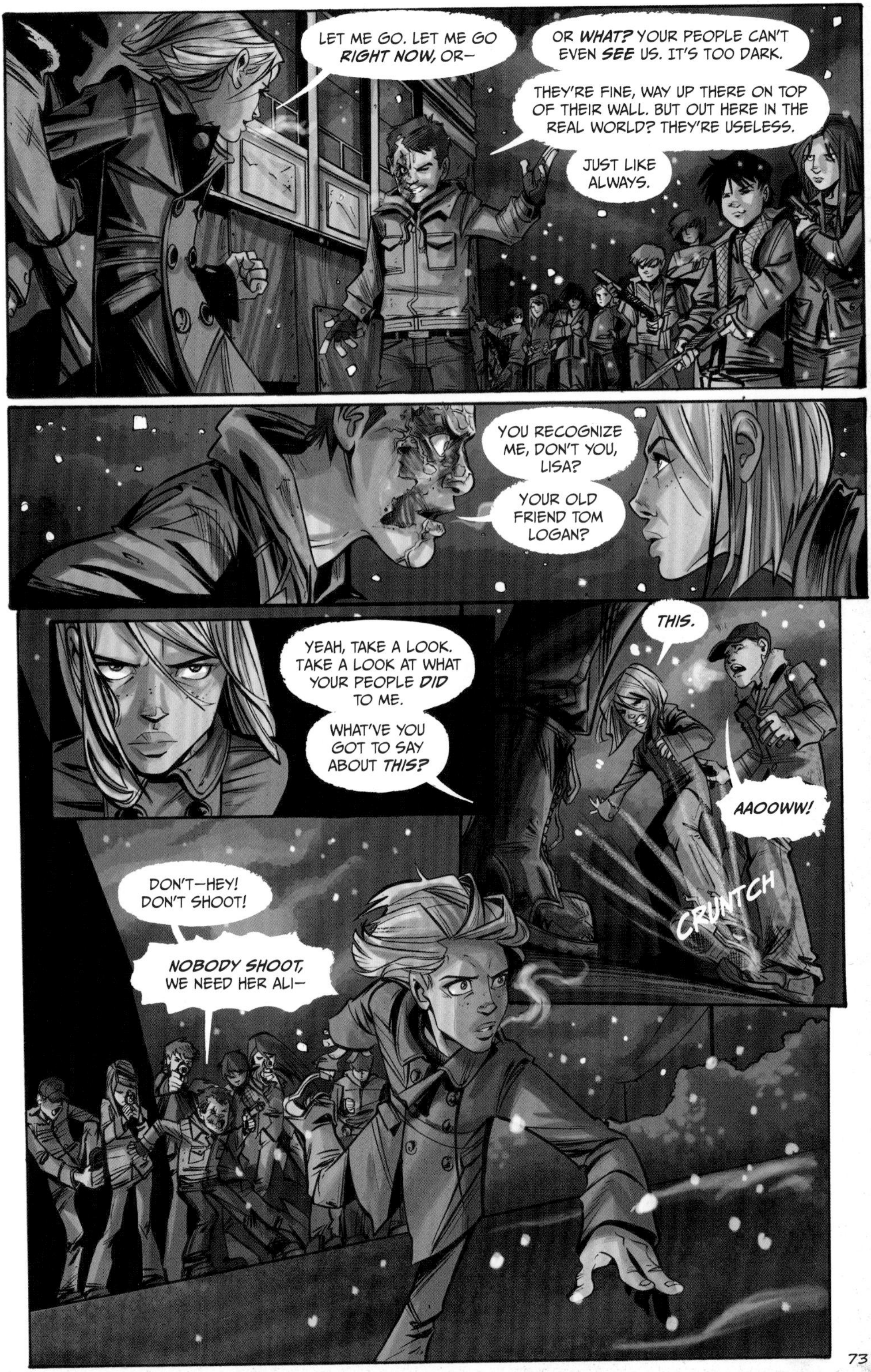
LET ME GO. LET ME GO RIGHT NOW, OR—
OR WHAT? YOUR PEOPLE CAN'T EVEN SEE US. IT'S TOO DARK.
THEY'RE FINE, WAY UP THERE ON TOP OF THEIR WALL. BUT OUT HERE IN THE REAL WORLD? THEY'RE USELESS.
JUST LIKE ALWAYS.
YOU RECOGNIZE ME, DON'T YOU, LISA?
YOUR OLD FRIEND TOM LOGAN?
YEAH, TAKE A LOOK. TAKE A LOOK AT WHAT YOUR PEOPLE DID TO ME.
WHAT'VE YOU GOT TO SAY ABOUT THIS?
THIS.
AAOOWW!
CRUNTCH
DON'T—HEY! DON'T SHOOT!
NOBODY SHOOT, WE NEED HER ALI—

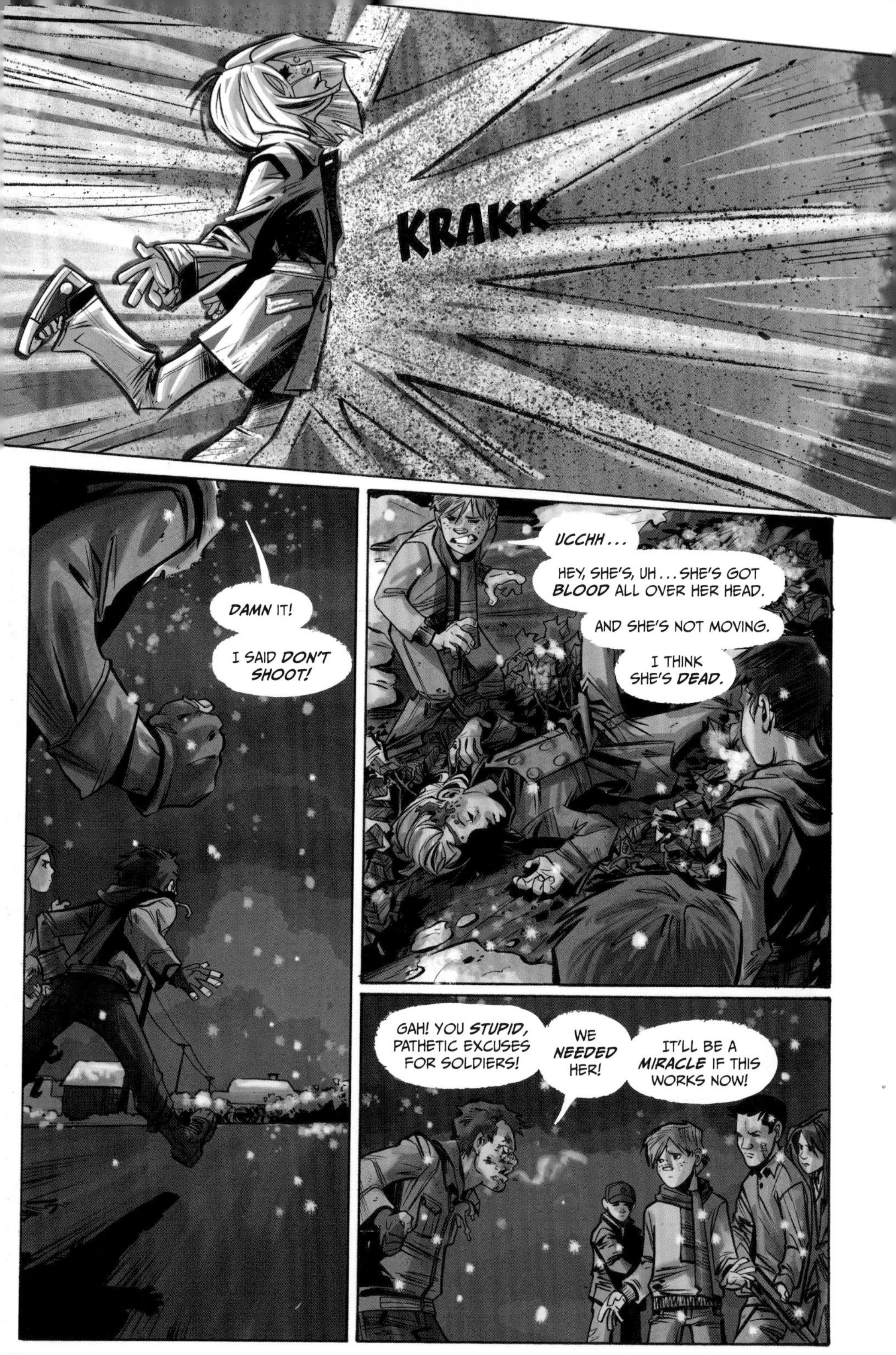
KRAKK
DAMN IT!
I SAID DON'T SHOOT!
UCCHH...
HEY, SHE'S, UH... SHE'S GOT BLOOD ALL OVER HER HEAD.
AND SHE'S NOT MOVING.
I THINK SHE'S DEAD.
GAH! YOU STUPID, PATHETIC EXCUSES FOR SOLDIERS!
WE NEEDED HER!
IT'LL BE A MIRACLE IF THIS WORKS NOW!

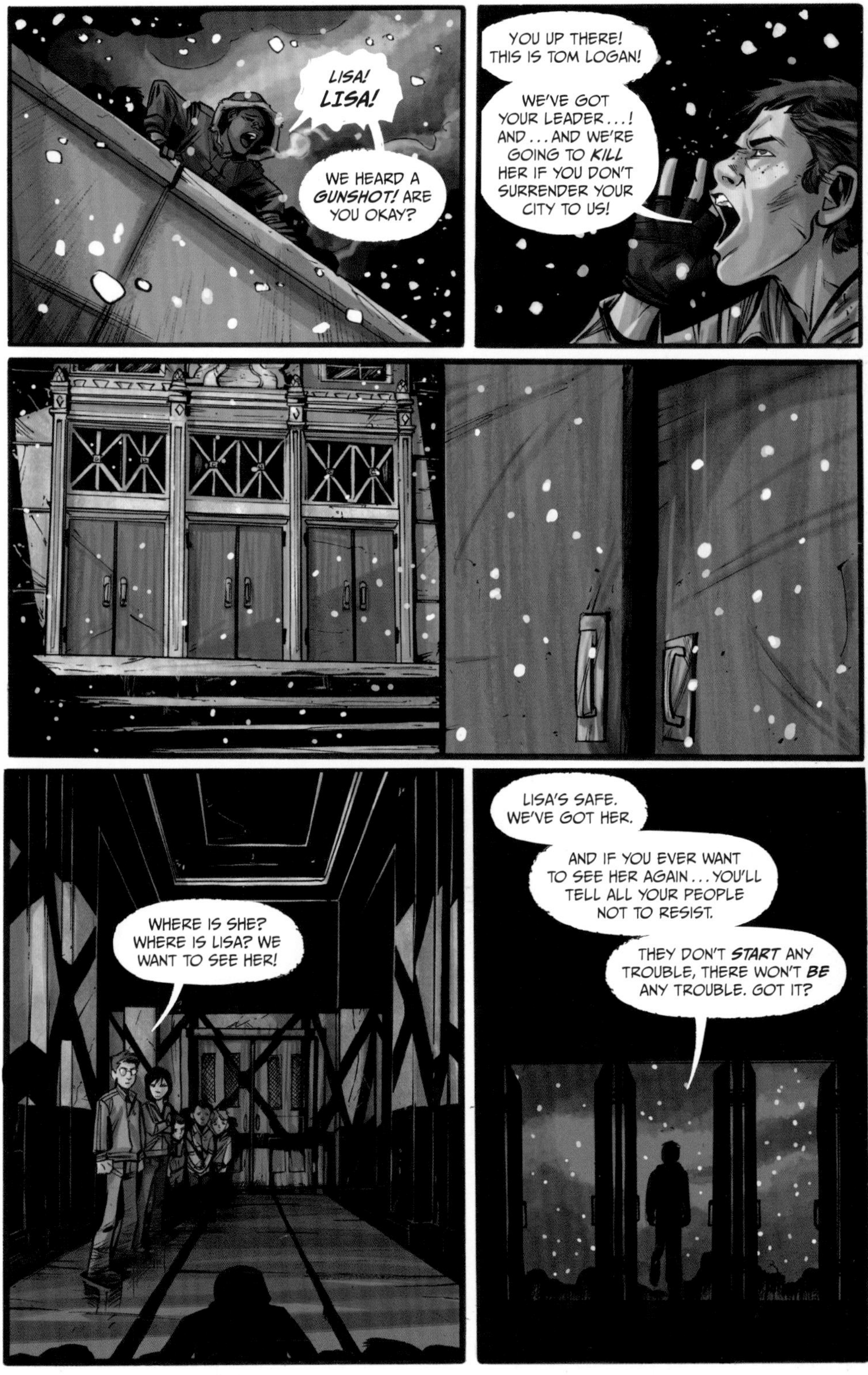
LISA! LISA!
WE HEARD A GUNSHOT! ARE YOU OKAY?
YOU UP THERE! THIS IS TOM LOGAN!
WE'VE GOT YOUR LEADER...! AND...AND WE'RE GOING TO KILL HER IF YOU DON'T SURRENDER YOUR CITY TO US!
WHERE IS SHE? WHERE IS LISA? WE WANT TO SEE HER!
LISA'S SAFE. WE'VE GOT HER.
AND IF YOU EVER WANT TO SEE HER AGAIN...YOU'LL TELL ALL YOUR PEOPLE NOT TO RESIST.
THEY DON'T START ANY TROUBLE, THERE WON'T BE ANY TROUBLE. GOT IT?

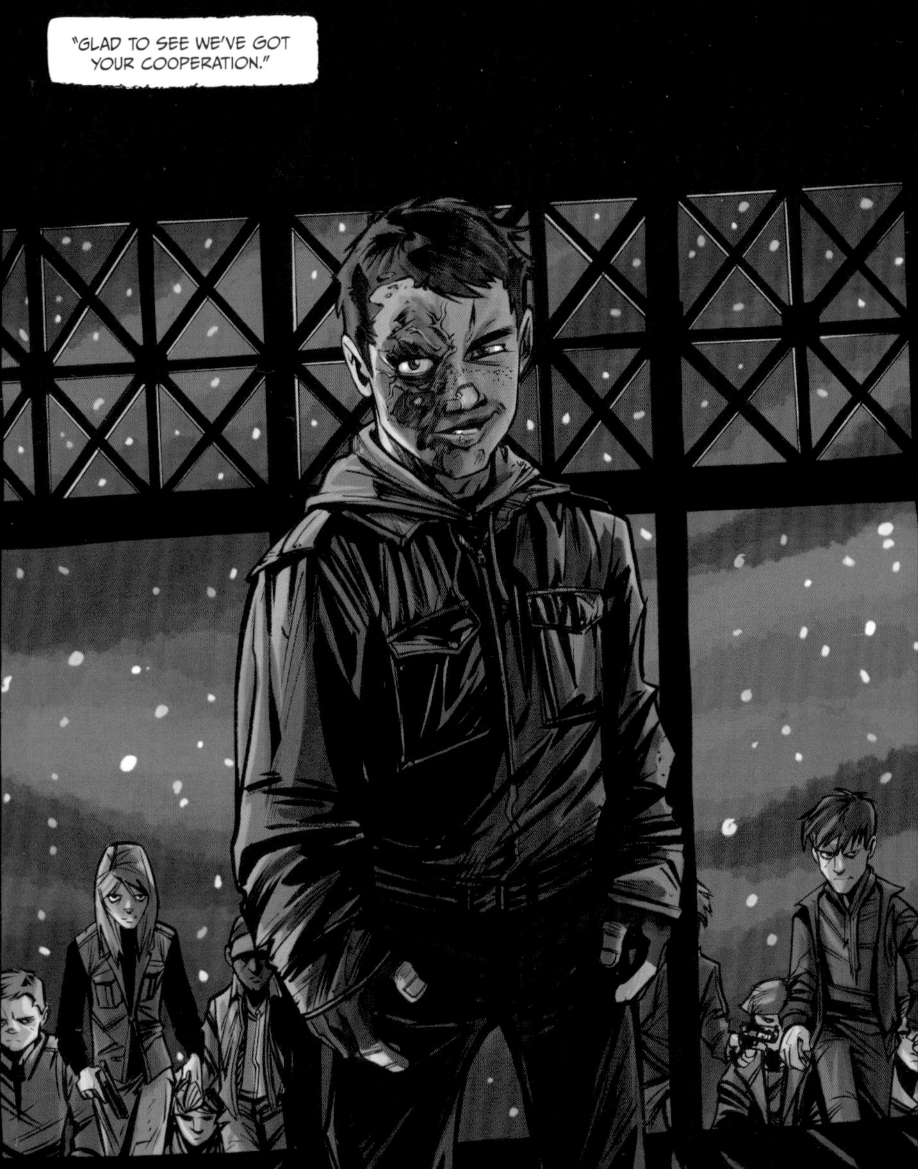
"GLAD TO SEE WE'VE GOT YOUR COOPERATION."

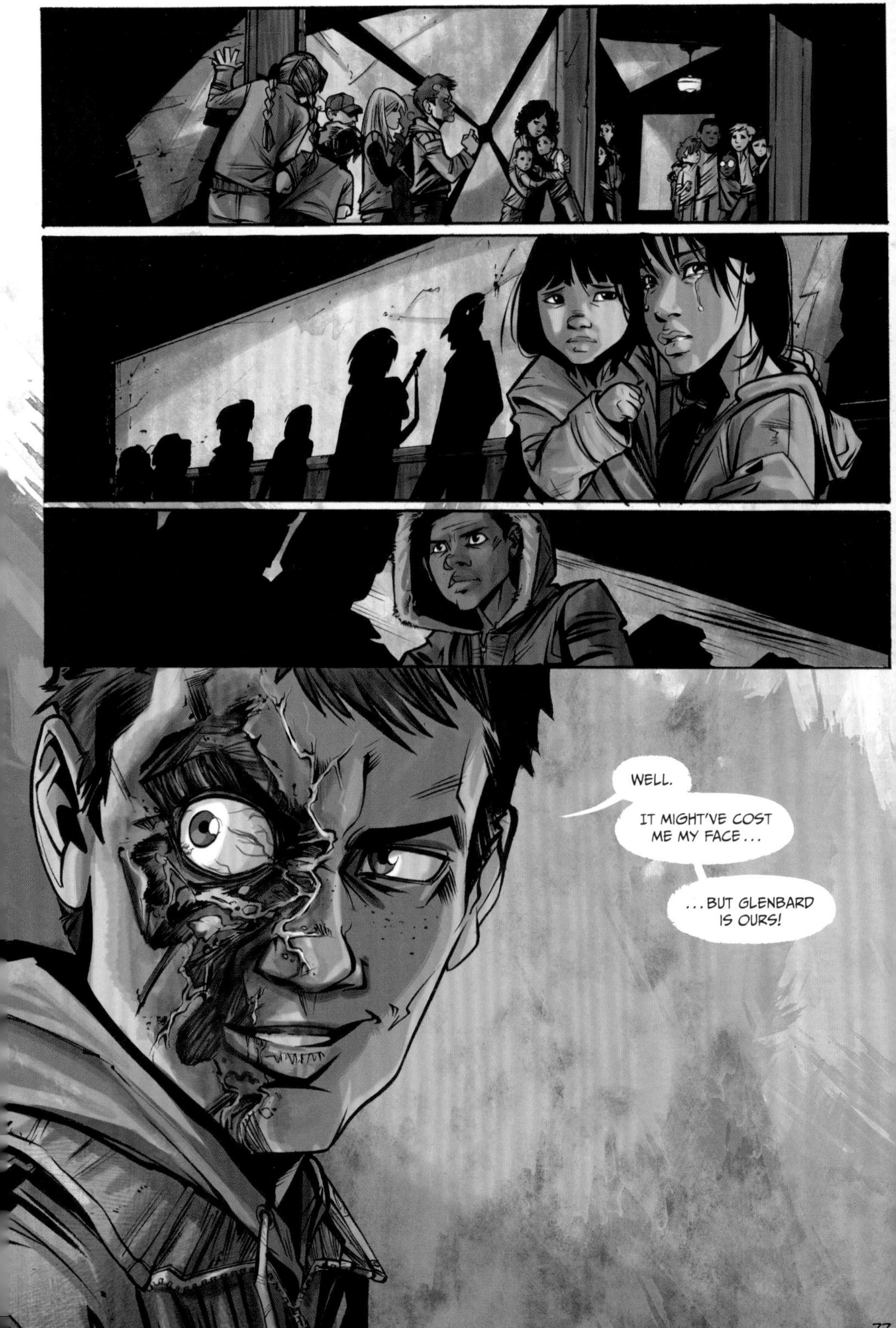
WELL.
IT MIGHT'VE COST ME MY FACE...
...BUT GLENBARD IS OURS!

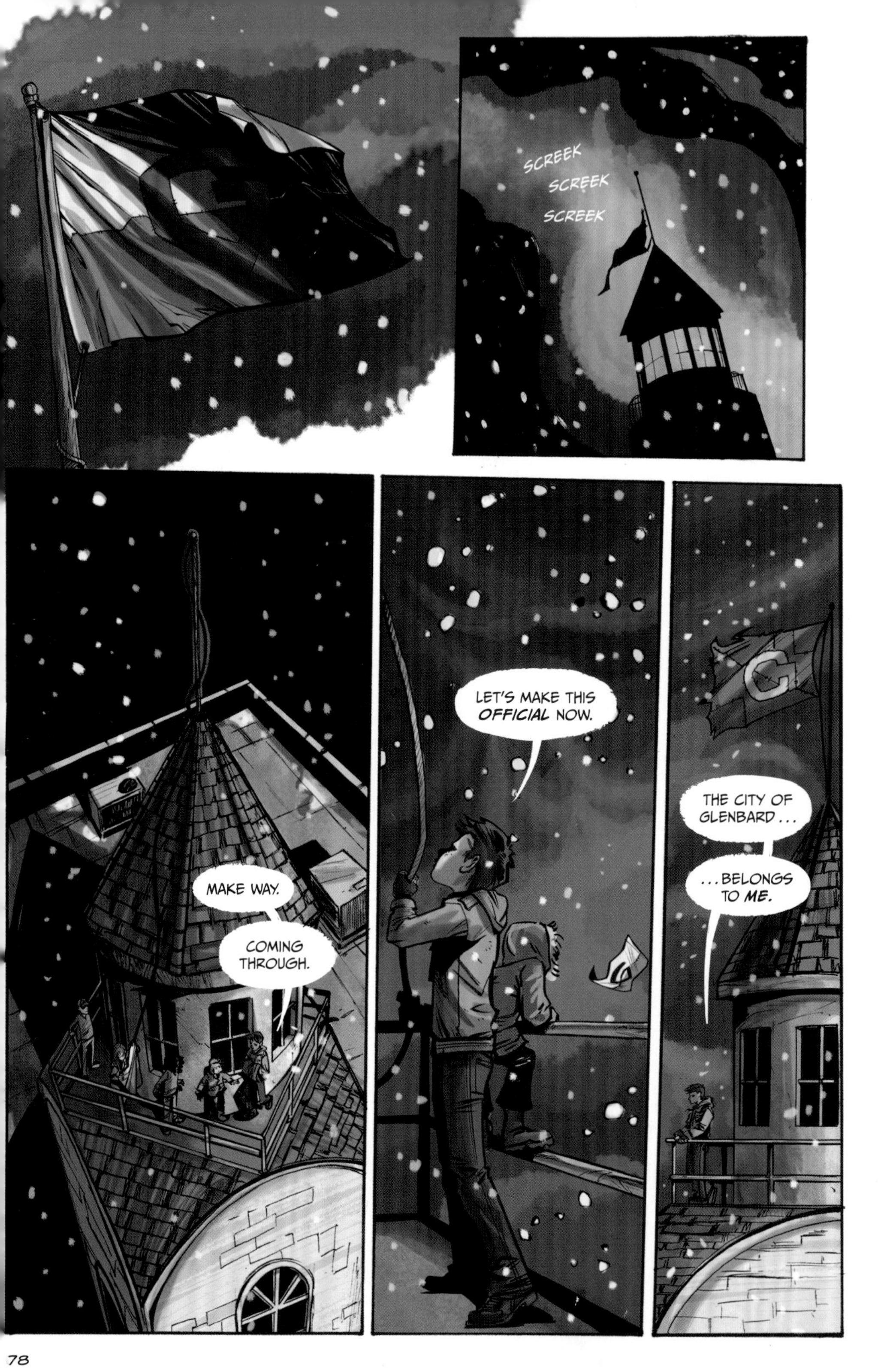
SCREEK
SCREEK
SCREEK
MAKE WAY.
COMING THROUGH.
LET'S MAKE THIS OFFICIAL NOW.
THE CITY OF GLENBARD . . .
. . . BELONGS TO ME.

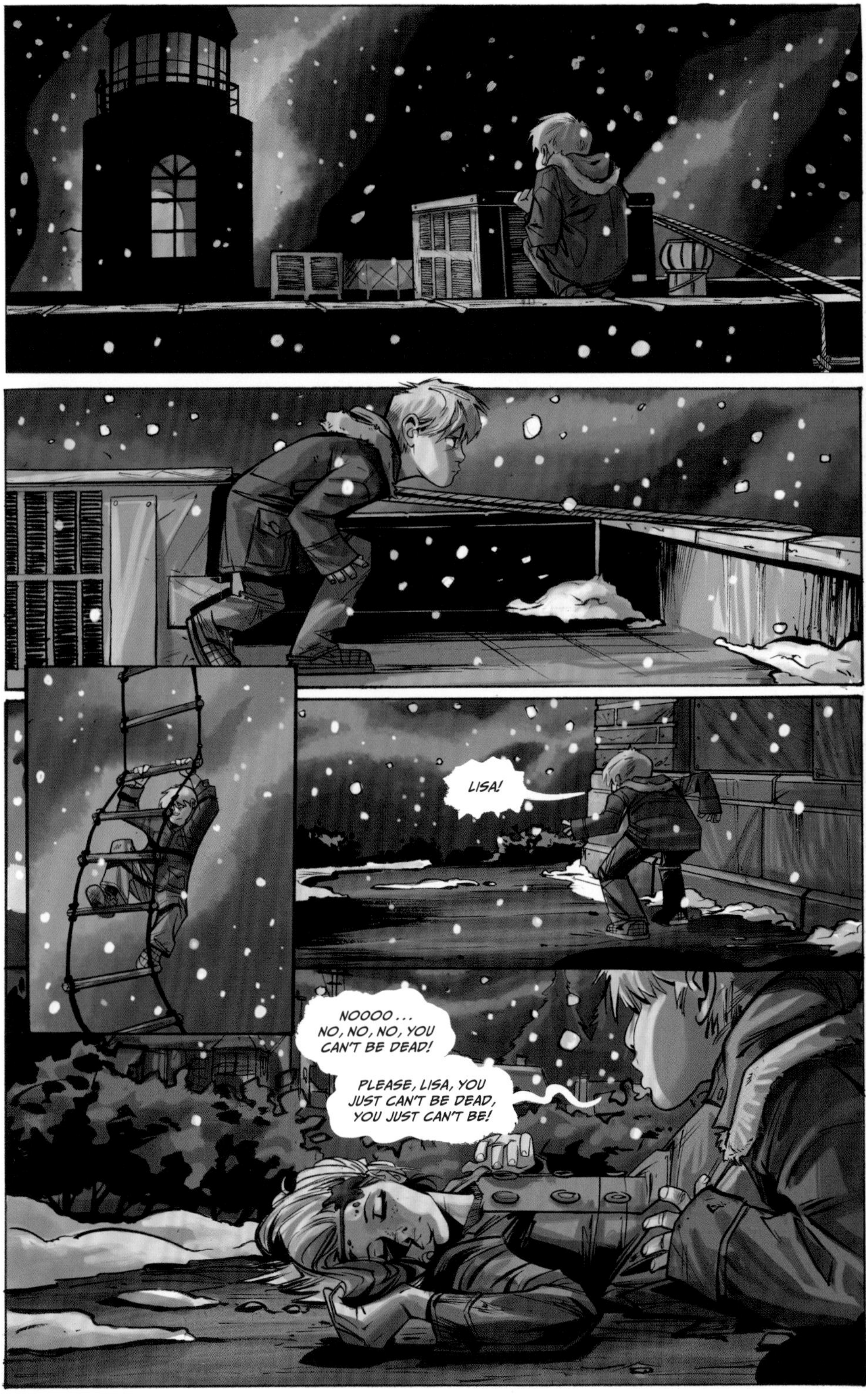
LISA!
NOOOO . . . NO, NO, NO, YOU CAN'T BE DEAD!
PLEASE, LISA, YOU JUST CAN'T BE DEAD, YOU JUST CAN'T BE!

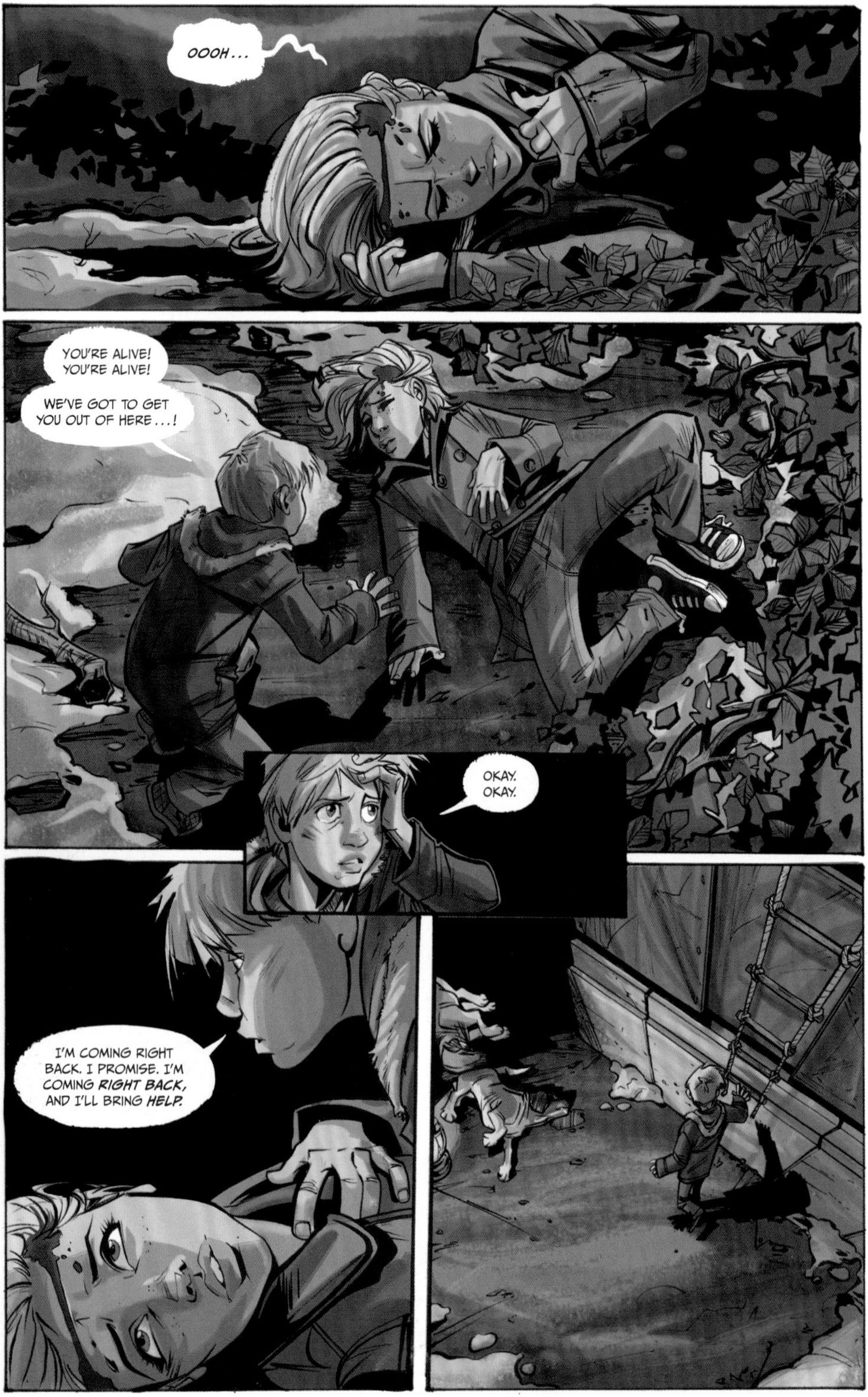
OOOH...
YOU'RE ALIVE! YOU'RE ALIVE!
WE'VE GOT TO GET YOU OUT OF HERE...!
OKAY. OKAY.
I'M COMING RIGHT BACK. I PROMISE. I'M COMING ***RIGHT BACK,*** AND I'LL BRING ***HELP.***

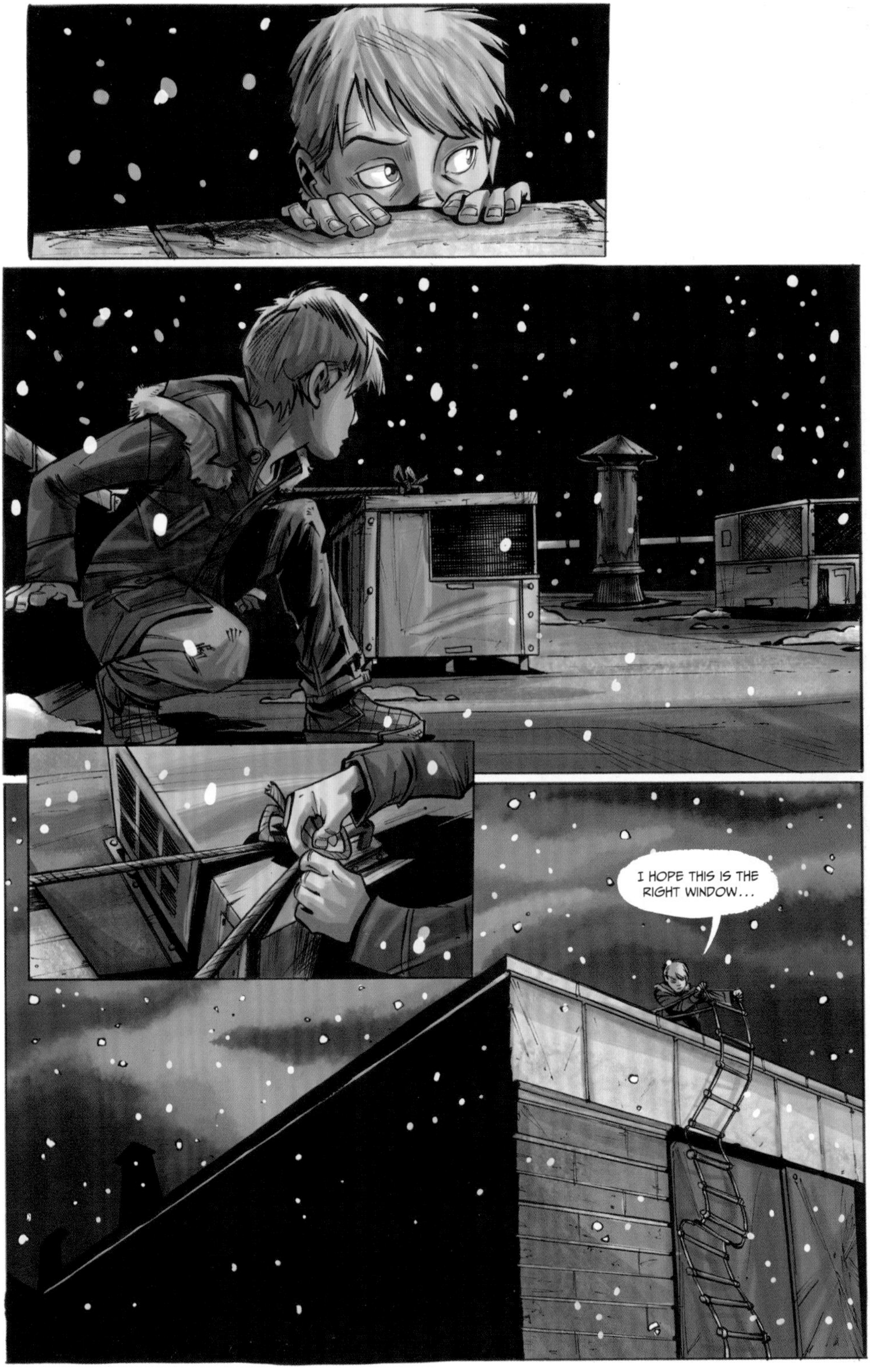
I HOPE THIS IS THE RIGHT WINDOW...

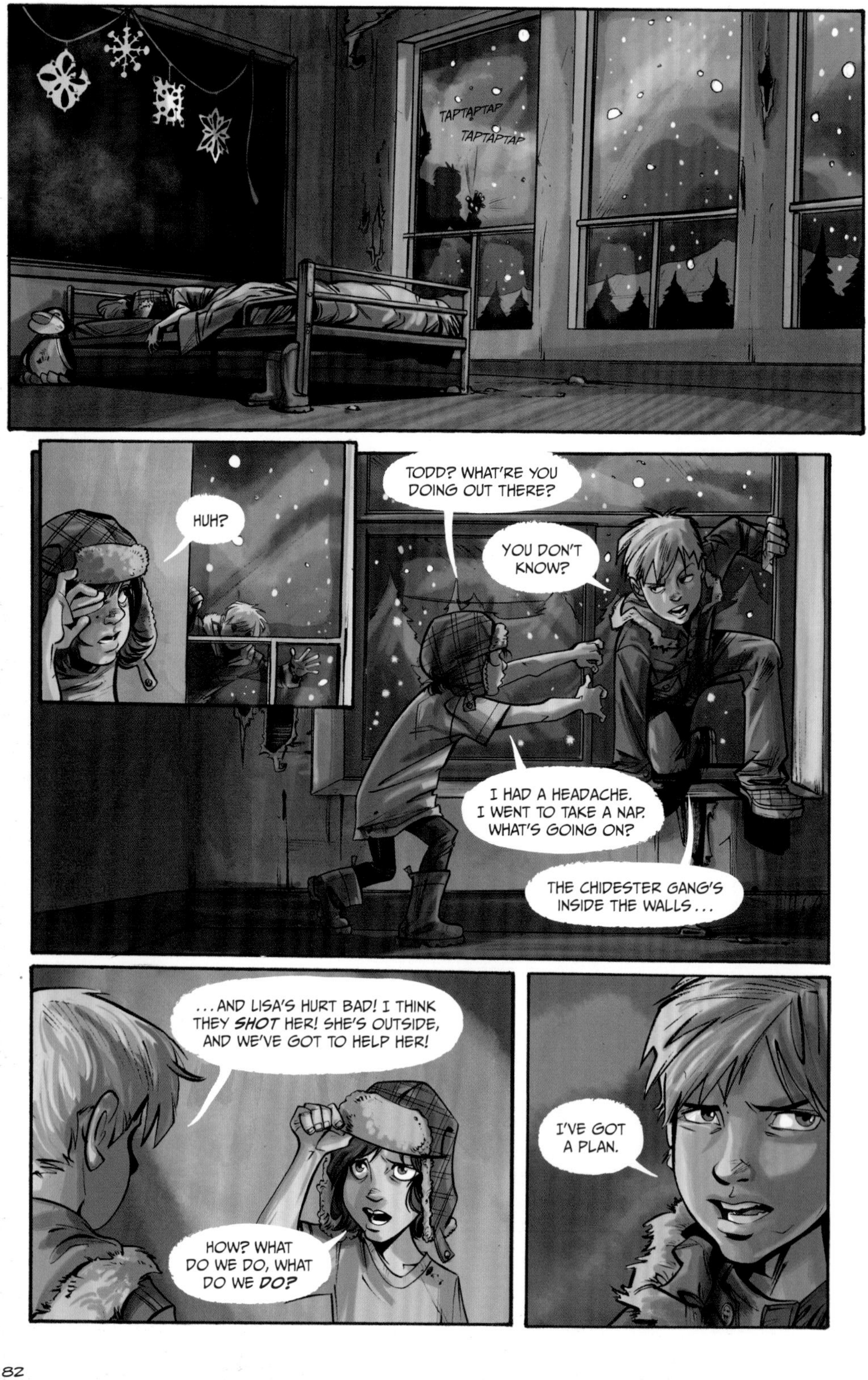
TAPTAPTAP
TAPTAPTAP
HUH?
TODD? WHAT'RE YOU DOING OUT THERE?
YOU DON'T KNOW?
I HAD A HEADACHE. I WENT TO TAKE A NAP. WHAT'S GOING ON?
THE CHIDESTER GANG'S INSIDE THE WALLS...
...AND LISA'S HURT BAD! I THINK THEY *SHOT* HER! SHE'S OUTSIDE, AND WE'VE GOT TO HELP HER!
HOW? WHAT DO WE DO, WHAT DO WE *DO?*
I'VE GOT A PLAN.

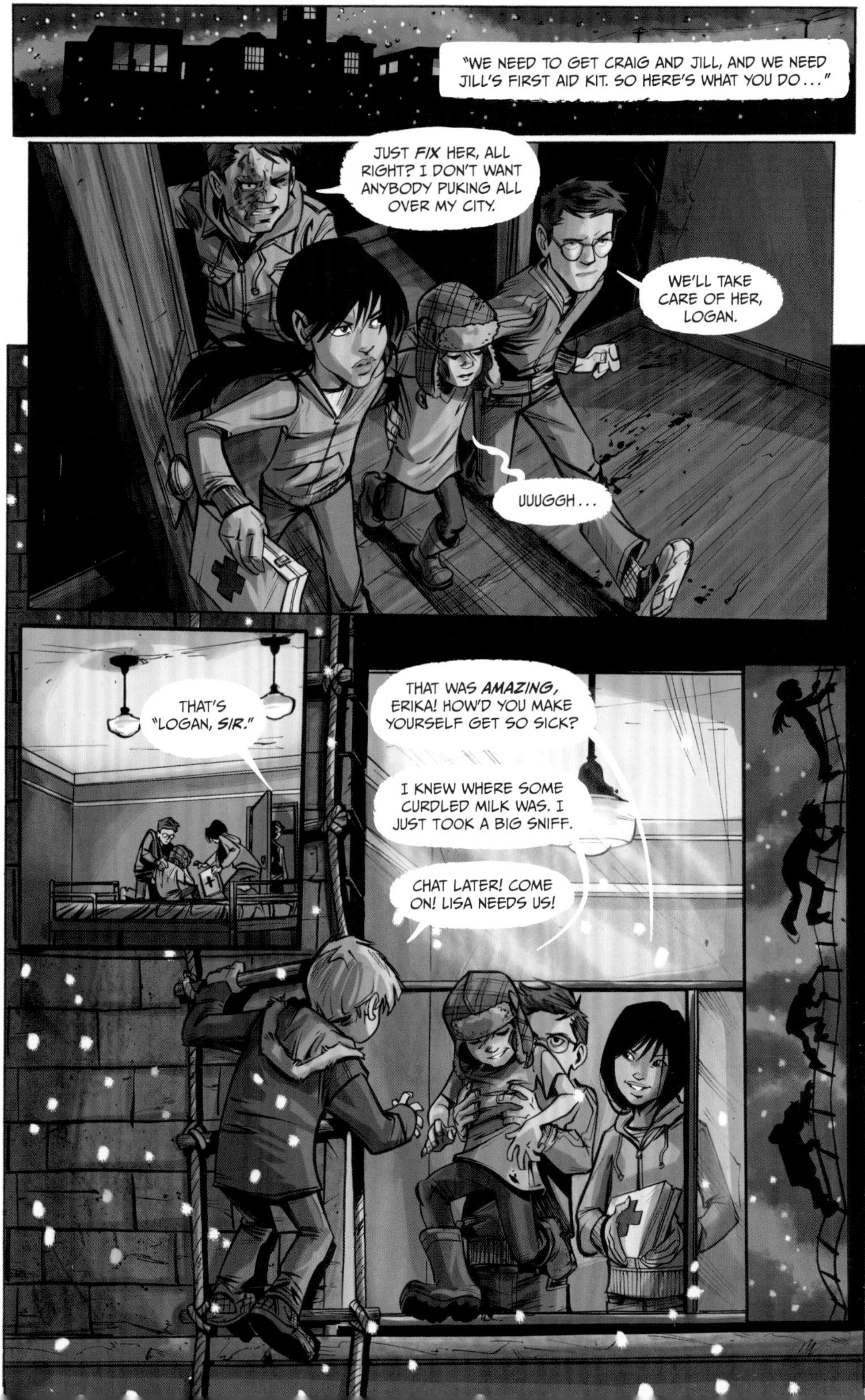
"WE NEED TO GET CRAIG AND JILL, AND WE NEED JILL'S FIRST AID KIT. SO HERE'S WHAT YOU DO..."
JUST FIX HER, ALL RIGHT? I DON'T WANT ANYBODY PUKING ALL OVER MY CITY.
WE'LL TAKE CARE OF HER, LOGAN.
UUUGGH...
THAT'S "LOGAN, SIR."
THAT WAS AMAZING, ERIKA! HOW'D YOU MAKE YOURSELF GET SO SICK?
I KNEW WHERE SOME CURDLED MILK WAS. I JUST TOOK A BIG SNIFF.
CHAT LATER! COME ON! LISA NEEDS US!

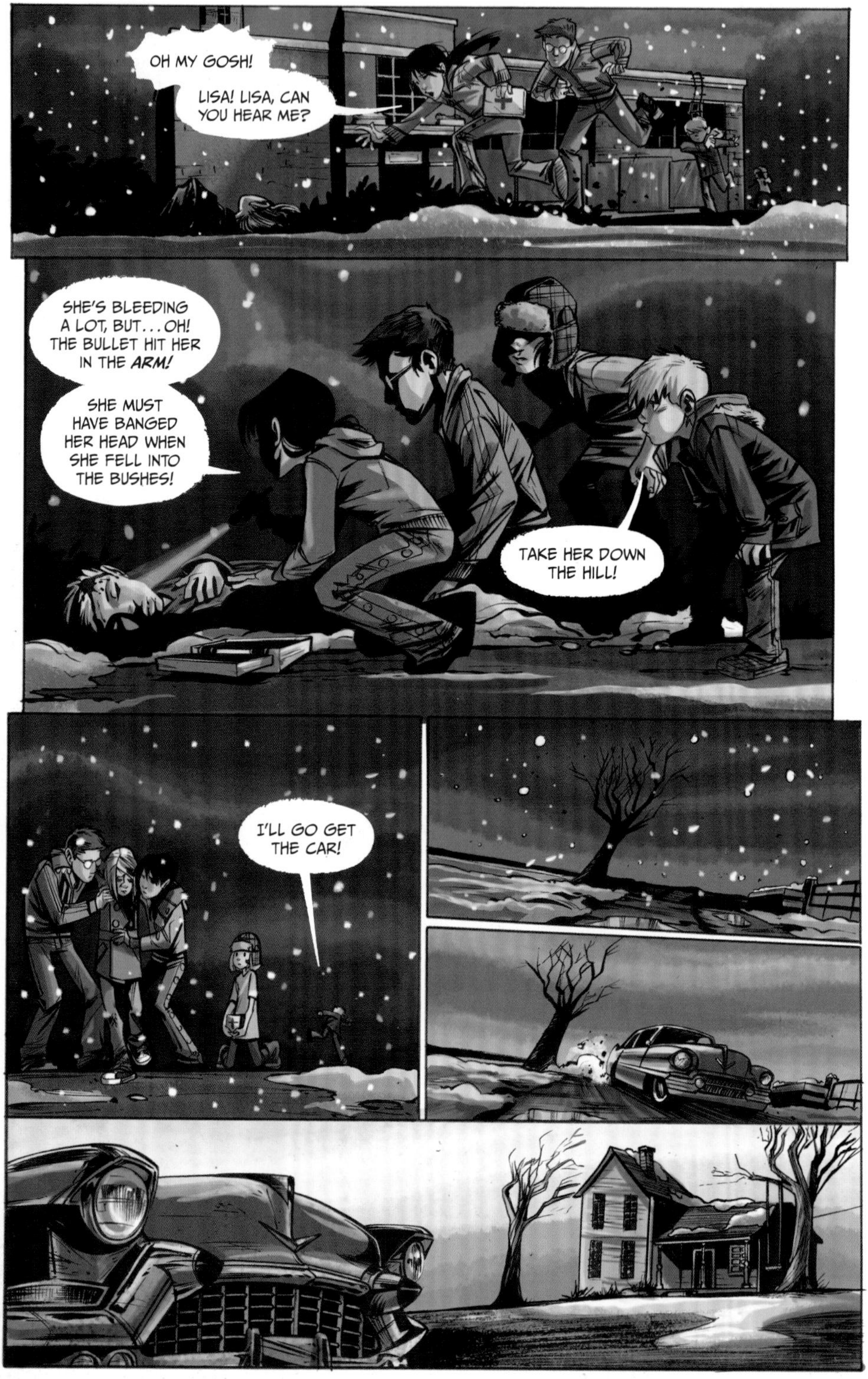
OH MY GOSH!
LISA! LISA, CAN YOU HEAR ME?
SHE'S BLEEDING A LOT, BUT... OH! THE BULLET HIT HER IN THE *ARM!*
SHE MUST HAVE BANGED HER HEAD WHEN SHE FELL INTO THE BUSHES!
TAKE HER DOWN THE HILL!
I'LL GO GET THE CAR!

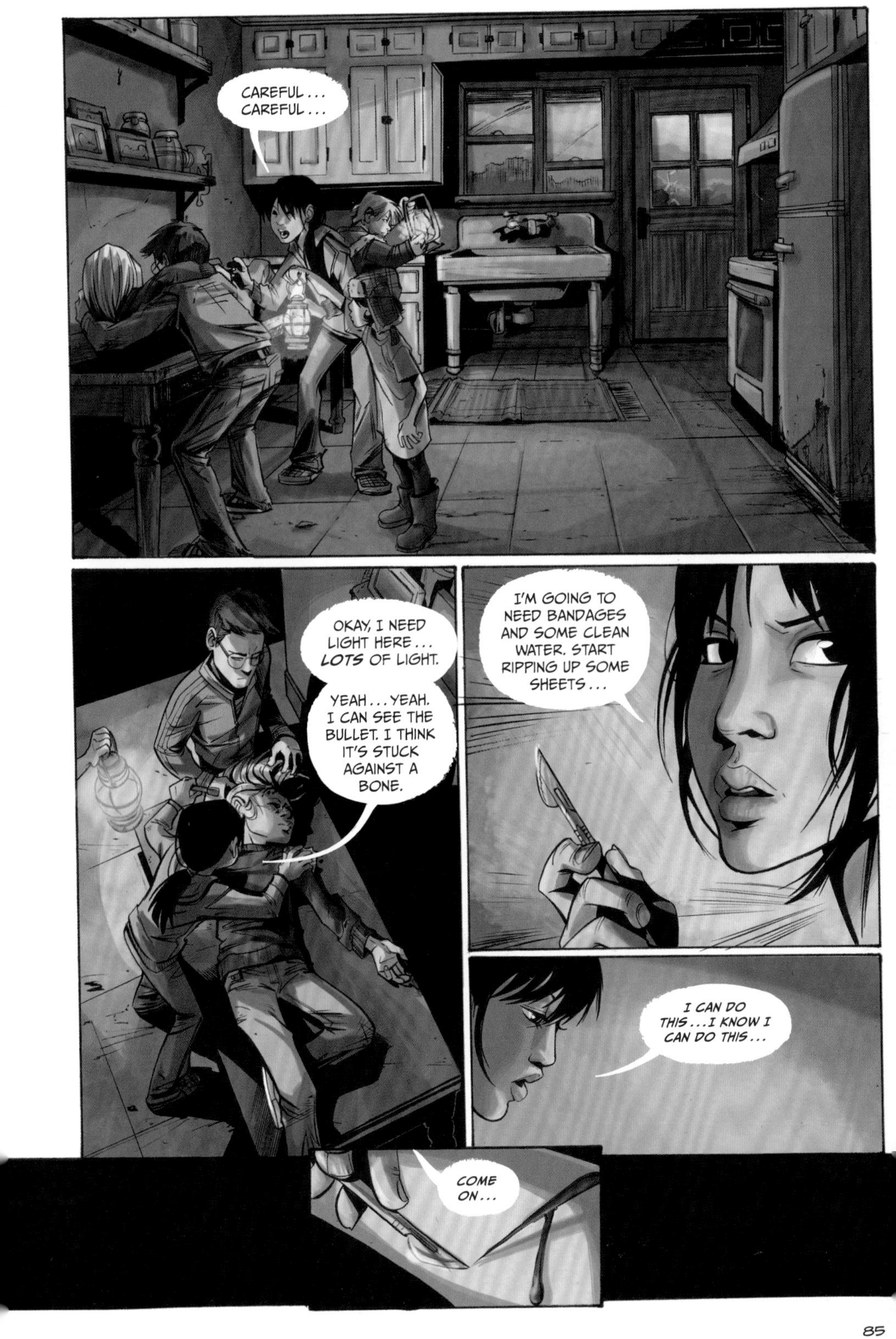
CAREFUL . . . CAREFUL . . .
OKAY, I NEED LIGHT HERE . . . LOTS OF LIGHT.
YEAH . . . YEAH. I CAN SEE THE BULLET. I THINK IT'S STUCK AGAINST A BONE.
I'M GOING TO NEED BANDAGES AND SOME CLEAN WATER. START RIPPING UP SOME SHEETS . . .
I CAN DO THIS . . . I KNOW I CAN DO THIS . . .
COME ON . . .

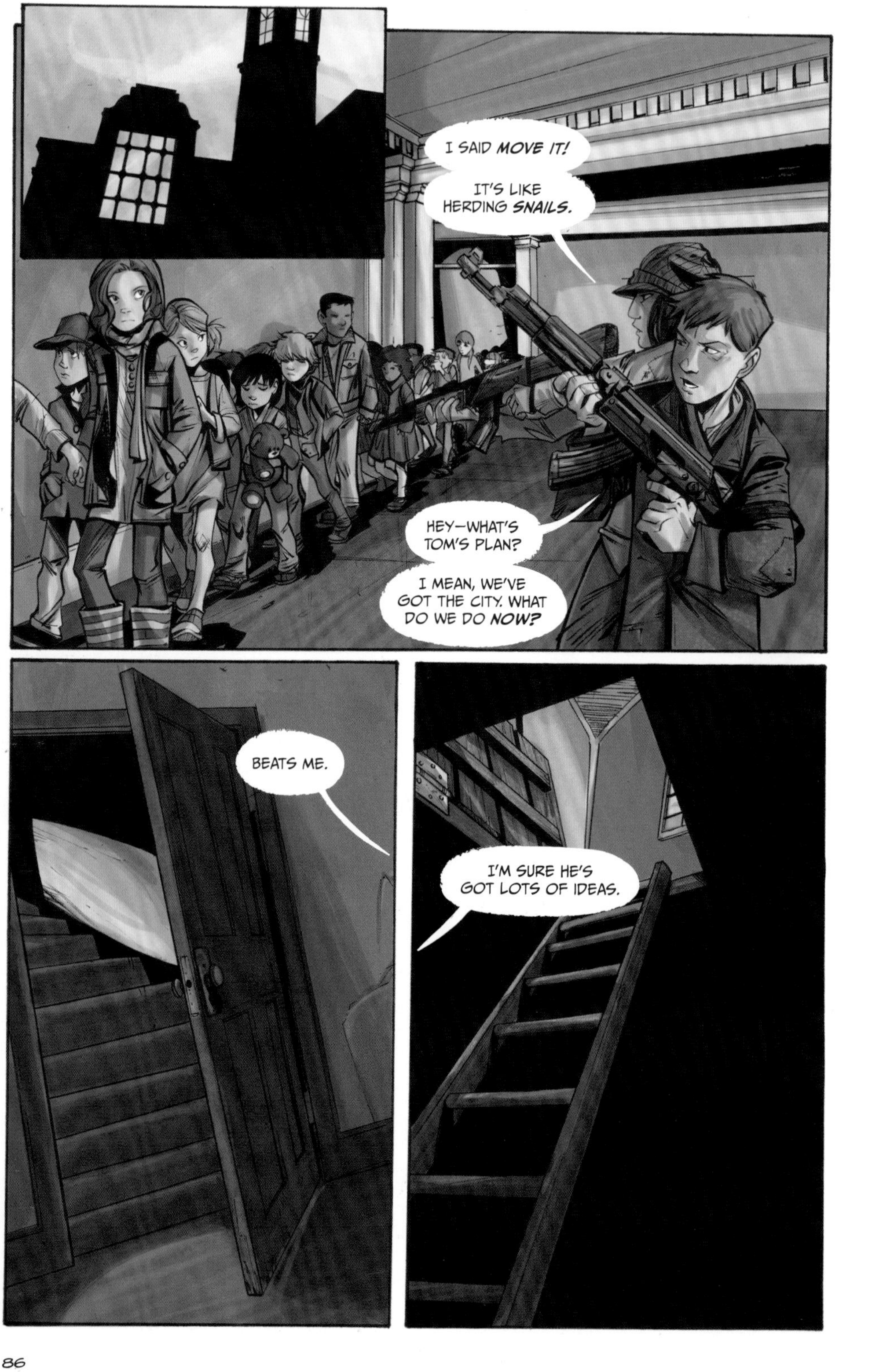
I SAID **MOVE IT!**
IT'S LIKE HERDING **SNAILS.**
HEY—WHAT'S TOM'S PLAN?
I MEAN, WE'VE GOT THE CITY. WHAT DO WE DO **NOW?**
BEATS ME.
I'M SURE HE'S GOT LOTS OF IDEAS.

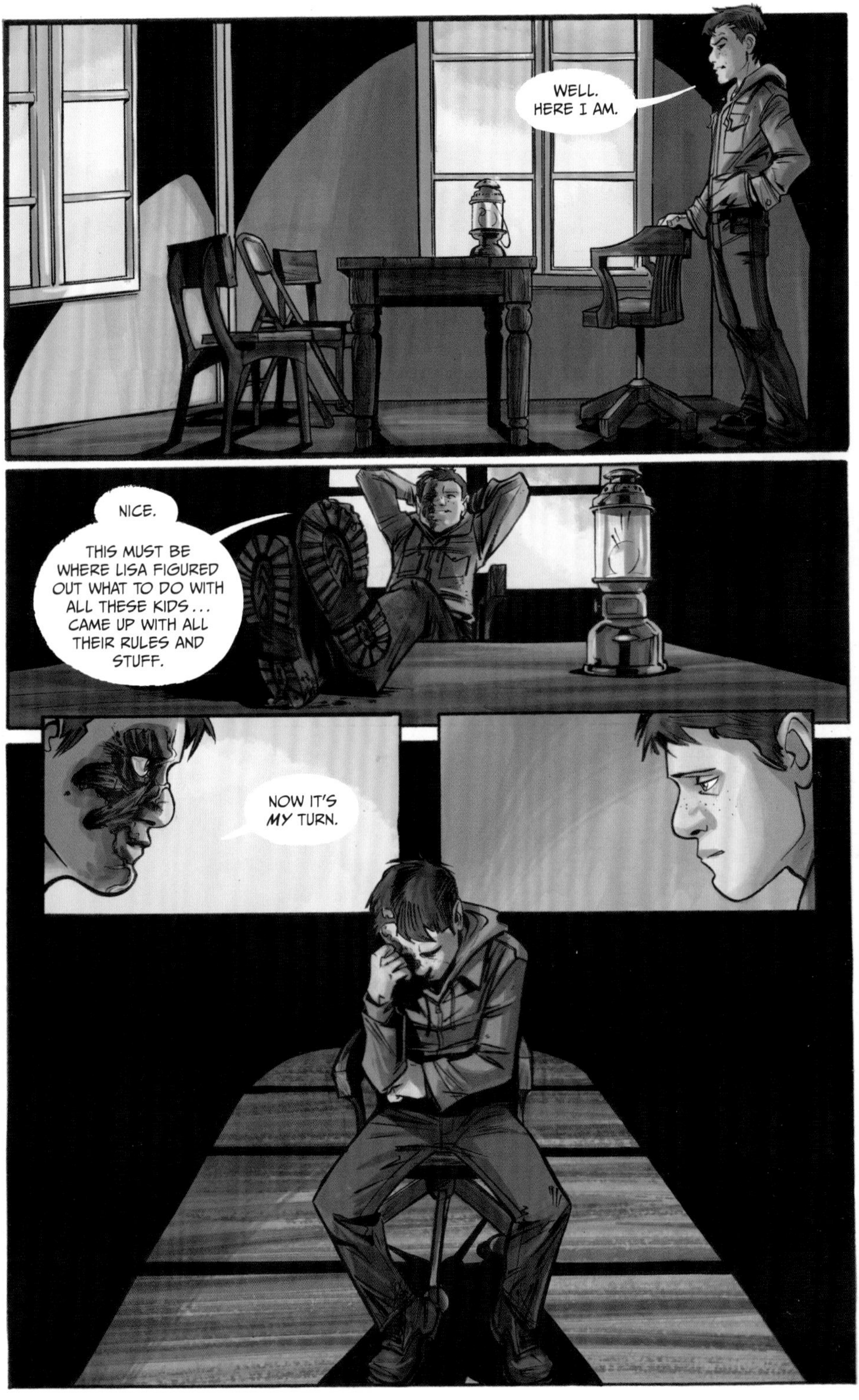
WELL.
HERE I AM.
NICE.
THIS MUST BE WHERE LISA FIGURED OUT WHAT TO DO WITH ALL THESE KIDS . . . CAME UP WITH ALL THEIR RULES AND STUFF.
NOW IT'S *MY* TURN.

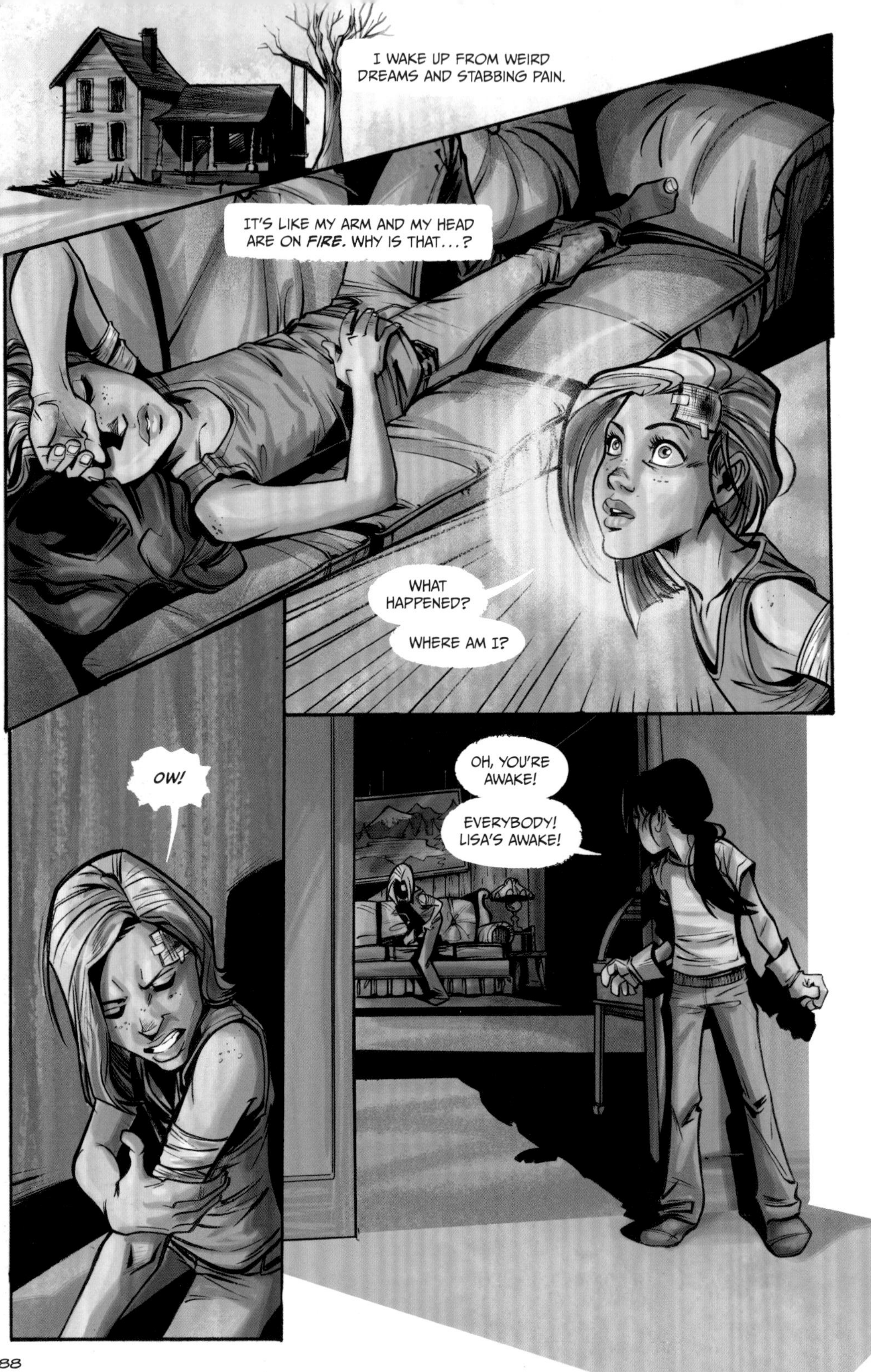

I WAKE UP FROM WEIRD DREAMS AND STABBING PAIN.
IT'S LIKE MY ARM AND MY HEAD ARE ON *FIRE.* WHY IS THAT...?
WHAT HAPPENED?
WHERE AM I?
OW!
OH, YOU'RE AWAKE!
EVERYBODY! LISA'S AWAKE!

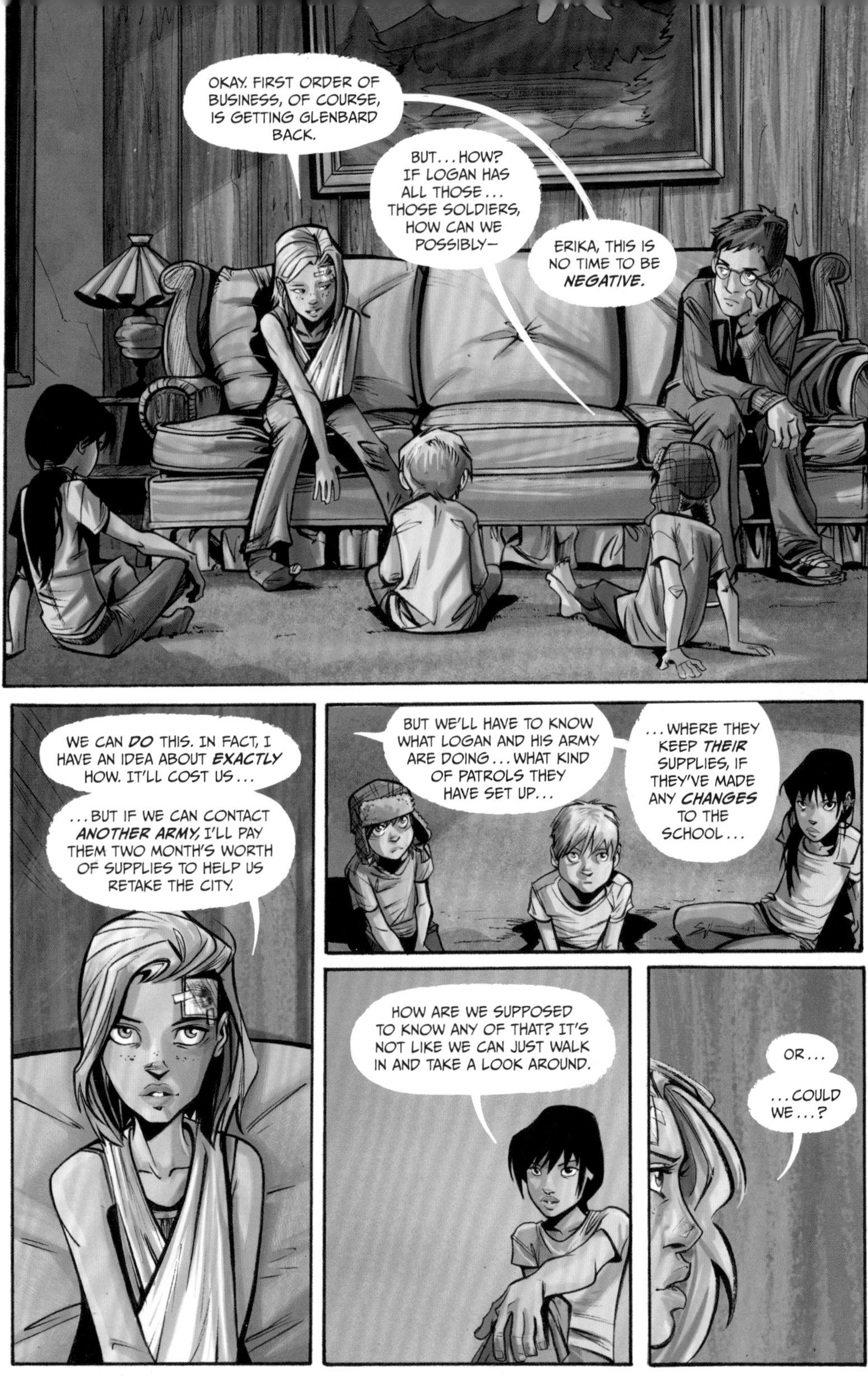
OKAY. FIRST ORDER OF BUSINESS, OF COURSE, IS GETTING GLENBARD BACK.
BUT... HOW? IF LOGAN HAS ALL THOSE... THOSE SOLDIERS, HOW CAN WE POSSIBLY—
ERIKA, THIS IS NO TIME TO BE *NEGATIVE.*
WE CAN *DO* THIS. IN FACT, I HAVE AN IDEA ABOUT *EXACTLY* HOW. IT'LL COST US...
...BUT IF WE CAN CONTACT *ANOTHER ARMY,* I'LL PAY THEM TWO MONTH'S WORTH OF SUPPLIES TO HELP US RETAKE THE CITY.
BUT WE'LL HAVE TO KNOW WHAT LOGAN AND HIS ARMY ARE DOING... WHAT KIND OF PATROLS THEY HAVE SET UP...
...WHERE THEY KEEP *THEIR* SUPPLIES, IF THEY'VE MADE ANY *CHANGES* TO THE SCHOOL...
HOW ARE WE SUPPOSED TO KNOW ANY OF THAT? IT'S NOT LIKE WE CAN JUST WALK IN AND TAKE A LOOK AROUND.
OR...
...COULD WE...?

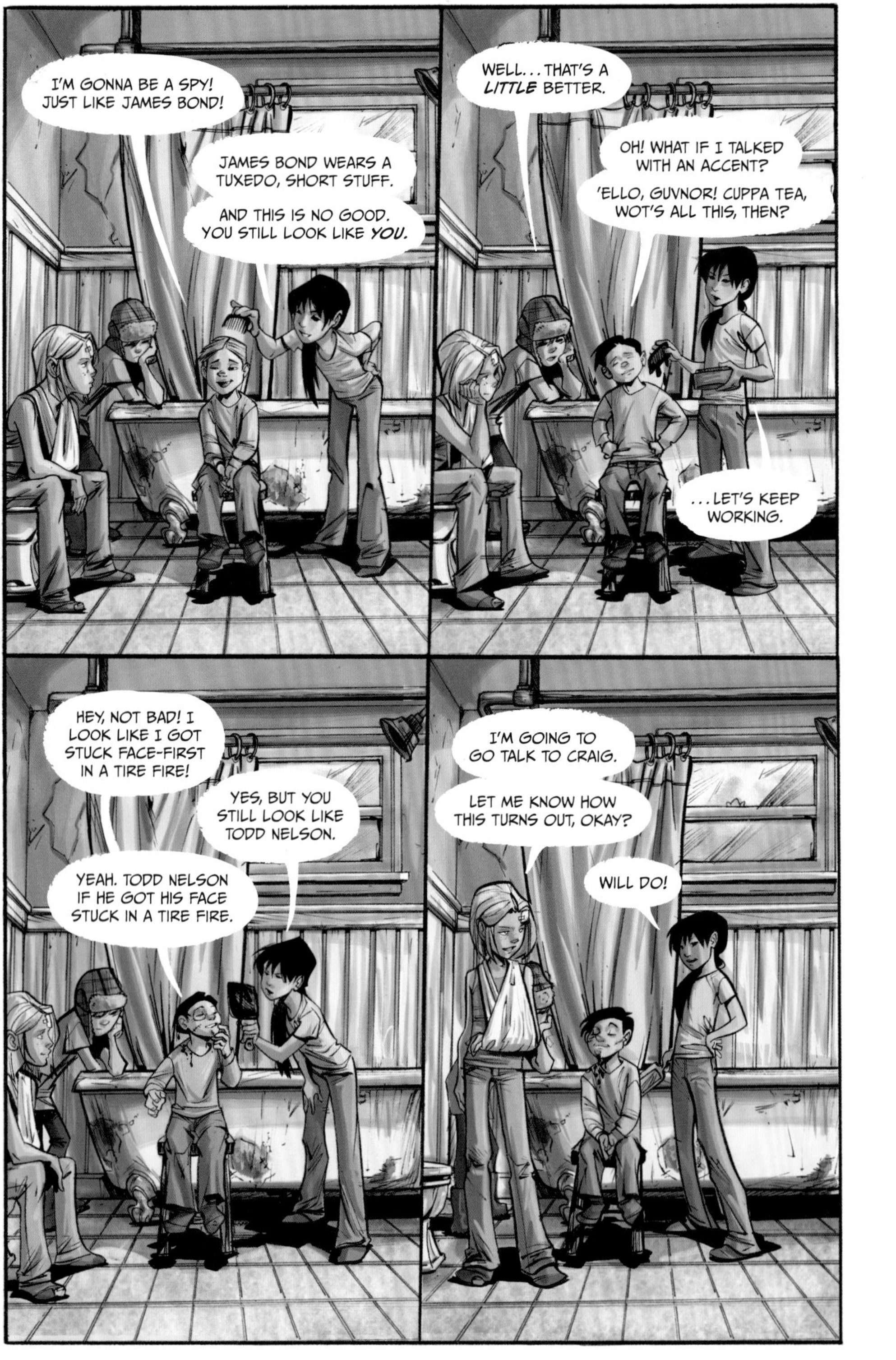
I'M GONNA BE A SPY! JUST LIKE JAMES BOND!
JAMES BOND WEARS A TUXEDO, SHORT STUFF.
AND THIS IS NO GOOD. YOU STILL LOOK LIKE *YOU.*
WELL... THAT'S A *LITTLE* BETTER.
OH! WHAT IF I TALKED WITH AN ACCENT?
'ELLO, GUVNOR! CUPPA TEA, WOT'S ALL THIS, THEN?
...LET'S KEEP WORKING.
HEY, NOT BAD! I LOOK LIKE I GOT STUCK FACE-FIRST IN A TIRE FIRE!
YES, BUT YOU STILL LOOK LIKE TODD NELSON.
YEAH. TODD NELSON IF HE GOT HIS FACE STUCK IN A TIRE FIRE.
I'M GOING TO GO TALK TO CRAIG.
LET ME KNOW HOW THIS TURNS OUT, OKAY?
WILL DO!

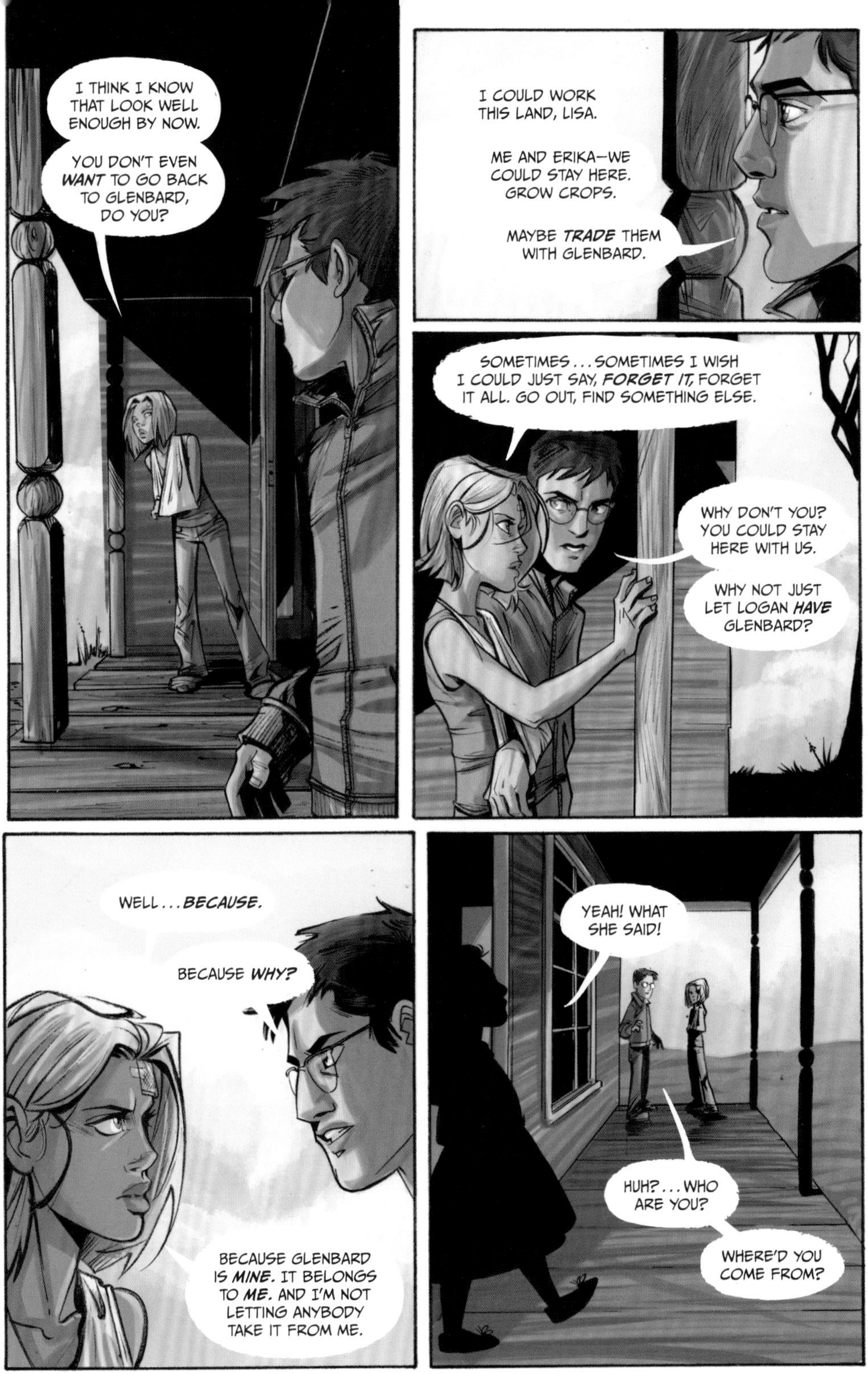
I THINK I KNOW THAT LOOK WELL ENOUGH BY NOW.
YOU DON'T EVEN WANT TO GO BACK TO GLENBARD, DO YOU?
I COULD WORK THIS LAND, LISA.
ME AND ERIKA—WE COULD STAY HERE. GROW CROPS.
MAYBE TRADE THEM WITH GLENBARD.
SOMETIMES . . . SOMETIMES I WISH I COULD JUST SAY, FORGET IT, FORGET IT ALL. GO OUT, FIND SOMETHING ELSE.
WHY DON'T YOU? YOU COULD STAY HERE WITH US.
WHY NOT JUST LET LOGAN HAVE GLENBARD?
WELL . . . BECAUSE.
BECAUSE WHY?
BECAUSE GLENBARD IS MINE. IT BELONGS TO ME. AND I'M NOT LETTING ANYBODY TAKE IT FROM ME.
YEAH! WHAT SHE SAID!
HUH? . . . WHO ARE YOU?
WHERE'D YOU COME FROM?

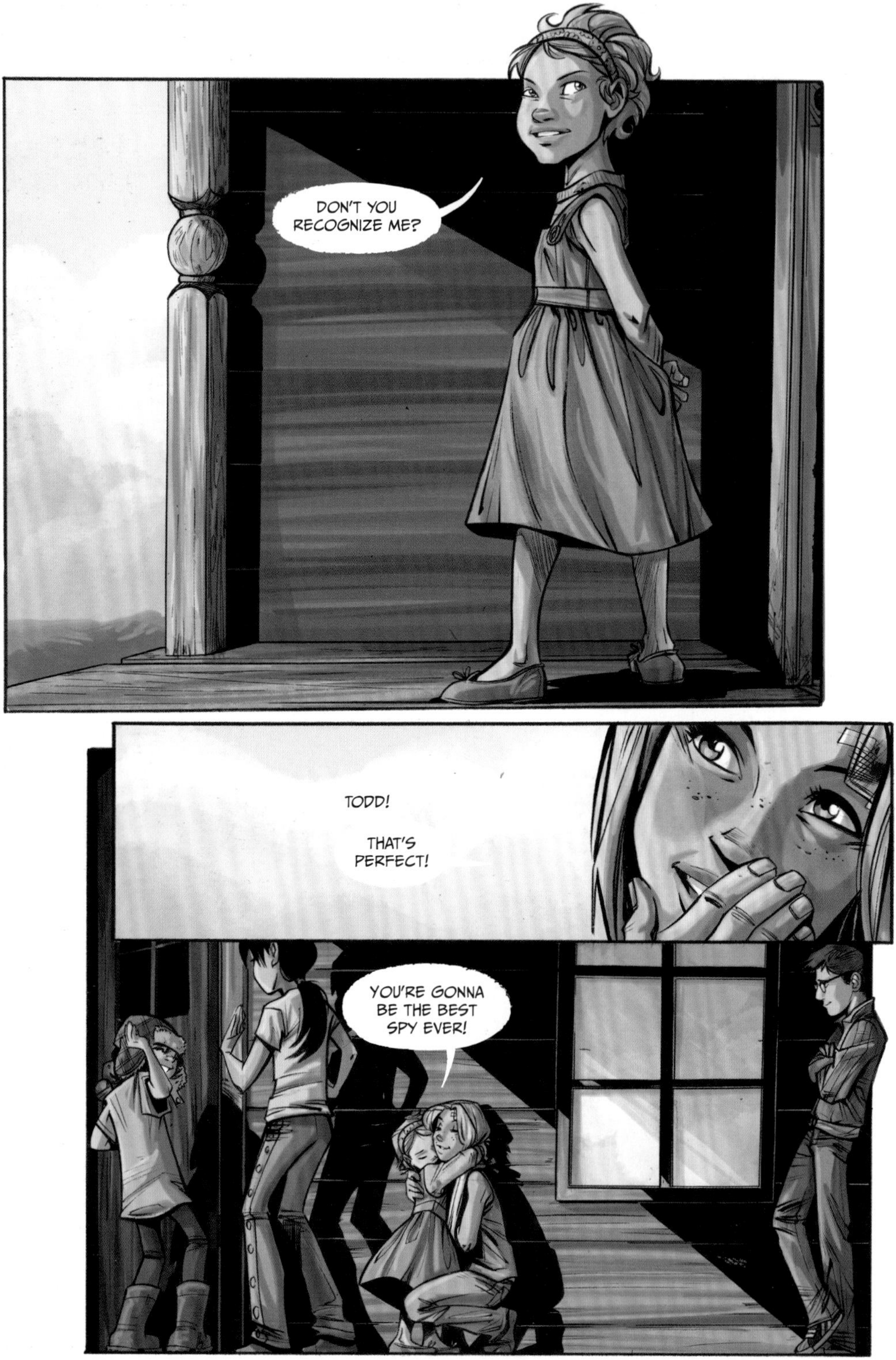
DON'T YOU RECOGNIZE ME?
TODD!
THAT'S PERFECT!
YOU'RE GONNA BE THE BEST SPY EVER!

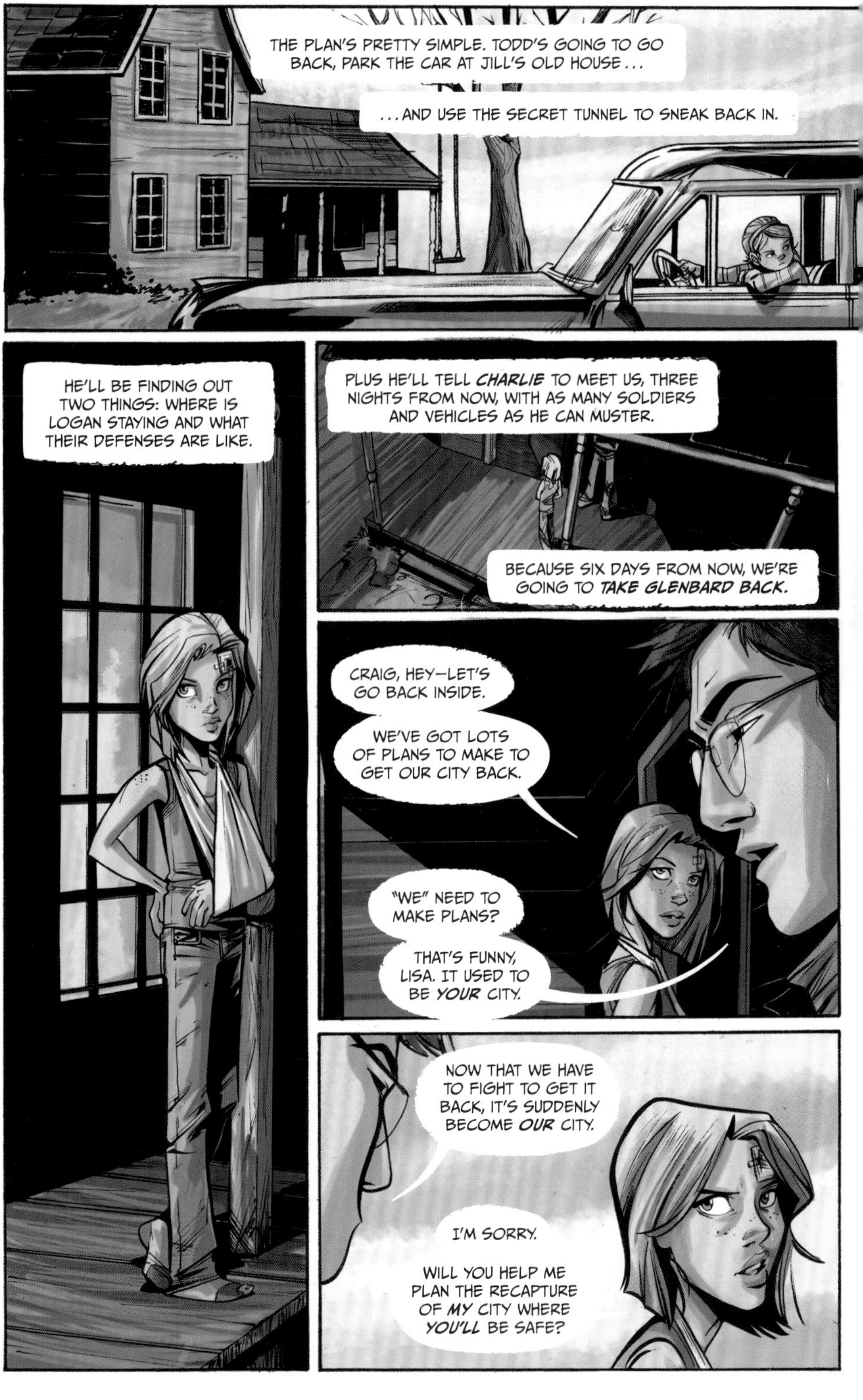
THE PLAN'S PRETTY SIMPLE. TODD'S GOING TO GO BACK, PARK THE CAR AT JILL'S OLD HOUSE . . .
. . . AND USE THE SECRET TUNNEL TO SNEAK BACK IN.
HE'LL BE FINDING OUT TWO THINGS: WHERE IS LOGAN STAYING AND WHAT THEIR DEFENSES ARE LIKE.
PLUS HE'LL TELL *CHARLIE* TO MEET US, THREE NIGHTS FROM NOW, WITH AS MANY SOLDIERS AND VEHICLES AS HE CAN MUSTER.
BECAUSE SIX DAYS FROM NOW, WE'RE GOING TO *TAKE GLENBARD BACK.*
CRAIG, HEY—LET'S GO BACK INSIDE.
WE'VE GOT LOTS OF PLANS TO MAKE TO GET OUR CITY BACK.
"WE" NEED TO MAKE PLANS?
THAT'S FUNNY, LISA. IT USED TO BE *YOUR* CITY.
NOW THAT WE HAVE TO FIGHT TO GET IT BACK, IT'S SUDDENLY BECOME *OUR* CITY.
I'M SORRY.
WILL YOU HELP ME PLAN THE RECAPTURE OF *MY* CITY WHERE *YOU'LL* BE SAFE?

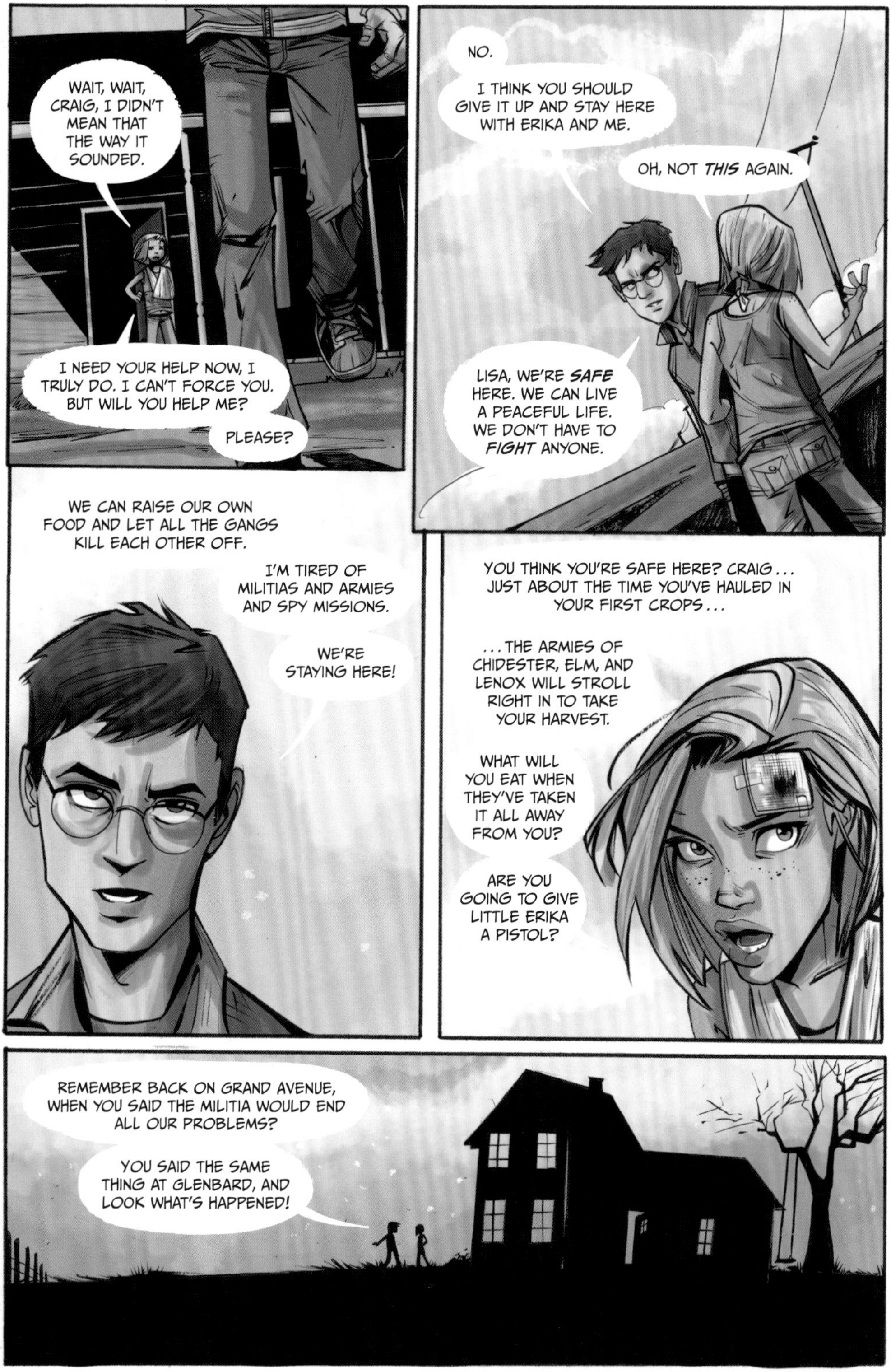
WAIT, WAIT, CRAIG, I DIDN'T MEAN THAT THE WAY IT SOUNDED.
I NEED YOUR HELP NOW, I TRULY DO. I CAN'T FORCE YOU. BUT WILL YOU HELP ME?
PLEASE?
NO.
I THINK YOU SHOULD GIVE IT UP AND STAY HERE WITH ERIKA AND ME.
OH, NOT *THIS* AGAIN.
LISA, WE'RE ***SAFE*** HERE. WE CAN LIVE A PEACEFUL LIFE. WE DON'T HAVE TO ***FIGHT*** ANYONE.
WE CAN RAISE OUR OWN FOOD AND LET ALL THE GANGS KILL EACH OTHER OFF.
I'M TIRED OF MILITIAS AND ARMIES AND SPY MISSIONS.
WE'RE STAYING HERE!
YOU THINK YOU'RE SAFE HERE? CRAIG... JUST ABOUT THE TIME YOU'VE HAULED IN YOUR FIRST CROPS...
...THE ARMIES OF CHIDESTER, ELM, AND LENOX WILL STROLL RIGHT IN TO TAKE YOUR HARVEST.
WHAT WILL YOU EAT WHEN THEY'VE TAKEN IT ALL AWAY FROM YOU?
ARE YOU GOING TO GIVE LITTLE ERIKA A PISTOL?
REMEMBER BACK ON GRAND AVENUE, WHEN YOU SAID THE MILITIA WOULD END ALL OUR PROBLEMS?
YOU SAID THE SAME THING AT GLENBARD, AND LOOK WHAT'S HAPPENED!

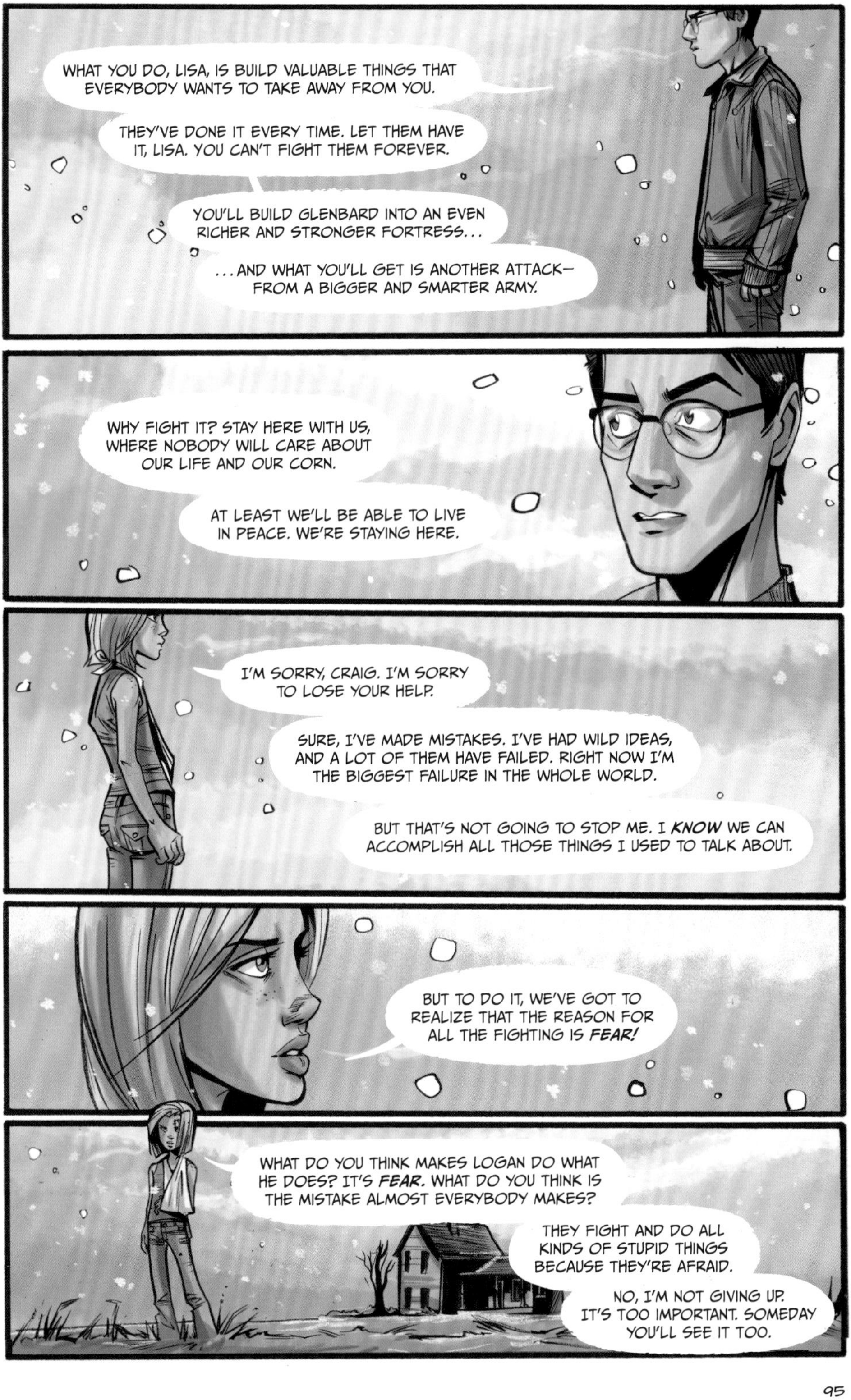
WHAT YOU DO, LISA, IS BUILD VALUABLE THINGS THAT EVERYBODY WANTS TO TAKE AWAY FROM YOU.
THEY'VE DONE IT EVERY TIME. LET THEM HAVE IT, LISA. YOU CAN'T FIGHT THEM FOREVER.
YOU'LL BUILD GLENBARD INTO AN EVEN RICHER AND STRONGER FORTRESS...
...AND WHAT YOU'LL GET IS ANOTHER ATTACK— FROM A BIGGER AND SMARTER ARMY.
WHY FIGHT IT? STAY HERE WITH US, WHERE NOBODY WILL CARE ABOUT OUR LIFE AND OUR CORN.
AT LEAST WE'LL BE ABLE TO LIVE IN PEACE. WE'RE STAYING HERE.
I'M SORRY, CRAIG. I'M SORRY TO LOSE YOUR HELP.
SURE, I'VE MADE MISTAKES. I'VE HAD WILD IDEAS, AND A LOT OF THEM HAVE FAILED. RIGHT NOW I'M THE BIGGEST FAILURE IN THE WHOLE WORLD.
BUT THAT'S NOT GOING TO STOP ME. I ***KNOW*** WE CAN ACCOMPLISH ALL THOSE THINGS I USED TO TALK ABOUT.
BUT TO DO IT, WE'VE GOT TO REALIZE THAT THE REASON FOR ALL THE FIGHTING IS ***FEAR!***
WHAT DO YOU THINK MAKES LOGAN DO WHAT HE DOES? IT'S ***FEAR.*** WHAT DO YOU THINK IS THE MISTAKE ALMOST EVERYBODY MAKES?
THEY FIGHT AND DO ALL KINDS OF STUPID THINGS BECAUSE THEY'RE AFRAID.
NO, I'M NOT GIVING UP. IT'S TOO IMPORTANT. SOMEDAY YOU'LL SEE IT TOO.

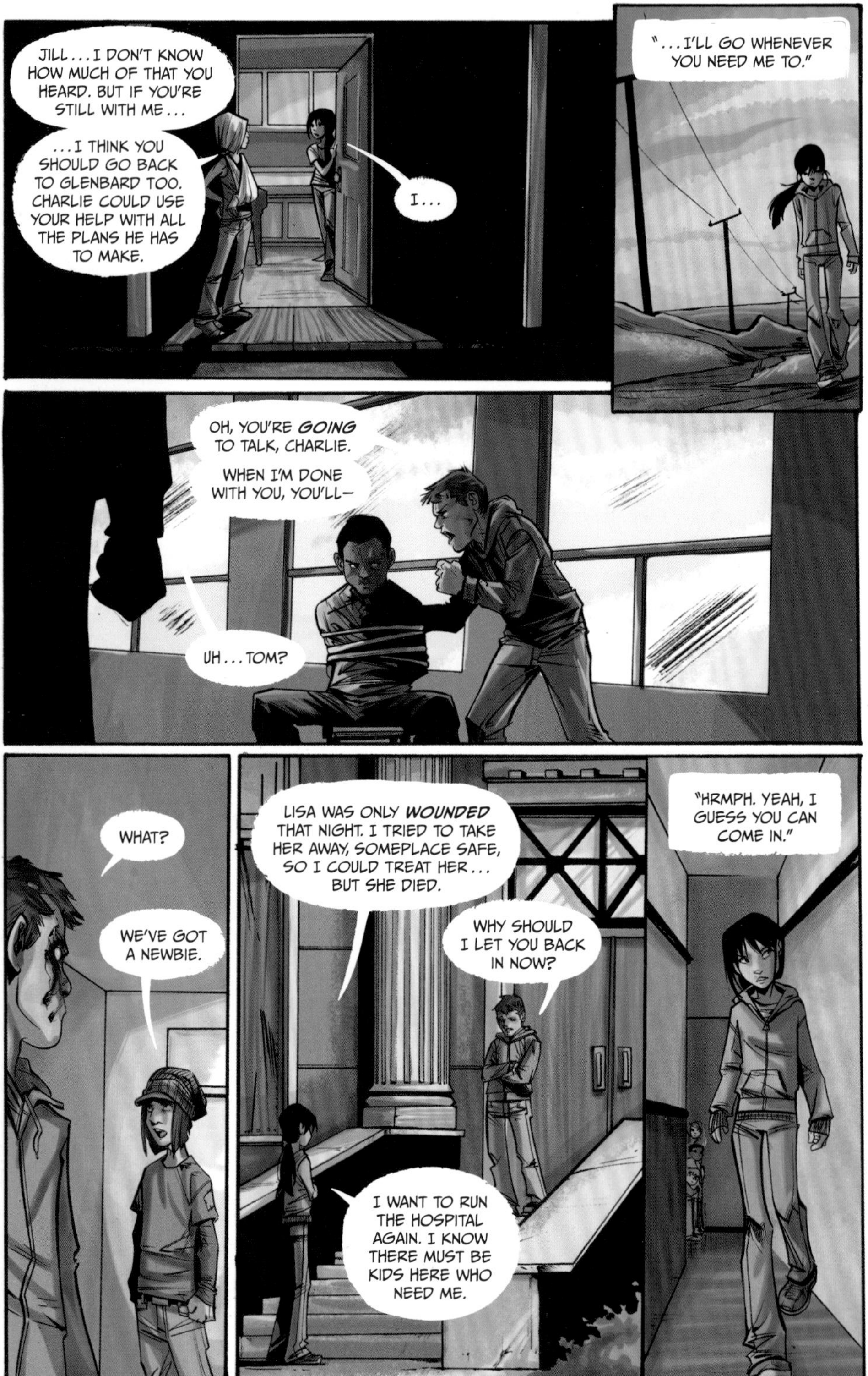
JILL . . . I DON'T KNOW HOW MUCH OF THAT YOU HEARD. BUT IF YOU'RE STILL WITH ME . . .
. . . I THINK YOU SHOULD GO BACK TO GLENBARD TOO. CHARLIE COULD USE YOUR HELP WITH ALL THE PLANS HE HAS TO MAKE.
I . . .
". . . I'LL GO WHENEVER YOU NEED ME TO."
OH, YOU'RE *GOING* TO TALK, CHARLIE.
WHEN I'M DONE WITH YOU, YOU'LL—
UH . . . TOM?
WHAT?
WE'VE GOT A NEWBIE.
LISA WAS ONLY *WOUNDED* THAT NIGHT. I TRIED TO TAKE HER AWAY, SOMEPLACE SAFE, SO I COULD TREAT HER . . . BUT SHE DIED.
WHY SHOULD I LET YOU BACK IN NOW?
I WANT TO RUN THE HOSPITAL AGAIN. I KNOW THERE MUST BE KIDS HERE WHO NEED ME.
"HRMPH. YEAH, I GUESS YOU CAN COME IN."

THINGS ARE PRETTY TENSE BETWEEN CRAIG AND ME, WAITING AROUND FOR TODD TO COME BACK.

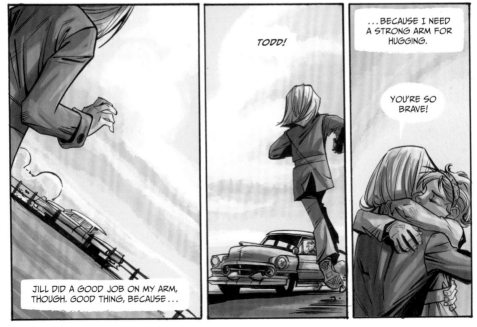

JILL DID A GOOD JOB ON MY ARM, THOUGH. GOOD THING, BECAUSE...

TODD!

...BECAUSE I NEED A STRONG ARM FOR HUGGING.

YOU'RE SO BRAVE!

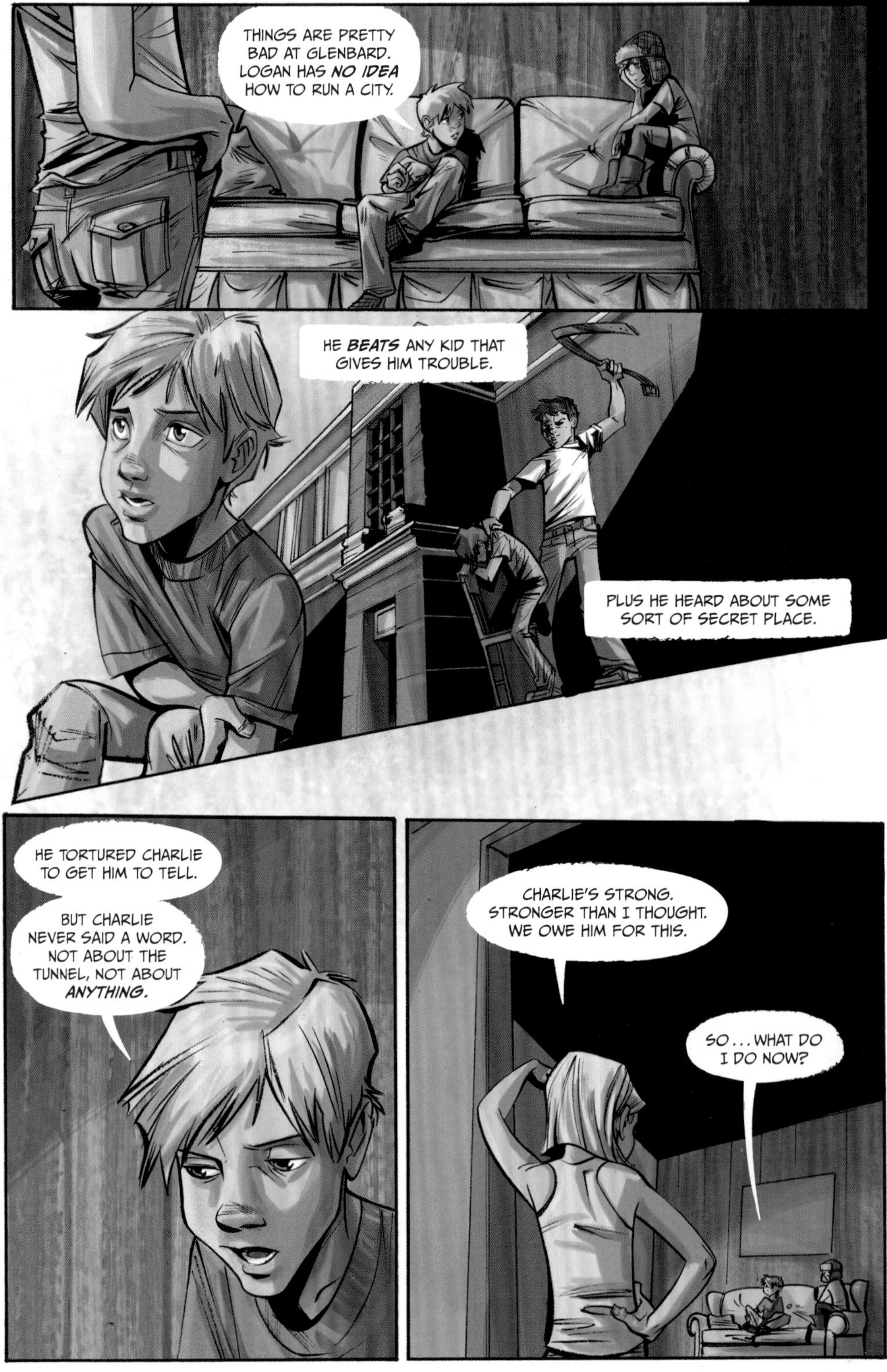
THINGS ARE PRETTY BAD AT GLENBARD. LOGAN HAS *NO IDEA* HOW TO RUN A CITY.
HE *BEATS* ANY KID THAT GIVES HIM TROUBLE.
PLUS HE HEARD ABOUT SOME SORT OF SECRET PLACE.
HE TORTURED CHARLIE TO GET HIM TO TELL.
BUT CHARLIE NEVER SAID A WORD. NOT ABOUT THE TUNNEL, NOT ABOUT *ANYTHING.*
CHARLIE'S STRONG. STRONGER THAN I THOUGHT. WE OWE HIM FOR THIS.
SO . . . WHAT DO I DO NOW?

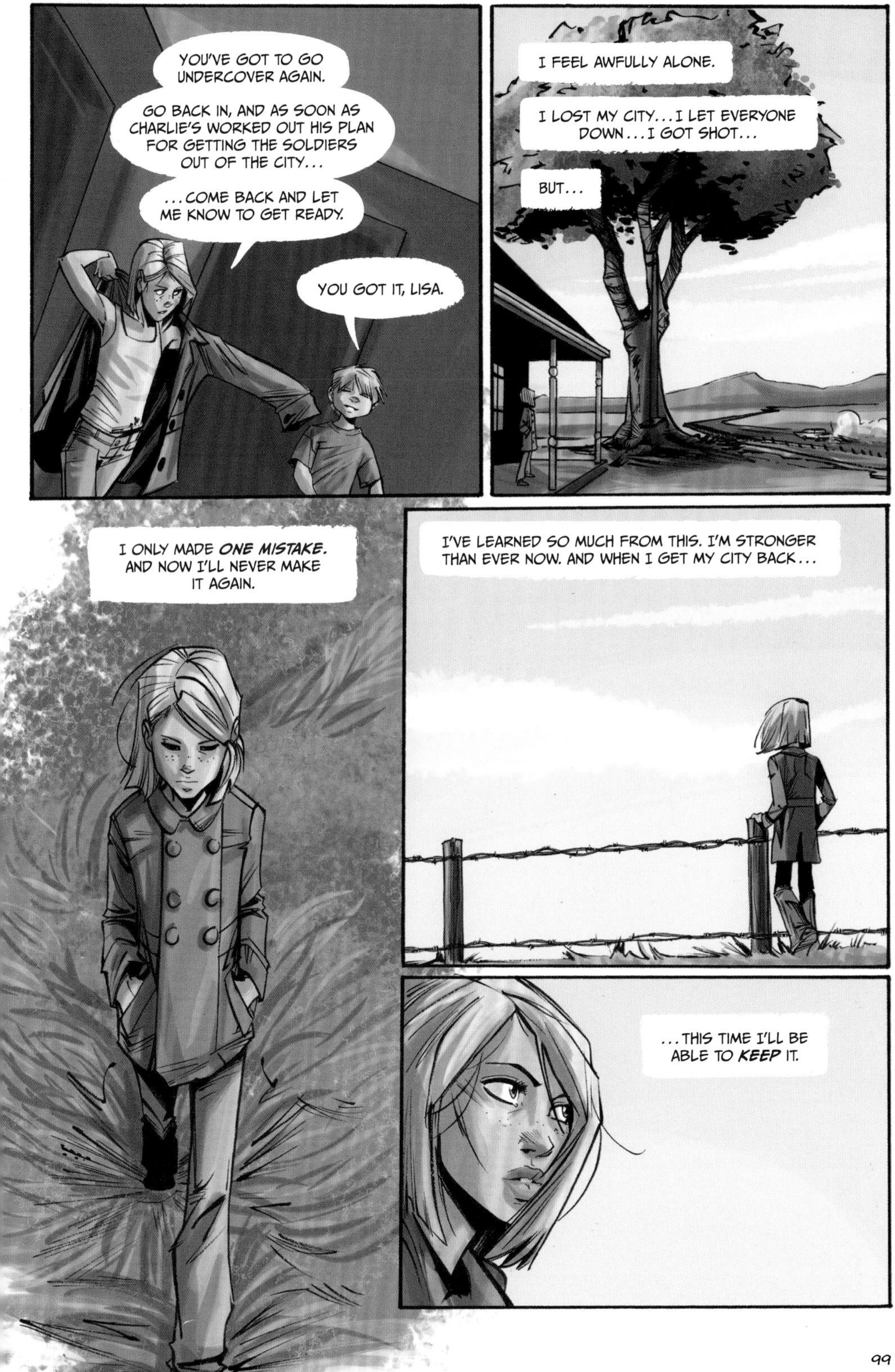

YOU'VE GOT TO GO UNDERCOVER AGAIN.
GO BACK IN, AND AS SOON AS CHARLIE'S WORKED OUT HIS PLAN FOR GETTING THE SOLDIERS OUT OF THE CITY...
...COME BACK AND LET ME KNOW TO GET READY.
YOU GOT IT, LISA.
I FEEL AWFULLY ALONE.
I LOST MY CITY...I LET EVERYONE DOWN...I GOT SHOT...
BUT...
I ONLY MADE ***ONE MISTAKE.*** AND NOW I'LL NEVER MAKE IT AGAIN.
I'VE LEARNED SO MUCH FROM THIS. I'M STRONGER THAN EVER NOW. AND WHEN I GET MY CITY BACK...
...THIS TIME I'LL BE ABLE TO ***KEEP*** IT.

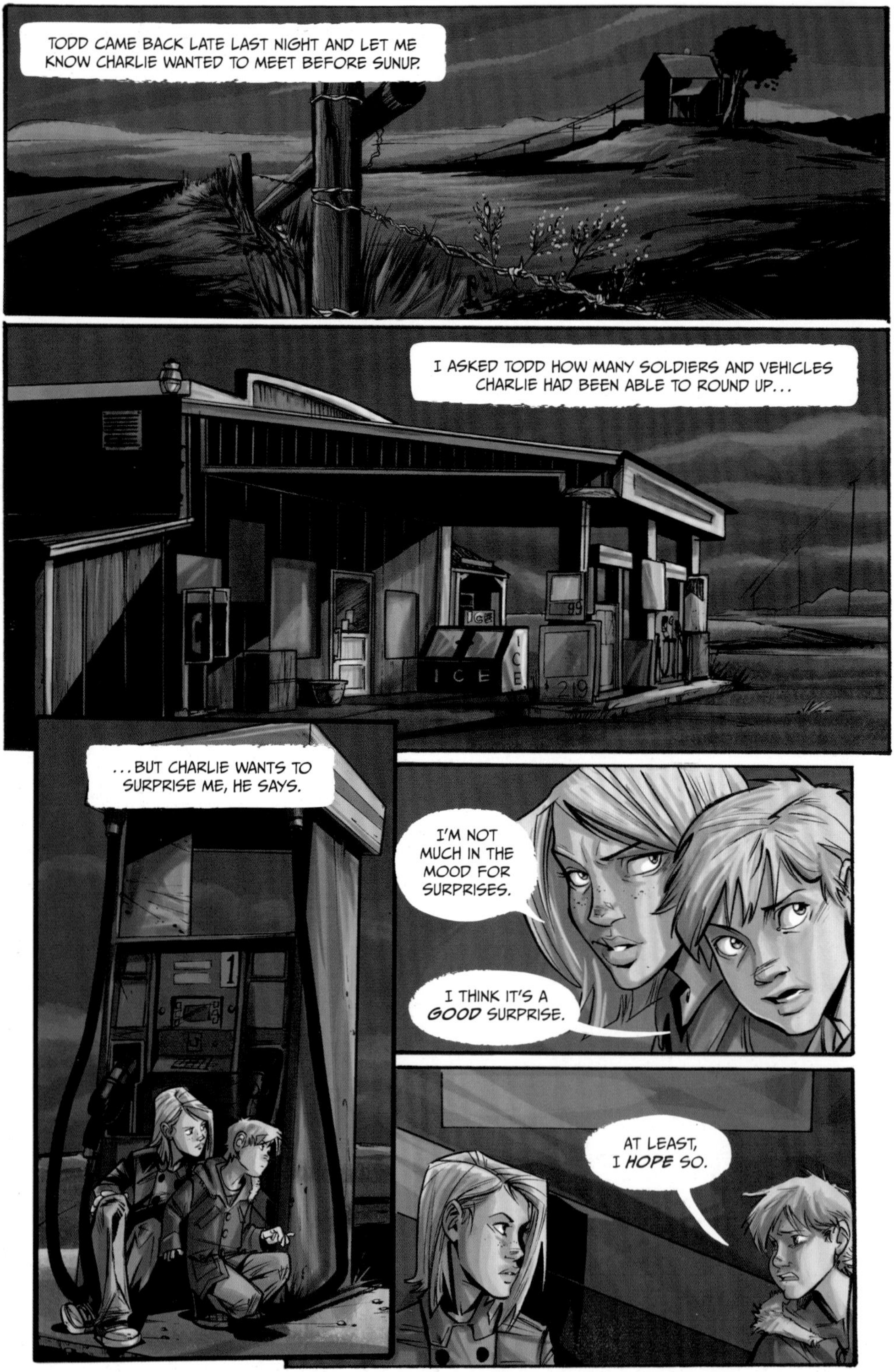
TODD CAME BACK LATE LAST NIGHT AND LET ME KNOW CHARLIE WANTED TO MEET BEFORE SUNUP.
I ASKED TODD HOW MANY SOLDIERS AND VEHICLES CHARLIE HAD BEEN ABLE TO ROUND UP...
ICE
ICE
...BUT CHARLIE WANTS TO SURPRISE ME, HE SAYS.
I'M NOT MUCH IN THE MOOD FOR SURPRISES.
I THINK IT'S A *GOOD* SURPRISE.
AT LEAST, I *HOPE* SO.

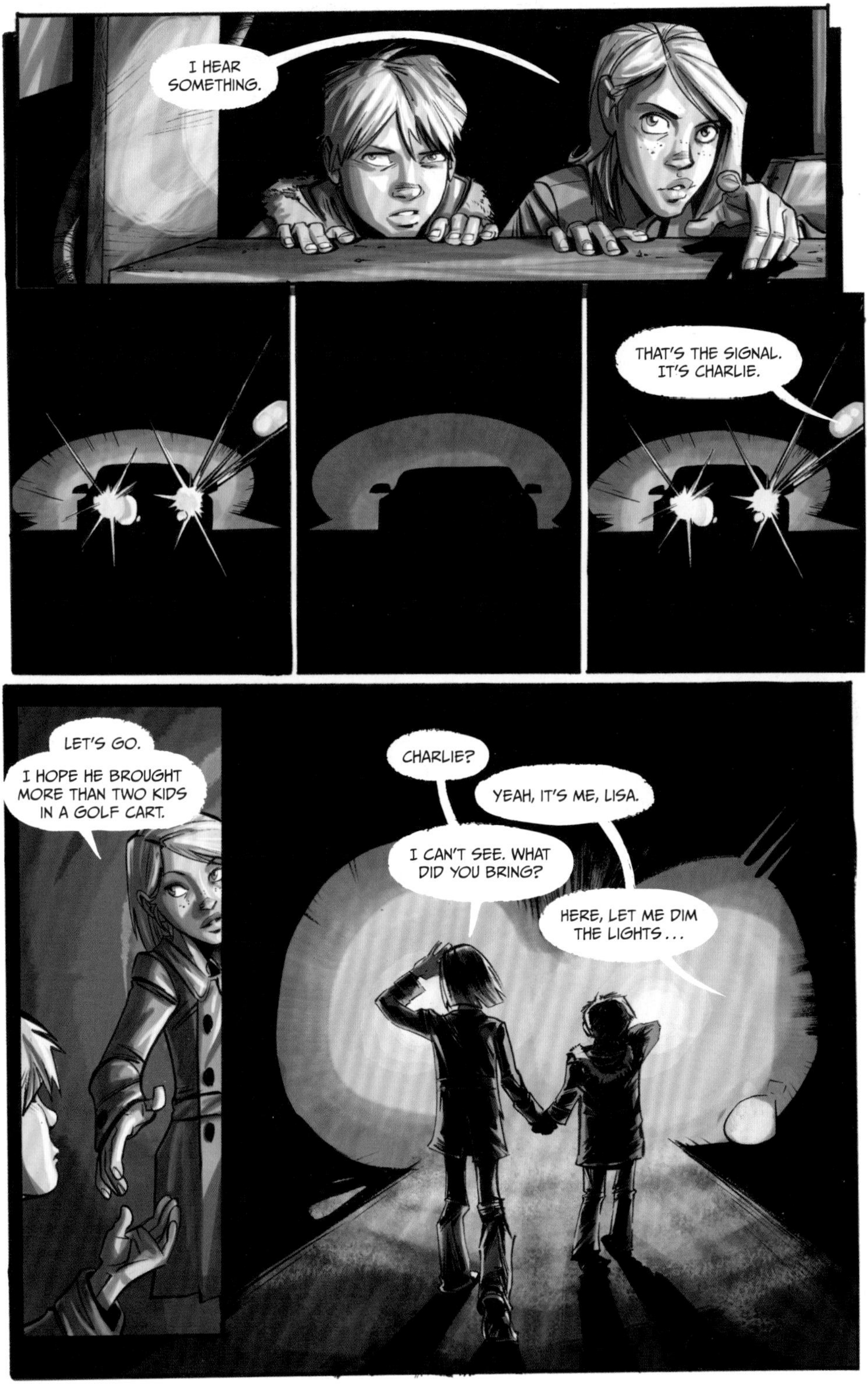
I HEAR SOMETHING.
THAT'S THE SIGNAL. IT'S CHARLIE.
LET'S GO.
I HOPE HE BROUGHT MORE THAN TWO KIDS IN A GOLF CART.
CHARLIE?
YEAH, IT'S ME, LISA.
I CAN'T SEE. WHAT DID YOU BRING?
HERE, LET ME DIM THE LIGHTS . . .

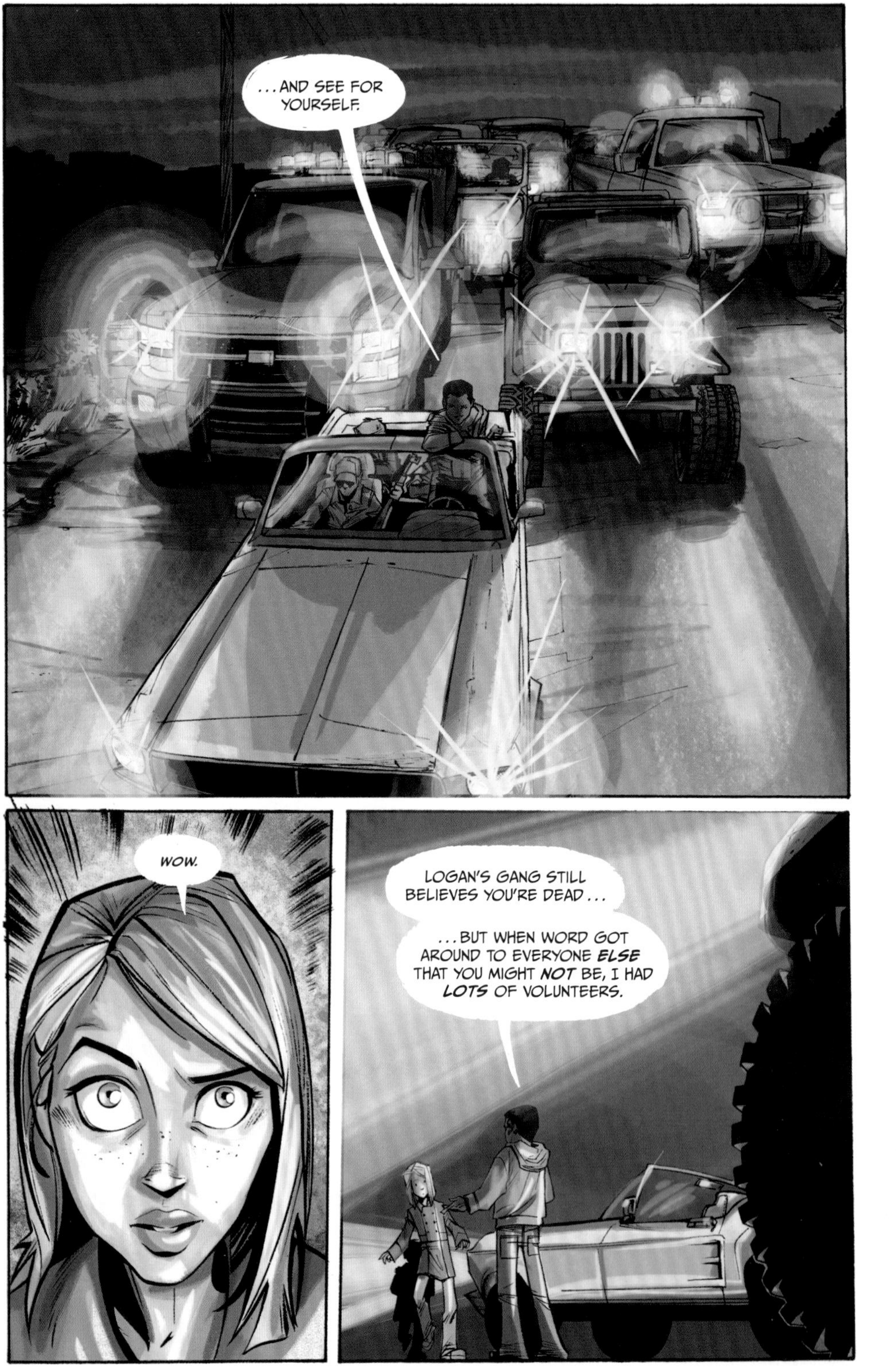
...AND SEE FOR YOURSELF.
WOW.
LOGAN'S GANG STILL BELIEVES YOU'RE DEAD...
...BUT WHEN WORD GOT AROUND TO EVERYONE ELSE THAT YOU MIGHT NOT BE, I HAD LOTS OF VOLUNTEERS.

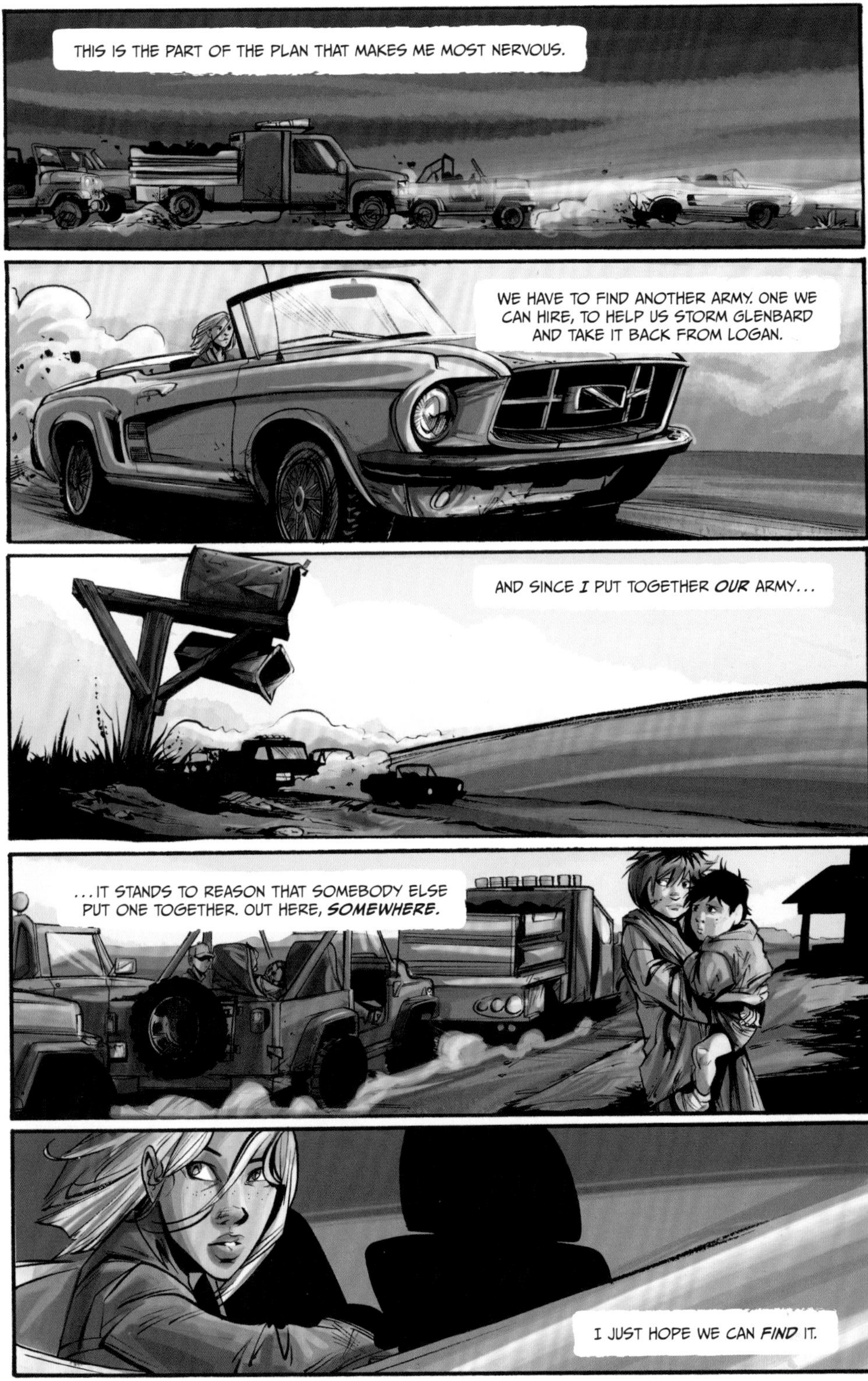
THIS IS THE PART OF THE PLAN THAT MAKES ME MOST NERVOUS.
WE HAVE TO FIND ANOTHER ARMY. ONE WE CAN HIRE, TO HELP US STORM GLENBARD AND TAKE IT BACK FROM LOGAN.
AND SINCE *I* PUT TOGETHER ***OUR*** ARMY...
...IT STANDS TO REASON THAT SOMEBODY ELSE PUT ONE TOGETHER. OUT HERE, ***SOMEWHERE.***
I JUST HOPE WE CAN ***FIND*** IT.

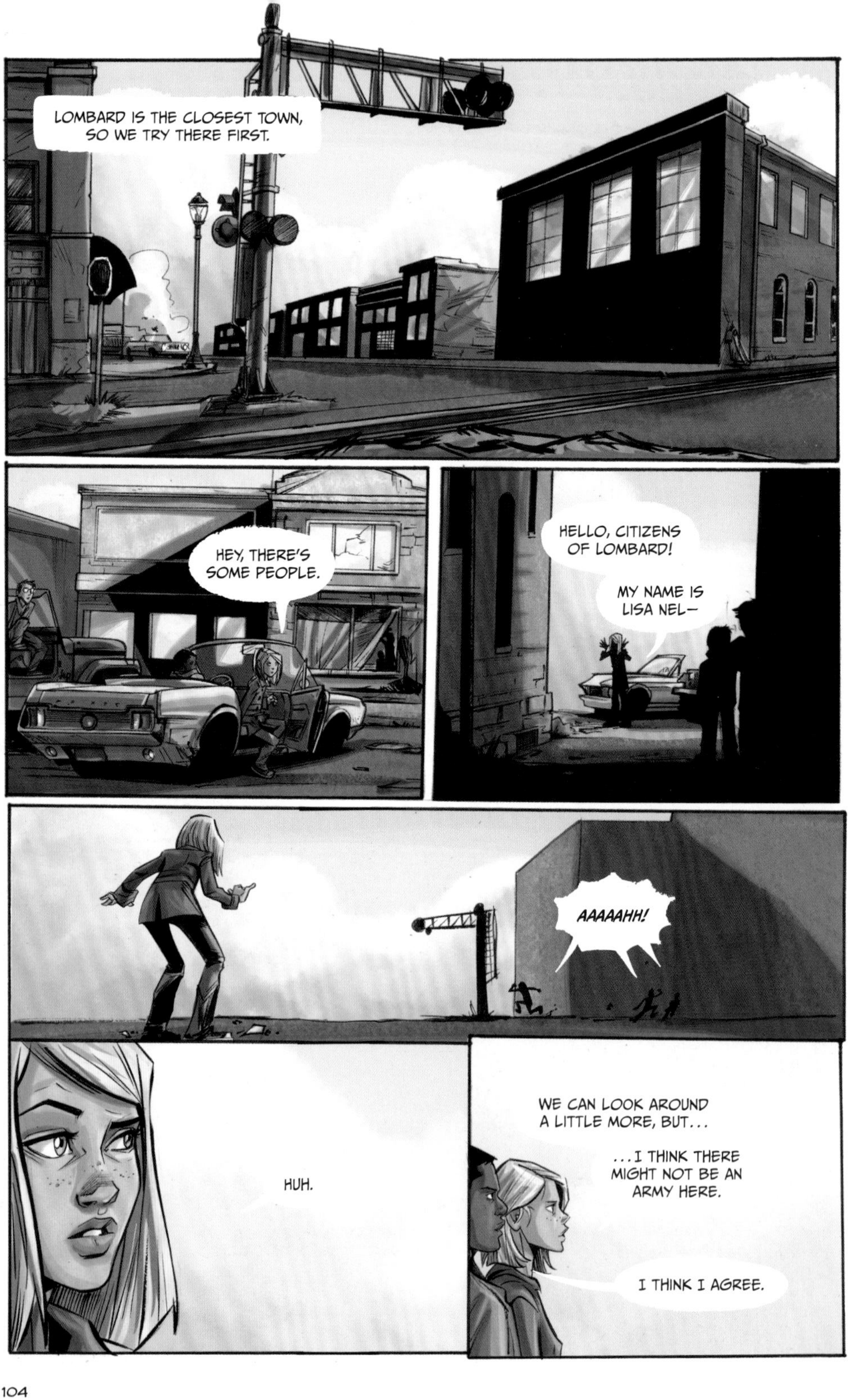
LOMBARD IS THE CLOSEST TOWN, SO WE TRY THERE FIRST.
HEY, THERE'S SOME PEOPLE.
HELLO, CITIZENS OF LOMBARD!
MY NAME IS LISA NEL—
AAAAAHH!
HUH.
WE CAN LOOK AROUND A LITTLE MORE, BUT...
...I THINK THERE MIGHT NOT BE AN ARMY HERE.
I THINK I AGREE.

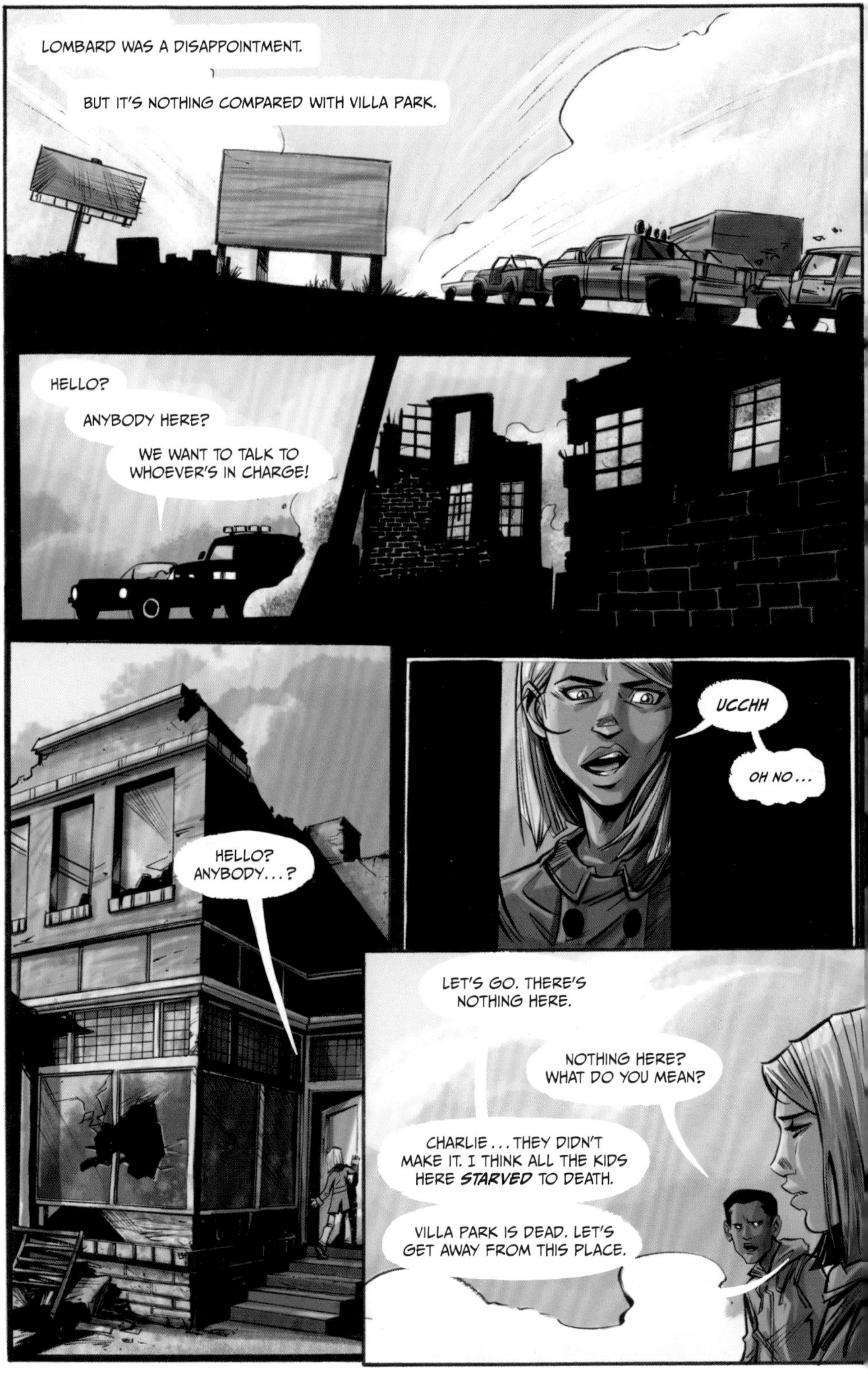
LOMBARD WAS A DISAPPOINTMENT.
BUT IT'S NOTHING COMPARED WITH VILLA PARK.
HELLO?
ANYBODY HERE?
WE WANT TO TALK TO WHOEVER'S IN CHARGE!
HELLO? ANYBODY...?
UCCHH
OH NO...
LET'S GO. THERE'S NOTHING HERE.
NOTHING HERE? WHAT DO YOU MEAN?
CHARLIE... THEY DIDN'T MAKE IT. I THINK ALL THE KIDS HERE STARVED TO DEATH.
VILLA PARK IS DEAD. LET'S GET AWAY FROM THIS PLACE.

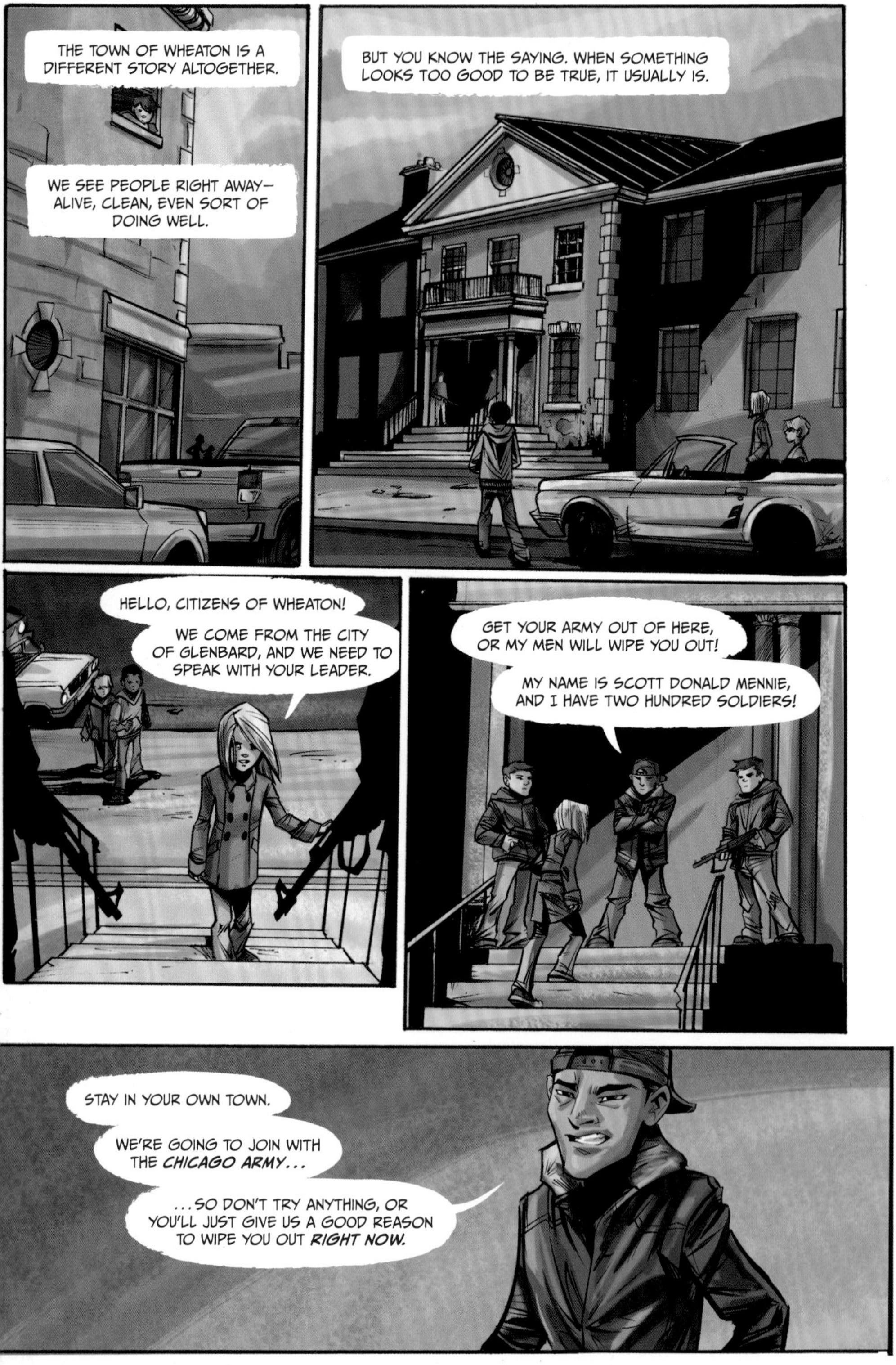
THE TOWN OF WHEATON IS A DIFFERENT STORY ALTOGETHER.
WE SEE PEOPLE RIGHT AWAY— ALIVE, CLEAN, EVEN SORT OF DOING WELL.
BUT YOU KNOW THE SAYING. WHEN SOMETHING LOOKS TOO GOOD TO BE TRUE, IT USUALLY IS.
HELLO, CITIZENS OF WHEATON!
WE COME FROM THE CITY OF GLENBARD, AND WE NEED TO SPEAK WITH YOUR LEADER.
GET YOUR ARMY OUT OF HERE, OR MY MEN WILL WIPE YOU OUT!
MY NAME IS SCOTT DONALD MENNIE, AND I HAVE TWO HUNDRED SOLDIERS!
STAY IN YOUR OWN TOWN.
WE'RE GOING TO JOIN WITH THE *CHICAGO ARMY*...
...SO DON'T TRY ANYTHING, OR YOU'LL JUST GIVE US A GOOD REASON TO WIPE YOU OUT *RIGHT NOW.*

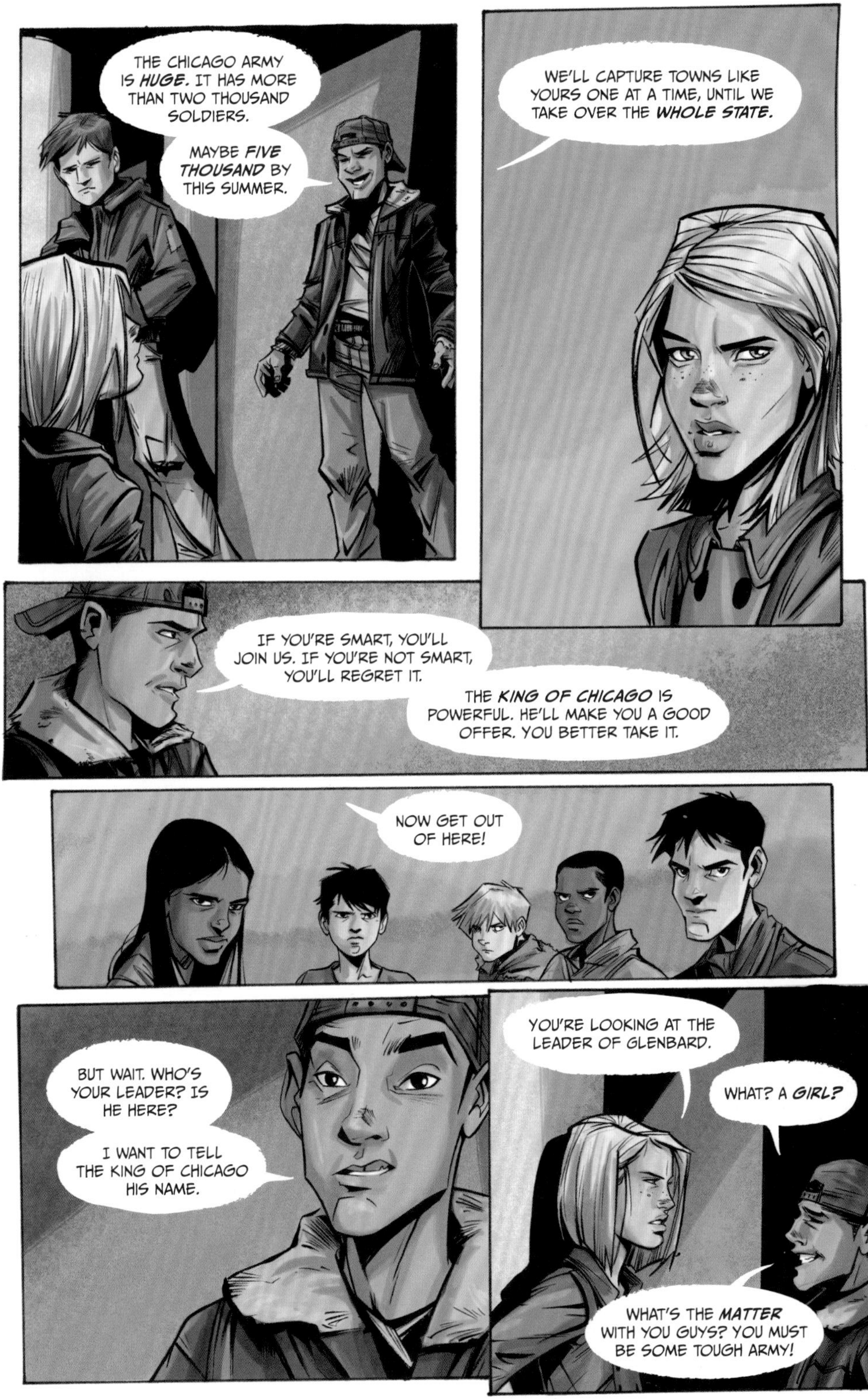

THE CHICAGO ARMY IS *HUGE.* IT HAS MORE THAN TWO THOUSAND SOLDIERS.
MAYBE *FIVE THOUSAND* BY THIS SUMMER.
WE'LL CAPTURE TOWNS LIKE YOURS ONE AT A TIME, UNTIL WE TAKE OVER THE *WHOLE STATE.*
IF YOU'RE SMART, YOU'LL JOIN US. IF YOU'RE NOT SMART, YOU'LL REGRET IT.
THE *KING OF CHICAGO* IS POWERFUL. HE'LL MAKE YOU A GOOD OFFER. YOU BETTER TAKE IT.
NOW GET OUT OF HERE!
BUT WAIT. WHO'S YOUR LEADER? IS HE HERE?
I WANT TO TELL THE KING OF CHICAGO HIS NAME.
YOU'RE LOOKING AT THE LEADER OF GLENBARD.
WHAT? A *GIRL?*
WHAT'S THE *MATTER* WITH YOU GUYS? YOU MUST BE SOME TOUGH ARMY!

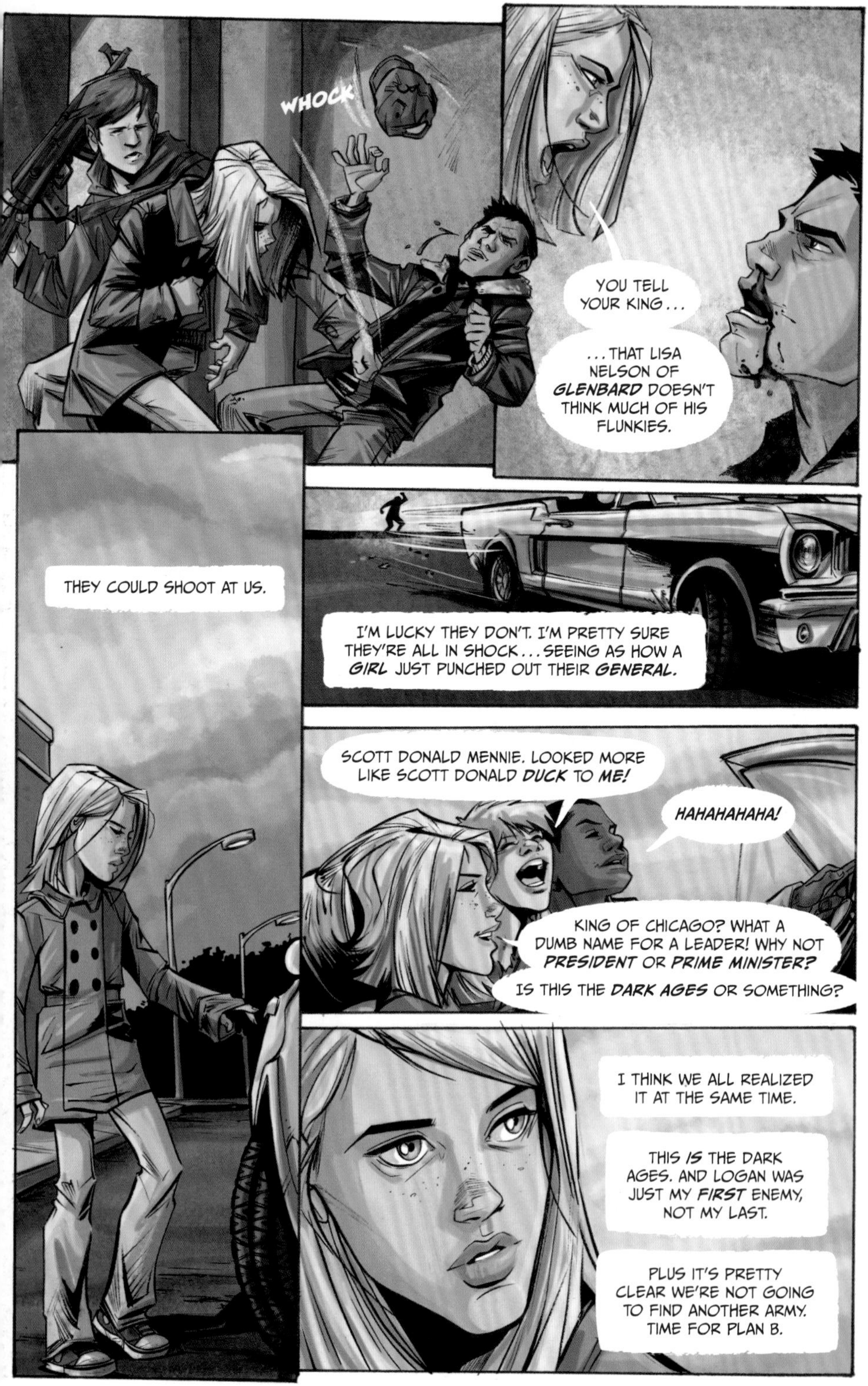

WHOCK
YOU TELL YOUR KING...
...THAT LISA NELSON OF GLENBARD DOESN'T THINK MUCH OF HIS FLUNKIES.
THEY COULD SHOOT AT US.
I'M LUCKY THEY DON'T. I'M PRETTY SURE THEY'RE ALL IN SHOCK...SEEING AS HOW A GIRL JUST PUNCHED OUT THEIR GENERAL.
SCOTT DONALD MENNIE. LOOKED MORE LIKE SCOTT DONALD DUCK TO ME!
HAHAHAHAHA!
KING OF CHICAGO? WHAT A DUMB NAME FOR A LEADER! WHY NOT PRESIDENT OR PRIME MINISTER?
IS THIS THE DARK AGES OR SOMETHING?
I THINK WE ALL REALIZED IT AT THE SAME TIME.
THIS IS THE DARK AGES. AND LOGAN WAS JUST MY FIRST ENEMY, NOT MY LAST.
PLUS IT'S PRETTY CLEAR WE'RE NOT GOING TO FIND ANOTHER ARMY. TIME FOR PLAN B.

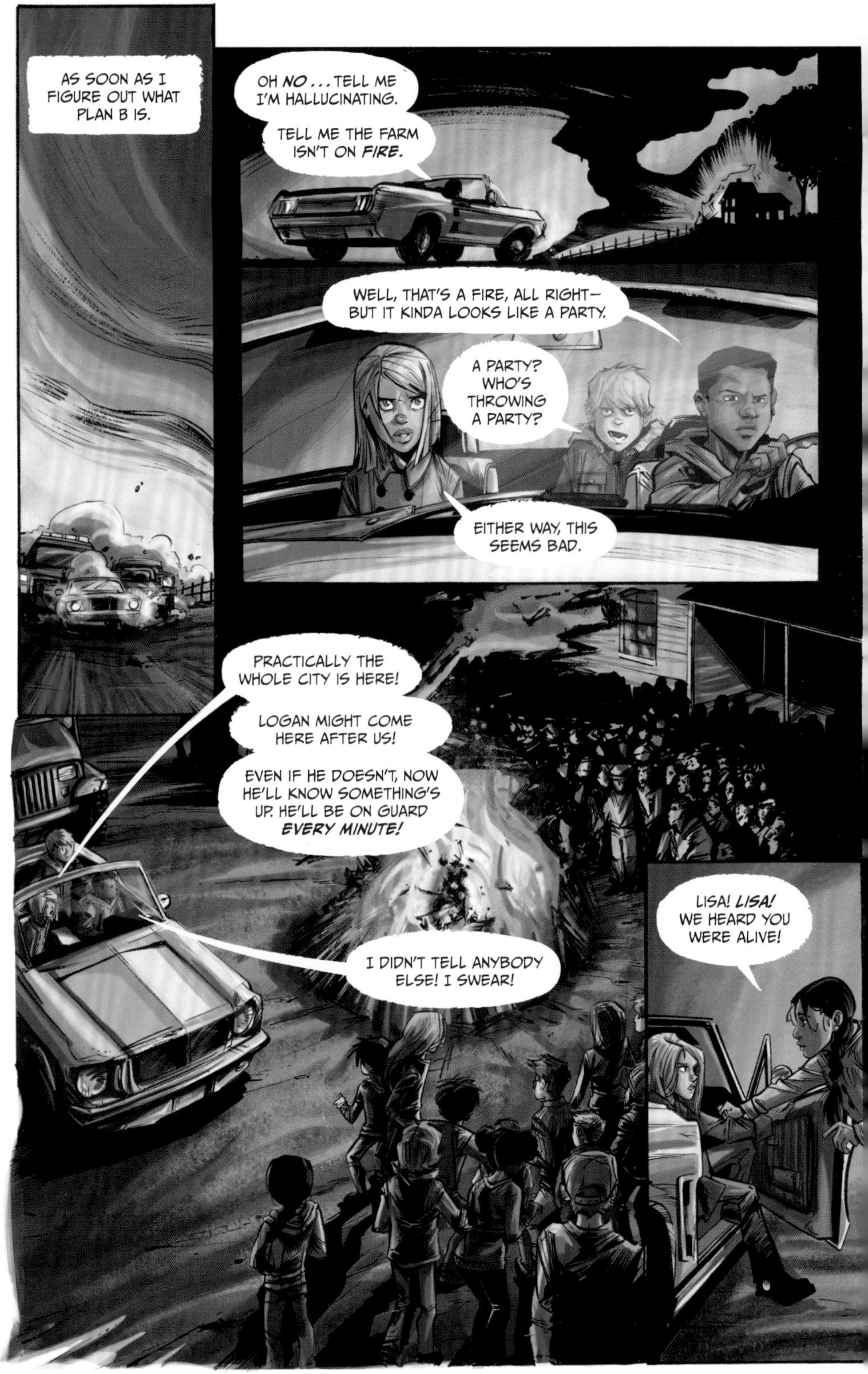

AS SOON AS I FIGURE OUT WHAT PLAN B IS.
OH NO . . . TELL ME I'M HALLUCINATING.
TELL ME THE FARM ISN'T ON FIRE.
WELL, THAT'S A FIRE, ALL RIGHT— BUT IT KINDA LOOKS LIKE A PARTY.
A PARTY? WHO'S THROWING A PARTY?
EITHER WAY, THIS SEEMS BAD.
PRACTICALLY THE WHOLE CITY IS HERE!
LOGAN MIGHT COME HERE AFTER US!
EVEN IF HE DOESN'T, NOW HE'LL KNOW SOMETHING'S UP. HE'LL BE ON GUARD EVERY MINUTE!
I DIDN'T TELL ANYBODY ELSE! I SWEAR!
LISA! LISA! WE HEARD YOU WERE ALIVE!

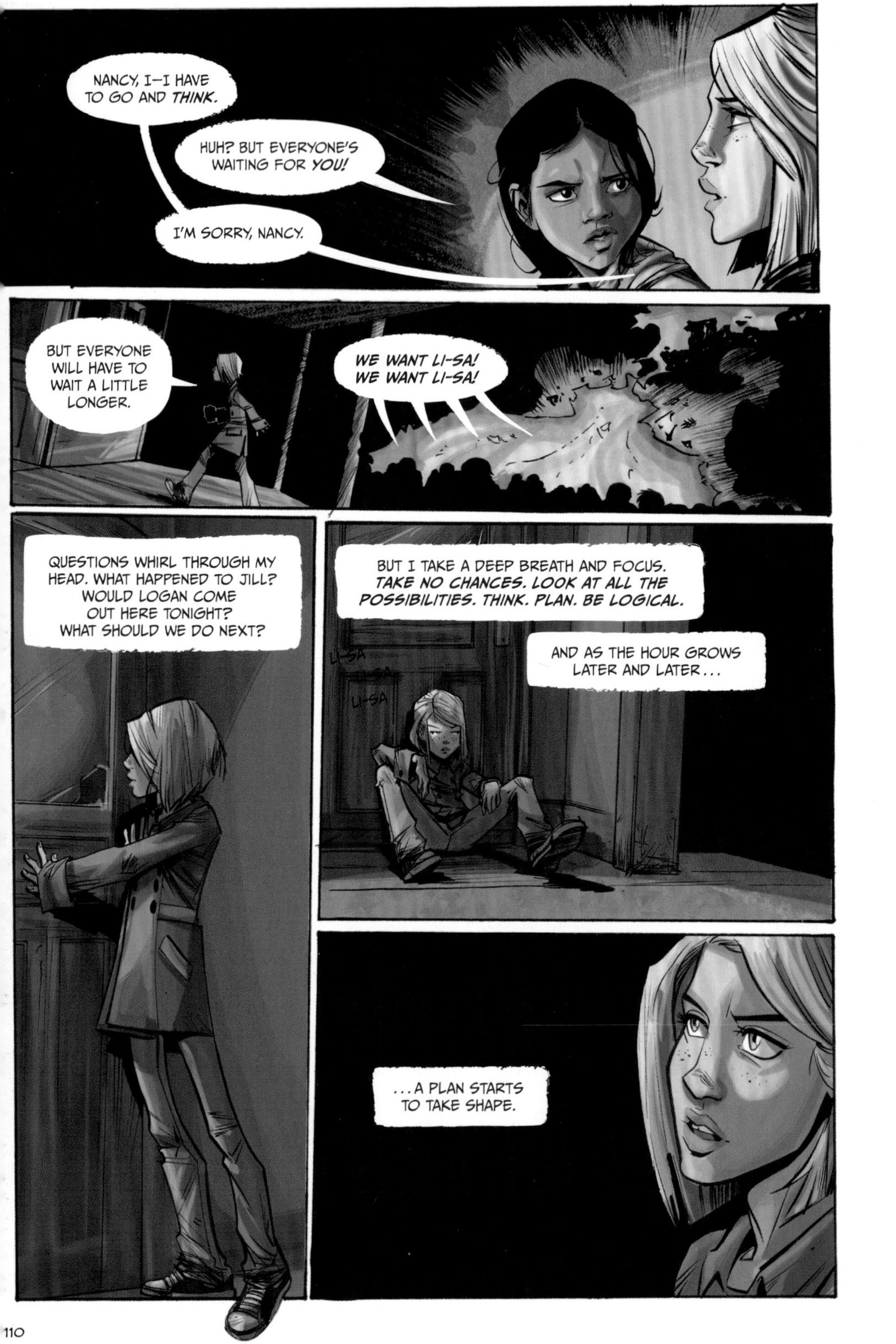
NANCY, I—I HAVE TO GO AND *THINK.*
HUH? BUT EVERYONE'S WAITING FOR *YOU!*
I'M SORRY, NANCY.
BUT EVERYONE WILL HAVE TO WAIT A LITTLE LONGER.
WE WANT LI-SA! WE WANT LI-SA!
QUESTIONS WHIRL THROUGH MY HEAD. WHAT HAPPENED TO JILL? WOULD LOGAN COME OUT HERE TONIGHT? WHAT SHOULD WE DO NEXT?
BUT I TAKE A DEEP BREATH AND FOCUS. *TAKE NO CHANCES. LOOK AT ALL THE POSSIBILITIES. THINK. PLAN. BE LOGICAL.*
LI-SA
LI-SA
LI-SA
AND AS THE HOUR GROWS LATER AND LATER . . .
. . . A PLAN STARTS TO TAKE SHAPE.

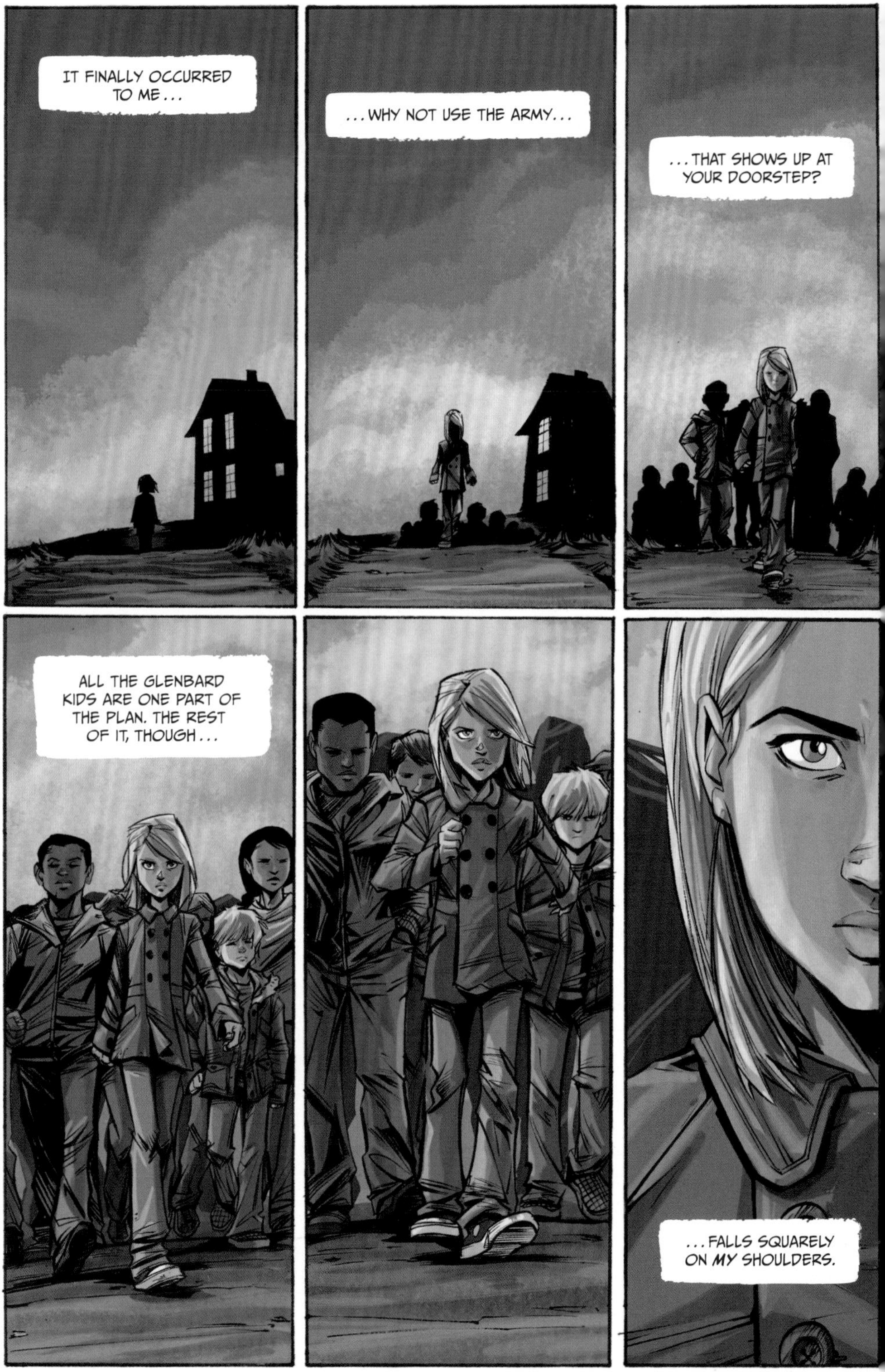
IT FINALLY OCCURRED TO ME...
...WHY NOT USE THE ARMY...
...THAT SHOWS UP AT YOUR DOORSTEP?
ALL THE GLENBARD KIDS ARE ONE PART OF THE PLAN. THE REST OF IT, THOUGH...
...FALLS SQUARELY ON *MY* SHOULDERS.

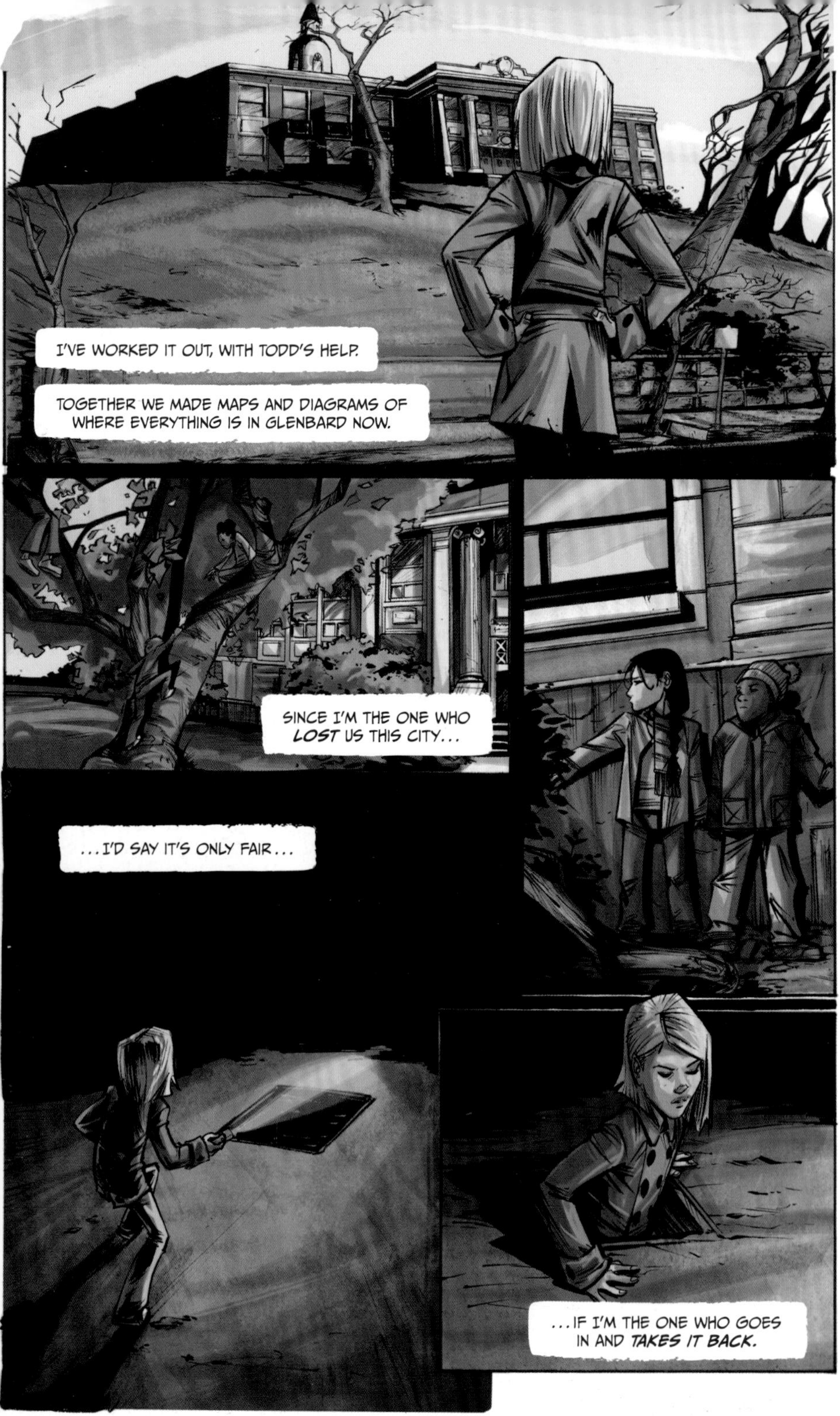
I'VE WORKED IT OUT, WITH TODD'S HELP.
TOGETHER WE MADE MAPS AND DIAGRAMS OF WHERE EVERYTHING IS IN GLENBARD NOW.
SINCE I'M THE ONE WHO *LOST* US THIS CITY...
...I'D SAY IT'S ONLY FAIR...
...IF I'M THE ONE WHO GOES IN AND *TAKES IT BACK.*

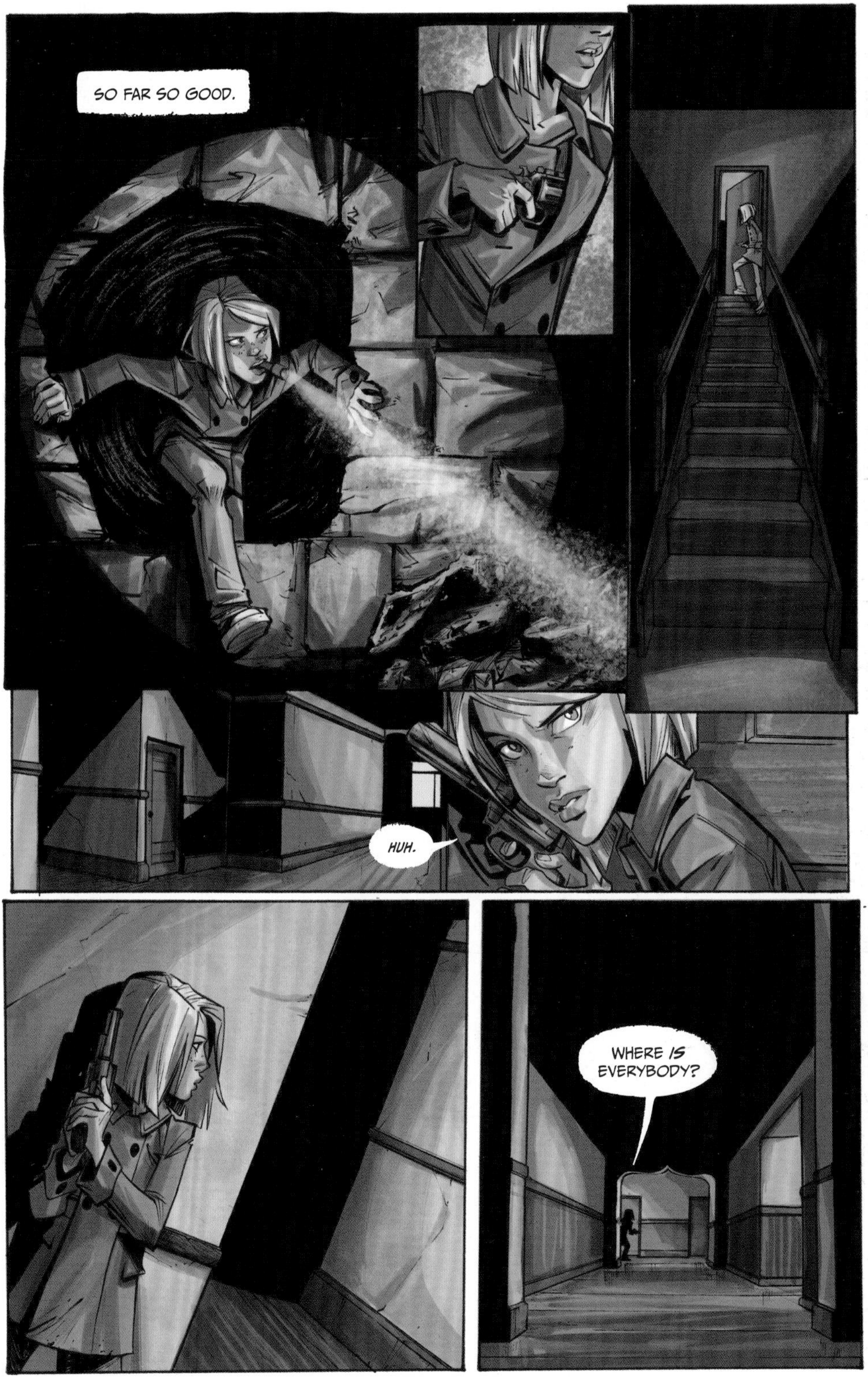
SO FAR SO GOOD.
HUH.
WHERE IS EVERYBODY?

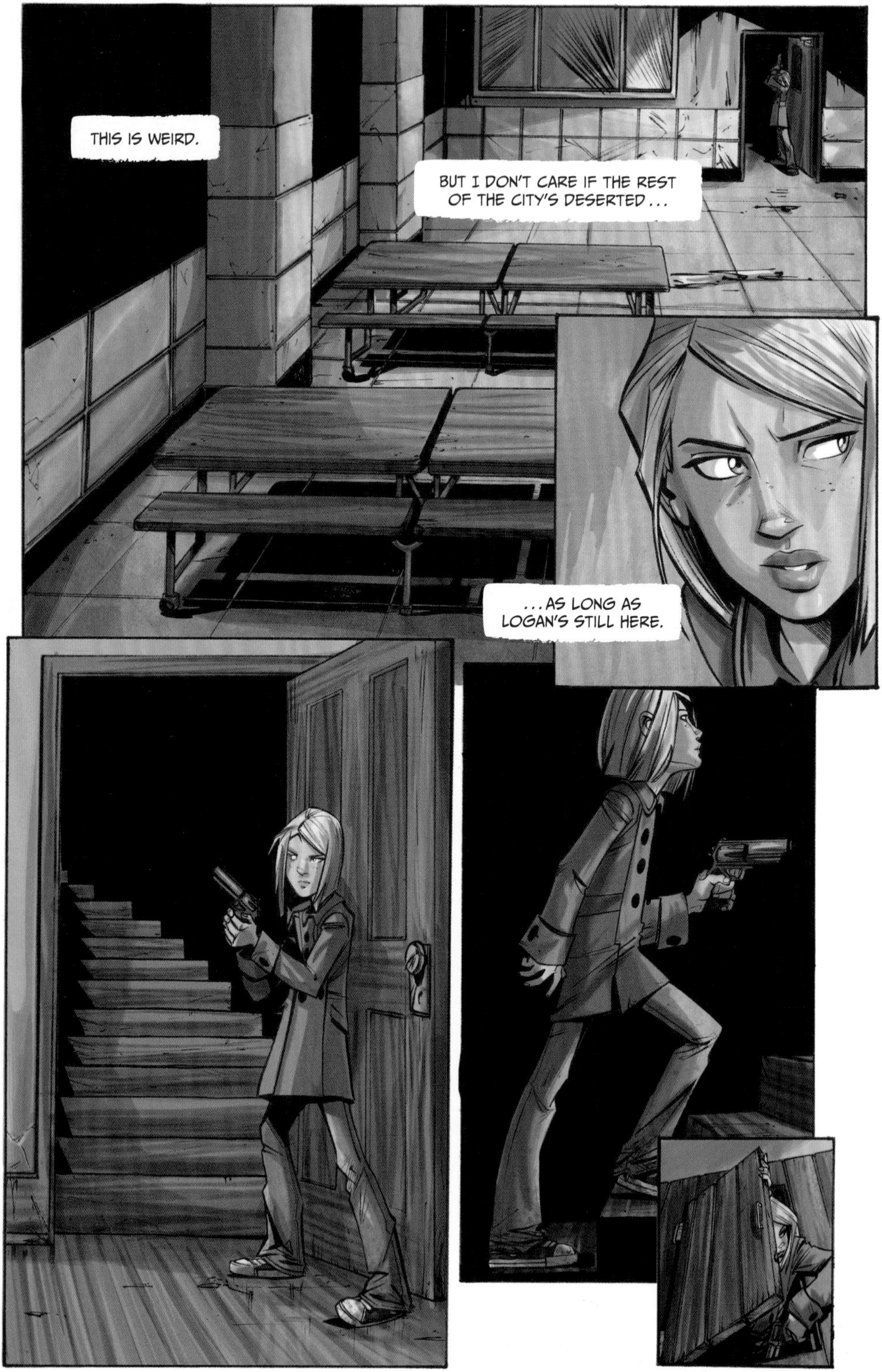
THIS IS WEIRD.
BUT I DON'T CARE IF THE REST OF THE CITY'S DESERTED...
...AS LONG AS LOGAN'S STILL HERE.

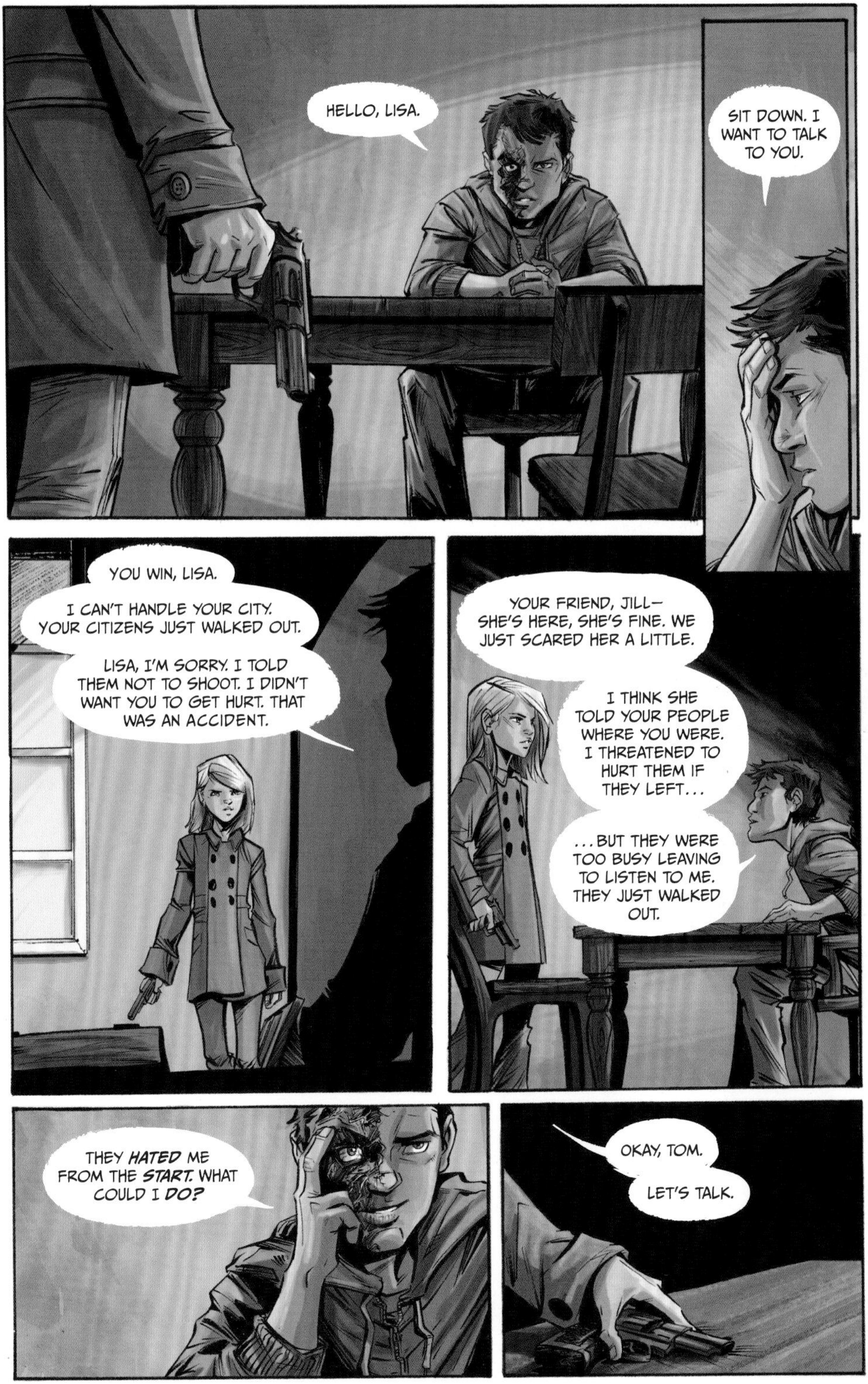
HELLO, LISA.
SIT DOWN. I WANT TO TALK TO YOU.
YOU WIN, LISA.
I CAN'T HANDLE YOUR CITY. YOUR CITIZENS JUST WALKED OUT.
LISA, I'M SORRY. I TOLD THEM NOT TO SHOOT. I DIDN'T WANT YOU TO GET HURT. THAT WAS AN ACCIDENT.
YOUR FRIEND, JILL— SHE'S HERE, SHE'S FINE. WE JUST SCARED HER A LITTLE.
I THINK SHE TOLD YOUR PEOPLE WHERE YOU WERE. I THREATENED TO HURT THEM IF THEY LEFT...
...BUT THEY WERE TOO BUSY LEAVING TO LISTEN TO ME. THEY JUST WALKED OUT.
THEY *HATED* ME FROM THE *START.* WHAT COULD I *DO?*
OKAY, TOM.
LET'S TALK.

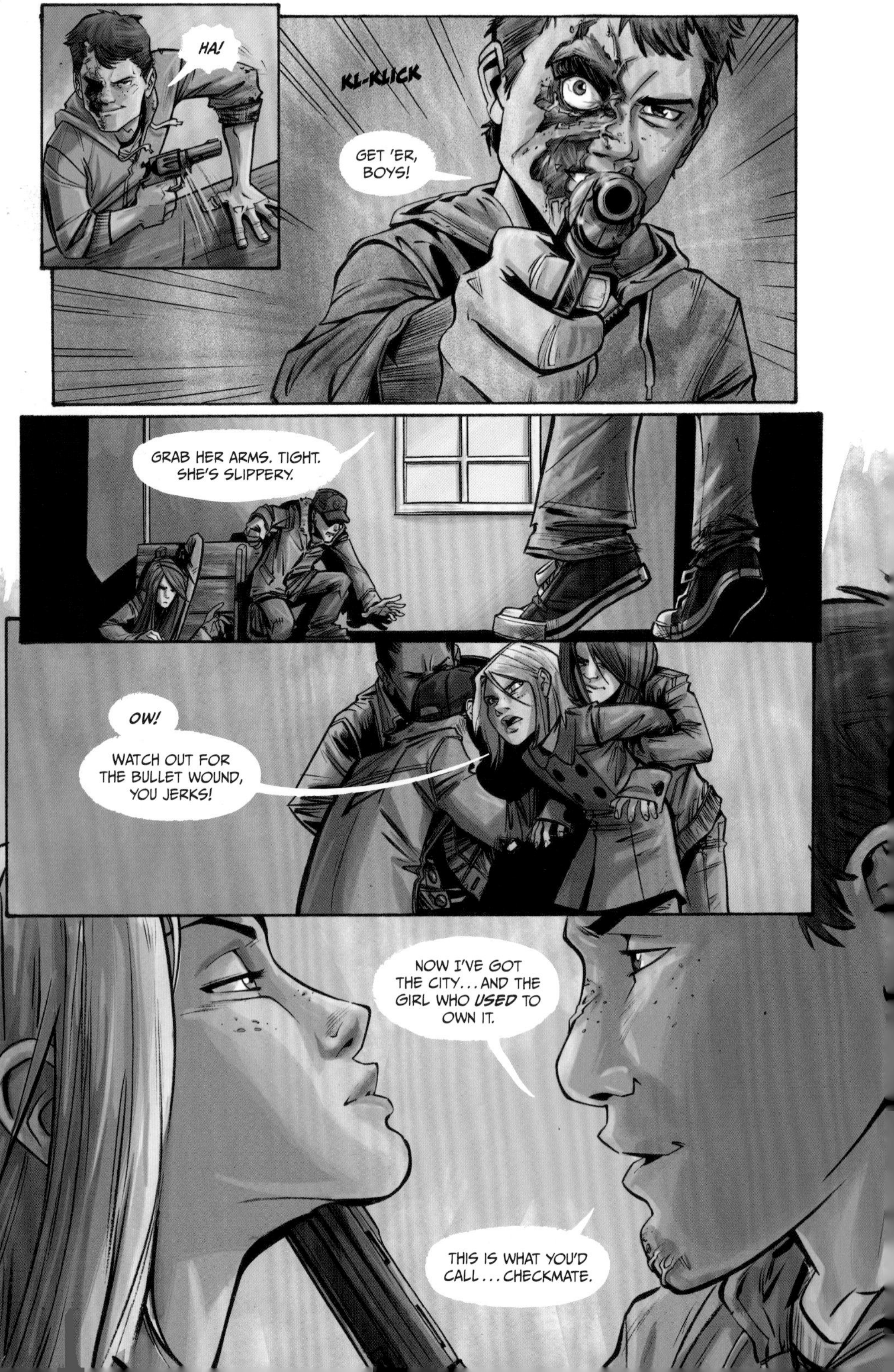
HA!
KL-KLICK
GET 'ER, BOYS!
GRAB HER ARMS. TIGHT. SHE'S SLIPPERY.
OW!
WATCH OUT FOR THE BULLET WOUND, YOU JERKS!
NOW I'VE GOT THE CITY... AND THE GIRL WHO *USED* TO OWN IT.
THIS IS WHAT YOU'D CALL... CHECKMATE.

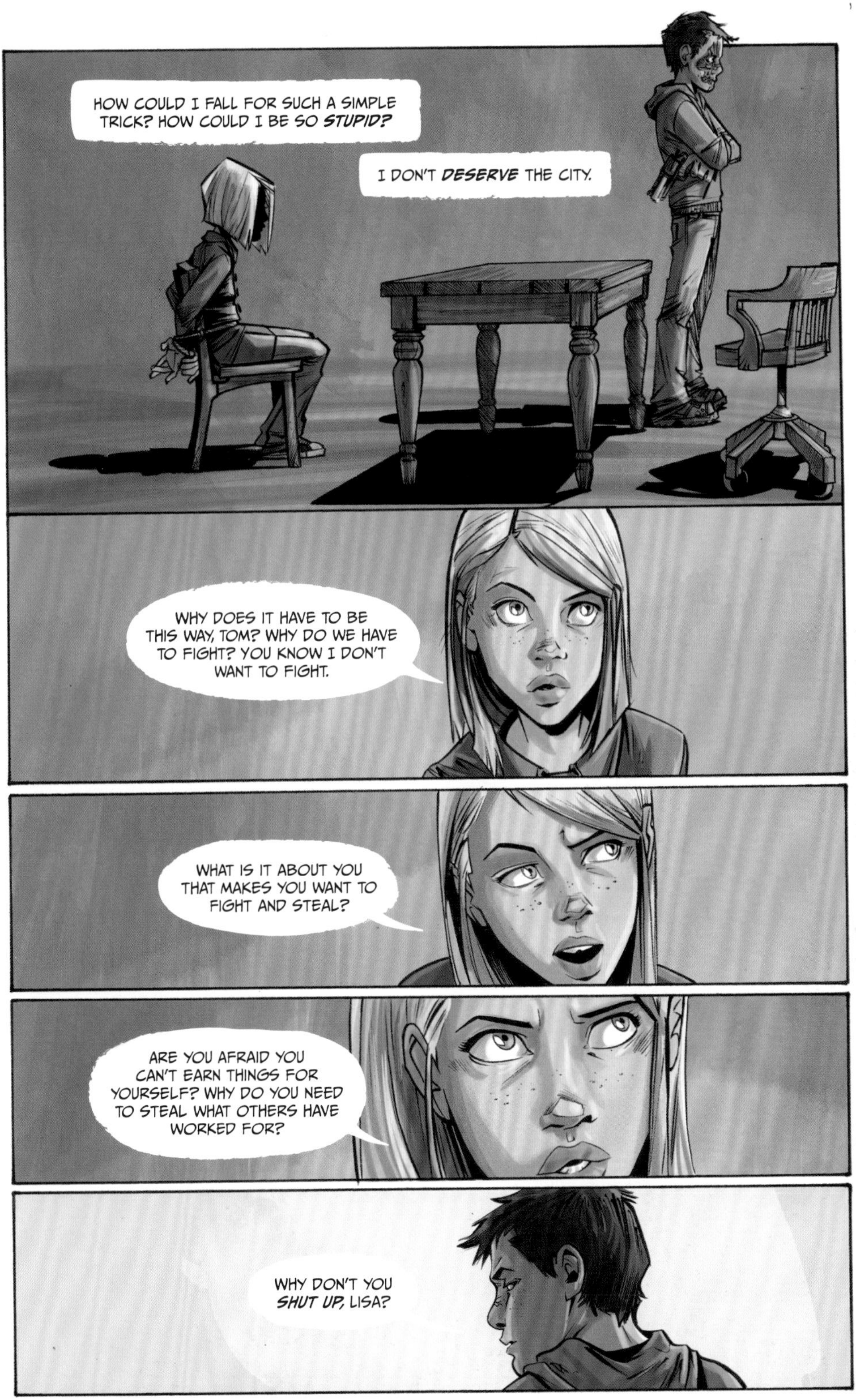
HOW COULD I FALL FOR SUCH A SIMPLE TRICK? HOW COULD I BE SO STUPID?
I DON'T DESERVE THE CITY.
WHY DOES IT HAVE TO BE THIS WAY, TOM? WHY DO WE HAVE TO FIGHT? YOU KNOW I DON'T WANT TO FIGHT.
WHAT IS IT ABOUT YOU THAT MAKES YOU WANT TO FIGHT AND STEAL?
ARE YOU AFRAID YOU CAN'T EARN THINGS FOR YOURSELF? WHY DO YOU NEED TO STEAL WHAT OTHERS HAVE WORKED FOR?
WHY DON'T YOU SHUT UP, LISA?

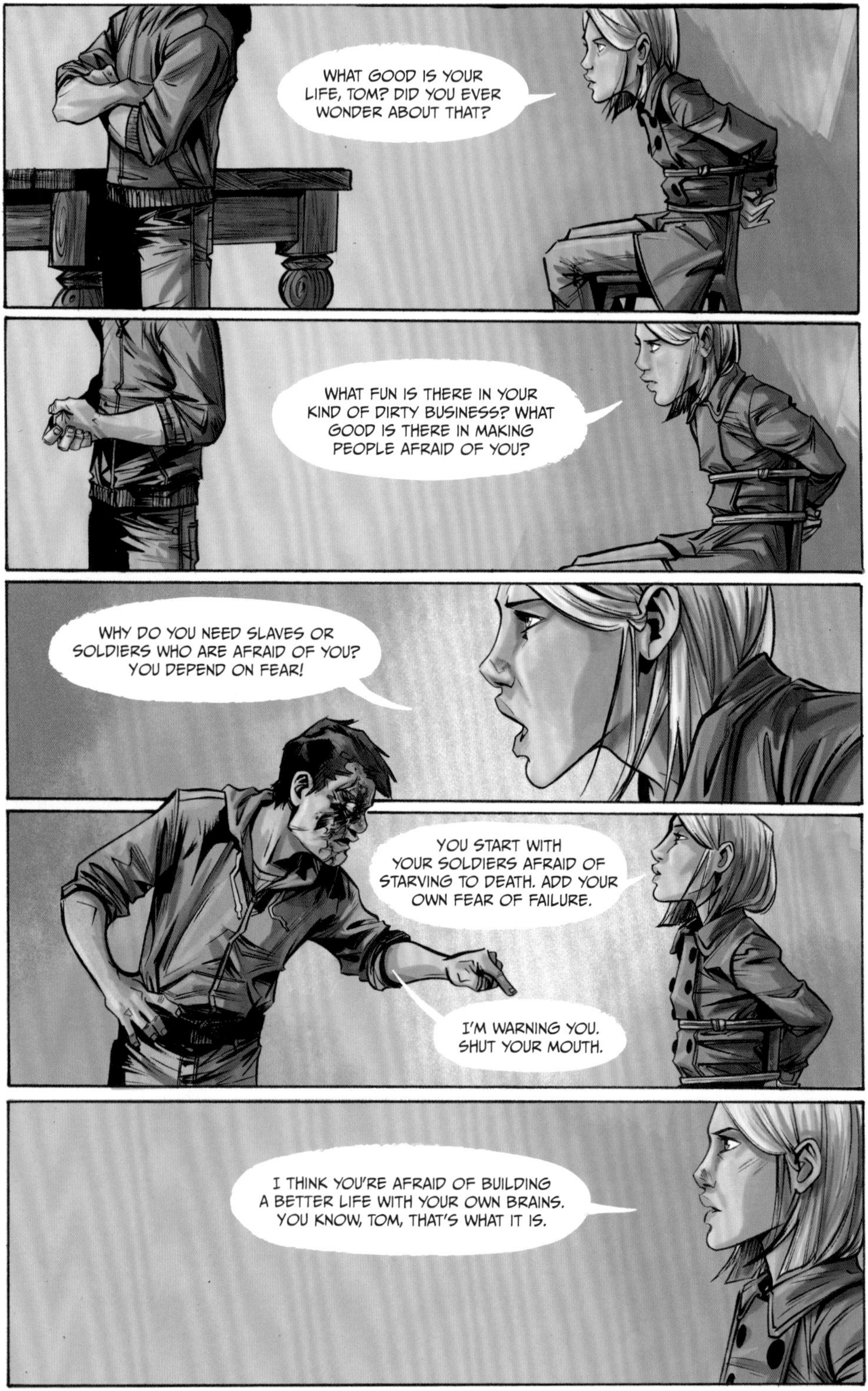
WHAT GOOD IS YOUR LIFE, TOM? DID YOU EVER WONDER ABOUT THAT?
WHAT FUN IS THERE IN YOUR KIND OF DIRTY BUSINESS? WHAT GOOD IS THERE IN MAKING PEOPLE AFRAID OF YOU?
WHY DO YOU NEED SLAVES OR SOLDIERS WHO ARE AFRAID OF YOU? YOU DEPEND ON FEAR!
YOU START WITH YOUR SOLDIERS AFRAID OF STARVING TO DEATH. ADD YOUR OWN FEAR OF FAILURE.
I'M WARNING YOU. SHUT YOUR MOUTH.
I THINK YOU'RE AFRAID OF BUILDING A BETTER LIFE WITH YOUR OWN BRAINS. YOU KNOW, TOM, THAT'S WHAT IT IS.

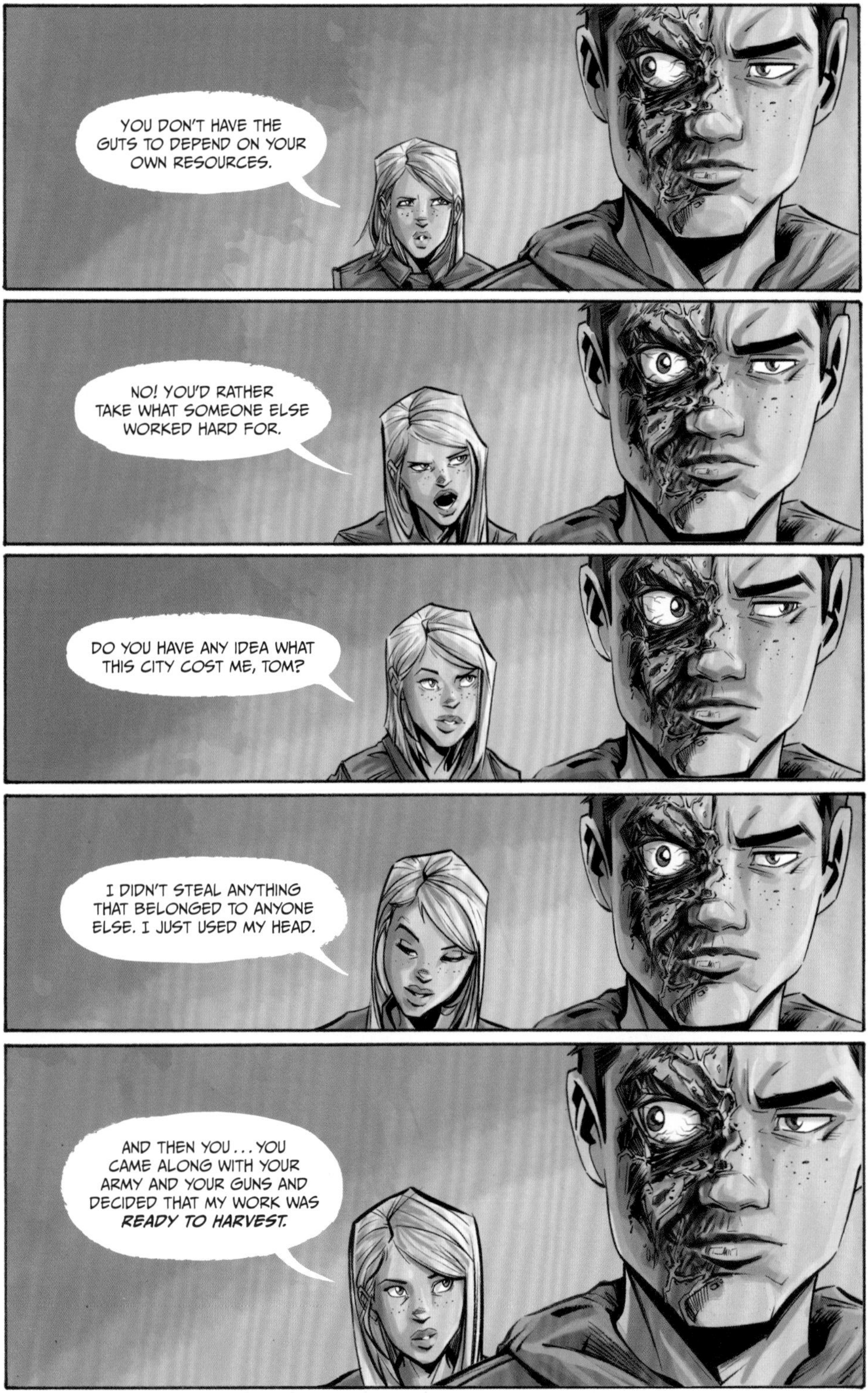
YOU DON'T HAVE THE GUTS TO DEPEND ON YOUR OWN RESOURCES.
NO! YOU'D RATHER TAKE WHAT SOMEONE ELSE WORKED HARD FOR.
DO YOU HAVE ANY IDEA WHAT THIS CITY COST ME, TOM?
I DIDN'T STEAL ANYTHING THAT BELONGED TO ANYONE ELSE. I JUST USED MY HEAD.
AND THEN YOU . . . YOU CAME ALONG WITH YOUR ARMY AND YOUR GUNS AND DECIDED THAT MY WORK WAS ***READY TO HARVEST.***

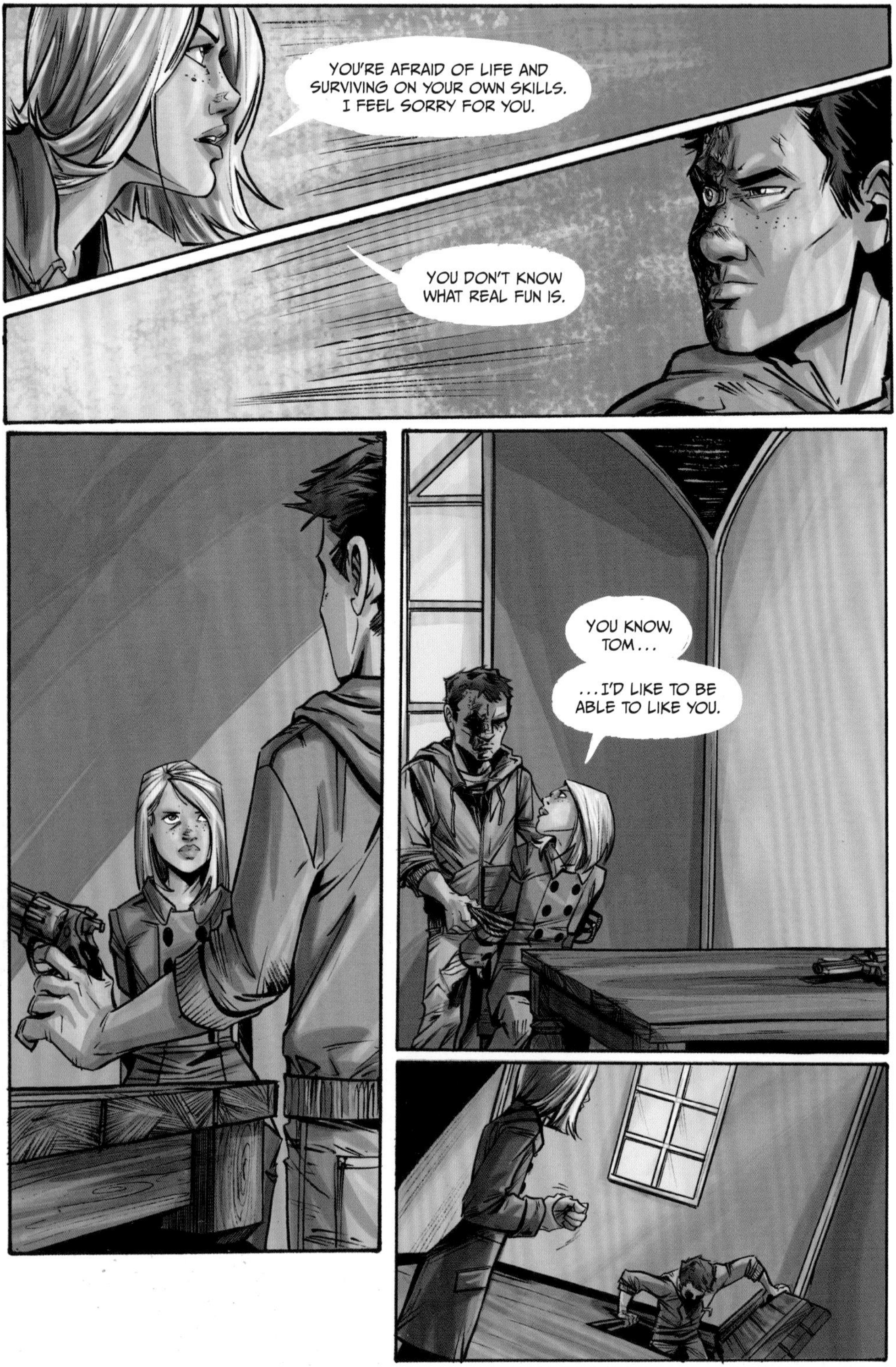
YOU'RE AFRAID OF LIFE AND SURVIVING ON YOUR OWN SKILLS. I FEEL SORRY FOR YOU.
YOU DON'T KNOW WHAT REAL FUN IS.
YOU KNOW, TOM...
...I'D LIKE TO BE ABLE TO LIKE YOU.

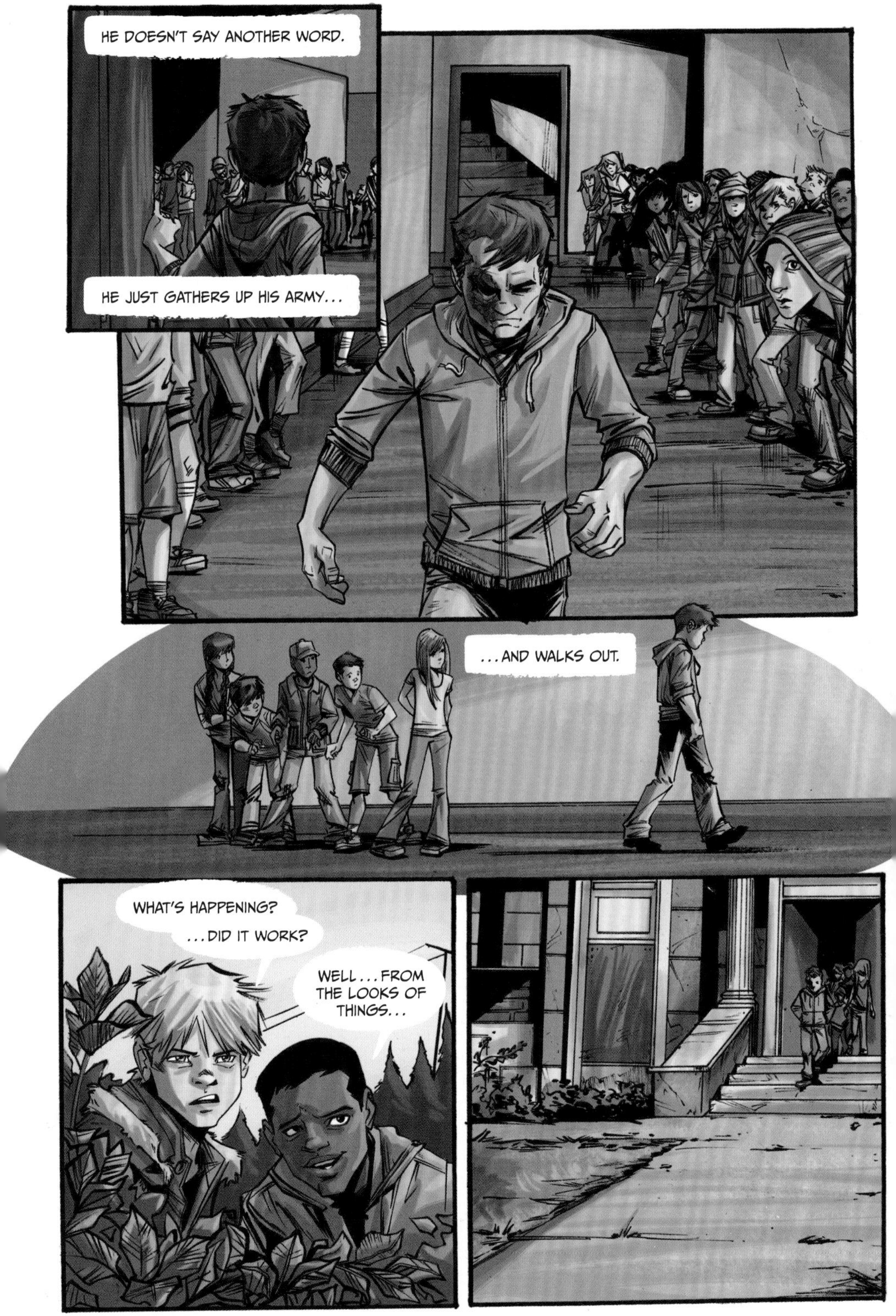
HE DOESN'T SAY ANOTHER WORD.
HE JUST GATHERS UP HIS ARMY...
...AND WALKS OUT.
WHAT'S HAPPENING?
...DID IT WORK?
WELL...FROM THE LOOKS OF THINGS...

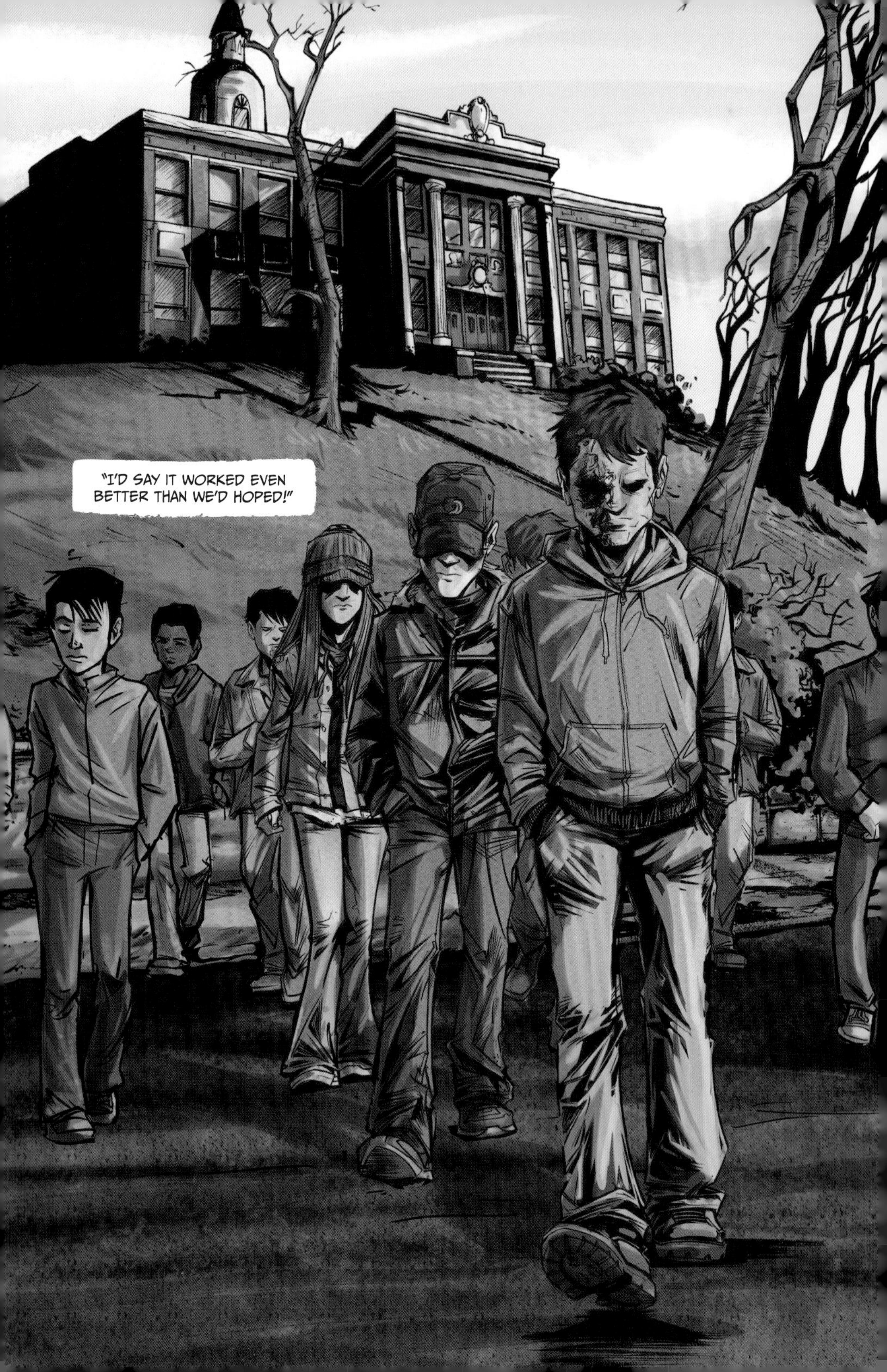
"I'D SAY IT WORKED EVEN BETTER THAN WE'D HOPED!"

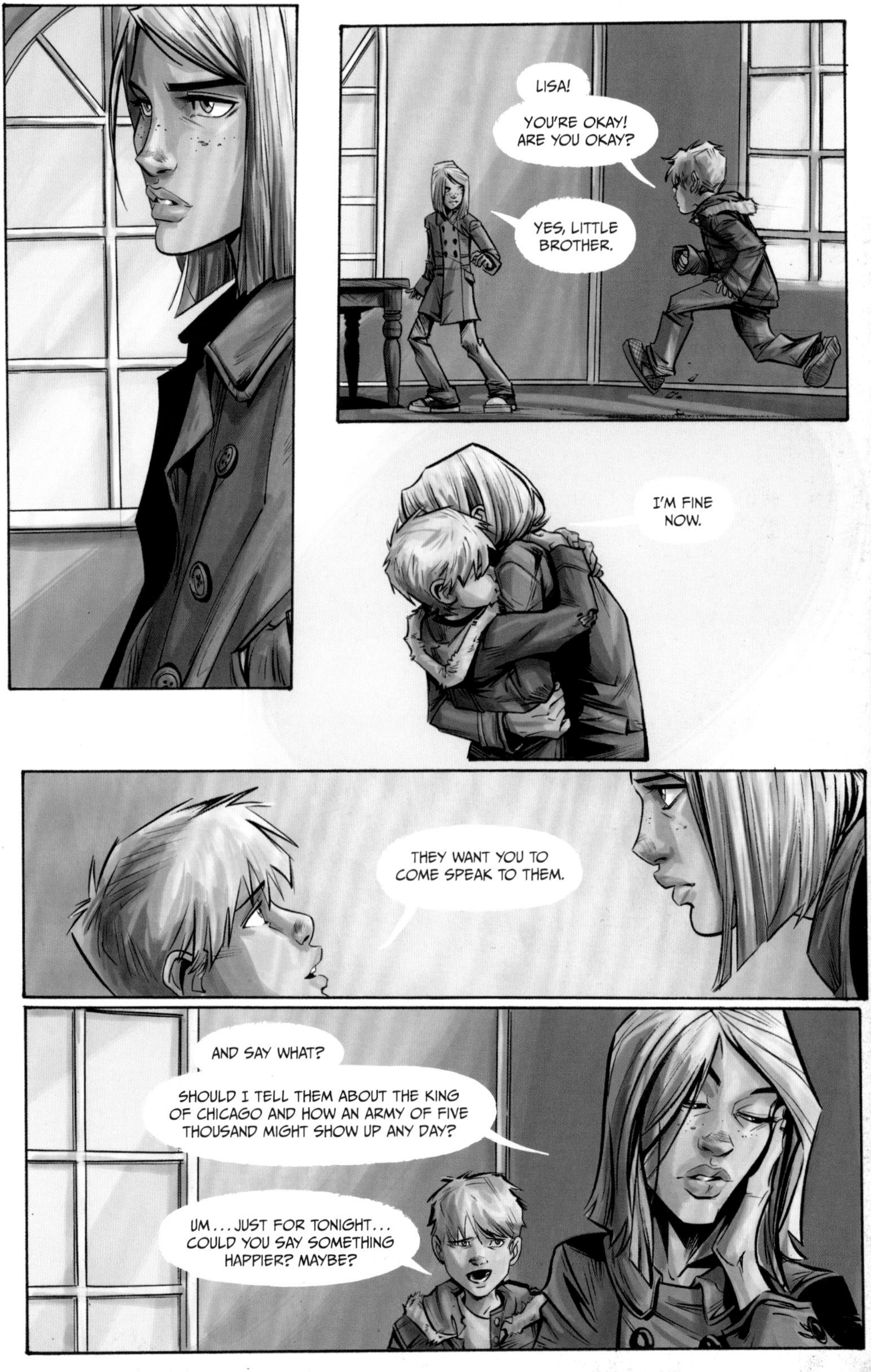
LISA!
YOU'RE OKAY! ARE YOU OKAY?
YES, LITTLE BROTHER.
I'M FINE NOW.
THEY WANT YOU TO COME SPEAK TO THEM.
AND SAY WHAT?
SHOULD I TELL THEM ABOUT THE KING OF CHICAGO AND HOW AN ARMY OF FIVE THOUSAND MIGHT SHOW UP ANY DAY?
UM... JUST FOR TONIGHT... COULD YOU SAY SOMETHING HAPPIER? MAYBE?

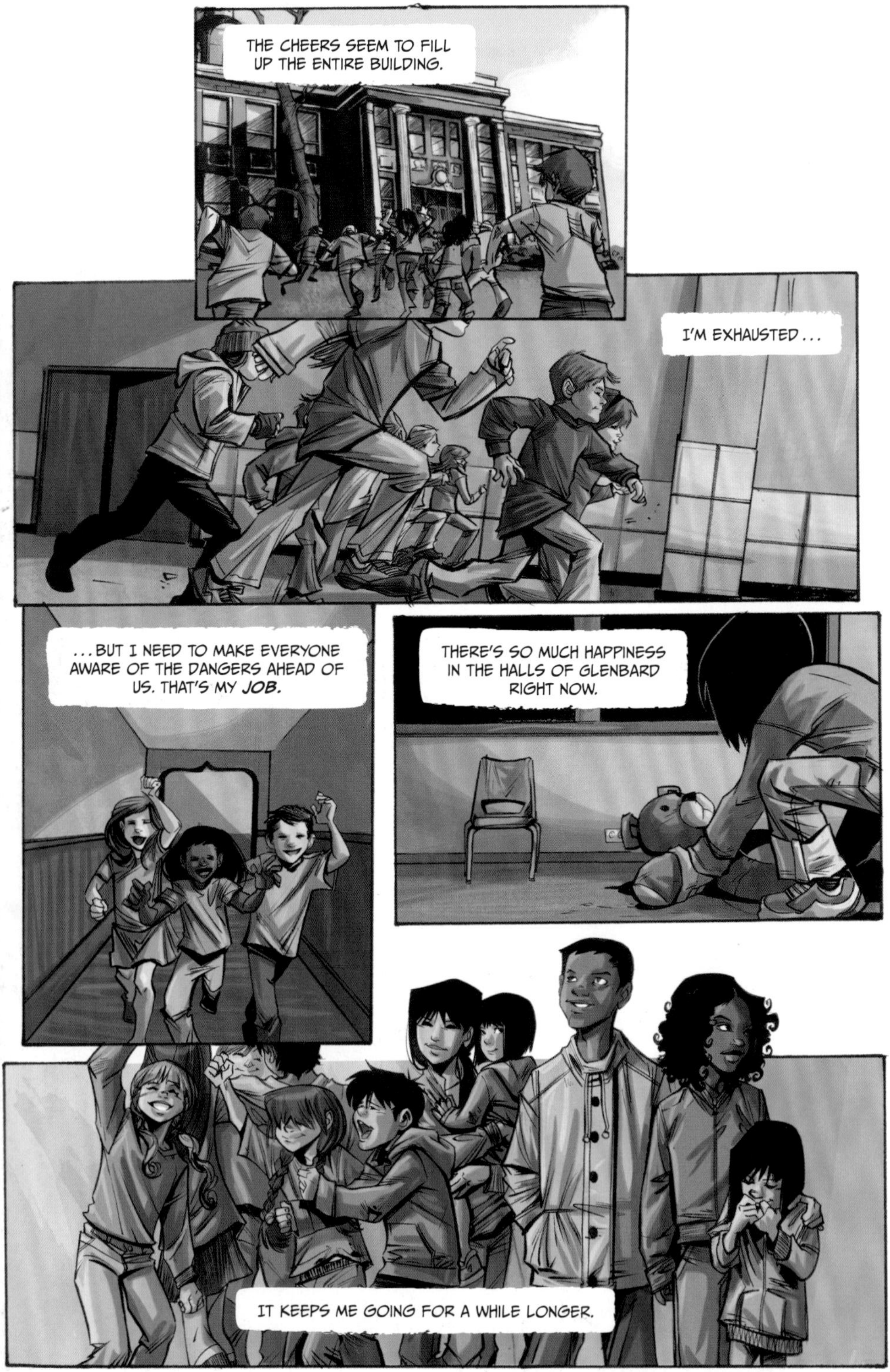
THE CHEERS SEEM TO FILL UP THE ENTIRE BUILDING.
I'M EXHAUSTED . . .
. . . BUT I NEED TO MAKE EVERYONE AWARE OF THE DANGERS AHEAD OF US. THAT'S MY JOB.
THERE'S SO MUCH HAPPINESS IN THE HALLS OF GLENBARD RIGHT NOW.
IT KEEPS ME GOING FOR A WHILE LONGER.

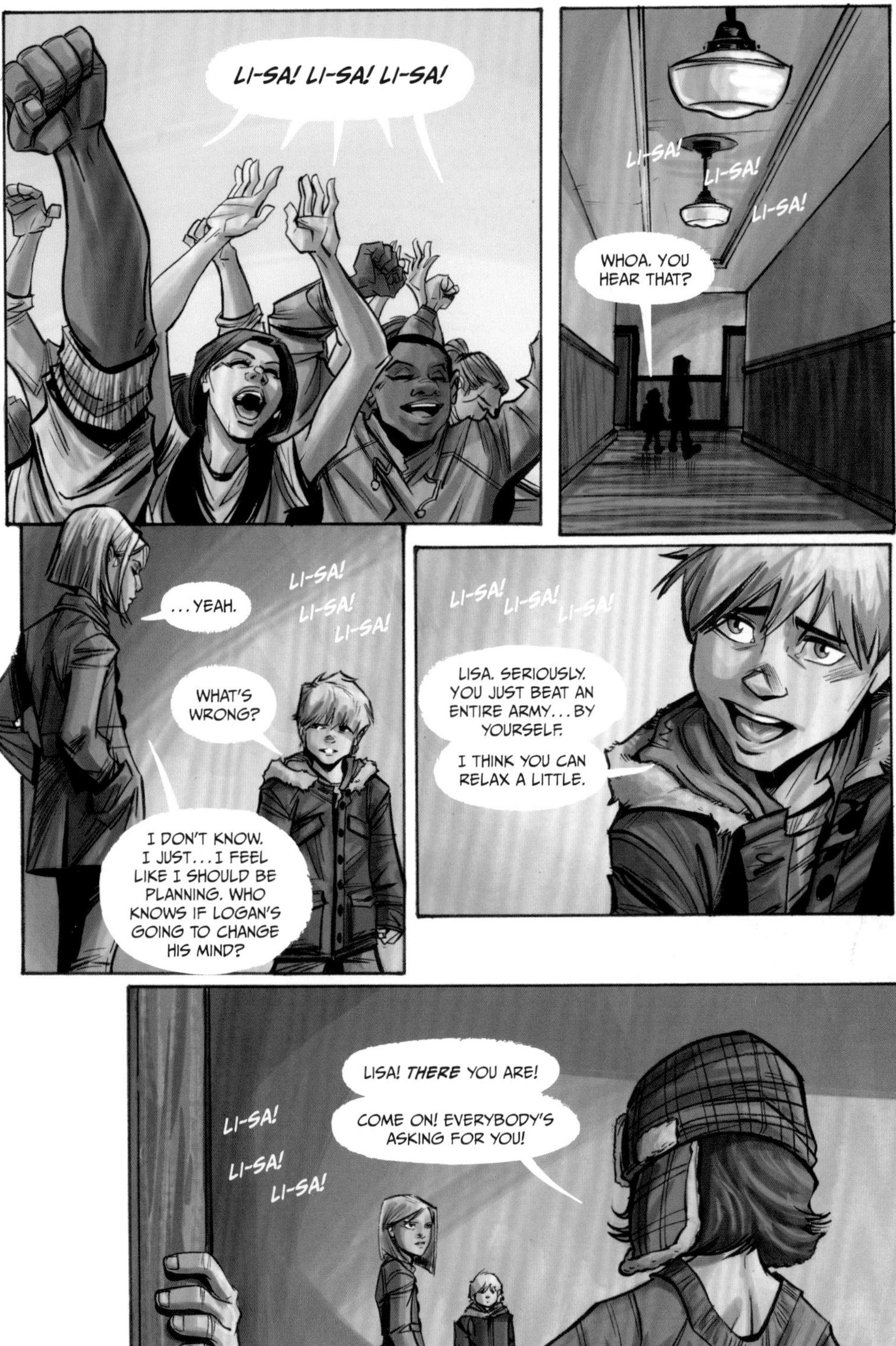

LI-SA! LI-SA! LI-SA!
LI-SA!
LI-SA!
LI-SA!
WHOA. YOU HEAR THAT?
LI-SA!
LI-SA!
LI-SA!
. . . YEAH.
WHAT'S WRONG?
I DON'T KNOW. I JUST. . . I FEEL LIKE I SHOULD BE PLANNING. WHO KNOWS IF LOGAN'S GOING TO CHANGE HIS MIND?
LI-SA!
LI-SA!
LI-SA!
LISA. SERIOUSLY. YOU JUST BEAT AN ENTIRE ARMY. . . BY YOURSELF.
I THINK YOU CAN RELAX A LITTLE.
LI-SA!
LI-SA!
LI-SA!
LISA! THERE YOU ARE!
COME ON! EVERYBODY'S ASKING FOR YOU!

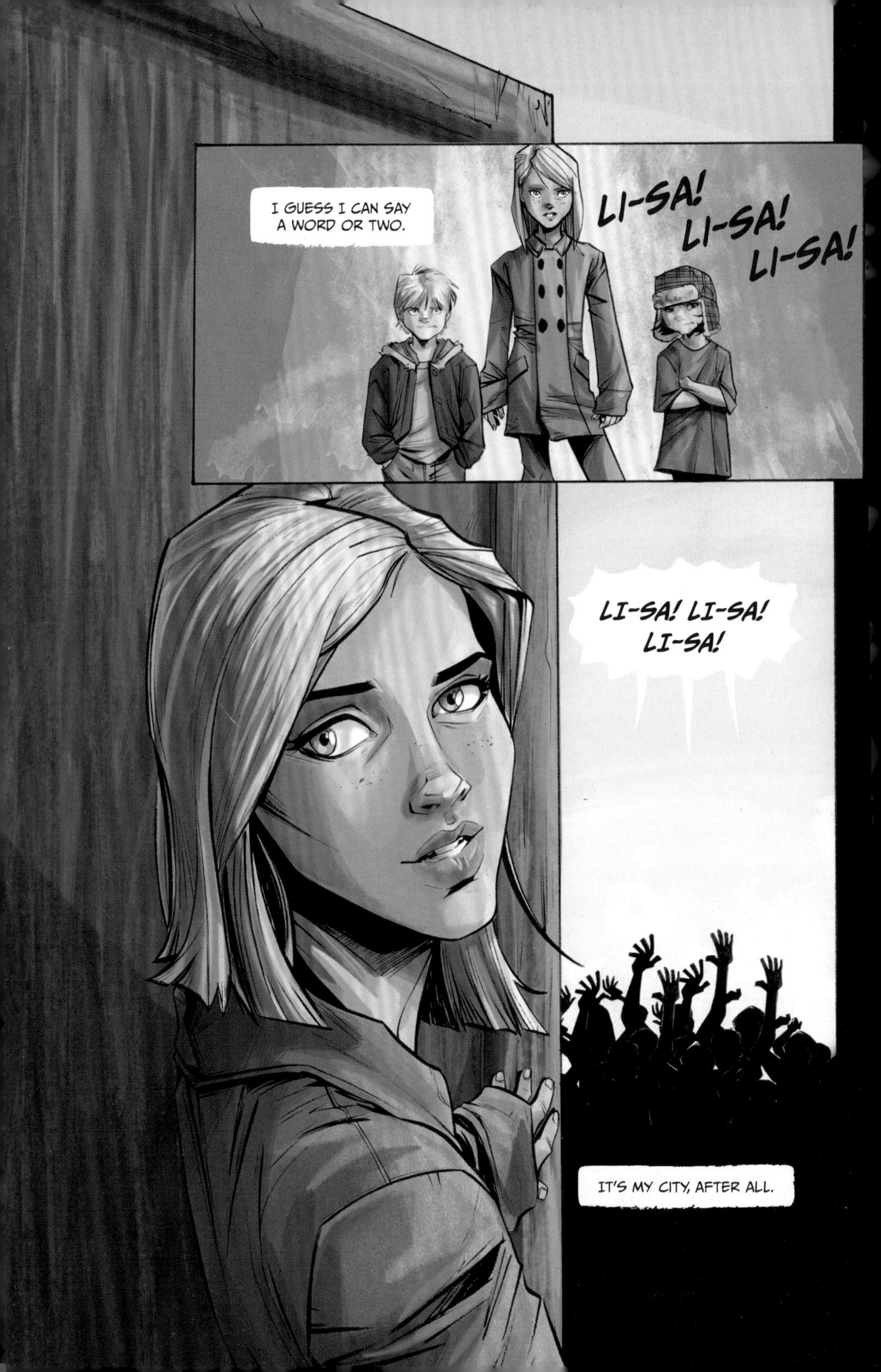
I GUESS I CAN SAY A WORD OR TWO.
LI-SA! LI-SA! LI-SA!
LI-SA! LI-SA! LI-SA!
IT'S MY CITY, AFTER ALL.